FIERCE DADDY

LAYLAH ROBERTS

Laylah Roberts.

Fierce Daddy.

Cover Design by: Allycat's Creations.

Photographer: Reggie Deanching.

Model: Derek Bryant.

Editing: Celeste Jones.

🏵 Created with Vellum

LET'S KEEP IN TOUCH!

Don't miss a new release, sign up to my newsletter for sneak peeks, deleted scenes and giveaways: https://landing.mailerlite.com/web-forms/landing/p7l6go

You can also join my Facebook readers group here: https://www.facebook.com/groups/386830425069911/

BOOKS BY LAYLAH ROBERTS

Doms of Decadence

Just for You, Sir

Forever Yours, Sir

For the Love of Sir

Sinfully Yours, Sir

Make me, Sir

A Taste of Sir

To Save Sir

Sir's Redemption

Reveal Me, Sir

Montana Daddies

Daddy Bear

Daddy's Little Darling

Daddy's Naughty Darling Novella

Daddy's Sweet Girl

Daddy's Lost Love

A Montana Daddies Christmas

Daring Daddy

Warrior Daddy

Daddy's Angel

Heal Me, Daddy

Daddy in Cowboy Boots

A Little Christmas Cheer

Sheriff Daddy

Her Daddies' Saving Grace

MC Daddies

Motorcycle Daddy

Hero Daddy

Protector Daddy

Untamed Daddy

Her Daddy's Jewel

Fierce Daddy

Harem of Daddies

Ruled by her Daddies

Claimed by her Daddies

Stolen by her Daddies (coming 2022)

Haven, Texas Series

Lila's Loves

Laken's Surrender

Saving Savannah

Molly's Man

Saxon's Soul

Mastered by Malone

How West was Won

Cole's Mistake

Jardin's Gamble

Romanced by the Malones

Twice the Malone

Men of Orion

Worlds Apart

TRIGGER WARNING

Please note that Tabby was in an abusive marriage. While this book doesn't go into any real detail and it's all in the past, this may be triggering for some readers. Please read with caution.

1

Someone was stalking her.

Or at least that's what it felt like. Turning, Tabby studied her surroundings.

Nothing.

However, as she started jogging again, a sense of urgency filled her.

Then a scream pierced the early morning.

Keep running, Tabby.

Not your problem.

If you get hurt, that's the end of your freedom.

Another cry, more muffled this time. But there was no mistaking the anger and fear in that sound. Tabby jogged in place.

How often did you wish someone would help you and they never did?

Fuck it. What did she really have to lose? So she got hurt and had to go back to Jared's house. He was expecting her to fail.

She wasn't going to, though. And she wasn't going to be the type of person who stood by while someone else got hurt.

Turning, she raced towards where she'd heard the sound.

There was a small park nearby and as she grew near, she spotted a large man trying to shove someone into a car. The vehicle had its lights off, but it was close to six in the morning and the sun was starting to lighten the darkness.

She reached into the pocket of her front pack and drew out her pepper spray.

"Hey! What do you think you're doing?" she yelled.

The big man froze. It was just enough for the person he held to break free of his hold. Tabby raced towards the kidnapper, who'd turned to chase his prey.

"Hey! You!"

When he turned, she raised the pepper spray, spraying it directly into his face before taking off, not wanting to wait around.

Perhaps she should have brought her stun gun. Maybe she needed a real gun.

Jared would have a freaking fit if he knew what she'd just done.

But as she raced away from the man, who was howling in pain, she smiled. This was the most alive she'd felt in years. Adrenaline pumped through her as she darted into some trees that were along one side of the park.

She'd actually done something. Something good. She'd helped someone.

It felt darn good.

"Psst."

Freezing, her heart racing, she turned her head carefully. Relief flooded her as she saw the person she'd rescued.

Well, the kidnapper was hardly going to call out, 'psst', was he?

"Over here."

Now that the rush of adrenaline was receding, she realized it was a feminine voice. Which made her feel safer.

Silly, really. Women could be dangerous too. But in Tabby's life, most of the people who had hurt her were men. It was men who had used and controlled her.

Abused her.

Yeah, she might have a few issues.

Glancing around for the big guy, who'd stopped screaming, she moved carefully to where the girl was peering around a large tree. How old was she? Tabby was slightly built and only reached five foot five, but she still felt like she was towering over this other girl.

"Come. We have to go before he starts searching. Do you know someplace safe we can go to?"

The other woman had a slight accent. Should she take her back to her apartment? Probably not. But where else?

"There's a twenty-four-hour diner not far from here," she told her.

"Okay, that might work."

Christ, Jared would have kittens if he knew she was being so reckless.

"Let's go."

Quietly, she started creeping out of the trees. The girl wasn't wrong about it being dangerous to stay here. That guy wouldn't be down for long. And this was the logical place to look.

It was growing lighter, which meant that they didn't have the cover of darkness. But neither did he.

She glanced back. She couldn't tell how old the other woman was. She wore a dark hoodie up over her head and she was limping.

"Are you hurt?" she whispered.

"I'll be fine. Keep going. Please."

Reaching the edge of the park, Tabby poked her head out and looked both ways. A car approached and she darted back, but she didn't think it was the same make of car as the one that guy had been driving.

"We're just going to have to make a run for it," the woman said, crouching. "Pretend we're out jogging, which it looks like you were already doing."

"You don't want to call the police?"

"Christ, no. My Papi would have a fit if I involved the cops."

Relief loosened the knot inside her. If she got involved with the police, Jared would drag her back to Chicago.

"Did that guy just randomly attack you?" If he had, that meant he might have already high-tailed it out of there.

"No. He'll be looking for me."

"Let's go, then." She still had her pepper spray in hand. They started jogging down the road. The other woman hissed.

Crap. She was injured. There was nothing she could do, though.

Tabby's heart pounded. Fear rather than exertion making her sweat.

"Fuck. How much further?"

"Just over there." Tabby pointed across the street. They'd made it to the other side of the road when another car started approaching. Shit. Was it him?

"Quick, inside," the woman stated.

They hurried inside and the car drove past. Tabby let out a sigh of relief. The diner was only about a third full, but she knew it would start getting busier from now on. She'd only lived in the area for a week, but she'd jogged past the diner enough to know it was popular.

The other woman strode toward a booth at the back. Probably a good idea. They'd have a good view of anyone who came through the door. Tabby followed, her gaze down, trying not to garner notice. She slid into the booth by the girl.

"Do you have any money?" the girl whispered.

"Yes. Are you hungry?"

"Starving. I could eat a horse."

Tabby shot her a surprised look. She'd expected her to say that she was too upset to eat. Although, now that she mentioned it, Tabby could maybe eat too.

"You're awfully chilled about all of this," said the girl, who still had her hoodie up. "Most people would have just called the cops and let Bert kidnap me. Even if they were brave enough to help me, I don't think they would be so calm afterward."

"I could say the same about you," she replied. "You're awfully calm for someone who was being kidnapped."

"It's not the first time," the other woman said glibly. She turned, then hissed. "Fuck."

"What is it? Do you need a doctor?" she asked.

"I'm fine. Could I borrow some money? I'll pay you back."

"Of course," Tabby said immediately. She was driven to help this girl. This was something she could do. Right in this moment, she didn't feel out of control or helpless.

She was aiding someone who needed it.

"Could I also borrow your phone? Do you know exactly where we are?"

Tabby dug her phone out of her pack and handed it over. She felt a bit gross sitting here without showering after her jog, but she didn't have much choice. She couldn't leave until she knew this girl was going to be all right. The girl tapped away on Tabby's phone as a waitress approached. She remained quiet, so Tabby ordered them both full breakfasts and coffee.

"And chocolate milk," the girl said.

"And two chocolate milks," Tabby added. It had been so long since she'd had chocolate milk, but right now, it sounded delicious.

The waitress nodded then looked down at Tabby's companion. Did she think it odd that the other girl didn't order for herself? Or look up from her phone? Or that she was sitting in the booth, slumped with a hoodie over her head? Then the waitress smirked. "I have a teenager just like that. Glued to their phones. Although mine wouldn't be up this early. Lucky if I can get her up to go to school."

"I know, right," Tabby replied.

Turning, she walked off.

"Teenager? Huh. I'm twenty-three years old." The other woman placed her phone on the table, tapping it with a nail that was painted bright blue.

"You are?" Tabby gave her a startled look. Mind you, she couldn't actually see the other woman's face. She was so slight.

"Yeah. People always think I'm young, though."

"Well, it helps in this instance. She just thinks you're a surly teenager, hiding because you didn't want to get up so early."

The other woman nodded. "I haven't seen Bert, at least. I think we might have lost him."

"Bert? You know the man who tried to kidnap you?"

"What? Oh no, Bert isn't his real name. There were two of them. So I nicknamed them Bert and Ernie. Although it's actually an insult to Bert and Ernie. These guys were thick as bricks. Ernie ate some bad chicken. His guts went while we were in the car. Jesus, I almost threw up, the stink was so bad."

Ew.

"So, Bert pulled over by that park because there's a public toilet. Ernie ran out to use the toilet and I took the opportunity to take off. They thought my hands were tied, but they're crap at tying knots. Unfortunately, Bert caught me. He was trying to get me back in the car when you called out. Thank you for that. Seriously. He probably would have knocked me out and shoved me in the trunk if it wasn't for you. That was really brave."

"I've never thought of myself as brave."

"Well, you were. I owe you. Big time."

The waitress brought them their drinks.

Tabby took a sip of chocolate milk. Yum. "You don't owe me. I'm just glad I could help you."

"You're a strange woman."

"So are you," Tabby told her.

As she turned, Tabby caught a glimpse of her olive skin and surprisingly bright green eyes. "I know. It's much more fun being different, right?"

Tabby wouldn't know. It felt like someone had always dictated how she should act, should think.

She had no idea who she was.

"You okay?"

"I guess. I'm Tabby, by the way."

"Oh my God, I'm Cat. Together, we're Tabby-Cat."

Tabby had to grin at that.

"Seems we were destined to meet, huh?" Cat nudged her arm, then groaned.

"What's wrong?" Tabby asked.

"Just some bruising. Seriously, I'll be fine."

Tabby's phone beeped and Cat picked it up, relief filling her face as she answered the call. She said something quietly that Tabby didn't understand. It sounded like she was speaking Spanish. Tabby had always wanted to learn another language but there had never been time.

Well, you've got time now.

True.

Too much time. With nothing to do. She sighed. What was the point in fighting to gain her freedom if she did nothing but sit at home, watch crappy TV, and go jogging? That wasn't living.

"Good news?" Tabby asked when the call ended. It was obvious the other woman held a lot of secrets. But in a weird way, it felt like they were kindred spirits.

"Yeah, someone will be here within the hour to get me. Will you stay with me until they're close?"

"Of course."

Cat sent her a smile. She was taken again by her beautiful green eyes. They were so distinctive.

Tabby knew she was rather plain. Ordinary brown eyes, dark-brown hair, pale skin. Average height. Average build.

She had a feeling that there was nothing average about Cat.

Their food soon arrived and they both dug in.

"Wow, you eat almost as much as I do," Cat commented. "Guess you were hungry after your jog and saving me, huh?"

"Oh, um, I guess." She usually ate a lot. She didn't know if it was all the jogging or just her metabolism, but she was pretty much always hungry.

"Well, I haven't eaten since yesterday morning. I'm starved. Damn, this chocolate milk is good."

"It sure is." Tabby drank hers down.

Cat let out a small laugh. "You're looking at it like it holds the secrets of the universe."

"I just forgot how good it tastes. Like I forgot what it's like to sit and eat breakfast in a diner with good company. Sorry, that probably sounds silly. I just . . . I've learned not to take the little things for granted."

Cat squeezed her hand briefly. "I'm really glad you were jogging by that park, Tabby. And that you're brave as fuck. Foolish. But brave."

Tabby let out a small bark of laughter.

"You know, you really shouldn't be jogging in the dark by yourself, right?"

Tabby shrugged. Yeah, she knew. But when you didn't think you were long for this world, then you didn't tend to worry as much about personal safety.

"They're fifteen minutes out," Cat said suddenly after checking Tabby's phone. She tapped away on it. "You should probably go now."

"And leave you?" She couldn't do that. "What if Bert comes back?"

Cat shook her head. "I'll be fine now, my Papi is close."

It was sweet how close she was to her dad. Tabby's father had been kind but distant. For most of her life, he'd been ill and her mother had spent all her time taking care of him.

"I've put my details into your phone. Text me if you ever need anything. I mean it. I owe you. And I mean more than just for breakfast."

Tabby shook her head, feeling shocked. "You don't owe me anything." She reached into her pack and pulled out some cash. "Are you sure?"

"Yeah, if you're here when they come, then my Papi will probably take you too."

"T-take me?"

Cat grinned at her. "You're smart, brave, and beautiful. I love my Papi, but he's arrogant and thinks he's always right. He'll take you and convince himself it's for your own good. That he's saving you."

"He c-can't just take me." Right? That sort of thing didn't happen. Except, Tabby knew better than most how many secret deals went down in the bowels of the underground. Where women were a commodity to be bartered. Where their wishes weren't respected.

Suddenly, she was worried for Cat.

"You can come with me. If you need a safe place, I can give you one."

Cat watched her with those amazing eyes. "You're a good person, Tabby. Maybe the best person I've ever met. But don't worry about me. I'm a survivor. Plus, I have Papi wrapped around my little finger. I'm terribly spoiled. I'm safe with him. I was only kidnapped because I went against orders." Cat grimaced. "I'll catch hell for that."

"Will he hurt you?"

"Nah, he'd never hurt me. He'll bluster a bit, though. But mostly, he'll be grateful I'm all right. Go now. And thank you. Really."

Tabby nodded and slid out of the booth, grabbing her phone and putting it away in her pack. "It was good to meet you, Cat."

"You too, Tabby. Be safe. No more jogging in the dark, huh?"

"No more getting kidnapped, hey?" Tabby replied back.

Cat grinned. "No promises."

Tabby couldn't help but snort out a laugh. Then she made her way out of the diner. She felt surprisingly sad as she walked towards her apartment. As though she'd lost a friend. Which was silly, since she just met Cat.

They weren't friends. And it was a show of how sad and lonely she was that helping a kidnapping victim was pretty much the highlight of her life.

"You've got to do something about this, Tabby," she muttered.

When she was a block away from the diner, she drew out her phone. There was no evidence of any strange calls or texts. But in her contacts list, she found Cat's number.

Tabby walked past the grocery store, then she stopped. For the past two weeks, she'd been living on frozen meals and take-out.

She was tired of it. She'd never learned to cook. But that didn't mean that she couldn't learn now. After all, she only had time on her hands.

After heading to her apartment, and showering, she started researching recipes on her tablet.

Coq au vin. She'd had that before a few times. It couldn't be too hard to make. After writing down the ingredients, as well as looking up some smoothie recipes, she had a list to go shopping with. She'd spotted a blender in the well-stocked kitchen, so she didn't have to get a new one for the smoothies she planned to make each morning.

Maybe she'd found her passion in life. Perhaps she could become a chef. She loved to eat. She loved food. So becoming a chef could be perfect for her.

Wouldn't that be something?

2

Life wasn't looking up.

Life was disastrous.

Leaning over the toilet, she threw up. Except she'd long since emptied her stomach, so all that was left was bile.

Groaning, she lay on her back on the floor.

She was dying.

This was it.

She was going to die lying on a bathroom floor. Hopefully, it wouldn't take too long for someone to find her. She didn't want to be too gross and decomposed. It would be nice to have an open coffin for the three people who would come to her funeral.

Jared and whichever two bodyguards were with him.

Oh Lord, her life was pathetic.

She was pathetic.

Is this what her life had come to? Dying, alone, on a dirty bathroom floor?

Well, the floor wasn't dirty because she had plenty of free time on her hands, and most of that was spent cleaning, jogging, or watching Scooby-Doo reruns.

She loved Scooby-Doo. What would he do right now?

Probably moan and groan about how sick he was. So they had that in common. If there was anyone around to listen, she'd be complaining right now.

Why did she think she could cook? And why hadn't she started with something simpler? Obviously, chicken was out. She hated chicken. She was never going to eat chicken again.

And she needed to stop thinking about chicken because yep, there went her stomach again. After vomiting this time, she waited ten minutes then decided to risk brushing her teeth. Managing to stand wasn't that easy and by the time she stumbled into bed, she was exhausted. She wanted to take a shower, to change her pajamas and her sheets, but she couldn't do anything except grab Snappy, her stuffed turtle, and curl up into a miserable ball.

Her head throbbed, and she knew she had to drink something because she was getting dehydrated, but the thought of getting back up made her cry.

This sucked.

This sucked so bad.

It sucked so much that she almost considered calling her cousin. Just for a moment. But this was the excuse he was looking for to drag her back to his house. Sure, it would be good for the immediate future. One of the house staff would take care of her. But once she got better, he wouldn't let her leave again. And she'd fought hard for her freedom.

A bit of food poisoning wasn't going to take that away from her.

She simply needed to ride this out. She could do it. If Luther didn't break her, then neither would this.

But it would be nice to have someone rub her back, bring her water, and help her get to the bathroom.

She closed her eyes. Yeah, her life needed a rethink. She couldn't go on like this. Sure, it had only been a week since she'd left Jared's, but what had she actually achieved? Nothing. She sat in her apartment and watched TV or did puzzles. She went out jogging. Cat was the first person she'd talked to.

This wasn't living. She might as well go back to Jared's for all the fun she was having. Only she had no idea how to turn her life around. All she knew was that she was lonely. She wanted someone she could call if she was sick and they'd worry over her. She wanted someone who'd be there if she was scared or angry or worried. She wanted to have more than three people at her funeral when she died.

But how did you go about meeting people? She wasn't looking for a relationship. She definitely wasn't signing up for one of those online dating services. Jared would have a fit. Which was actually a point in favor of signing up.

But no, that just scared her. Maybe she could join a club? But what? And how? And would she even be able to talk to people? Talking to people wasn't one of her skills.

Did she have any skills? Nope. Could she get a job?

Maybe her career as a chef was over. But that didn't mean she couldn't do something else. Snuggling Snappy tight, she closed her eyes and decided she'd figure something out once she was feeling better.

IT WAS Saturday afternoon before Tabby felt well enough to get out of bed. Carefully making her way downstairs, she grabbed some Gatorade from the kitchen then sat on the couch. The ground floor level was an oversized garage, easily big enough to fit eight vehicles. Upstairs was a loft-style apartment. There was an open-plan living area with spiral stairs leading to a level with three bedrooms, each with an attached bathroom. It was way too big for one person.

Switching on the television, she managed to find a cartoon she liked watching. It wasn't Scooby-Doo, but it would do.

Then she picked up her phone. Urgh. Dead. She hoped Jared hadn't texted. After plugging it in to charge, she grabbed her laptop.

She thought she had figured out what she needed to do. She had to get a job. That would help her meet people, right? Perhaps she could even make some friends.

Having people you care about is dangerous, Tabby. They could be used against you.

She remembered her mother giving her that advice when she was just seven and wanted to go to her best friend's house for a sleepover.

Jared had bought this place for her. He'd insisted on installing a shitload of security as well. It was the first time she'd ever lived on her own. There wasn't anyone around to dictate to her, to watch her.

To hurt her.

Nobody was going to hurt her again.

She looked through the job ads. It was useless, though. She had no qualifications or experience. Feeling completely dejected, she closed the laptop and picked up her phone.

Jared could help. But he likely wouldn't. He didn't want to make it easier for her to stay here. He wanted her back home, where he could keep an eye on her.

His words. Not hers.

What he'd really do was smother her.

Besides, she'd prefer to get a job on her own.

But how was she meant to do that when she had no skills and didn't know anyone?

That's not quite true, though, is it?

Scrolling through her phone, she brought up Millie's number.

The woman who Luther had wanted to destroy. Who Tabby had helped save.

She closed her eyes briefly. But what would she say? Not like she could just call her up and ask to be her friend. Or if she knew of any jobs.

But what else was she to do?

Everything she had, Jared had paid for. To get out from under his well-meaning protection, she needed money.

Sighing, she grabbed her purse and reached inside for the card she'd kept there for all these months. It was worn, almost smudged.

On the front was an image of a motorcycle. She didn't know her bikes at all. But it was gorgeous.

Montana Custom Bikes.

Pretty simple name. And there in the corner was his name. Owner: Razor Samuels.

There was a phone number, probably for the shop. But on the back of the card, he'd scrawled his personal cell phone number. She'd looked at this card so often, had dreamed of calling him.

She'd never dared to, though.

Going online, she looked up the website listed. Wow, the bikes he built were gorgeous. She clicked on the profile page and scrolled down. Maybe she should get a bike. That could be fun, right?

Then she spotted it.

Help Wanted. Looking for someone to work the front desk. Must be reliable with good customer service skills. Knowledge of motorbikes a bonus, but not necessary. All training provided.

Could she?

It was a stupid idea, right? She had no training. She could be terrible. And he knew who she was. That she was Jared Bartolli's cousin.

He wouldn't want her working for him.

So what's the worst that can happen? He says no? Not like you ever have to see him again.

And he might just say yes. Likely out of pity. But a pity job was still a job, right? Lord, she didn't know if it was a smart or stupid thing to do. However, if she didn't try, she'd never find out.

MONDAY MORNING, she pulled up out front of the garage.

Shit.

She could tell this wasn't the best area. Why would he set up shop here? It was obvious that his custom bikes sold for a lot. She remembered Luther talked about buying a bike once, and he'd went on and on about how much it was going to cost.

Of course, if he'd spent less money on booze and drugs, he'd probably have been able to afford it.

Asshole. She tightened her hands around the steering wheel of the BMW SUV that Jared had given her.

Luther was gone now. He wasn't coming back.

Stepping out of the car, she took another look around. Graffiti covered the building across the street, it badly needed a coat of paint. In comparison, the garage she was sitting in front of looked crisp and clean. There was a large wrought-iron gate that had been pulled back, letting people drive right up to the office that was in front of the building.

But she parked on the road, not wanting to draw too much attention to herself.

Whether her car would be in one piece when she came back out, she wasn't sure. But Jared would have insurance, right?

Moving towards the shop, she heard someone let out a low wolf whistle. Her shoulders tightened.

"Hey, there, sweet thing," a voice called out. "You need help? Because I'd be happy to give you some."

She glanced to her right as a heavily-tattooed man with a shaved head leered at her. He appeared to be cleaning something mechanical. Oh Lord, how could she expect to work here? She hesitated.

The man continued to leer, making her stomach tie up in knots.

"Tommy, shut up, asshole." Another man stepped out of the garage, which was set up with six bays. All of the doors were pulled up except for one.

"What?" Tommy snarled, staring at the other man. "You're not the fucking boss of me. A fine piece of ass walks along and I'm gonna admire it. She likes it, don't ya?"

Did he really expect her to agree with him? She glared at him. His eyes were too close together and his nose was overly large. He looked like a weasel.

Then she turned her gaze to the man who had come to her defense. Her mouth went dry. This guy, he was terrifying. She'd be lucky to reach the top of his shoulders. And those shoulders were broad. He had his blond hair pulled back. Tattoos covered his arms and went up his neck. He had a thick beard.

"Yeah? You want to explain to Razor why you ran off a customer with the bullshit that just came out of your mouth?"

Weasel gave the other guy a sullen look. Wait, that wasn't a good name for him. Weasel breath. Weasel jerk.

Weasel dick.

Ah, perfect.

"I suppose you're gonna go tell him, huh?" Weasel Dick whined.

"I'm no rat," the other man growled, before turning his dark gaze to her.

Tabby resisted the urge to turn and walk away. This wasn't exactly a great beginning to her quest for financial freedom. Her insides were trembling, but she knew better than to let on how scared she was.

Men like Weasel Dick fed on fear. You couldn't ever show them weakness.

"You looking for a bike for your old man?" her rescuer asked.

That was a bit insulting, assuming that she wasn't after one for herself, but Tabby didn't point that out. Because she wasn't actually looking to buy a bike. She couldn't afford one. Well, the credit card Jared had forced on her probably had no limit, so technically, she could.

But he'd have kittens if he discovered she'd bought a motorcycle.

Hm. Might be worth it just to see the look on his face.

"Actually, I'm here to see Razor. Do you know if he's around?" She hoped he was because she wasn't certain she could work up the courage to come back.

The big guy raised an eyebrow. "You know him?"

"I've met him before."

"Oh, I bet you've met him," Weasel Dick said slimily, looking her up and down then licking his lips.

What. A. Dick.

"That lucky bastard. Don't know what you see in him, but you need to try some younger dick. We get it up quicker and it stays up longer."

"What the fuck did you just say?" the big guy boomed before he slapped Weasel Dick around the back of his head. Then he shoved him.

Tabby was used to violence. She'd seen it, she'd experienced it.

But she still didn't like it. Taking a step back, she moved her gaze from one man to the other, watching worriedly.

"Sav! Tommy! Everything okay out here?" a firm voice called out.

And there he was. Tall and broad. His dark beard had some

gray in it, but that just added to the gorgeousness that was Razor Samuels.

Butterflies flew through her tummy. Could she do this? Speak to him? Ask him for a job? See him on a day-to-day basis? Hell, she was practically tongue-tied.

She didn't know what it was about him. He was twenty years older than she was. Maybe more. Old enough to be her father. That should turn her off, right?

But it didn't. Oh no, not in the slightest.

He was sex on two legs. But even more appealing than his looks, was his calm, confident manner. She'd only spent a few hours with him, but he'd made her feel safe. For someone who had rarely felt that in her life, it was priceless.

"Everything's fine. Tommy just needs to remember how to speak to a client," Sav told Razor with a scowl.

She thought Tommy needed to remember how to speak to other people, period. But she didn't say anything.

None of your business, Tabby.

"We've talked about this, Tommy," Razor said in a cold voice. "Do we need another chat?"

"No, boss, I'm good. Sorry, missus."

She didn't think he was at all sincere, but she nodded. If she was lucky enough to get this job, then she'd have to work with Weasel Dick.

Maybe she should rethink this idea.

No. She could do this. She had thick enough skin to put up with some sexist comments. As long as he didn't try to touch her.

"Hey, I'm Razor, the owner. Can I help you?" he asked politely, his southern drawl faint.

Oh, great, he didn't recognize her. Her stomach dropped.

"Thought you knew each other," Sav said. What kind of name was Sav? A name like Razor, she guessed.

"Oh, well, I, um . . ."

Razor studied her, frowning. "Do I know you?"

Then she realized she had on her big sunglasses. She liked to hide behind them, but she couldn't expect him to recognize her all these months later with them on. So she slipped them up onto her head. She thought she heard Tommy mutter something, but Sav said something to him and it shut Weasel Dick up.

She forced herself to meet Razor's gaze. "I don't know if you remember me, I'm—"

"Tabby," he breathed out the name. "You're Tabby."

3

Tabby was here.

In his office.

What was she doing here now?

Was she here to commission a bike for her new man? Unless she was here for herself? But no, she was tiny. Delicate. He couldn't imagine her on a bike.

The protective instincts that she'd stirred the night he'd met her reappeared.

He couldn't stand assholes who picked on those weaker than them. His hands clenched into fists.

Easy. That bastard, Luther, is dead.

He wished he'd done it himself, though. Jared Bartolli, her cousin, had killed Luther. Something he should have done long before then.

The last time he'd seen her, she had been traumatized. Abused and beaten. He'd wanted to do whatever he could to ease the fear on her face. It had killed him when she'd decided to leave with her cousin.

He hadn't gotten it then. Didn't get it now.

But right now, that didn't matter. Not when she was sitting across his desk from him.

She was so serious as she stared at him, that it made his heart ache. Life was so short. Too short to spend it being sad.

Fuck, listen to him. Getting fanciful in his old f age, wasn't he?

Practically philosophical. Maybe he should look at writing this shit down.

Life according to Razor: A guide of what not to do.

Tabby shifted around, giving him a nervous look. Her cheeks were pale. She appeared tired. Worried. Her dark hair was pulled back in a tight braid.

Suddenly, he realized he was just sitting here, staring at her. Shit. No wonder she seemed like she was about to bolt. He cleared his throat and she half-jumped out of her seat.

"You don't need to be scared of me, Tabby," he told her. Then he rolled his eyes at himself. Her husband had been the lowest fucking scum in the pond. Of course she was nervous. She didn't know him well. Sure, he'd never touch a hair on her head, but she didn't know that.

He cleared his throat. "I'd never hurt you."

"I know that," she whispered. Then she gathered herself, straightening her shoulders and staring him in the eye. Her transformation surprised him and made him inexplicably proud. She was obviously intimidated by him, but she was trying to push that aside. "I wouldn't be here if I thought that."

Studying her, he tilted his head to the side. Why was she here, then?

"If you're here for a bike, then—"

She shook her head, her ponytail flicking back and forth. He wondered how long her hair was when it was down? Really long, he was guessing. "I'm not here for a bike. Not right now, anyway. Maybe one day."

Okay, then. So . . . something occurred to him and he leaned forward. "Are you in trouble? Do you need help? Are you trying to escape from your cousin?"

Surprise filled her face. "Why would I need to escape from Jared?"

"I know who he is," he reminded her.

"I don't need to escape Jared. He wouldn't hurt me."

Hm. He wasn't so convinced. He'd thought about trying to contact her, but then he'd remembered the look on her face as she'd said goodbye. The firmness in her tone as she'd told him she would be fine.

She wasn't his to worry over. Just because he'd felt protective of her, didn't mean that she owed him anything.

"Why are you here after all this time?"

She jumped slightly, even though he'd spoken in a calm voice.

"I'm not here for a bike, and I'm not here for help or to escape my cousin. He's not a bad man."

"So, why are you here? Haven't heard from you once all this time. Thought you must have thrown my card away."

"I tried to," she whispered. "I probably should have. I shouldn't even really be here. It was a stupid idea." She stood and started moving towards the door.

"Tabby," he said in a low voice. "Freeze."

She stilled. He'd expected she might. But he didn't want her obeying him because she was afraid. No, he wanted her to obey him because she wanted to.

That thought came as a surprise. He wasn't interested in her.

Sure, she was gorgeous. But she was also a lot younger than him. Vulnerable.

Turning, she glared at him fiercely. There was something in the way she held herself that told him that while she wasn't completely confident in her own skin, she was getting there.

He was fucking proud of her.

"Why are you here? You kept my card, I'm guessing. Looked

me up. Decided to come here. You're not really going to leave without assuaging my curiosity, right?"

"Right," she whispered. "Well, I'm actually here about the job."

The job? What?

Oh. Hell.

His eyes widened. "You want a job? Here?"

"Yes." She nodded woodenly and it was clear that she was braced against rejection. "I saw it advertised and I wondered if you had filled it. But you likely have. Or you probably want someone with more experience. I don't have any. I've never even had a job before. I'd probably be crap at it."

His eyes widened as she continued to talk.

"Sorry," she finally said. "I'll just leave now."

"Tabby, wait." She continued to walk through the outer office towards the door. "Tabby, come back here."

Turning, her hands clenched into fists at her side. "It was a stupid idea and I apologize for wasting your time. I don't know what I was thinking."

She was timid. Shy and quiet. His guys were rough. They swore a lot, the things they talked about weren't for her ears. And some of his clients weren't much better.

She had no experience. Not great when there was a lot he needed her to do quickly.

She was gorgeous and sweet. He'd prefer someone that his guys wouldn't drool over.

And yet . . .

Standing, he sighed. Then he realized she'd already left. Fuck. He raced out of his office, through the other room and outside, where he spotted her opening the driver's door on a late model beamer.

Shit. She'd driven a hundred-thousand-dollar car into this neighborhood and left it here? The boys must have kept an eye on it for her while they were working.

"Tabby, I said wait." He was too old to chase after her.

She froze by the door, but she wouldn't look up at him. Her gaze was kept on her feet.

Fuck, he hated that.

"Tabby, look at me."

"It was a stupid idea. Don't know what I was thinking. Why would you want me to work for you? Idiot."

Oh, hell no.

He scowled, then went to reach for her chin with his finger. Until he remembered her bruised face after Luther hurt her. And how she'd curled into herself. How often had she been abused by that asshole?

He wouldn't touch her without her permission. Not when he didn't know her well.

"Tabby, don't talk about yourself like that," he told her in a low, coaxing voice. "I don't like it. And it's definitely not true. You are not an idiot."

She slowly raised her head, her hazel eyes meeting his. "I am, though. I'm sorry you wasted your time."

Again, he raised his hand then dropped it. A stricken look filled her face before it disappeared. She'd likely learned to hide her emotions.

"I think the question should be, why wouldn't I want you?" he asked her.

She held up her fingers, ticking them off. "I've no experience. I've never had a job. I don't know a thing about motorbikes. Or about any systems you might use."

"You know, seeing as you've never had a job, you might not know how a job interview works. But generally, you tell a prospective employer all the reasons why they should hire you, not all the reasons they shouldn't."

He grinned to let her know he was joking. He got a small smile back. He took that as a victory.

"So, you have anything good to tell me about yourself for why I should want to hire you?" he asked after she was silent for a good few minutes. He was going to hire her. He didn't know how she'd gotten out from under Bartolli's thumb, but she had. And he wouldn't allow anyone to take advantage of her. The world was a fucking harsh place, which she knew all too well. If he could shield her from some of that, though . . .

"No," she told him.

Shit. That hurt. She couldn't think of one good thing to say about herself when she should be full of them? That was just wrong. On so many levels.

He wanted to change that.

"Except, I'll work hard. I promise. I can learn things quickly, and I'll keep working at it until I do. I'll come in early and leave late. I have no life, so that's not a problem."

He ran his hand over his face and looked back at the shop. Christ. This was probably a bad idea. But he'd had people help him when he'd needed a start. And there weren't many people who'd hire a twenty-something-year-old with no experience or skills.

"Okay, how about this? You start at eight, finish at four. We'll do a trial of a month, make sure it all works out. After three months, if you decide to stay longer, you get a raise. Okay?"

"You mean . . . I have the job?" she whispered, looking so shocked that it actually hurt him.

"Yeah, you have the job. Although there's something I have to tell you. The guys that work for me, they don't have the best pasts. Some of them have been in jail. Others were in gangs. They're all trying to turn their lives around, but you should know what you're dealing with."

"I can deal with that."

"You won't be out in the garage much, anyway. You'll deal

mainly with me or Dart. He runs the place when I'm not around. I'll introduce you to him tomorrow."

"Thank you," she said again. "You won't regret this."

"I know I won't. Now, is this the only car you have?"

She blinked up at him. Lord, she was gorgeous. So beautiful, it was almost like someone had drawn her because she was too perfect to be real.

"Um, yeah. Is there something wrong with it?"

"Just sticks out like a sore thumb in this neighborhood. I don't want you leaving it on the street. Drive it into the lot. All right?"

"Yes, sir."

"Razor is fine. Go home. Get some rest. I'll see you at eight tomorrow. Not before, though, understand?"

"All right. Should I wear anything in particular?"

"No dress code. Just wear something comfy."

She gave him a nod and climbed into her car. He forced himself to move, telling himself that he couldn't watch her drive away. And that she'd be fine.

She didn't need him going all over protective on her ass.

Much as he might want to.

Christ, now he needed to go have a chat with the guys about toning their language down around her.

That was going to go over well.

SHE CELEBRATED her new job with pizza and chocolate milk. She might have a new addiction.

"Cheers, Snappy." She held up her glass of milk to her toy turtle. Maybe she should think about getting an actual turtle. Her mom had bought Snappy for her when she was little. He was pretty much the only thing she had from her childhood.

"Maybe a turtle is too much commitment right now. I could get a goldfish. What do you think?"

She'd never had a stable enough life for a pet. But maybe it was time to start turning that around. Yeah, maybe she'd look into a goldfish. Perhaps one of those fish tanks. That could be quite fun.

"Things are looking up, Snappy. I think this could be the turning point. Razor is, well, he's sexy as hell. But I shouldn't really notice that, right? He's my boss."

It had kind of hurt when he'd gone to touch her, then pulled his hand back. She shouldn't take it as a rejection, but she did.

"I really think I'm going to ace this job. It's going to be fun."

S he wasn't having fun.

And she definitely wasn't acing this job. In fact, she thought it was fair to say she pretty much sucked at it.

Three days she'd been here and she didn't have a freaking clue what she was doing. She'd barely seen Razor. She'd figured he would show

her what to do, but instead, this condescending jerk called Matthew had given her an hour-long whirlwind tutorial on everything she needed to know, then left her to it.

Apparently, he used to have her job, but he'd recently moved on to somewhere else. He'd come in specially to train her so she didn't feel she could ask him to explain everything again. She also didn't want to call him when she was stuck. So, she spent a lot of time online trying to understand the accounting software they used and looking up the different mechanical parts and terms.

Maybe it would have been easier if Razor had been in the office. But he was out in the shop, working frantically on a custom job that they'd gotten behind on. She'd seen him on the first day when he'd introduced her to Matthew. But otherwise, he'd been mostly absent.

She knew he felt bad, he'd apologized. But why should she expect any special treatment? She was an employee. She'd claimed that she'd be able to learn quickly and that's what she'd do, damn it.

She wished she didn't feel like an idiot for not understanding any of this, though.

"Tabby."

She looked up as Razor walked in, rubbing the grease off his hands. He looked slightly stressed. Quickly, she swallowed her mouthful of granola bar.

"Hey," she said quietly.

"Reckon you can call around and find me a part? I'll get one of the boys to pick it up." He drew a piece of paper out of his back pocket. She looked down at his chicken scrawl in dismay. What the hell did that even say?

"Can you read it?" he asked.

"Not really."

He huffed out a laugh and moved around behind her. Bending over, he placed his hand on the desk and she got a whiff of his aftershave.

Oh, Lord, help her.

Was it weird that she hadn't felt any real arousal in years, yet his scent, his closeness, sent her body into overdrive?

She was pretty sure that she shouldn't feel this way about her boss.

"Did you get that?"

"Yep, sure." She crossed her fingers because she hadn't heard a freaking word.

Fuck. Fuck, fuck, fuck.

He eyed her. Then he told her what he needed again, while she could feel her face heating. He knew she was messing this up, that she hadn't been listening.

Crap. Do better, Tabby.

"Sure you're okay?"

"I'm fine. I have this."

She didn't. She really didn't.

"Good. Can you please grab the guys' lunch orders too? It's gonna be a long day and I want to keep them happy. Take the money from petty cash."

"All right."

"Anything you need? Matty go through everything with you all right? He didn't seem to be here long, you must pick up things quick."

She nodded, while her brain screamed at her to confess that she had no idea what was going on.

"You know where the list of preferred suppliers is?"

No clue.

But it seemed like something she should know, so she nodded again. By now, she was crossing her toes as well. Not literally, but it was the thought that counted.

"Do you want me to do the lunch orders first or find the part?" she asked.

"Find the part, first. When you do, tell Tommy, he can go get it."

Great. Weasel Dick. Her favorite person.

All the guys that worked here were rough around the edges. She'd only met them briefly when Razor had taken her on a quick tour on her first day. But Tabby was used to being around coarse men. And she knew the worst thing you could do was show fear.

"Um, Tabby?" He looked at her strangely.

"Yes?"

"Is there something blue on your ear?" He reached out and rubbed at her ear.

Oh God. Oh God.

Mortification filled her and she knew her face went red. He raised an eyebrow as his lips twitched.

"Maybe." Was this really happening? This couldn't be happening!

"There a reason why there's blue stuff on your ear?"

"Smoothie accident," she muttered.

"A smoothie accident?" he drawled.

More like a smoothie disaster. After her jog this morning, she'd decided to make herself a healthy smoothie, with blueberries and a banana. Only, she obviously hadn't put the lid on properly. It had blown off, spraying blue juice everywhere. By the time she'd cleaned up the kitchen, she'd been running late. She could have sworn she'd washed all the blueberry off her, though.

Obviously not.

"Yeah, I didn't put the lid on properly. It exploded everywhere. I thought I had gotten it all."

"Think it's all off now," he reassured her. "You've got to watch those blenders."

"Yeah, I've figured that out." To say that her experiments in the kitchen were going well would be an outright lie.

After Razor left, she slumped down in her seat, banging her head lightly against her desk.

Dummy.

After finally finding the list of preferred suppliers, she called around to find the part and wrote the name of the place and address on a piece of paper for Tommy.

Right. Now to go find Weasel Dick. Grabbing a pen and paper, she figured she'd also take everyone's lunch order at the same time.

She found Tommy out the back having a smoke break. She frowned. Everyone was frantically working inside and he had time to smoke? That didn't seem right. But she shook it off.

"Hello, sweetness," he said in a fake-deep voice that he probably thought sounded sexy.

She thought he sounded like he was constipated.

"Razor wants you to go get this part," she told him, holding out the piece of paper. "I've put it on hold. Here are the details."

He ignored the paper, his gaze eating her up. "You want to go get a drink after work?"

"No, thank you," she said as politely as she could manage. He made her skin crawl.

"Come on, sweetness. You'll have fun with me. You're uptight, I'll loosen you up."

Ew. She thought she'd puked a little.

Calm. Don't rock the boat.

"Go get the part."

His eyes narrowed as he stared at her. "Uppity bitch, aren't you?"

Her shoulders straightened as he glared at her.

Don't show any fear. Don't back down.

"Razor said you would get it. I'm just passing on what he wants."

"Say please and I'll do it," he told her.

Yeah. That wasn't happening.

"No."

Anger flooded his face. "Best not cross me, bitch. I'm not a person you want as an enemy."

He threw the smoke on the ground and, snatching the piece of paper out of her hand, stomped away. With a grimace, she ground out the glowing cigarette with her shoe then let out a shaky sigh.

Then she realized she didn't have his lunch order. Oh well, she'd be sure to get him something really gross. Moving into the shop, she went around to the other guys. Razor had ten guys working for him, which was far more than she'd expected.

Last, she walked over to where Sav and Razor were standing,

discussing something. Both men were frowning. Razor had his arms crossed over his chest, making his biceps bulge.

Wow, that was hot.

Get your mind off your hot boss. Jeepers.

"Hey, Tabby," Razor greeted her gently, his frown disappearing as soon as he saw her.

She managed a shaky smile as Sav nodded at her.

"Lunch orders?"

They both rattled off what they wanted from the sub shop.

"You find that part?" Razor asked.

"Yeah, Tommy's gone to get it. I'll go grab lunch now."

Sav wasn't looking at her, but Razor gave her a nod. "Thanks, kid."

She had to hide a wince. Kid? Really?

WHEN SHE RETURNED thirty minutes later with a pile of subs, she'd bought Tommy an extra spicy one, Razor and Tommy were out front, discussing something. Both men stared over at her as she got out of her car. Razor appeared confused while Tommy looked smug.

Her stomach tightened.

Uh-oh.

"Hey, Tabby, why'd you send me on a wild goose chase?" Tommy called out.

"What? What do you mean?" she asked.

"That place you sent me to didn't have the part on hold and they had no record of you calling them."

"But I put it on hold. It should have been there. I'll call them."

"No point," Tommy told her. "I was just there. Waste of fucking time."

"Watch it," Razor warned. "It was just a mistake."

"They said they had the part, though," she said frantically, feeling ill. "I'll call them again, then go over myself and get it."

"Don't worry," Razor told her gently. He ran a hand over his face, looking tired. "I'll sort it and go get the part, okay? It's no issue. All part of learning."

He walked into the office and she watched him, that sick feeling in her stomach growing.

Shit.

She hated that she'd messed up.

"So, what did you get me for lunch?" Tommy asked, swaggering over to her.

"That part really wasn't there? You went to the place I wrote down?"

"Course I did. I'm not stupid. Don't know how you fucked it up, but it's not my fault. And I've lost an hour out of my day."

"Right. Sorry." She handed him the sub and he nodded his thanks.

THAT NIGHT, when she dragged herself into her loft apartment, she felt exhausted. She'd tried to stay late. Some of the guys were staying to finish up a job and it didn't feel right to leave. But Razor had walked into the office around five and ordered her to go home.

Probably worried she'd mess something else up. She couldn't blame him for that.

Grabbing Snappy from her bed, she moved into the attached bathroom and ran a bath. She added her favorite bubbles. Yeah, they were kids bubbles and tutti-fruity-scented but she didn't care.

She needed cheering up.

How had she messed up something so simple?

She stayed in the bath until her fingertips were wrinkly and the water was cool. Climbing out, she got ready for bed, pulling on her favorite soft pajamas. They had images of Scooby-Doo all over them.

She knew she should eat. But she was just too tired, and her stomach was still tied up in knots. As she fell back into bed, clasping Snappy close, her phone rang. Who the heck would that be?

Well, actually, there was only one person it was likely to be. She grimaced. Awesome.

Why now?

She didn't have the strength to deal with him. The ringing ended, but then she saw he'd called her three times while she was in the bath. Shoot. If she didn't answer him now, he was going to send someone around.

Or come himself.

Fuck it.

She called him back, putting him on speaker.

"Hey, Jared."

"Tabitha, why didn't you answer your phone?" he snapped. "What's wrong?"

"Sorry, I was in the bath. Nothing's wrong." She made sure she made her voice light and cheerful.

"You sound weird. Why do you sound like that? Is someone there? Are they threatening you?"

She closed her eyes. Christ. She was about to give him a coronary. As well as finding herself dragged back to his house.

"Jared, I'm fine. Promise. There's no one here."

"That's what you'd say if someone was threatening you."

"But they're not. Here, I'll switch to camera." She turned the camera on, waving at him. "See? Fine." She flipped it, showing him the empty room, before flipping it back. She studied her cousin. He was probably a handsome guy. If you were into tall, dark, and cold as ice.

He frowned at her.

"How are you?" she asked.

"Fine," he said brusquely, as though he didn't have time for niceties. He likely didn't. She wondered what had happened to the boy who used to protect her.

"When are you coming home?"

She sighed. His house wasn't her home. It wasn't even his home. It was a place he sometimes slept. It was cold and uninviting and she hoped that she wouldn't ever be going back there.

"I'm not."

"Tabitha, this has gone on long enough, don't you think? You need to come home where you'll be safe."

And smothered. Likely used as a pawn again. Jared wouldn't mean to. He'd probably convince himself it was in her best interest. But no doubt, he'd arrange for her to marry someone else.

Not happening.

"I'm safe. Nobody knows I'm your cousin." She crossed her fingers at that lie. "I'm careful." Another lie. Whoa, she was going to be in trouble if he ever found out. "Nothing exciting happens in my life. I just sit around doing puzzles and watching bad TV."

No way was she telling him about her job. Eventually, he'd find out. She was actually kind of shocked he didn't have someone watching her. But if he did, then she figured she would have already caught hell for her early morning jogging. Not to mention her job.

There was another voice in the background. She couldn't see the person or properly hear what they said but Jared frowned. "I have to go. Be careful. Call me if you need me."

The call ended and she slumped back into bed. Not only was she messing up at her job, but she was lying to her cousin. A cousin who could take away everything she had.

Unless she earned it herself. Unless she broke free.

And to do that, she really needed to keep this job.

Reaching for her turtle nightlight, she turned it on. It had stars and planets cut out of the shell, and when she turned off the main light, it was like she was outside under the sky. She hadn't been able to sleep in the dark for years. Something that Luther had unfortunately discovered and tortured her with.

Why hit someone when you could gain their cooperation and misery by locking them up in the dark?

Of course, he'd actually enjoyed hitting her, so she guessed he didn't care.

Put him out of your head.

She tossed and turned for what felt like hours. She'd fall into a light sleep, only to wake up gasping for breath and sweaty.

In the early hours of the morning, she gave up and got up. She'd go for a jog. It was the only way she'd found to clear her head. To give her a bit of peace.

Even if just for an hour.

Running was her stress relief, a way of easing all the restless energy she had. She pulled on her workout clothes. Then grabbing her pack that held her phone, pepper spray, and a stun gun, she set off. She'd started carrying her stun gun after that incident with Cat.

Immediately, she knew it was a bad idea. Her head thumped and her body didn't want to move. Pausing, she leaned against the front of a building, trying to gather in some air. Crap.

The sound of footsteps approaching had her tensing. She reached into her pack and grabbed hold of her pepper spray.

"Hey there."

She glanced up, relaxing slightly when she saw who it was. Not that she knew the guy who was jogging in place in front of her. But she'd seen him a few times. He had a short beard, and he always carried around a backpack and had a cap pulled down on his head.

Which she'd always thought a little odd. But maybe he just liked wearing caps.

"You okay?"

"Oh yeah, I'm fine."

"Not to sound rude, but you don't look okay. Have you got some water?"

"No. But I'm fine, really." As much as this guy seemed okay, she still didn't like standing around alone in the dark with him. A car approached, the lights shining bright in her eyes.

Great. That didn't help her headache. She groaned.

"Here, have some of my water."

A metal drink bottle was held out in front of her.

"Oh no, really, I'm fine."

"I haven't drunk anything out of it," he reassured, pushing it towards her. She took hold of it because it seemed the polite thing to do, but didn't open it.

She wasn't silly enough to take a drink out of an unsealed bottle. "Really, I can't. I've had a bit of a sore throat lately."

"Should you be out jogging with a sore throat?" he asked sternly.

She flushed at the chiding tone. "Um, likely not."

The man grunted but took the drink bottle back. "Probably why you had to stop. You should go home and rest. Take it easy."

"I'm going to go do that. Thanks for stopping." Just because he was a bit bossy didn't mean she wasn't appreciative.

"I better go. You can get home all right?"

"Yep. Thanks."

"Oh, I'm Reynard, by the way."

"Tabby."

"Nice to meet you, Tabby. I'll see you."

She took off at a fast walk. Her throat was parched, but she knew she'd made the right choice not taking a sip of his water. He'd seemed nice, but then likely so did serial killers and rapists.

When she made it home, relief filled her. Now, she just had to find the energy to get to work.

SHE STILL FELT exhausted when she pulled into work at seven-thirty. She didn't even have the energy to drive around and wait until eight. At least some painkillers had taken care of her headache. The gates were shut, so she parked on the street. Maybe she'd just sit here for a moment and rest her eyes. The sound of a vehicle approaching made her sit up, watching as Razor pulled up to the gate in his truck and entered a code, making the electric gate slide open.

He climbed out of his truck then pointed at her and crooked a finger before pointing into the parking lot.

Right. Stop sitting around, Tabby. It's weird.

Driving into one of the spaces that were meant for customers, she turned off her car. Suddenly, her door opened and Razor frowned down at her. A gorgeous-looking dog stood beside him, wagging her tail, whining eagerly.

He reached down to pat her head. "Easy, Luna."

It shouldn't be a turn-on, watching him pat his dog, hearing that note of affection in his voice. But it was. A guy that was good to his dog had to be a good guy, right?

Reaching into the car, he undid her seatbelt.

She froze. That was a surprisingly intimate gesture. Especially from someone who was usually very careful not to touch her. So careful, it was almost insulting.

"Come out, please."

There was something stiff in his voice. Formal. Oh no, was he going to fire her? Because of one little mistake? But it was a mistake that had cost him valuable time, so could she really blame him?

But she desperately needed this job.

Climbing out of the car, she shut the door. His dog made a whining noise, looking like she wanted to pounce.

"Stay, Luna," he said sternly.

"Gorgeous dog," she told him nervously.

"Thanks. She spends some days here and some days with my neighbor or friends."

She nodded. "I'm really sorry about yesterday. It won't happen again. I'll be extra careful next time."

Lord, she wished she'd stopped for more caffeine this morning. Her brain felt all fogged up. This wasn't going to help her concentrate on work today.

"Tabby, I'm not upset about what happened yesterday."

"You're not? You should be. I cost you valuable time. I'm meant to be helping, not making things harder for you."

His lips twitched. "Are you wanting me to tell you off, kid?"

She clenched her jaw in irritation. Yeah, she was younger than him. In years. But not necessarily in life. She hadn't been a kid for a long, long time. Not since her mom died.

"I'm not a kid," she told him forcefully. Shit. She probably shouldn't have said it like that. Luna whined and pushed her head against Tabby's hand. Tabby patted her absentmindedly, taking comfort from the dog.

Boss. He's your boss.

Razor pushed his sunglasses up onto the top of his head. "I didn't mean to offend you."

"No, I'm sorry. I'm just a bit out of sorts this morning."

He shook his head. "You should tell me if there's something you don't like. I shouldn't be calling you a kid when you're not. I apologize."

She stared at him, flabbergasted. When was the last time someone had apologized to her? When had a *man* had apologized to her? Even Jared hadn't apologized for taking so long to get her away from Luther.

"Tabby? You okay?"

"Um, yeah. Sorry. I just, you don't have to apologize. You're the boss."

"That doesn't mean I don't make mistakes. Or mean I can get away with anything I want." He grinned, his white teeth gleaming. Wow, he had gorgeous teeth.

Tabby, Tabby, you have got it bad. His teeth, seriously?

Maybe she needed to think about dating. Or at least buying a vibrator.

But she'd have to wait until her first paycheck to get that. She wasn't buying it on her cousin's credit card.

Mind you, that could be kind of funny.

"Not saying it wouldn't be nice to have that much power." He winked at her and she felt her entire body sigh.

Lord, oh, Lord.

Help her.

"But if there's something I or anyone here does that makes you feel uncomfortable or is out of line, I want you to tell me, hear? Should have made that clear before now."

She thought about Tommy. But he wasn't exactly out of line, was he? It was hard for her to judge. It wasn't like he'd touched her.

"Like I told you, all of these guys have been in the system or they were in gangs. I'm trying to give them a way out. To earn money. But not all of them will stick with it. Any of them bother you, I want you to tell me. Hear me?"

He spoke in a firm voice, which she wasn't used to from him.

"Okay."

"Mean it, Tabby. I won't be happy if you don't. You've been warned."

Why the heck did that send a shiver up her spine?

Two vibrators. Maybe she needed two. And a big box of batteries. Lube.

Sheesh, Tabby. Making up for the last few years of no sexual arousal, huh?

"You okay?"

"Um, yes, of course."

He studied her intently. Oh God, she hadn't said any of that out loud, had she? Mortification filled her and she could feel herself growing red.

"Should I ask why you're blushing?"

"I think it would be best if you didn't," she replied primly.

He barked out a laugh that flooded her with happiness.

"All right then. I won't ask."

Thank the Lord for that much.

"What time is it, Tabby?"

Huh? She looked down at her watch. "Um, seven-forty-five."

"What time do you start work?"

"Eight. But, I—"

"And what time did you work to last night?"

"Five, but—"

"And what did I say to you last night when you left?"

"That I should come in later this morning," she said reluctantly. "But I wanted to stay late last night, it was the least I could do after I messed up."

"Tabby, you made a small mistake. Not the end of the world. Everyone makes them and you're just learning. You don't owe me anything. I don't want you coming early and leaving late, all right? I definitely don't want you alone in this neighborhood, understand?"

"I would have waited in my car."

"Not the point. Leave early this afternoon, understand?"

"Yes, sir," she whispered before she could help herself.

Razor just grinned at her. "Razor will do." He studied her closely. "Now, you want a coffee? Because I do."

"Um, yes, but I'll make them."

She expected a comeback from him, but he just nodded. "Won't say no to that. I take it black with one sugar. I think it's a yes, but do you mind having Luna hang with you?"

He glanced down at where she was patting the dog without even realizing it.

"Yeah, I'd like that."

THAT NIGHT, she went online and bought a vibrator, some lube, and a clit tickler.

Please, let that help her.

And please, don't let Jared find out she was spending his money on adult toys.

5

Razor had just climbed out of his truck when he heard the scream.

With the music and other noise from the garage, he knew the others likely wouldn't have heard. Opening up the back his truck, he pulled out his baseball bat. No, he didn't play baseball. But he did carry around a ball and mitt as well, just in case he was ever questioned about it.

Luna started barking as he opened the office door. It was kind of sweet how attached she'd gotten to Tabby in a short while.

He raced in, the bat held high as he stared around, searching for the threat.

To his shock, Tabby was standing on the desk while Luna continued to bark at the small kitchen area he had set up in here. It was basically just a bar fridge, microwave, and coffee machine, along with a cupboard to store stuff.

"What's going on? Why did you scream?"

He lowered the bat, his heart racing as he realized there was no immediate threat.

"Luna, quiet," he ordered in a calm voice as he walked closer to

Tabby. The normally composed and serious girl was trembling and pale. She'd worked here for a week and a half now, and he hadn't learned much about her. She kept to herself mostly, not talking much unless it was work-related. He'd invited her out last Friday night for drinks, but she'd declined. Not that he blamed her. She probably had better things to do with her time than hang out with her workmates.

So it was a surprise to find her up on the desk, looking like she was about to vomit.

"Tabby? You okay?"

"N-no."

"What is it? What happened? Did someone threaten you?"

Luna was still sniffing around the kitchen area. And it suddenly clicked. "Wait, are you up there because you saw a—"

"Mouse!" she cried, pointing.

He started to turn, but then he found himself holding a trembling woman. She wrapped herself around him, legs clasping his waist, her arms strangling his neck.

"Mouse! Mouse!"

Luna was barking excitedly as he put one arm around Tabby, his other hand still held onto the baseball bat. The damn mouse shot across the floor. Luna, rather than giving chase, bounced up and down, pouncing as though she thought this was some great game.

It was utter chaos.

And so it was at that moment that Reyes walked in the door.

"Well, this isn't something you see every day," Reyes said with amusement.

SHE KNEW she was being ridiculous.

It's just a mouse, Tabby. An itty-bitty mouse. Can't do you any harm.

But it could run up her leg. A mouse had done that to Luther once. He'd been wearing his boxers around the house. They'd been a size too small and they'd put everything on display. The sausage and the mounds of mashed potatoes.

Wait . . . she didn't think that was the saying. Oh, whatever. It didn't matter. The last thing she wanted to think about right now was Luther's dick.

"Did she just say that she was thinking about Luther's dick?" Reyes said. She remembered him from that night at Millie's house. He'd been there along with Razor. Back then, he'd stared at her with pity. Right now, he was looking at her like she'd lost her mind.

Maybe she had. All it had taken was a mouse to send her over the edge.

"No! I didn't! I don't want to think about his dick at all! I wish I'd never seen it. Oh Lord, I'm losing it. I'm so sorry. It's just, this mouse once ran up Luther's leg when he was standing around in his boxers. And he tried to get it off and it bit him. Not on the dick. I wish it had. That would have been a reason to cheer the mouse on. No, it bit him on the hand. And then the bite got infected. It was gross. And I didn't want it to bite me! I'm so sorry, Razor! I know this is so unprofessional," she wailed.

Luna let out a howl at her words, obviously in sympathy.

Oh, Lord. She was making such a fool of herself. This was terrible. She didn't dare look at Razor, not wanting to see how horrified he was at her behavior. So she turned to Reyes. He was a good-looking guy, but a bit scary. And she was acting like an idiot.

"Luna, quiet," Razor told the dog firmly.

Luna stopped howling and then looked up at Razor, her tail wagging back and forth.

"You want me to go get some mouse traps?" Reyes asked.

Razor sighed and shook his head. "Nah, I've got some in the shop. I'll grab 'em."

"I'll get them, man. You take care of this." Reyes' lips twitched. Was he laughing at her?

Probably. She was making a spectacle of herself.

"Tabby, gonna put you on the desk, okay?" Razor said gently.

Not okay. She was happy where she was. Maybe a bit too happy. Yeah, she should probably let go of him. She couldn't spend the rest of the day in his arms.

As nice as that sounded.

"Okay," she whispered.

Razor set her down on her desk and she forced herself to let him go. She eyed the corner where she'd last seen the mouse.

"Tabby, eyes on me."

Her gaze rose at those words, surprised at the firm tone. Not that she could blame him, she was acting like a lunatic. "Tabby, a mouse will only bite if it feels cornered."

She knew that. But it still didn't make her feel any better. She didn't want it to run up her leg. She should have worn tights today.

"Hey, eyes back on me."

Whoops, she hadn't realized that her gaze had strayed to the corner again. She raised her eyes to meet dark gaze.

"It's more scared of you than you are of it."

Was he sure about that? Because she wasn't. She was pretty damn scared. Although, she was starting to feel more than a bit foolish. It was just a mouse. She was far bigger than it.

"Sorry for embarrassing you."

"You didn't embarrass me," he reassured her.

That was kind of him to say, but she wasn't sure it was true.

"Sorry for jumping on you."

His lips twitched. "Can't say I was expecting it, but you don't have to be sorry."

"I didn't hurt you, did I?"

"Hurt me?" Uh-oh, now he sounded offended. "Just how would you hurt me?"

"Well, I kind of just flung myself at you. I didn't hurt your back or anything, did I?"

His gaze narrowed and he crossed his arms over his chest. "Are you implying that I'm not strong enough to hold you up?"

"I'd never imply that." She shook her head. Nope. Not her.

He grunted. In satisfaction or annoyance, she wasn't sure. "Damn right, you weren't implying that. Because I caught you just fine."

The door opened and Reyes walked back in. His intense gaze moved over her before he looked at Razor and held up two mouse traps still in their packaging. "Found these. They do?"

Razor nodded. "Tabby, do you remember Reyes?"

"Ah, yes. Hi."

Reyes nodded to her. Then he turned to Razor. "She's shaking."

Razor eyed her.

"I'm fine," she said, embarrassed that Reyes had noticed.

Razor moved around her desk and opened up her snack drawer, rustling through it. What was he doing? He came back with her emergency chocolate bar. Then he opened it. She gave him a disgruntled look. She would have shared if he'd asked, but it seemed a bit presumptuous to just open it and help himself, right?

But then he held a piece up to her mouth. "Open." Reyes made a strange noise and Razor turned to look at him. "Got something to say?"

"Me? Nope. Never."

Razor grunted.

She stared at him in shock. He'd gotten the chocolate for her? Why?

"Tabby, open your mouth," he urged.

Her mouth opened before she even thought about it. But she didn't want chocolate. Only as soon as the sweet, creamy goodness hit her tongue she felt better.

"You just need a bit of sugar to settle down," he told her,

breaking off another piece and feeding it to her. If he was trying to settle her, he was failing, because having him feed her like this was awakening something else deep inside her.

"That's enough for now. Have a feeling we might need the rest of this later." He wrapped up the chocolate and put it away. "Tabby, why don't you go home early? I'll set these up before I leave and hopefully catch the mouse overnight."

"I'll be all right here," she told him, licking her lips. As long as she kept her legs up at all times.

He shook his head. "There's not much left to do. I'll be in the office now, anyway. Go home."

"Will the . . . will the trap hurt it?"

His eyes widened and he stared at her. "What?"

"Will the trap hurt it? I don't want it to be hurt. Just for it to not be here. With me. You won't hurt it, will you?"

Both of them were staring at her incredulously.

"I thought you were scared of mice?" Reyes asked.

"Well, yes, but I still don't want it hurt."

SHE DIDN'T WANT him to hurt it?

Was she kidding right now? But the look on her face said she wasn't. She was perfectly serious.

He still couldn't believe that she'd thrown herself at him like she had. Mostly, she shied away from touch. Although, she seemed to be growing more at ease with him.

Still, it had been a shock to find her pressed up against him. A nice shock.

Stop thinking about how much you enjoyed holding her. Perv.

"Um," he said, mind scrambling.

"We'll go get some humane traps," Reyes suddenly said.

That shocked him. He raised his eyebrows at Reyes, who gave him a calm look back.

"You will? But that's a hassle for you." She worried at her lip. He hated when she did that. When she got that look on her face like she was expecting someone to yell at her. Or worse.

That bastard, Luther, had a lot to answer for.

"Why don't you go get some," he suddenly suggested.

"I . . . are you sure you don't need me?"

He nodded. "Go get the traps, bring them back. Then go home." He firmed his voice, giving her a look that told her he meant business.

To his surprise, she actually gave in.

"All right," she whispered. Then she looked to the corner where the mouse had run to and carefully got to her feet.

He thought about offering to carry her, but that probably wasn't appropriate.

Reyes stepped aside and opened the door for her. She paused and gave the other man a surprised look. Razor hated that she wasn't used to simple courtesies. That having someone do something for her surprised her.

"Nice to meet you, Tabby," Reyes told her.

"You too," she whispered. He noted that she took a wide berth around the other man. Reyes noticed that too, his eyes narrowing.

When she was gone and the door was shut, Reyes turned to him. "Got something to tell me?"

"Nope," Razor replied, knowing what he was implying. "She's an employee."

"Hm, when was the last time you fed one of the guys chocolate because they were a bit shaken up?"

Razor glared at him. "She was upset."

"Hm. She's jumpy."

"Wouldn't you be? With the life she lived?"

Reyes frowned. "Why the fuck did Bartolli not do something about that asshole she was married to?"

"Because he's an asshole."

"I don't know. From what I've heard, he doesn't hold with violence towards women. Apparently, he's not like his old man."

He raised his eyebrows. "You're defending him?"

"No. I don't know him. Just telling you what I've heard. Do you think it's just a coincidence that she's here?"

Razor frowned. He'd told the others on Saturday night that he'd hired her. He'd already had four calls from Millie asking how Tabby was doing, and if she wanted to come to Reaper's with them one night. He'd promised to ask her.

"You think she's been planted? By who? Jared Bartolli? What reason would he have to do that?"

"I don't know. I just find it odd."

"You see plots everywhere. I think it's likely she saw the ad for the job and thought she'd try her luck since she knew me. She doesn't have any experience or other references, so likely no one else would hire her."

Reyes shook his head. "You were suckered into hiring her, weren't you?"

"She's a hard worker and a quick learner," well mostly, "I'm glad I hired her."

"All right. But just be careful. I don't know if there's any reason why Bartolli would send her here, but I still think we should be cautious. Yeah?"

"Fine. How is Emme?"

"Good. Getting a bit frustrated by the fact that she has to have a constant guard." All of the girls were being closely watched after Mr. X kidnapped Jewel and gave her a warning for Markovich. Back off or he'd retaliate.

Probably a good thing Razor didn't have anyone special to protect. Because if he had someone like that and she was threatened, he'd lose his goddamn mind.

"Things will be better once we can figure out who Mr. X is."

"Yeah, but Emme will always have to be watched, because of

who her father is. She gets it. Just sometimes it's hard for her." Reyes shook his head. "But yeah, I'll sleep better once we know who this asshole is. Then we can take him out."

"Heard anything from the Fox?" he asked quietly.

"He's following up on a way of getting into the auction. Said it's taking him longer than expected."

"He'll get there."

Reyes just grunted. None of them were exactly fans of the Fox, Duke especially. But he did get results. How he went about getting those results was definitely not legal. But Razor wasn't going to question his methods. He might be a bad guy, technically. But since he was using his skills to take out worse guys, didn't that make him more gray than black?

Or had Razor lived so long in the gray he could no longer see anything else?

Damned if he knew.

"So, you ever gonna tell her that wasn't a mouse?" Reyes asked.

"Hell, no. Could you imagine her reaction if she knew it was a rat?"

Reyes just grinned, then he sobered. "If you like her, Razor—"

"It's not as simple as me liking her, and you know it. There's her past. The fact she works for me. And the threat from Mr. X."

"We can guard her. If she's who you want."

Razor shook his head. "It would be selfish of me to start anything with her. It's my job to protect her."

"You're never selfish, man. And maybe it's time to stop punishing yourself for the past."

"Her safety is more important than my happiness."

"I think you can have both. Just think about it."

"SOMETHING SMELLS GOOD."

Tabby looked up with a small smile as Razor walked into the office. Luna glanced up and wagged her tail as he patted her head.

Tabby was heating up her lunch. She'd made it last night and although she hadn't tasted it yet, she had to say that she thought it smelled good too.

In fact, she was feeling pretty upbeat about this cooking thing now. She'd mastered scrambled eggs and French toast. Okay, they weren't the hardest thing to cook. And they were only breakfast foods. But she'd come a long way from food poisoning and blueberry explosions.

"Would you like some?" she asked.

Since the mouse incident two days ago, she'd been avoiding him as much as possible. It helped that he was still busy out in the shop helping the guys catch up on their orders. What had she been thinking, jumping into her boss's arms like that?

Yikes.

"Wouldn't want to take your lunch," he told her. Although there was a hopeful look on his face.

"It's all right. I have plenty."

She pulled out the microwave dish and opened the top.

"Careful," he told her, gently pulling her back as steam rose. "What is it? Chili?"

"Yep. I cooked it in the crockpot last night. I haven't eaten any yet, though." She put some into two bowls. "Oh, and I have some cornbread. I bought that, though."

She passed him some cornbread that she'd wrapped up in foil and brought with her.

"Can't wait to try it." He sat on the sofa they kept in the office for when people had to wait. Which wasn't very often. She sat at her desk, where she usually took her lunch. She stirred hers, waiting for it to cool. But Razor dipped straight into his. She waited impatiently to hear what he thought.

She hoped he liked it.

"Milk."

"What?" she asked. His voice was croaky so she didn't think she'd heard him correctly.

But he'd already set the chili down and jumped to his feet, racing over to the fridge. She watched in amazement as he grabbed some milk and gulped it down. Straight out of the bottle

.

Sweat glistened on his forehead as he turned to her. He strode over and grabbed the spoon right out of her hand, then he picked up the bowl of chili.

"Hey! What are you doing?" she asked. She stood, prepared to chase after him. What was his problem? She hadn't even gotten to taste the chili and she'd been looking forward to it. She thought chili might be her signature dish. It hadn't been hard to make and she'd managed to put her own unique twists on it.

"How many chili peppers did you put in this?"

"What? Oh, just three."

"Just three? What kind did you use?"

"I got them from this specialty shop. They're called Carolina Reapers. Have you heard of them?"

His eyes nearly bugged out of his face. Then he drank down some more milk. That was kind of gross. She thought about asking him if he wanted a glass, but the milk was almost gone and it wasn't like anyone else was going to drink it now anyway.

It was all his.

"What's the matter? Why did you take my chili? If you don't like it, then you don't have to eat it."

She couldn't help but feel a bit offended, though. She didn't have to share her chili with him, after all.

"Tabby, Carolina Reapers are the hottest chili peppers in the world."

"What? No, the sign said they were mild."

"Then the sign was wrong or you read the wrong one, I don't

know. I like hot stuff, but that chili is hot enough to burn the skin off your tongue."

Oh no. And he'd eaten it.

"I'm so sorry!" she cried. "I thought I'd bought very mild chili peppers. I don't even like things that hot. I can't believe I got that so wrong. Sit down. Are you okay? Do you need anything?"

"There any more milk?"

He sat and took another mouthful of milk.

"Yes, here you are." She grabbed another bottle of milk out of the fridge and handed it to him. "Razor, I'm so sorry. I didn't realize it was so hot. Really. Are you all right? Do you need to go to the hospital?"

"No." He shook his head. "I'm fine."

He didn't look fine. He looked ill and he was still talking like he had a sore throat.

"I feel terrible. I didn't know. I'm so sorry."

"Hey, come here." He crooked a finger at her. She didn't know if she should go over to him. He didn't look mad, but . . .

Then realizing what she was doing, she forced herself to walk to him. Razor wouldn't hit her no matter how upset he was. And if she thought he would, then she shouldn't be working for him.

No, she was just upset and it was messing with her instincts. She stepped over and he pointed at the coffee table. "Sit."

She sat. When he used that low, firm tone, it was hard not to do what he said. She had no idea why.

"This isn't your fault. It was an accident, okay?"

"But I fed you really hot chili. I wish I'd eaten it first."

"Well, I'm glad you didn't eat it first. At least I'm used to hot stuff. Unless you've got a cast-iron stomach?"

"I probably would have died if I'd eaten it. Well, not literally." She shook her head. "I'm still sorry, Razor. I feel terrible."

"Stop," he told her sternly. "No more apologies."

"I think I need to give up on this cooking thing. First, I give myself food poisoning by not cooking chicken properly. Then my smoothie explodes all over the kitchen. I didn't clean it off the ceiling quick enough, and now I think it's got permanent blue splotches. I'm going to have to get a ladder and get up there to paint the whole thing. Oh, and now I almost put you in the hospital with too-hot chili."

"You didn't almost put me in the hospital," he told her gruffly.

"I could have given you a heart attack," she wailed.

Luna started up a howl. Razor shook his head at them both. "Luna, hush. And you hush your mouth too."

She raised her eyebrows. "Did you just tell me to hush my mouth?"

"Yeah, I did. Because you're talking nonsense."

Nonsense? Really? Where did careful Razor go? The one who watched what he said, and kept a safe distance? Now, he was ordering her to come here, telling her to hush and that she was talking nonsense.

She should probably take offense.

"My heart isn't so fragile, it can't handle some hot chili peppers," he told her in that delicious drawl of his.

"Are you sure? They say as you get older that you should take better care of your heart."

He stared at her.

Oh.

Oops.

Had she just implied that her boss was old?

"You wanna run that past me again?" he asked in a deep voice.

She jumped to her feet. "Nope. Don't believe I do. What I should do is go get you more milk. Yep, I'll get onto that right away. Bye." She raced out of the door and was at her car before realizing that she didn't have her keys or her handbag.

Oh Lord. Had she really just done that?

A throat clearing had her slowly turning. Razor stood there, arms over his chest. Then he nodded back at the office. Did he want her to go back inside so there were no witnesses to him throttling her? Because in that case, she was going to have to decline.

"Go get some money from petty cash. Buy us both lunch. Something without chili peppers or chicken. And grab some more milk." Then he strode off towards the shop.

She had a feeling she'd just been given a reprieve.

Note to self, don't call your hot boss old.

Or hot.

Dear Lord, she was in trouble.

6

"Tabby?"

She spun and started choking on the bite of apple she'd just taken.

Alarm filled Razor's face as she attempted to heave in a breath. Luna sat up, whining. Razor raced over and started whacking her back.

"Cough it up. Right. Now," he demanded, holding a cupped hand in front of her mouth.

What did he think she was trying to do? He couldn't just expect her body to obey him. Except as he smacked his hand on her back, she managed to cough the piece of apple up. It landed in his hand.

Ew.

So attractive, Tabby.

"Good girl," Razor praised, now rubbing his hand over her back.

Oh, Lord. How could she be getting aroused now? All he was doing was trying to soothe her.

He grabbed a tissue to clean his hand as he walked over to the small kitchen area to grab a bottle of water. Returning to her, he opened the water and held it to her lips.

"I can do it," she told him, reaching for it.

Frowning, he drew it away. "You're shaking. You'll spill it all over yourself."

Well, he wasn't wrong there. But it was embarrassing as hell to have him holding the bottle for her. Like a baby being given a bottle. However, the water felt nice and soothing on her throat.

Razor put the water down, screwing the cap back on. Then he reached over her, his arm brushing against her breasts as he opened her snack drawer.

Don't react. Don't react.

Did he know how he was affecting her? He couldn't know, right?

That same block of chocolate he'd grabbed after the great mouse incident—yes, that's what she was calling it—appeared in his hand.

He broke some off and gave it to her. "Open."

She opened her mouth and he placed the chocolate inside. "Suck."

Her eyes widened at the same time his did. Some red actually filled his cheeks and he snatched his fingers back from her mouth, as though worried she might start sucking on the digits.

Ouch. Rejection hurt. But it especially hurt when she felt this insane attraction towards him.

Suck it up, Tabby. You've been hurt worse. This is just a blip on the radar.

Razor slid his hand behind his neck as he took a step back. "Feel better?"

She nodded, busy sucking. The chocolate soothed the back of her throat.

"I should check your throat, make sure you didn't hurt it."

"It's fine."

His gaze narrowed as though he was thinking. She'd seen him do that a few times. He looked ruffled. He'd been in his office all morning, dealing with paperwork. Which tended to make him a bit grouchy. Which was kind of cute.

Not that she'd tell him that.

She'd brought him in his coffee but otherwise hadn't spoken to him. She'd been here for just over two weeks now and it had become their ritual. She made certain to get to the garage around five minutes before eight to start the coffee brewing, which wasn't so early that Razor grumbled at her.

Of course, he didn't know about the hours of research she did at home at night. But she figured that was on her, anyway. He'd hired her with no experience, the least she could do was try to catch up. She was finally getting the hang of the accounting system and learning some of what they did here.

She didn't realize that a boss could be like this. She'd thought he would be happy for her to work extra hours for free. But it turned out that Razor didn't want his employees to slave away for their job. He actually cared about their lives. When he was in the office, it wasn't unusual for one of the guys to come in and talk to him about something going on in their lives.

So he wasn't just a boss to these guys, he was a mentor, a safe place, and a freaking miracle worker.

"I could get Hack to come check on you," Razor said thoughtfully.

He wasn't for real, right? She remembered Hack. Could still hear the noise as Luther knocked him unconscious. It had been a cowardly move. The other man hadn't even seen Luther coming.

"I don't need anyone to check me."

Razor frowned.

"Once, Luther kicked me so hard in the back that there was blood in my pee, but he wouldn't let me go to the doctor. I survived. I'll be fine."

The thunderous look that filled his face made her still.

Oops. She probably shouldn't have said that.

"What?" His voice was chilling.

"Nothing." She gave him a bright smile. Totally fake. And the way his gaze narrowed told her that he wasn't buying her bullshit.

There went that tick by his eye. Shoot.

"Repeat what you just said."

"Um, nothing."

His hands clenched, then released. She eyed him, worried about his blood pressure.

"Please don't look at me like that."

She jolted in surprise at the pleading in his voice.

"Like what?"

"Like you think I would hurt you. I'd never harm a fucking hair on your head."

"I know you wouldn't. I know you're not going to hurt me."

"Then why do you look so worried?"

"Um, I guess I was concerned about you."

He stared at her for a long moment. "Me?"

"You're upset. It's not good for your blood pressure. Maybe you should sit down. I'll get you some water." She stood and hustled him into her chair. Then she grabbed him a bottle of water. "Here you are. Drink that down."

"Thanks, I just . . . wait!" He stood and glared at her. "What are you doing?"

"What?" she asked innocently.

"Oh, you know what. You're trying to distract me because you don't want to repeat what you said before about Luther. But it's not working."

Drat.

"Okay, you're onto me. But it wasn't important."

"It was fucking important. I . . . ." His voice trailed off and he took a deep breath. "Sit. I need to go for a walk. I want all that water gone by the time I get back. Luna, stay."

He strode out of the office before she could say anything. Now, she felt terrible. She wished she'd never said anything to him about Luther.

Sitting, she looked down at Luna, who came over to rest her head on Tabby's lap. "I think I upset your Daddy."

Luna just whined.

She kept working and sipping on her water, watching the front door. About fifteen minutes later, it opened and Luna rushed over to Razor, who patted her.

"Good girl, Luna."

Darn it. Was she jealous of a dog?

Then he turned his dark gaze to her. "I'm sorry I reacted like that. Hope I didn't scare you."

"You didn't. I know not all men are abusive. I know *you're* not."

"Good. Sure you're okay? Do you need to go home?"

"No, I'm fine."

Another nod. He seemed subdued, a bit distant, and she didn't like it. Not one bit. Darn it, why had she mentioned Luther?

"I had a piece of paper with me earlier. Have you seen it?"

"Um." She looked around her desk, then saw it on the corner. "Here."

"That's it. Could you put through this order for me? I've got to go run some errands."

"Sure thing," she told him.

"Actually, first, could you grab the lunch orders for the guys and phone it in? I'll pick the stuff up on my way back. Come on, Luna. You're with me."

The dog licked her hand on the way out, almost like giving her a kiss goodbye. It was seriously cute.

He was buying them lunch again? Surely, most bosses weren't

like this. As he left, she grabbed up a pen and a pad and walked out to the garage.

A long, low wolf whistle greeted her. She looked over at Tommy, who was leering at her.

"Hey, sexy thing, you want to come out with me tonight?"

Urgh, she'd rather roll around in pig shit.

"No, thanks."

"Aww, come on. I'll make it good for you, promise." He made a crude gesture with his hand, then erupted into a braying laugh. She glanced around. It wasn't that she was shocked by the gesture or his come-on. But she was surprised he was being so blatant in front of the others. But then she noticed that Dart and Sav, the two people most likely to take him to task, were down at the other end and unable to hear him.

A couple of the guys looked over at them with frowns, but didn't say anything.

Seemed she was on her own then. Well, she was used to that.

"Yeah, I'll pass." She looked him up and down, then turned away.

"What the fuck was that look about? Am I not good enough for you, princess?"

Just ignore him. Keep moving.

She definitely wasn't ordering him any lunch. The asshole could starve.

"Fucking snobby bitch." That last part was muttered, and she was the only one close enough to hear it.

But she couldn't ignore it. She'd been taught to be silent. To put up and shut up.

She didn't have to follow those rules anymore.

Turning, she sneered at him.

"Yeah, Tommy. That's right. You're not good enough for me. I'd rather go out on a date with a pig than you. That clear enough for you?"

He turned red as a few of the guys started chuckling. She moved around, taking everyone else's orders.

She skipped Weasel Dick.

Asshole.

Fifteen minutes later, she'd hung up with the sub place and was about to start putting through the order that Razor had given her when the phone rang.

"Hello, Montana Custom Bikes, you're speaking with Tabby."

"Put Razor on."

Her eyebrows went up at the demand. "Who can I say is calling?"

"Get him. Now."

"I'm afraid he's not here, currently. If you'd like to leave a message—"

"Listen, girlie, I don't care if he said to hold his calls. I want to talk to him. Get him now."

"Sir, if you'd just tell me your name, I'll leave him a message."

"Stop trying to think, and get him on the damn phone, you little bitch."

Oh, hell no.

She hung up. Then she winced as she realized what she'd done. Shoot. She really should have gotten Dart and let him deal with the rude asshole. There was no way he'd talk to the gruff giant that way.

What if he was a big client? Had she just hung up on someone important?

Crap.

She went back to her list, but her mind wasn't on it and she was shaking. Maybe she should go tell Dart about the call? But he was busy, and the asshole hadn't called back. She nearly had the order ready to send through when the door slammed open and an older man walked in. He'd probably been muscular once, but all that muscle had mostly gone to fat. He wasn't attractive, with a bulbous nose and broken blood vessels across his cheeks.

He stormed over. The stench of booze hit her nose, making her grimace. "You the bitch that hung up on me?"

Shit, shit, shit. "Excuse me?"

"Don't give me that uppity tone. Go get Razor. Now. My money is as good as anyone else's and I'm this far from going somewhere else." He held up a finger and thumb.

She swallowed nervously. But she made herself stand her ground. She wished Luna was here with her. "Razor isn't here right now, as I told you on the phone."

"I want to speak to him. I want to know why the fuck he's not taking my job and I want to know now."

He attempted to storm past her to get into Razor's office. She didn't know why she did it. It wasn't like Razor was in there. Or that there was anything of importance that Razor wouldn't want this guy to see.

But that was Razor's office. And since he wasn't here, she wasn't going to let this asshole inside.

So she jumped out of her chair and stood in front of the door, arms splayed wide. Like she could actually stop this bulldozer of a guy.

She stood her ground. Until he grabbed hold of her arm. Hard.

"Get out of my fucking way!"

"Let go of her," a chillingly calm voice said from behind the big man.

The smelly boar in front of her dropped her arm and half-turned. "I'm here to talk to Razor."

She peered around the other man to see Sav standing in the doorway of the office. He looked calm, his arms crossed over his chest. But there was something in his eyes that made her think he could snap at any moment and that wouldn't be good for any of them. She didn't know Sav's story. He was quiet and kind of brisk. But she didn't want him getting into trouble.

"Razor's not here," Sav stated.

"I don't care about his excuses, I want my bike."

Sav's eyes narrowed and she gulped. Uh-oh.

"You've got to pay for your bike," Sav replied.

"I paid a deposit."

"And the rest is owing. You got three payments to make. You missed the last two, so no bike."

"That's fucking robbery! And I'm not leaving until I get my damn bike."

"That so?" Sav drawled.

This was going nowhere good. She scooted around the asshole and got between the two men.

"Tabby," Sav warned.

"It's time you left," she said to the drunk boar. "You're getting nowhere here."

"Listen, bitch, I'm not leaving until I get my bike."

"It's not here," Sav told him. "Tabby, get over here."

She shook her head. If she moved, she was worried about what Sav would do. This guy wasn't leaving without force, and she couldn't let Sav make the first move.

"Where is he?" The other guy swayed, unsteady on his feet. Just how drunk was he?

"Razor isn't here. And you need to go before I call the cops and have them escort you off the premises." She crossed her fingers behind her back, knowing she wouldn't call the police.

"Nobody is making me fucking leave."

He swung out with his fist. But he was slow and clumsy and she was used to ducking punches. She crouched and then moved to the side.

She felt rather than heard Sav move. The big, drunk guy let

out an enraged roar that quickly turned into a high-pitched squeal.

Turning, her heart raced as she saw that Sav had the asshole pinned to her desk. His face was squished against the wood as Sav held his arm twisted against his back.

"Get Dart, babe," he told her.

Nodding, she raced out of the office and into the shop. The music was pumping, and they didn't have a clear view of the office, so she guessed they hadn't heard the drunk guy's yells.

She had to be thankful that Sav had come in when he had, or she hated to think what might have happened. She always had pepper spray in her handbag, as well as a stun gun, but her bag was locked in a drawer.

Maybe she should start carrying some pepper spray in her pocket.

Just as she started toward the garage, she heard a truck behind her, turning she saw it was Razor. Relief filled her. She rushed over to him as he got out, Luna beside him. He was staring at the red truck parked in front of the office.

"Razor! There's a drunk man inside. He's very insistent on seeing you. Sav is in there. He might need help."

"Stay out here. Luna, stay with Tabby." Razor rushed inside.

Screw that. Tabby quickly put Luna back in the cab of Razor's truck then ran in after him. Inside, she found Sav still had the asshole pinned down. He didn't look strained at all.

Razor half-turned, frowning at her. "Tabby, I told you to stay outside."

Yeah. She wasn't doing that.

"Let me go!" the smelly boar yelled.

"What's going on?" Razor demanded.

She moved up beside him.

"Tabby, stay behind me."

"Let me go, asshole!" the jerk yelled.

"Shut up," Razor said in such a cold voice that she actually felt a chill. She stayed beside him, though. It wasn't like this guy was going anywhere. He wasn't a threat.

"He came in, stinking of alcohol and yelling, then he tried to hit Tabby," Sav explained.

"What? Are you hurt?" Razor turned to her. "Where did he touch you? What happened?"

She shook her head. "He didn't hit me."

"Grabbed her arm, though."

Darkness entered Razor's gaze and she gulped at the sight. She'd been around evil. Razor wasn't evil, but he definitely looked like he was about to commit murder.

"He didn't hurt me. I swear, I'm fine." She glared over at Sav. What was he trying to do? Rile Razor up? Couldn't he see he was near the edge of his control?

"I just want my fucking bike! It's mine!"

"Tabby, go outside," Razor told her calmly.

Oh no, she didn't think that was a good idea. She shook her head. She needed to be here to make sure Razor and Sav were okay. And that they didn't do anything crazy.

Sav raised his eyebrows as he stared at her then up to Razor to see what he was going to do.

"Tabby, go outside."

"I'll stay."

"You'll go outside. Now."

Shock filled her at the dominant tone of his voice. She'd never heard him talk like that. Not even when he was telling her off for starting work too early.

"What are you going to do?"

Razor turned and opened the door. Then he just stared at her.

Frowning, she kept her gaze down so he couldn't see the disgruntled look on her face. He was still her boss.

But she just wanted to help. To protect them. What if they needed a witness? Well, she could still lie and say she was there.

A taxi pulled up outside and sat there as she stood by the truck. Just as she was going to go ask the driver if he needed something, the door to the office opened and Razor walked out with the surprisingly subdued drunk man. He was walking kind of funny, leaning against Razor as though he couldn't stand on his own.

Razor gave her a firm look. As though telling her to stay put.

She got it. He didn't want her anywhere near the guy. The asshole turned to glare at her. Razor drew him close and whispered something in his ear that made him pale. A terrified look entered his eyes.

The jerk got into the taxi without a word. Razor said something to the driver, then the taxi left. He turned and looked at her.

Uh-oh.

She got the feeling she was in trouble.

RAZOR WAS TRYING VERY, very hard not to lose it.

She'd already been exposed to enough anger and violence today. She had to have been terrified by that asshole's behavior.

He'd left her alone and vulnerable. He sat at his desk and closed his eyes as he thought of everything that could have happened.

What if Sav hadn't come in then?

What if that jerk had touched her?

What if she hadn't managed to avoid that punch?

Deep breath in. Deep breath out.

"Razor? Are you all right?"

He opened his eyes to find her still standing across from him. Sav had gone back into the shop. Fuck, he owed the other man big time.

Tabby held a bottle of water in one hand and the rest of her chocolate bar in the other. He'd insisted she take both. At this rate, he was going to need to buy shares in a chocolate factory.

"Sit down. Drink your water. Eat your chocolate."

She gave him a puzzled look but sat. He wished she'd obeyed him that quickly earlier when he'd told her to leave. What had she been thinking? She obviously had no sense of self-preservation. That guy had been dangerous. He could have hurt her and instead of getting herself to safety, she'd dared to shake her head at Razor when he'd given her an order.

He wanted to take her over his knee and spank some sense into her.

Easy, man.

She wasn't his sub. She'd had trauma in her past. She was his employee.

One he'd failed to keep safe.

"That won't happen again."

Her gaze narrowed. "You mean he won't be back?"

"I mean, you won't be left alone here in the office again. If I have to leave, one of the boys will come in here with you. If I'm out in the shop, then you can lock the office door and call me if someone arrives."

Her mouth dropped open. "You're not serious!"

He just looked at her.

"You're serious. Like really serious," she muttered. "But why? Because of one angry customer? I can handle guys like him."

He hated the calm way she said that. As though it was an everyday occurrence. She shouldn't have to put up with shit from guys like Gary.

Razor wished he could have taken the guy out back and taught him a lesson. In his younger days, he wouldn't have hesitated to break the bones in his legs in retaliation for touching something that belonged to him.

Shit.

Tabby doesn't belong to you.

But he was possessive over everyone who worked for him. And, of all of them, she was the most vulnerable.

"He touched you."

"He just grabbed my arm, it was nothing."

"Sav said you tried to stop him from getting into my office."

"He thought you were hiding in there from him. As if you'd hide from someone like that. You could easily take him."

"I'd never hide," he commented arrogantly. He was pleased with her faith in him. "But you should have just let him in there. You're not to try and defend me, understand? That's my job. To protect you."

She gave him a startled look. "But why?"

"Because you work for me."

"And you think that means you need to protect me?"

"Exactly." And she was to obey him when it came to her protection.

"That's just stupid."

He stared at her. She flushed red. "Um, I probably could have worded that better."

Razor placed his arms on the desk and linked his fingers together. "And how could you have worded that?"

"Well, I, um, it's not your job to protect me," she blurted out. "That's not what an employer does."

"It's my job to make sure my employees are safe in their work-place. You wouldn't have been exposed to that asshole if you weren't working here, correct?"

"I suppose so, but—"

"There are no 'suppose sos' or 'buts' about it. That's the damn truth."

"But you didn't know he was going to turn up here. Or that

he'd be violent or drunk. And it's probably my fault for not telling anyone that he'd called."

"Yes, you should have called me straight away then gone and gotten Dart. Anything like this happens again, that's what you do. You find someone and tell them. You do not try to keep some asshole out of my office. You also don't situate yourself between said asshole and one of my guys." She went to speak and he held up his hand. "I'm speaking right now."

She grumbled something under her breath then put the water and chocolate on his desk before slumping back with her arms folded over her chest.

Damn. That was actually cute. She looked so disgruntled. He wished he could pull her onto his lap and hold her tight, tell her never to do that again.

What was wrong with him?

It's because you feel responsible for her. That's all.

"And you definitely do not ignore an order given by me for your safety, understand?"

"You're overreacting."

"Understand?" he asked in a lower voice, injecting some Dom into his tone.

She immediately seemed to take notice, sitting up straight and uncrossing her arms. He tried not to read too much into that. Her eyes couldn't meet his. That was something he'd noticed she did a lot. Dropped her gaze.

But he wasn't sure why. Because she was a sub? Because that's what she'd been taught to do? Was it out of fear? He hated that thought.

Or was it that she was trying to hide her true feelings?

"I understand."

"Good girl." Shit. If she objected to being called a kid, then she wouldn't like being called a girl either.

But she didn't say anything. Then she raised her gaze. "What did you say to him to get him to calm down? He was spitting mad when he got here and he didn't say boo when he left. Did you hit him?"

He blinked in surprise at her matter-of-fact voice then he remembered her background. Shit. How much violence had she seen? Experienced?

"I just made a few things crystal clear to him."

He'd reminded that asshole of who he was, and why he didn't want to cross him. Then he'd told him exactly what would happen if he ever showed his face here again, came near any of Razor's people, or so much as breathed in Tabby's direction.

Asshole had nearly pissed himself by the time Razor had gone into a great deal of detail about what would happen to him if he broke any of the rules.

Part of Razor almost hoped he would. He'd enjoy working a bit of his temper out on that dick.

But not at his place of work. And definitely not with Sav around. He wasn't risking his parole. Or the other guys who worked here either.

Although, he might have landed a couple of gut punches. In retaliation for the asshole almost hitting his girl.

Not yours.

"Right," she said skeptically.

This time, she managed to meet his gaze with her own. It only lasted a few seconds, but he took that as a positive sign.

"Now I've made that clear, you can gather your stuff up and head home."

She grew so pale that he nearly jumped up, worried she was about to keel over.

"I'm fired?" she whispered hoarsely.

"What? No! Of course not. I want you to go home and rest."

"Why?" She looked puzzled.

"Because you've just been threatened, and manhandled, and

you were nearly hit." He thought it was obvious why she should go home and rest.

"But he didn't hit me. I feel fine. I need to finish ordering those supplies."

"I'll do it. You're going home. Do you need someone to drive you? I don't want you driving if you're shaky. Eat your chocolate. Drink more water."

She glanced down at herself as though searching for any shakiness. "I'm fine. I don't need to go home. And I don't need chocolate. You know it doesn't fix everything, right?"

He ignored that. Doing something made him feel better, even if it was just feeding her. "You're taking the rest of the day off. You're going to rest. If I see you back here before eight tomorrow morning, I'm not going to be happy."

"What happens when you're not happy?"

"You don't want to find out." He was hoping she didn't push him on this, because he really had no way of showing his displeasure. It wasn't like he could put her in time-out, or make her write lines, or spank her ass.

Yep, highly inappropriate thoughts there, you dick.

"Maybe you should take tomorrow off too. Have a long weekend."

"I don't need a long weekend. I don't need to take tomorrow off."

"All right, then I'll see you tomorrow morning. If you wake up and don't feel up to coming in, then call me." He stood and moved to the door.

She rose, looking slightly dazed. Moving past him, she gathered up her stuff.

"Sure you can drive? Sav could take you and get a taxi back."

She just shook her head.

"Words, please," he said gently.

Her shoulders tightened. Was he pushing too much? Upsetting

her? But when she turned to look at him, he was surprised at the temper in her face. He had to bite his lip to hide a smile. He didn't want her to think he was laughing at her.

Damn, she was cute, though. She was trying desperately to hide her annoyance. And failing.

It was far better than her usual, closed-off look. He'd much rather see her emotions than try to guess what she was thinking. He figured that she'd learned to hide what she was thinking in order to avoid punishment.

Fuck.

"I'll be fine."

"I'll call you later to check on you. Tabby," he called out as she reached the door that led outside.

She paused and looked back.

"Rest. Eat. Let me know if you need anything. All right?"

Turning, she muttered something he couldn't hear and figured wouldn't be at all flattering. When the door closed, it was safe to let a smile slip free.

Yeah, she was cute.

TABBY WAS grouchy as she drove home.

What the hell? Why was she being sent home like an errant child? She hadn't done anything wrong.

Okay, so maybe she should have listened when he told her to go outside. But she'd only been trying to help.

Feeling out of sorts and needing something to cheer herself up, she pulled into a local mall. She wandered aimlessly through a clothing store. Nothing seemed to interest her. Instead, she walked out and spotted a pet store.

Maybe she should get a fish. Walking over, she stared at all the fish, not having a clue what she wanted.

"Can I help you?"

Turning, she smiled at the assistant. "Yes, I'd like to buy some fish and a fish tank and food. And whatever else I need."

Over an hour later, she walked out with a receipt for her purchases. The fish tank, accessories, and fish would all be delivered later this afternoon. She was gonna be a fish mama.

Feeling better about everything, she headed towards the exit. She walked past a toy store then stopped.

Snappy could use a companion.

But that was silly, right? A stuffed toy didn't need a companion. And a twenty-seven-year-old woman didn't need another toy.

Right? Right.

Only...

Turning, she walked in. If anyone asked, she'd tell them she was buying some things for her niece. Besides, she was really just looking. If anywhere could cheer you up, surely it would be a toy store, right?

Right.

But then she found it. The area of her dreams. It was filled with Scooby-Doo toys. There were stuffed animals. Masks. Dress-ups, which would be silly to buy since they were all child-sized. She wondered if it would be possible to find some adult outfits online.

She'd look when she got home. But, for now, she grabbed a stuffed Scooby, a replica of the Mystery Machine van with figurines for all the characters, and a Scooby-Doo money jar and cookie jar.

Feeling like that was probably enough, she rushed through her purchase at the counter then hurried out to her car. As she was driving back to her apartment, her phone rang and she hit accept, thinking it was likely the pet store people.

"Hello?"

"Tabby?" Razor's voice filled her car. Her entire body relaxed. Damn, she loved that man's voice. The accent. The calm tone.

She might have to use her vibrator when she got home. They were amazing. The first time she'd used the one with rabbit ears, she'd come three times.

"Razor? Everything okay? Do you need me to come back?"

"Are you still in your car? Why aren't you home yet?"

Oh. Shit. She bit her lip. She'd been sent home from work to rest. Not shop.

"Oh yeah, I had to stop on my way home for some groceries." She crossed her fingers at the small lie. It was basically a white lie, right?

"Can you pull over safely? I don't like you talking and driving at the same time," he said firmly.

Her eyebrows rose at the question, but she found herself pulling into a parking lot.

"I'm on my Bluetooth."

"It's still distracting. When you're driving, you should only be driving. Not talking at the same time. Do you do that often?"

Never. Mostly because no one ever called her. In fact, in the last month, she'd only received calls from her cousin, her power company, and now Razor.

Wow. That was sad. She really needed to think about how closed off she'd become from everyone. Was she really that worried about getting hurt that she'd rather isolate herself than risk getting harmed?

"So you never use Bluetooth?" she asked suspiciously.

"We're talking about you. Not me."

Ahh, she got it. One rule for him and one for her, huh? She frowned.

"You left three hours ago. How many groceries did you need?"

"Um, not many. But then I ran some other errands." There, now it was definitely just a white lie.

She still kept her fingers crossed. She wasn't about to break that sacred law of lying.

"I sent you home to rest."

"I'm going home to rest right now."

"What was so important you had to stop?"

"Sanitary products," she blurted out, crossing her fingers at the lie.

Jesus, Tabby. You're normally a better liar than this.

Why was she so rattled? Why hadn't she just told him the truth? It wasn't like she was doing anything wrong. But nooo, she had to make something up and now he thought she was on her period.

If she'd thought he'd start stammering or acting awkward because she'd mentioned the words, 'sanitary products,' she was very mistaken.

"Ah, poor baby. You need anything?"

That was a very un-bosslike thing to say. Or at least, she didn't think an employer usually showed sympathy for someone on their period. Or called them baby. But damn, she liked hearing him call her that.

"Sorry, that was really inappropriate, huh?"

He sounded upset. Instantly, she wanted to help him feel better.

"It's fine," she told him. "I know you just care."

"Yeah, but it's not acceptable. I'm your boss."

"Razor, you're a great boss. You're the best boss I've ever had."

"I'm the only boss you've ever had," he replied dryly.

"You'd still be the best, even if I'd had others."

He let out a scoffing noise, but she was sure she could hear a smile in his voice. "Right."

"Do you need me to come back to work, boss?" She didn't know how she'd manage the delivery of the fish tank if he did, but she was certain she could figure something out.

"No, I was just calling to make sure you were all right."

"See? Best boss ever. I should get you a mug that says that."

He laughed. "Thanks, Tabby."

"For what?" she asked, surprised.

"Making me feel better. I really am sorry about what happened today."

"It really wasn't your fault," she insisted.

She heard someone call his name.

"You should go."

"You're heading home now?" he queried.

"Sure am, boss."

"And you'll rest." It wasn't a question.

What was his obsession with her resting? She shook her head in confusion. "I'll rest."

If by rest, he meant would she get a space ready for her fish tank, attempt to make potato and leek soup, then watch reruns of Scooby-Doo. Then sure, she'd rest.

"And you don't need anything?"

"No, I don't need anything." She was slightly puzzled by what exactly he meant.

"Heat pad? Extra Ibuprofen?"

Oh Lord.

Was that the sweetest thing ever, or what? Was he really offering to bring her stuff to help with her period pains?

Not that she actually had period pains. And now, she felt lower than dog poo. Shoot.

"I, um, no, that's okay. Thank you," she said quietly.

Someone called out his name again.

"Call me tomorrow if you don't feel up to coming in, all right? And anytime if you need anything."

"I will."

He was so sweet she wanted to cry.

"Go straight home and rest. No answering any more calls while driving." The call went dead.

And there he was.

So bossy.

She smiled the entire way home.

THAT NIGHT, Tabby curled up under a soft blanket and watched the Scooby-Doo movie with Scooby on one side and Snappy on the other.

Snappy was in a mood because he didn't like the addition of her new fish. She stared down at the sulking stuffy.

"I told you, Snappy, I'm not buying you a girlfriend. Can you believe him, Scooby?" When she realized who she was talking to, she smacked her forehead with the palm of her hand. "I'm losing my mind. Maybe I should have gotten a puppy. At least talking to your puppy is acceptable. Talking to your stuffies, not so much."

That made her think about Luna, Razor's dog. She was adorable. And the way she stared at Razor was just too cute. She figured you could learn a lot about a man by the way he treated his dog.

Or his employees.

Razor was a good person. And she really had to stop lying to him. Even small, white lies with her fingers crossed.

Now, the poor guy thought she had her period. And she was probably going to blush as soon as she saw him in the morning.

But talking to her fish was more acceptable. She reached in for a handful of buttery popcorn. She'd made soup for dinner, with enough left over for lunch tomorrow.

She turned her attention back to the movie. "Ooh, it's starting to get good. Are you watching this, Daphne, Fred, Shaggy, and Velma?"

Yes, she'd named her pet fish after the cartoon characters. She'd also managed to find an adult-sized Scooby-Doo onesie online. She just hoped that Jared wasn't paying attention to her credit card bill. He hadn't mentioned anything when she'd talked to him yesterday.

It was payday on Tuesday. Her first paycheck.

Life was really starting to look up. She had a job she was finally starting to get the hang of. A great boss. Mostly good co-workers, Weasel Dick didn't count. She had some fish. And a vibrator.

What more could a girl want?

7

S hit. Shit. Shit.

She took it all back. Life was not looking up. At all.

How had she made this mistake?

This was the worst Monday morning ever.

"This isn't what I ordered. I promise."

She couldn't even look at Razor. He was staring from his hand-written note to the invoice that had been printed off from what had arrived from the supplier. Along with the supplies. Which were vastly more than should have been ordered.

"It doesn't matter," Razor told her. "We can send back the excess. At least everything is here."

"I should have double-checked the order before I sent it."

She'd come in on Friday morning, entered the last two items, then she'd intended to send it off, but a customer had come in. And then she'd gotten caught up in the accounting system. And she'd just sent it off.

This was all her fault.

"I'm so sorry, Razor." She felt ill.

Great. She'd been here three weeks. She shouldn't make fuck-ups like this anymore.

"It's not a problem, Tabby," he said quietly, even though he looked tired. "We'll just return what we don't need. Call the supplier first, then book a courier. Just make sure they take it off the invoice. Okay?"

It wasn't okay, though. She felt sick to her stomach.

"Hey, look at me."

She couldn't, though. She didn't want to see any disappointment in his eyes. Or pity. So she raised her gaze to his chin instead.

Razor sighed. "Tabby, it's a simple mistake. Everything is here that we need to continue on. It's fine, all right?"

She nodded.

"Now, you coming for a drink Wednesday night for Tommy's birthday?"

"Ah, no, I don't think so."

"Tabby, stop worrying. And think about coming for a drink, all right? We're going to Reaper's Bar, where the Iron Shadows members hang out. Millie goes some weekends, she's been asking after you."

She raised her eyes up, feeling startled. "She has? She remembers me?"

"Of course she remembers you." Razor's eyes filled with a tender look that she assumed had to do with Millie, not her.

She'd like to see Millie again, but did she really want to go to a bar filled with bikers? Not really.

"I'll think about it."

"You feeling okay?"

What, other than feeling like a complete and utter failure? Sure, she was feeling hunky-dory.

"Sure. I feel great." She tried to smile.

"Good. Let me know if that changes. And if you need to use a heating pad, you go right ahead."

Lord. She was an idiot. He still thought she had her period.

Damn it. How could he still be so nice when she'd fucked up so royally?

TABBY DROVE past the closed gate for the garage with a yawn. She'd known nobody would be there yet, it was barely six-thirty. She wasn't even sure what she was doing here.

But she'd been unable to sleep, going over and over her mistake in her head. Even playing around with her vibrator hadn't helped.

And when she'd finally nodded off, she'd had dreams about Luther all night. He'd been laughing at her, calling her names.

So about five this morning, she'd headed out on a run, making certain to take her pepper spray and stun gun.

As she was going past, something caught her sight. The gate was partially open. Was there someone there? But none of the lights were on anywhere. She parked up in front of the gate and got out, looking around.

Should she call Razor? Probably the smart thing to do. Drawing out her handbag, she grabbed her phone. And her pepper spray.

Then, before she could call him, she saw someone running past the office.

"Hey! What do you think you're doing?" she cried out. Shit! Should she run after him? But what if there was more than one of them?

She had her pepper spray, though. And this was Razor's business. Razor, who'd given her a job. Who'd been so kind, even when she'd messed up.

The sound of something smashing filled the quiet.

Crap.

"Hey, get out of there! You're trespassing." Someone raced towards her and she was too slow to get out of his way. He slammed into her, sending her flying backward. She landed on her ass with a groan.

That was going bruise later. Getting onto her knees, she searched around for her pepper spray and phone. She'd dropped both when that jerk slammed into her. She found her pepper spray, but before she could locate her phone, there was another smashing noise.

"Stop! Get lost! I've called the cops!"

Shit! Where was her phone? As she got to her feet, two more figures rushed out at her. They were dressed all in black, with hoodies up over their heads, obscuring their faces.

They raced past, one of them knocking into her again. Only this time, her ankle turned under her and she crashed to the ground. Her hands scraped along the asphalt and she let out a cry of pain, tears filling her eyes that she wouldn't allow to spill.

Toughen up, Tabby.

You've been through worse.

Grabbing her ankle, she sat up with a groan. She was such an idiot. What had she seriously expected she would be able to do?

She helped one person, and now she thought she was freaking superwoman?

Stupid. So stupid.

The roar of a bike sounded, and then a headlight lit up her car before the bike turned into the concreted parking area.

Shoot. Razor was going to kill her.

RAZOR WAS ALREADY ON EDGE, having been woken by his alarm company. Then having to race into work.

And now . . . his eyes had to be deceiving him, right?

Because that could not be Tabby's car sitting in front of the opened gate.

And that could definitely not be Tabby sitting on the ground, holding her ankle and staring up at him with a pale face.

Turning off his bike, he pushed down the stand and hopped off. Then he raced over towards Tabby, who was trying her best to get up off the ground.

"Tabby! Baby, what happened? Are you all right?"

"I'm so sorry, Razor. I tried to stop them. But one of them slammed into me. I lost my phone and my pepper spray. I found my pepper spray, but I don't know where my phone is. If I could have, I'd have stopped them. I don't know what they did."

Stop them? What was she talking about? Stop them?

His heart raced even faster. Had she seriously attempted to stop the people who'd done this?

He was going to kill her.

Why weren't the security lights on? Even with the sun rising, they should still be on. He glanced quickly around, but couldn't see her phone. And he had more important things to worry about right now.

"Where are you hurt?"

"I twisted my ankle when one of them knocked me over."

"I'm going to fucking kill them," he swore, crouching in front of her. Forgetting why he shouldn't just touch her, he ran his hands over her legs then her arms. "Are you hurt anywhere else? Is it just your foot? Did you get a good look at them?"

"They wore all black, with hoodies up over their heads. I'm so sorry, I couldn't see their faces."

"It's all right, it doesn't matter. Are you hurt anywhere else?"

"Just my hands." She turned her hands over. He needed to get her somewhere warm and light so he could properly check her.

"Come on, baby. Let's get you inside." Right then, all he cared about was making certain she was safe, and that she wasn't hurt worse than she was letting on.

Because he knew that she definitely underplayed things. She'd done that when Gary had scared her, nearly hitting her. She'd acted unaffected. But he'd seen the way the skin around her eyes had pinched, the small tremble in her hands. She wasn't as unaffected as she liked to act. Maybe she believed her own lies, but he knew differently.

He slid a hand under her legs and around her back, lifting her.

"Razor, you shouldn't lift me! Put me down!" she cried out, even as she wrapped her arms around his neck. He liked that. Having her close. Having her cling to him. Her scent, something sweet, teased him.

"Why can't I?" he asked in a soothing voice. She sounded as panicked as he'd ever heard her. And she was clinging to him like he was an anchor in the storm. Not that he was objecting.

Not at all.

Pervert.

"You'll hurt yourself."

Oh, hell no. She didn't just say that.

"You trying to say I'm too old to carry you?" he growled.

"Um, no, of course not."

He grunted. That was exactly what it sounded like she was saying.

"I could carry you for hours and be fine," he boasted, walking towards the front door of the office. "And there's nothing wrong with my damn back."

"Sorry. I didn't mean to insult you. I'm just not used to anyone taking care of me. Not like you do. Luther never cared if I was hurt or injured. I mean, I guess that could be because most of the time he was the one to cause the injury . . ." she trailed off as though realizing what she'd just said.

"He can't ever hurt you again."

"I know," she whispered. "Just wish he'd never had the opportunity to hurt me in the first place."

He set her carefully down while he drew the key out of his pocket.

"Me too, baby girl. Me too." He opened the door then grabbed her again.

"I really can walk."

"No. You can't," he replied firmly. He carried her into the office and set her down on her desk before turning on a light. He grabbed the first aid kit from a cupboard. Opening it, he drew out one of those snap ice packs.

"You need to go check what they did," she told him urgently. "You have cameras, right? Do you want me to call the police?"

She tried to slide off the desk and he reached for her. "What do you think you're doing? Sit down."

"I'm fine. I want to know what damage they did."

"Whatever they did can wait until I make sure you're all right," he told her firmly. He handed her the ice pack. "Put that on your ankle."

She stared up at him, eyes wide. "But I'm okay. It's just a twisted ankle and some scraped palms. Seriously, I've had a lot worse."

And he hated the thought of that. Grasping hold of her hand, he turned it over, hissing.

The need to take care of her warred with his need to ensure that there was no further danger outside. But right now, she wasn't suffering from injuries that needed immediate attention. So her safety came first.

"Just stay right there. Do not move, understand me?"

"But there's nothing wrong with me."

Nothing wrong with her? Her pants were torn. Her palms were bloody and she'd hurt her ankle. Nothing wrong?

"I'm going to go check that there's no one else around," he told her. "You're to stay right here and not move, understand me? I'll lock the door again, just in case."

"But, I—"

"I mean it, Tabby," he warned. "You move and I'll put you over my knee."

It wasn't until he was outside that he dropped his head and groaned. What the hell was he thinking? Seriously? He'd just threatened to put her over his knee? He'd be lucky if she didn't sue him for sexual harassment. Or if he didn't terrify her into quitting.

Sure, she'd made a few mistakes. And she really didn't have any clue about what they did here.

But he liked having her around. He looked forward to seeing her every morning.

And he hated that she'd been hurt.

But threatening to spank her? Way out of line. Way, way out of line.

"Idiot," he muttered.

Look at him. He was pathetic. He was practically shaking. A mix of rage and fear rushed through him.

Why was he feeling so emotional? He never got this worked up. Not anymore. He'd learned to control his temper. Sure, he might like to flirt. And when someone he truly cared about was threatened he could be a scary son-of-a-bitch. Or so he'd been told.

But he barely knew Tabby.

This was more than just her working for him. Than her being vulnerable.

He'd come to fucking care about her.

Shit.

He quickly made his way over to where one of the doors had been forced up. What he didn't understand is how they knew to take out the security lights. Or how they'd gotten through the front gate since it required a pin code.

Unless someone who knew the pin code had given it to them.

Could this be an inside job?

But as he walked around, switching on lights, all he saw was destruction. He'd need to check with Tabby about whether any of them were carrying anything, but as far as he could see, all they'd done was destroy the place. There was graffiti sprayed across the walls and a couple of bikes they'd been working on. And one bike looked like someone had taken to it with a crowbar or something similar.

It could have been worse. They hadn't gotten to the bikes locked in the back room, the ones that were waiting to be picked up or delivered. Not wanting to be away from Tabby for long, although he wasn't sure what reception he'd get, he headed back to the office.

He took a deep breath. She'd be within her rights to tell him to stay the fuck away. Or to file a complaint against him.

He just hoped like hell that she wasn't scared of him.

When he walked in, to his shock, she was still sitting on the desk where he'd left her.

He raised his eyebrows as she stared at him. She wasn't in tears. She hadn't thrown anything at him. And she wasn't screaming at him to get out.

So, that was positive.

But he could tell she was concerned about something.

"What did you find?" she asked him, sounding anxious. "Did they take anything? Are the bikes still there? Equipment?"

Wait. She was worried about the shop?

He shook his head as though to clear it.

"What does that mean? That they didn't take anything?" She let out a frustrated noise. "I'm going to go look for myself." She wiggled forward on the desk.

"Nope. Don't you move." He pointed at her.

"Or what?" She huffed, crossing her arms over her chest. "We both know you wouldn't actually spank me."

Oh, she thought that, did she? Well, he wouldn't actually do that without her agreement. He'd never touch her like that without permission. Ever.

"Tabby, I'm gonna ask you a favor."

"What's that?"

"Don't push me right now, okay? I shouldn't have said what I just did and I apologize. I had no right to ever imply that I'd touch you without your permission. I hope you know I wouldn't. But you're within your rights to have me up on sexual harassment charges."

Her eyes widened. "I'm not going to do that. You only said that because I worried you. I know you didn't mean it."

"Thing is, I did."

"W-what?"

"Not that I'd spank you." He held his hands up. "I'd never spank anyone without their permission. But a naughty submissive, yeah, I'd spank her if it was an agreed-on punishment for breaking the rules or putting herself in danger."

"You're a Dominant?"

"Yeah. But I should never have said what I did. So like I said, you can make a complaint about me. Or you can leave this job. I'll pay you out for the next two months and give you a reference. I'll totally understand."

Her mouth opened and closed. "No, I like it here. And I . . . I trust you."

"Really?" That was big, considering her past.

"I think I trust you the most out of anyone. I know that's pathetic when we barely know each other. But over these past few weeks, I've gotten to know you better. And, well, you're a good guy, Razor."

"You're not scared of me?"

"What? No, not at all."

"Then how come you can't look me in the eyes?"

"I . . . I have problems with that."

"Okay, baby, I mean Tabby, shit."

"It's okay." She managed to give him a tiny grin. "Really, Razor. You don't have to tiptoe around me. I'm a big girl. I'm not going to faint or cry if you call me baby or tell me you're going to spank me."

"You sure?"

"I'm sure. I'm not going to break. I'm stronger than you think. And I don't offend all that easily."

"All right. But I'm going to try to be careful not to cross any lines. I've called Dart and Sav, they should be here any minute. So let's take a look at your hands, yeah?"

WHAT IF I want you to cross the line?

She'd just managed to stop herself from asking him that. She was kind of shocked at herself, if she was honest. It wasn't that she wanted him to spank her.

Right?

She'd been in an abusive relationship. She wasn't ever going to repeat that. In fact, she didn't intend to ever be in another relationship again.

But she knew that BDSM wasn't abuse. Not that she had any experience with it. But she'd read some books with BDSM scenes in them. It was hot to read about it, but would she like any of it in real life?

Razor just started cleaning her right hand when she heard some bikes approach. He set the cloth down and she expected him to leave her to fend for herself. He had more important things to attend to, after all.

Instead, he pulled off his jacket. "You're shivering. Why didn't you tell me that you were cold?"

She wasn't cold. Right?

"I'm not cold. I don't know why I'm trembling."

He put his jacket around her and warmth flooded her. Oh, that was so nice. His scent surrounded her, easing the knot in her stomach. It was like being enveloped in a giant hug. She could only imagine how good that would feel. When was the last time she'd been hugged? She couldn't even remember.

No, wait, yes, she could. It was from Millie. The night that she'd knocked Luther unconscious, just before she'd left to go back to her cousin.

Millie had hugged her. Maybe being carried in Razor's arms counted as one, though. It was kind of a hug, right?

"Adrenaline drop." He moved to her snack drawer and drew out a bag of chocolate kisses. When had they gotten in there? He unwrapped one and she immediately opened her mouth.

Shoot. She'd done that without even thinking. A blush filled her face.

"Tabby, look at me."

She shook her head. "I'm fine. You should get out there and deal with what's going on."

"Sav and Dart have things under control out there. Right now, you're my priority."

She gaped up at him.

"What? What is it?"

Tabby cleared her throat. "Um, nothing."

Had she ever been anyone's priority before?

"Right, let's check out this ankle." He grabbed her chair and wheeled it around so he could sit in front of her. Then taking gentle hold of her foot, he eased her shoe off. She made certain not to let any noises escape. But shit, that hurt.

"You don't have to hide your pain from me," he told her without looking up from her ankle.

How had he known?

"I'm fine. Really."

"Really? Does this look okay?" he countered. He moved back slightly so she could see her foot more clearly.

Aw, shit. It was swollen to twice its size.

Damn it.

"Guess I won't be running for a while," she said with a sigh. "Shoot."

"You run?"

"Yeah, every morning," she replied as he set the ice pack back on her foot. "Where did the chocolate kisses come from?"

"I bought them," he told her. "Let's sit you on the chair, then get you another chair to put your foot on." Standing, he lifted her down before she could attempt to move, settling her on the chair.

He disappeared into his room while she held the ice pack on her foot. He wheeled his chair back into the room and was putting her foot on it as the door opened and Dart stomped in.

"Mother-fucking bastards. Should have chased after them and run them down," he snarled.

She stared up at him in shock. She'd never heard the man say more than a word or two at a time. And he was always polite.

"Dart, Tabby's here," Razor said sharply. He picked up her other hand and started cleaning it gently.

Ouch. She tried not to flinch, but it wasn't easy.

"I'm sorry, baby," he said to her without raising his head. "But it has to be done. I'll be as gentle as I can."

She stared down at his bent head in amazement. Did he really think she was worried about how rough he was? He'd already shown her more care than anyone.

Then she remembered that Dart was there. And he'd just heard Razor call her baby. What would he think of that?

But when she looked up at the big man, he had his gaze on her hands. "Sorry, Tab," he muttered. "What the hell happened?"

"Oh, nothing. I was just clumsy."

"It's not clumsy when someone bowls into you and shoves you over," Razor countered as he cleaned her other hand.

"What the hell?" Dart snapped, his eyes widened. "Those asswipes pushed you over? They touched you?"

"I'm all right," she reassured him. It was sweet that he cared. They'd barely spoken. Most of the time, she didn't think he knew she existed.

"You're not okay," Razor told her. "And you need to stop acting like you are. Just look at her fucking hands. They're ripped to shreds."

That was an exaggeration. She had a few grazes, that was it. These two were acting as though she'd lost a finger or something. It was kind of amazing. Even as a child, she'd have been left to clean injuries like these up herself.

"And you should see her ankle. It's damn well three times its normal size."

Dart walked around and lifted the ice pack. She tensed, waiting for him to touch her. Razor lifted his head, obviously sensing that something was wrong. He watched her for a moment, then turned to Dart, who was carefully replacing the ice pack.

"Looks damn sore."

Razor nodded. "I reckon so."

She'd noticed that his accent became more obvious when he was upset.

She shook her head. "It's really not that bad, guys. I've had worse."

They both scowled down at her, obviously upset at the idea of that. Her insides filled with heat.

She decided not to mention her bruised knees. That might just send them over the edge.

"What happened?" Dart asked.

"I was driving past when I saw the gate was open. I pulled up, and I was going to call Razor, but then I caught sight of someone. I had my pepper spray in one hand and my phone in the other, but as I got out of the car, one of them slammed into me and I dropped them. Then I heard something smash and I yelled out. Two more came running at me. I got knocked over again and my ankle turned. Then Razor turned up."

Silence filled the room. And she forced herself to raise her gaze from her lap. Both men were staring at her. Dart looked shocked and Razor looked . . . mad?

"Is there a lot of damage? What did they do?" Were they upset with her because she hadn't been able to stop them? She'd panicked and hadn't been thinking clearly.

Razor seemed to be taking deep breaths. She got the feeling he was trying to calm down, but she couldn't understand why.

"Is there something wrong?" she asked. "Why aren't either of you saying anything?"

"She really have no idea?" Dart said to Razor.

"I don't think she does," Razor replied.

"You gonna change that?" Dart asked.

Razor sighed. "Fuck. Gonna try."

"Good," Dart replied.

She stared at them in confusion. She had no idea what they were talking about. "What are you going to change? I don't understand. What is it that I have no idea about?"

They just stared down at her. All right, now she was starting to get irritated.

"Dart?" Razor said.

"Yeah?"

"I'm going to take Tabby to the emergency room." Razor sounded like he had something in his throat. Was he getting ill? "Can you find her phone? Then I need you and Sav to take care of shit here. Take photos of everything that was damaged. We'll need a police report for insurance."

"Damn," Dart said. "That's the last thing we need."

Razor sighed. "Take a look around, see what the damage is. If you think we need to claim insurance, let me know. I'll call and deal with them. But warn the boys it's a possibility. Might be best if Sav and Axel weren't here since they're on parole. Don't want them getting blamed for shit."

Dart grunted. Then he looked down at her and shook his head. "Girl, you got to know your worth."

Huh? What did that mean? What worth?

But before she could ask him anything, he left.

That was weird.

She turned her gaze to Razor, but he didn't say anything.

"Where's Luna?" she asked suddenly.

"Left her home. I'll call my neighbor soon to go get her."

He grabbed some painkillers which he handed to her. "I'll get you some water, then we'll need to take your car to the emergency room since I'm on my bike."

"I don't need to go to the emergency room," she told him.

"You're going." He handed her a bottle of water from the small fridge they kept in her office.

She looked down at the pills with a grimace. Nausea bubbled in her stomach.

They're just pills.

"Take the pills."

"I don't need them."

"Tabby," he said warningly. "Take the pills."

No way.

"What were you doing here so early, anyway?" he asked before she could come up with an excuse not to swallow the damn pills.

"I'm sorry," she said quickly. "I couldn't sleep, and I was just going to drive past and maybe go to the diner down the road."

There, it wasn't exactly a lie. She'd had no intention of going to the diner, but then again, she might have.

She didn't think she even had to cross her fingers over that.

"At the moment, that's the least of your transgressions," he told her.

What? What the heck did that mean? What transgressions? What did she do?

Did he mean because she hadn't stopped those guys from trashing the place? Surely not. Razor wasn't an asshole. Now, Luther, he'd be spitting mad at her.

"Are your keys in your car?"

"Yes, but I don't need to go to the emergency room."

"I'm not arguing with you."

Okay, then. She kind of thought he would put up more of a fight about her going to the emergency room.

That wasn't hurt she felt. She was getting her own way. Getting upset because he wasn't insisting on taking her to the emergency room was just ridiculous.

She was an adult who could make her own decisions. She slipped the pills into the pocket of her pants.

Sneaky, yes.

But also, necessary. Pills made her gag. Luther had forced her to swallow some pills the same night that he'd lost his mind and threatened Millie. Now she grew nauseous at the sight of them.

The door to the office opened and Dart walked in with her phone and handbag. "Landed face up, so screen's all right."

"Thank you."

Dart just nodded and left

"Right, let's go." Razor grabbed hold of the ice pack and then handed it to her before picking her up into his arms.

"I really don't need to go anywhere. I can still work."

Razor didn't reply. Great, she guessed he planned on taking her home. He carried her out to her car. Sav jogged over to open the passenger door.

"Not sure how long I'll be. Call if you need help. If we need to bring in the cops, then lay low, yeah?"

Sav just nodded, frowning down at her. "How bad?"

"She'll be okay," Razor said before she could speak.

"I'll be all right," she told Sav. "Everyone's overreacting. It's a few scrapes and a twisted ankle. That's all."

Sav raised his eyebrows as Razor set her in the passenger seat.

"I'm sure I can drive."

"I'm sure you can't," Razor countered. Reaching over her, he buckled up her seatbelt. Then he grabbed hold of the ice pack and placed it on her ankle.

"I'm fine." She huffed out an irritated breath and he gently caught her chin.

"Enough. You're going to do what's best for you. Understand?"

Her eyes widened, especially when Sav gave a satisfied nod. What? Was he agreeing with him? What was happening here?

The door shut before she could demand to know if they'd both had their brains taken over by aliens or something. Then Razor spoke briefly to Sav before knocking his fist against the other man's and walking around the car. He climbed into the driver's side.

"I'm not sure if you're on my insurance," she told him.

He just shot her a look before backing out. He laid his arm over the back of her seat and turned, looking back.

"Um, there's a backing camera."

No reply. He headed off. In the wrong direction.

Okay, maybe he didn't like having something obvious pointed out to him. She got it. Luther had been the same.

Not that she was saying Luther and Razor were alike. Not at all. Luther would have left her lying on the ground while he threw a fit, likely blaming her for everything. And then she'd have had to drag herself inside, hoping he didn't turn his little temper tantrum onto her.

Yeah. Those were definitely times she didn't miss. Razor was the polar opposite. He was obviously upset about something and instead of ranting and raving about it, he'd gone silent. She didn't like that. She wished he'd just tell her what the problem was.

"We're going the wrong way."

"No, we're not."

"But if you're taking me home, my place is that way." She pointed in the opposite direction.

"Told you, going to the emergency room."

"Razor, I really don't need to go." She hated the ER. Well, she guessed for most people it wasn't their favorite places. But she had bad memories attached to them.

She twisted her fingers together.

"I'm not arguing."

"So you get to just make the decision and I get no input," she said quietly.

He was silent for a long moment, then he drew her car off to the side of the road. "Fuck." Closing his eyes, he took a deep breath. He looked hurt. As though he was in physical pain. Was that her fault? Had she done this to him? This strong, resilient, kind man?

Then he turned to her, opening his eyes. "You're right. I'm sorry. I have no right to make decisions for you. No right to just dictate like some asshole. If you were . . ."

"If I was what?"

"Doesn't matter. What matters is what you want to do. I really wish you'd let me take you to the emergency room. I'm worried about how much your ankle has swollen. I just want you to get checked out, to ease my mind."

"You're really worried about me?" she asked in amazement.

"Of course I'm worried. What sort of monster would I be—

actually, don't answer that. I know what kind monster wouldn't have worried about you if you were hurt. Asshole."

"I really hate emergency rooms, they hold bad memories."

He blanched.

"Not just for me. I didn't often end up in one. He didn't usually hurt me that badly."

His hands tightened on the steering wheel, and she watched him for a moment, worried.

"My dad was sick. He'd often be in pain, and my mom would call an ambulance. For most of my childhood, that's all I can remember—having to be quiet so dad could sleep. Or not being able to leave the house because dad needed my mom at home. When he died, Uncle Fergus took mom and me in. I think we were broke. I can remember mom trying to sell stuff off. I guess I should be thankful he did that. Of course, then he forced me to marry an asshole just like him, so . . . yeah."

He didn't say a word, but his knuckles were white with how hard he was holding onto the steering wheel.

"Are you all right?" she whispered.

"Am I? Am I all right?"

"Yeah? Are you? You look stressed. If you have to go back to the garage, I understand."

"I . . . shit . . . baby," he said in such a tender voice that tears entered her eyes. "Baby, I'm fine. You don't need to worry about me, okay?"

"But you worry about me."

"Yeah, and to my way of thinking, not enough people have worried about you in your life."

"I can't remember the last time someone did. Jared, he worries in his own way, I guess. If I'd twisted my ankle, he'd get one of his men to take me to the doctor, I'm sure."

"Do me a favor? Don't mention your cousin to me. He should have protected you from that asshole, Luther."

"Jared's not a bad person."

He shot her a look.

"Not like Uncle Fergus," she amended. "He just has a different way of looking at things."

"He should have protected you."

"At the time, he thought he was. He thought Luther was the lesser of two evils. Luther was dumb, but he was also careful to make sure I never had a chance to tell Jared what was going on. He isolated me. And when he . . . when he hit me then he was usually careful to do it in places which could easily be hidden by clothing."

"And your cousin didn't think it weird that he was isolating you?"

"Jared thought that was better than me becoming a target of the deranged asshole trying to murder him."

One beat of silence. Two.

"Are you serious?"

"Yeah. I am. See, Jared thought Luther was the lesser of two evils. And in a way, he was right."

He reached over then paused. "Can I touch you?"

"Y-yes," she said, unsure what he planned to do. He gently placed his hand on top of hers. Oh, that was nice. She could get used to this touching thing.

"Will you let me take you to the emergency room to get checked out?" he asked her. "Please?"

"All right," she agreed.

"Thank you. It will make me feel a lot better."

And she realized she'd do a lot to make him feel better.

8

Tabby looked down at her bandaged foot in frustration.

The doctor had insisted on wrapping it up to help it heal and bring the swelling down. And she'd been ordered to keep off it as much as possible for at least three days.

Just awesome.

Looked like she was going to be doing a lot of hopping over the next few days. Her hands and knees had smaller bandages. They were just grazed.

They were back in her car and Razor was tapping his fingers on the steering wheel. Thankfully, the ER wasn't overly busy on a Tuesday morning, so it hadn't taken long for them to see someone.

She'd told Razor that he didn't have to stay, but he'd just given her that look.

The one that told her she was completely bonkers.

"My place is just up here." She pointed down the street. "I have a car park underneath. Pull in here."

Razor looked around. She wondered what he was thinking. Her house didn't look like anything on the outside. Just another concrete building. That was part of Jared's plan when he'd bought it.

She hit the button on the garage door remote. There was also a camera that read her license plate. If it was the wrong license plate, the door wouldn't open despite the remote being hit.

Razor drove down into the garage. The door shut behind them. Razor let out a whistle as he took in the garage. "I was expecting something cramped and tiny. How many people live in this building?"

"Oh, just me."

He parked close to the elevator door then turned to her. "Just you?"

"Yeah. Jared bought it for me. Part of his stipulations for me being able to live on my own is that I had to live in a secure building. That meant no close neighbors since they posed a risk. And a security system with cameras."

"Well, at least he protects you this much."

"He does." She nodded. "He bought this car for me as well. It's actually got bullet-proof glass. I think he's gone a bit overboard, but he's been paranoid ever since that psycho stalked him. He doesn't want anyone knowing I'm his cousin. I use my dad's last name."

"I'm surprised he let you move out on your own."

"He didn't want to. I guilted him into letting me leave."

"What does your mom think of all this?" he asked.

"She died."

"Oh, Tabby-baby, I'm so sorry."

Tabby-baby, that was sweet. "Thank you, it was a long time ago now."

"Doesn't mean that it doesn't hurt," he replied. "How old were you?"

"Thirteen."

"That's such a hard age to lose your mom. Not that any age is easy." He sounded like he was speaking from experience.

"What about your parents?"

"My dad died when I was young. My momma worked three jobs to keep food on the table. I was the oldest, so as soon as I could, I went out to work to bring in money to feed my younger sisters."

"How many do you have?"

"Four."

"Oh wow. Do any live close by?" she asked.

"No. They're all back in Georgia. My momma still lives there too."

He climbed from the car and she undid her seatbelt, cursing herself for asking too many personal questions. She knew what it was like not to want to talk about your family. She grabbed her handbag as he opened her door. Crouching, he picked her up.

"Razor! You have to stop doing that!"

"I'm fine."

He shut the door to her car with his hip and it locked automatically as he carried her to the elevator.

"I need to put in my pin," she told him, wriggling to get down. "And it has a retina scanner."

"Good to know." Setting her down, he kept hold of her waist to steady her as she stood on one foot. He looked around in interest. "Your cousin has someone monitoring the cameras constantly?"

"No, I have panic buttons everywhere and there's a code I could have put in if you were coercing me or something. Then they'd check the cameras."

Razor nodded. The elevator doors opened and he picked her back up. It came out on the main floor of the loft.

He whistled. "This place is enormous. Nice."

She shrugged. "Yeah. It's pretty good." Not exactly her taste, but she wasn't going to complain.

"Where's your bedroom?"

"Upstairs," she told him in surprise. Why would he want to know that?

"I'll carry you up so you can pack a bag. Unless you trust me to do it."

"Pack a bag?" she asked.

"So you can come stay with me."

Her mouth opened. Closed. "Razor, I'm not coming to stay with you."

"Yeah, you are. Now, are you packing your bag, or am I?"

Had she not just pointed out that he couldn't make decisions like that for her a few hours ago?

"Razor, I'll be fine here. It's just a twisted ankle."

"The doctor said you had to stay off it for a few days. How are you going to get up to your bedroom? Make yourself food? Get to the bathroom?"

"I can hop," she pointed out. "And I'll sleep down here on the couch."

He gave her an appalled look. "You're not sleeping on the damn couch."

"It's really comfy. You should try it. I don't mean you should sleep on it. But sit on it. Can you put me down, please?" She didn't know if she'd ever felt this flustered before.

He set her down on the sofa, then he dragged the coffee table over. He grabbed a cushion off the couch and placed it on the table. Her foot went on top of the cushion.

"Now, what's this nonsense about you staying here?"

Lord, give her some patience.

"I'm not going home with you."

"You are."

"Razor, you're being unreasonable."

"You need help, you can't be on your own."

"I'll be fine." Why was he so insistent on her coming home with him?

Maybe the question should be why was she so insistent on stopping him? Here's someone who actually cares about her.

Hang onto him and don't let go.

She wished it was that simple.

"Tabby, you aren't fine. You can't walk. You hurt yourself while trying to protect my business. Which we'll be having words about. But the least I can do is take care of you."

Oh. Right.

That's why he wanted her to come stay with him. Because he felt guilty.

Silly her.

Why would it have been anything else? She was nothing special.

His phone rang and he drew it out of his pocket, checking the screen before putting it back. He had to go. He had to have a hundred things to take care of.

"You shouldn't feel guilty. I chose to chase after those guys. It's my fault I got hurt. Not yours."

He scowled. "Why did you get out of your car?"

She opened her mouth. Closed it. Then stared at him in surprise. "Why?"

"Yeah, why? Why put yourself at risk like that? Why not stay in your car and call the cops?"

"Because I don't exactly trust the cops." The way she'd been raised had taught her that they were the enemy, even though she knew, logically, that they weren't. "And they were up to no good."

He lowered his eyebrows, giving her a stern look that sent a shiver through her. "And you think that's an acceptable reason to put yourself in danger?"

"What do you consider an acceptable reason?"

"Nothing. Nothing is an acceptable reason, young lady."

Young lady? Was he serious right now?

"What you should have done was stay in your car and called me. You shouldn't have gotten out. You shouldn't have even stopped at the garage. You should have driven past, gone to a safe place which was well lit with people, then called me."

"But they would have been long gone by then."

"So? It is not your job to protect my business. It is your job to keep yourself safe. You didn't do that today. Promise me you won't do that again."

"I was going to call you. It's just, I thought I might be able to scare them. Then one of them crashed into me and I lost my phone. Then I heard something smash and I...yeah, you're right. I should have called you straight away. I just...I didn't..."

"You didn't think about your own safety, did you?"

"It's never really been a priority."

"I want you to change that. Your safety should always be a priority, understand? Now, you can't stay here alone. I'll worry about you. Can we pack a bag and get you back to my place? I need to ... shit." He drew out his phone as it rang again. "I'll just take this."

He walked off towards the kitchen and she shuffled over to where Snappy and Scooby sat on one end of the sofa. He hadn't even given them a second glance. But then, lots of adults had stuffed toys. Her uncle's last wife, Angie, had owned this big whale she'd called Wally.

After her uncle was killed, Angie had disappeared. Jared had been preoccupied, and she'd somehow slipped away.

At least, that's what Jared told her.

God, she hoped she wasn't dead. She'd liked the other woman, who'd only been a few years older than Tabby. She hadn't deserved to be married to Uncle Fergus. The warthog.

That was probably mean to warthogs.

When Razor returned, he was frowning.

"Razor, you don't need to be worrying about me on top of everything else. I'll be fine here."

"I really don't like to argue, Tabby."

She sighed. "How are you even going to take care of me? You'll be at work all day."

He ran his hand over his face. "Shit. Well, I'll figure it out."

"I guess I could go to work during the day. I could just sit at my desk. That would actually work. I mainly sit all day anyway."

"You're not going to work," he told her firmly. "Not until you can weight bear on that foot."

"But I'll just be sitting at home anyway, and you're going to be short-handed."

"No," he told her. "No work. I'll shorten my work days. And get someone to check on you during the day."

"You can't shorten your days. You're already behind schedule, and you've spent most of today dealing with me." Now, she was really starting to regret what she'd done. She'd made his life so much harder.

Idiot.

"It will be fine. I'll get someone to check on you, help you to the bathroom and feed you lunch. Yeah, that will work."

Feed her lunch? Seriously?

"And I'll just do all the paperwork at home, which means I should be able to come home earlier."

She shook her head.

"It's either that or I move in here. With Luna. Which would you prefer?"

Move in here? Was he serious?

She could tell from the way he looked down at her that he was. So what were her choices?

With a sigh and a glare, she nodded. "Fine, I'll move in with you. But only until Thursday."

"We'll see. You're only leaving once you can walk on that foot."

"Fine." She'd be walking on her foot in two days, come hell or high water. "What about my fish though?"

He turned to her fish tank. "They're cute."

"Yeah, the clumsy, orange one who keeps bumping into stuff is Shaggy. Then that one is Fred. That one is Daphne and the smallest one is Velma. Honestly, I think Shaggy is actually a girl and Daphne is a boy, but I'm not sure. I forgot what they told me at the pet shop."

"They're cute. You like Scooby-Doo, huh?"

She tensed. Would he think that was weird? It was, right?

"Yeah."

He just nodded and then turned to look at her. "How often do they need to be fed?"

"Once a day."

"Can you give me access through the security system?"

"I don't know how," she told him. "And I don't think it would be a good idea to call Jared and ask him." And by not, she meant it would be a terrible, very bad idea.

"Oh, wait! I have an automatic feeder." She didn't know why she'd bought it. She'd just bought everything the shop assistant suggested. He'd probably totally fleeced her.

But it was coming in handy now.

They set up the fish feeder, then he carried her upstairs and left her to get packed. After about ten minutes, he knocked on the door before entering. "Got everything?"

She was hopping around and he frowned at her, coming over and steadying her. "Easy, you're going to hurt your other foot. Why didn't you call out for me?"

"I'm fine. I'm all packed now, and you were on the phone."

"Dart called the cops. Said the damage is too much to be replaced without insurance."

"I'm sorry."

"Not your fault." He pointed at her sternly. "Not going to let you take responsibility for it, understand?"

She gave him a sassy salute. "Yes, sir." Wait. Where did that come from? She had no idea. "Why did you say that Sav and Axel should lay low if Dart called the cops?"

"Because they're on parole."

"But they didn't do anything wrong."

He shrugged. "Some of the local police don't like me much, or my guys. We've all been in trouble with the law at some stage."

That wasn't fair.

"But Axel and Sav are the most vulnerable because they're still on parole. So they get protected the most."

"I bet they love that."

"Well, I've never told them." He grinned. Then he crossed his arms over his chest, looking stern. But she thought she saw a twinkle in his eyes. "Now, are you going to be a good girl and let me help you or are you gonna give me trouble?"

"I'm a good girl," she told him sassily.

Whoa. Where had that come from? She didn't know who was more surprised by her reply. Razor or her.

He cleared his throat. "All right. You need anything else? Stuff from the bathroom? Got your toothbrush? Any medication?"

"I've got it all."

As he carried her downstairs, she realized there were two things she didn't have. Shoot. Should she ask him to get them? Would he think she was odd?

Well, he probably already did.

"Could I bring Snappy and Scooby?" she managed to ask.

Instead of heading to the elevator, he walked over to the sofa and bent so she could grab the toys.

She snatched them up into her arms.

And he never said a word.

JUST AS HE got her settled in the car, pulling her seatbelt over her again, his phone rang. He shut the door and started pacing. Then he paused, his hand at the back of his neck.

God, he was sexy.

If only he felt more for her than responsibility. If only he wanted her to come stay with him because he cared about her.

But, she didn't blame him. She probably seemed like some silly child. Too young and foolish to bother with. Look at all the trouble she'd caused because she hadn't stopped to think through the consequences before running off into a dangerous situation.

Razor climbed in with a sigh.

"Everything okay?"

"You know how there are days when everything goes fucking wrong?"

He started up the car and she shrank back into her seat. Yeah, she got that today had been a mess. And that she'd caused half of the mess. He had dozens of more important things to do. Instead, he'd had to take her to the hospital then back here. And now he was having to drive her to his place. And she'd slowed him down with her arguments.

Why'd she do that? Why couldn't she have just followed along with what he wanted?

Silly girl.

"Shit," he muttered as they emerged onto the street. "Tabby, I didn't mean that the way it sounded."

"I know I goofed up today. I'm really sorry for all the issues I caused."

He reached over and took hold of her hand. Her skin tingled where it touched his. What would happen if he touched her somewhere else? Like her face, her neck, her breast?

Okay, you need to stop thinking about him touching your breast.

Now she wished she'd packed her vibrator. What was she going to do? Living with him was going to be hard. She wasn't a saint, after all.

"Stop. I'm not upset because of you. Well, I'm upset that you put yourself in danger. Gonna be a while before I get over that. And that you didn't see anything wrong in putting yourself in danger. Yeah, wasn't happy about that."

"So, in other words, there is plenty you're upset at me about," she told him dryly.

He sent her a half-grin. "Okay, maybe. But that has nothing to do with why this day is fucked up. How's your ankle?"

"Oh, it's fine." Throbbing. Painful. But she wasn't going to tell him that.

"You sure? Because it's been a while since you took those painkillers. You're due some more."

Hm. Rats. She'd forgotten that she'd pretended to take those pills.

Oh, Tabby. You really are in trouble.

"I don't need any yet."

"Let me know when you do. I don't want you in unnecessary pain."

Seriously. Who was this guy? It was like someone had created the perfect man for her. Only they had a fine sense of irony, since he didn't seem to feel the same about her. In fact, she wondered if he'd have ever noticed her if they'd met under different circumstances.

"Unfortunately, we have to make a stop at the shop," he told her.

"That's okay. If you need to work, I can wait in the office."

He didn't even reply to that. He looked so huge in her car. Out of place and yet not. Because Razor made any place he entered better just because he was there.

Oh Lord. Getting fanciful now, Tabby.

"It's not because I need to get to work. But the cops have turned up and they want to take your statement."

"That's fine." Not her favorite thing to do, but she'd get through it.

She studied him as he clenched his jaw. "One of the cops, his name is Detective Shane Andrews. He's an asshole. He's got it in for me. Has been trying to pin shit on me for a while. Doesn't like that I employ ex-cons. A while ago, one of my guys was at a bar with his girl and this other guy started harassing her. Cayden hit him, and a brawl started. It was a mess. Detective Andrews' brother was the guy Cayden hit. He was fine, but he's had this grudge since."

"That's ridiculous."

"I know. And for some reason, he's decided to take an interest in what happened at the shop this morning."

That was insane.

Razor pulled into her usual parking spot. "I don't want you to worry about him, all right? I won't let him bulldoze you, and I won't leave you alone with him."

"I'm not worried about some detective with a grudge," she reassured him.

"I'm still not going to let him intimidate you," he grumbled. "Wait there. Do not move."

Okay, bossy Razor was piloting the ship right now. She decided it might be wise just to let him get his way for a while. He obviously felt like he needed some control. And she could give him that. With all that she owed him, it was the least she could do.

Still, she wouldn't let him get away with being so bossy all the time. That wouldn't be a good idea if he wanted to fit his already big head through doorways.

She had to giggle at the idea of a giant-headed Razor trying to move around.

He would probably still look hot as a big bobblehead.

Maybe she'd change that coffee mug she was going to get him from Best Boss Ever to Bossiest Boss Ever.

RAZOR WASN'T sure why she was giggling when he opened her door, but he was glad she wasn't fretting over talking to the detective. He couldn't believe this asshole was still sniffing around, trying to find something to pin on him.

Jerk.

He pulled Tabby into his arms, cradling her against his chest.

She opened her mouth, and he gave her a quelling look. "If you tell me again that I'm going to hurt my back, then I'm going to …"

"What?" she asked. There was a sparkle of something in her eyes.

"Well, I guess I can't threaten to spank you. I have a once-a-day policy on threatening to spank employees."

She giggled, and he winked down at her. "Can I be there when you threaten to spank Sav?"

"Dear God, woman. I like my balls where they are, thanks. Ah, hell, probably shouldn't have said balls to you. And now I said it again."

He winced. Jesus. What was he thinking?

"Uh, Tabby, sorry, I didn't—"

Reaching up, she put her hand over his mouth. "It's okay. You think I don't hear worse every time I go into the shop?"

He frowned and she dropped her hand quickly. Damn, he liked when she touched him.

"What do you mean, you've heard worse? From who? I told them to clean up their damn language."

She grinned up at him.

Yeah, he got the irony.

But fuck, it was worth it to see that smile on her face. God, she was gorgeous.

A throat clearing had him turning. And there he was.

Detective Shane Andrews. The asshole.

"Am I interrupting?" The detective ran his gaze over Tabby. Razor stiffened, not liking the look in his eyes.

"Yeah, you are, actually," Razor told him. "Thought you'd be in the office."

"Wanted some air." Andrews smirked at him. "And I needed to make some calls."

"If we're keeping you from your work, then you can feel free to fuck off."

"Razor," Tabby said quietly.

Yeah, he got it. He needed to ease up a bit. But the asshole deserved it. Razor didn't like the way Andrews was staring at her. Like he wanted to eat her up.

Tabby was his.

Not yours. Ease down.

"You must be Miss Smarts," Andrews said to her. "I heard you hurt your ankle when these assholes ran into you. I'm sorry you were hurt."

"Um, thanks," she said hesitantly.

"Perhaps we should go inside so Razor can set you down. I'm sure you don't want to be held by him any longer than is necessary."

Really? Fucker thought he was going to goad him by implying that she didn't want him touching her?

He knew fuck all.

"In fact, perhaps I should take her. Don't want you to drop her. Must be a strain, holding her."

Andrews reached out as though to grab Tabby. She shied back against Razor, pressing into him.

Satisfaction flooded him. Even as he told himself not to read too much into it. He knew Tabby didn't like to be touched. She'd barely tolerated the doctor at the hospital touching her, and she'd insisted that Razor stay with her the whole time.

It wasn't that she didn't want the detective to touch her. It was most people. But Andrews didn't need to know that. A red flush filled his cheeks, and he stepped back.

"Brainwashed her, have you?"

"I haven't done anything. She just doesn't seem to like your winning personality," Razor told him. "But yeah, let's go inside."

9

Tabby wished she hadn't shied away from the detective's touch.

But then he would have touched her. Her skin crawled at the thought. She wouldn't have trusted the detective even without Razor's warning. There was something slimy in his gaze.

"You're all right," Razor reassured her quietly as he carried her into his office. "I wouldn't have let him touch you."

She patted his hand in thanks. But it might have been easier to let him touch her. Because he had a funny look in his eyes as he stared at her now. And when he turned his gaze to Razor, that look became more of a sneer.

Tabby could remember her uncle yelling derogatory things about the cops, blaming them for whatever had gone wrong.

Logically, she knew there were plenty of upstanding, wonderful police officers who were out there protecting the public.

However, she wasn't sure the detective was one of them.

It wasn't reasonable for him to blame Razor for something one of his men had done a while ago. This Cayden didn't even work here anymore. So what was the detective's problem?

"Razor, I'm going to have to ask you to leave so I can talk to Tabitha in private."

"That's Miss Smarts to you," Razor told him. He'd set her down in his chair, and now he was leaning against the wall behind him, arms crossed over his chest. "And I'm not going anywhere."

"You can't stay. My witness can't be expected to talk freely in front of you."

"Your witness? This wasn't a murder," Razor stated. "Just what do you think is going on here?"

"Why don't you tell me? Why do you think someone broke in here? What were they looking for?"

"I'm guessing they were looking to destroy the place," Razor told him. "And maybe steal some bikes. But Tabby probably interrupted them before they could force their way into the backroom."

The detective glared at Razor from where he sat across her desk and she tensed. She wished she could reach back and touch Razor to reassure him, but she didn't want to give the detective more ammunition to use.

"Really? And that's all they were after? Some bikes?" the detective asked skeptically.

"Some very expensive bikes," she said smoothly. Obviously, it was going to be up to her to keep this conversation on-topic. These two seemed like they could snap and snarl at each other all night. "And yes, that seems to be what they were after. Or maybe they just wanted to destroy some property, I'm not sure. You'd know better than me why a criminal might act the way they do. I'm sure as a detective you're very good at reading people."

Urgh. Her stomach rolled at her efforts to flatter him. But she wanted to defuse the situation, and the detective seemed the type of guy who would like to have his ego stroked.

Sure enough, Detective Andrews moved his glare from Razor

to look at her. His shoulders relaxed at her words. "And that's why I can't understand why they'd bother to break into a place like this without stealing anything."

"I guess I interrupted them. Perhaps you could take my statement, though? It has been a trying day, and I'd really like to go home and rest my ankle."

"Of course, Miss Smarts. If Razor would leave, we can get on with that."

She didn't miss the sneer in his voice when he said Razor's name.

"I'm not leaving," Razor told him.

"I can do this down at the station if I need to," the detective said.

"You've got no cause to take her into the station."

"I think she'd be more comfortable there, away from your influence." The detective stood, glaring over at Razor.

"Detective, I'm not sure what you're trying to say." She gave him her best clueless smile. "But I'm perfectly fine giving my statement here. Going to the station is just going to prolong things, and the doctor wanted me to rest."

"Of course." He gave her a stiff smile as he sat again. "But I have to insist on taking your statement. Alone."

Before Razor could object, she turned to him, giving him a quelling look. "I'll be fine on my own."

"No," Razor said.

"Razor, I'll be all right."

"I'm not leaving you with him on your own."

"Are you implying something?" the detective snarled.

"He's not implying anything, he's just very protective," she explained.

"Really? Is there something between the two of you I should know about?"

"That's none of your business," Razor snapped at him.

"Actually, I think it's very pertinent to what I'm investigating. Are you in a relationship with Razor, Miss Smarts?"

"No, I'm not. I'm his assistant. But like Razor said, that's not any of your business. And I find the question rather odd."

"Do you?"

"I also find it odd that a detective would come out for a break-in. Quiet day?" Okay, she wasn't going to get anywhere like this. "Detective, could we have a couple of minutes?"

He glared at them both but got up and stomped out. Sheesh. It was a bit like dealing with a toddler having a tantrum. She didn't say that, though.

"Razor, I'm fine talking with him on my own."

"Not happening." Razor glared at the door.

"It's obvious he thinks there's something going on. I can find out what he's thinking."

"I don't care what he's thinking. He's a damn douche." Then he grimaced. "Sorry."

"Like I said, heard worse."

"Those boys really have to clean up their language. I'm not leaving you with him, Tabby."

"And he's going to think that everything I say is what you want me to say. He'll think you're coercing me—just ten minutes. I want to get this over and done with. Please. Trust me. I've dealt with far worse people than some jacked-up detective on a power trip. Believe me."

Razor grunted. "And you shouldn't have had to. Someone should have protected you from those people."

Yep. He was the sweetest person she'd ever met.

"I couldn't protect you then. But I will now," he muttered, almost to himself.

Did he mean that night he met her? When Luther had beaten her? But he hadn't even known her.

"Razor, he's not going to hurt me."

"I don't trust him."

"Neither do I," she told him. "But you'll be just outside the door. You'll hear if I yell out. And I can't see him physically harming me. Can you?"

Razor reluctantly shook his head.

"Let me just get this done and then he'll leave. Otherwise, he might insist on me going to the station and I don't want to do that. Please?"

He grunted. "Fine."

Thank the Lord. She really didn't think he was going to give in. "But if he scares you, if he even looks at you funny, then he's in for a world of pain. Get me?" He gave her a stern look, but she wasn't worried. He was only worked up because he felt protective of her.

"I hear you. You need to trust me to look after myself."

He shot her a look of disbelief. "You can really ask me that after today?"

All right, she could understand his doubt in her. "I know I messed up today. That won't happen again."

"Damn right it won't."

Striding over to the door, he opened it. "Detective, you can come in."

Detective Andrews walked past Razor, giving him a slightly wary look. So he did have some brains in his head.

"I'll be right outside the door, Tabby." Razor gave her a firm look that she guessed was meant to be a warning to call out if she needed him. She wouldn't. She could handle Detective Andrews with one hand tied behind her back.

The detective waited until Razor shut the door to lean over her, resting his hands on the desk. She knew what he was doing. He thought this gave him a position of power.

She barely held in a smirk at the move. She wasn't concerned. She didn't know why she felt so safe. It may be because she'd been around much scarier people than the detective. Or maybe it had to do with the man on the other side of the door.

Let him play his petty games.

"I can get you out."

"Out of where, detective?"

"Here. Away from them. I'll put you into protection. All you have to do is tell me what's going on here." He leaned in further.

"You mean, that we're creating amazing, custom motorbikes," she whispered.

"I'm talking about the drugs."

"What drugs?" she asked.

He sat in his seat, shaking his head. "I can't tell whether you really don't know what's going on or you're trying to lie for him. But either way, you're being foolish. There's got to be drugs here or some other contraband substance."

"Why does there have to be?"

"Because there's a bunch of criminals working here."

The way he spoke, he made it sound like she was dumb for not working that out for herself.

"Ex-criminals," she said stiffly.

A cagey look crossed his face. "Right. Ex-criminals."

"Nothing illegal is going on here, detective."

"Sure, there's not. If you're not willing to talk to me, I think we're done here."

"Aren't you going to ask me questions about the intruders this morning?" she asked.

Did he seriously think that the shop was a front for drugs? Simply because many of the men that Razor employed had been in jail at one time?

"Right. Sure. Tell me what happened this morning."

She went through everything, even though she could clearly see it was pointless. He wasn't interested in what had actually happened here. He was just looking for something else to pin on Razor and the guys. Basically a fishing trip.

She wasn't giving him any bait.

Not that there was any.

"So did they say anything?" he asked.

"No."

"Were they carrying anything?"

"I don't think so."

He gave her a disgruntled look. "So basically, you didn't see their faces. Didn't hear anything. And there wasn't anything distinctive about them."

"Sorry to disappoint you, detective."

He sighed. "Can't be helped. If you think of anything else or you change your mind, and you're finally ready to talk about what is really going on here, here's my card." He slid it across the desk at her. She took it, nodding.

Of course, there was nothing to call him about. But she thought it might be a good idea to keep his number anyway.

Getting up, he held out his hand. "You seem like a smart, nice girl. You shouldn't be hanging out with people like them."

"People like them."

"Yeah, you know exactly what I mean. Think about what I said. You've got to have other options. You don't need to work here. All they'll do is drag you down."

"I'll take what you say into consideration, detective."

She waited until he left to grimace. "What a dick face."

"What?" Razor asked.

She looked up, startled. "Oh, I didn't realize you were there. Not you. Him. Detective Dick Face."

His lips twitched up into a smile. "Detective Dick Face. I like it."

"I don't like him. He thinks you guys are dealing in drugs here.

He wanted me to tell him what's really going on behind the scenes. And he wasn't at all interested in the break-in this morning."

"Drugs? Seriously?"

"Yeah, he doesn't understand why a bunch of ex-cons, his words not mine, would work here unless there was something illegal going on."

"Not much I can do about Detective Dick Face right now. What I can do is get you back home and resting. Come on."

10

She stared out the windshield of her car in shock.

This was Razor's house?

This was not what she'd expected.

Razor turned off the car. They'd brought her car since Razor only had his bike at work and he told her that she wasn't getting on the back of that with a sore ankle.

Razor didn't like to argue. So whenever she said something he disagreed with, he'd just give her that look. And it seemed that for some reason, she found herself giving in.

Big Bossy Boss.

Another mug possibility.

"This is your house?"

"Yep."

"Does Red Riding Hood ever come to the door looking for grandma?"

She said it without even thinking. Then she froze as soon as she realized what she'd said.

"Did you just imply that my house is grandmotherly?"

"No, no, I didn't imply that."

She'd totally implied that. It looked like Little Red Riding Hood was about to skip her way up the footpath and knock on the door.

"Are you lying to me, little girl?"

Little girl? Where had that come from?

"Fuck," he muttered before climbing out of the car and walking around the hood to her side. He opened the passenger door, but instead of helping her out, he crouched down.

"Tabby?"

"Yes?"

"You comfortable staying with me?"

That wasn't what she'd expected him to say.

"I kind of feel like I railroaded you into staying with me."

Well, he did. But in the nicest possible way. Because how could it be anything but nice when he was obviously worried about her?

She shook her head. "You didn't. I'm fine. I'm comfortable."

"Sure? If you'd rather stay with a friend . . ."

Right. Because she had so many of those. Who could she stay with? Cat, the mysterious woman whose life she'd saved? She'd said that Tabby could call her if she needed something. But she never intended to do that. And did she really think that sort of favor extended to this? Or jogger guy who possibly offered her a water bottle that was drugged. Would he be happy to look after her? Millie? Who she'd met once?

Yeah, her possibilities were endless.

Actually, more like they were a dead end.

"I know it could be weird staying with your boss. Don't want you to feel awkward. Nothing that happens here has anything to do with your job, okay?"

"So what you're saying is that if I leave the toilet seat down, then you're not going to fire me?" she joked.

"No. Although if you feed me Carolina Reapers again, I'm gonna start to think that you're trying to off me." He winked to let her know he was joking. "How about while you're staying here, we're not boss and employee. We're just friends, yeah?"

"Yeah." She smiled at him.

"Good. Gonna go open the front door, then I'll come back and get you. Stay there."

She saluted him and his eyebrows rose.

Yeah. She should probably stop doing that. Just like she shouldn't have implied that his house looked like something the grandma from Little Red Riding Hood would have lived in.

But it so did. It was a wooden house painted cream. The window shutters were a pretty duck egg blue and so was the front door. The whitewash porch had pots filled with flowers. It was so darn cute that she sighed happily.

This was the sort of place she'd often dreamed of living. She could see herself in the rocking chair on the porch. Reading a book and watching people walk past. Maybe calling out a greeting because this was the type of neighborhood where people knew one another. Where kids went trick or treating on Halloween and the neighbors had a friendly competition about who had the best outdoor Christmas lights.

Razor had taken her bag with him into the house and it wasn't long until he returned to pick her up.

Yeah, she could definitely get used to him carrying her around. He walked in through the front door. There were hardwood floors and the walls were painted a soft gray with white trim. It was seriously her dream house. And that it belonged to this man was mind-boggling. This was so not the sort of house she'd pictured him having.

She guessed she'd misjudged him. She'd thought he would have a bachelor pad. Maybe an apartment with zero maintenance. Something a bit rough and rundown.

Not something beautiful.

He carried her through to a large living space. There was a big leather sectional that faced a log fireplace. Above it was a wooden mantel that she thought would look amazing with stockings hanging from it. To the right was a huge TV, and to the left was a bookcase that was overflowing with books.

Yep, she'd totally misjudged him. And she felt pretty crappy about it.

"You like reading?" she asked as he set her down on the sectional. He raised her foot up, putting a cushion beneath it.

"Yeah, feel free to read anything I have. You like to read?"

"Sometimes. It's a good escape from real life. For a while, I get to live a completely different life."

"Get what you mean."

"I mostly read romance, though. You probably don't have any of those."

"I think you'll find one or two up there," he told her.

Was he blushing? Oh Lord, that was the cutest. The big, bad biker was blushing because he owned some romance books.

She really thought he'd been created just for her.

And she didn't want to hand him back.

Nuh-uh. Finders keepers and all that sort of stuff. Maybe she should lick him. If she licked him then he was hers, right?

And she wanted him to be hers.

Calm down. You can't keep him. He's not a stuffed toy you found at the playground. He's a person.

"I'm going to get you set up here. Sav should be here soon on my bike and I have to take him back."

He stood and grabbed the TV remotes for her, placing them down on the coffee table, which he dragged closer.

"Where's Luna?" she asked, realizing the dog would have been out to greet him the second he opened the door.

"Still with the neighbor. You want me to get her before I go?"

"Yes, please, if it's not too much bother."

"No bother." He stood and moved to the bookcase, choosing a

few romances, which he also set on the coffee table. "I'll get you some painkillers, you must be in a lot of pain by now. What do you want to drink? Eat?"

"Oh, I'm fine." She wasn't. She was starving. But she didn't want him running around for her.

"When was the last time you ate?" he asked her.

"Um, you got me some food when we were waiting in the emergency room."

"So about four or five hours ago?"

"Yep. Not that long ago."

"How long do you usually go without eating?" he asked.

"I don't know."

"Oh, I think you do know. Just like I think you're starving and not saying anything because you don't want to be a bother."

Drat.

He gave her a stern look. "Can't take care of you properly unless you're honest with me."

Now she felt terrible. "Sorry."

"You're forgetting I've been working with you for three weeks. I know how much you eat."

"Hey!" she protested.

He grinned. "Not really sure I've got enough food in the house to feed you."

Her mouth dropped open, he did not just say that.

"Might have to go get some groceries. Stock up."

She grabbed a cushion off the sofa and flung it at him without even thinking. It hit him straight in the face and he didn't say anything for a moment.

Horror filled her. "I-I'm s-sor—" she managed to get out before he broke into laughter.

"Good aim there, Tabby-baby," he told her.

Warmth filled her at the name and she blushed. "Sorry. But I don't eat that much."

He raised an eyebrow. "You forget I've seen your snack drawer."

Whoops. So he had.

"I feel funny if I go too long without eating," she defended.

"You do? You ever seen a doctor about that?"

"Oh yeah, a while ago. He said I'm fine. I just need to make sure I snack regularly."

"Then you need a snack right now. Apple and peanut butter?"

"Thanks, that sounds good."

He returned quickly with some sliced apple and peanut butter on a plate, along with some carrot sticks and cheese slices with crackers.

Yum.

There was also a bottle of water, some Gatorade, and those horrid pain killers.

"This looks delicious, thank you." To her embarrassment, tears flooded her eyes.

"Hey. What is it? Don't you like it?"

"What? No!" She hugged the plate of food close as he reached for it. "Hands off. Mine."

He held his hands up in surrender. "Whoa. Okay, no one is taking your precious."

"Good. Yummy. Mine."

"Right. Didn't realize you were so possessive of your food."

Well. He knew it now.

You're acting insane, Tabby.

"Sorry, this is really nice of you. I'm just not used to it. Thank you."

"Fuck."

What was it? Had she done something to upset him?

"Razor?"

"I'm going to go get you a blanket. Back in a minute."

He was gone longer than a minute and she was starting to think she'd said something wrong.

When he returned, he held a blanket as well as Snappy and Scooby, who had been resting on top of her bag. She blushed, but he just tucked the blanket around her before handing her the stuffed turtle. "Sorry about before. Upsets me when you say things like that."

Like what? That she wasn't used to people being so nice to her? Oh.

That upset him? That was so . . . sweet.

"Do you need anything else? Got to go to the bathroom?"

"No, I'm fine."

She heard the sound of a bike approaching.

"There's Sav," he said needlessly. "I need to get going. Sure you don't need to pee?"

"I'm good." Sheesh.

"All right. Got your phone? It's charged?"

Her bag was on the coffee table and she drew out the phone to show him.

"No moving unless it's necessary. Call me if you need me. I'll grab Luna now and put her inside. Remember, stay put." He pointed a finger at her.

Jeepers.

SHE LAY in bed that night, unable to sleep.

After he'd returned from dropping Sav back to the shop, Razor had made them both dinner. Then they'd played a game of Scrabble and watched an episode of a house renovation show that both of them were addicted to.

He was pretty much all of her fantasies and wishes in one sexy package.

Well, except for his bossiness. But sometimes, that could be sweet. When it didn't stop her from doing what she wanted to do.

She rolled over. He'd insisted on carrying her around. Hell, he'd even run a bath for her. She'd had to put her foot down, figuratively, not literally, since he wouldn't let her down, when he'd wanted to help her in and out of the bath.

That wasn't happening, buddy.

Although, now she was kind of hot thinking about it. About him touching her, running his strong hands over her skin, her breasts, down her stomach to her pussy.

Sheesh.

Reaching down, she cupped her pussy. Then she ran a finger under her panties and along her slit.

Could she touch herself? She never got much satisfaction from her fingers, but she hadn't brought her vibrator with her. Maybe she could give it a go. If she could take care of this arousal coursing through her, then perhaps she'd be able to sleep.

Her mind was too busy and maybe it would relax her. She drew her panties down slightly and started to pinch her nipple. Oh, that felt so good. She let out a small sigh.

Make sure you're quiet.

She brought up her fantasy again. Only, this time instead of being in the bath, she was in the shower.

Razor was behind her, washing her. His hands ran down her body then up to cup her breasts. Her hard nipples pressed into his palms. She groaned.

Then she realized she'd actually groaned out loud. Not just in her head.

She paused, her heart racing. Had he heard that?

There was no noise from his bedroom, which was next to hers. Finally, she moved her fingers again. Pushing a finger into her pussy, she pinched her nipple at the same time.

Now, where was she?

Oh yeah. She and Razor in the shower. Both of them naked. Slippery and wet.

He turned her around to face him. "On your knees."

Slowly, she complied, then looked up at him, waiting for his next command. Grasping hold of his cock, he ran the head over her mouth.

"Open."

That voice, deep, gravelly, and full of command, sent a thrill through her and she opened her mouth, taking him inside her.

Moving her finger to her clit, she rubbed it, flicking it up and down.

He drove his cock deep into her mouth, until she could hardly breathe. Hunger filled her. She loved that he was in control. That he wasn't letting her make the decisions.

So freeing.

In and out of her mouth, he thrust.

She moved her finger against her clit with firmer, faster strokes.

So close. So close.

Razor came in her mouth. "Swallow me down. Don't you miss a drop, baby girl."

A shockwave rocked through her body as she shook with her orgasm. A groan escaped before she could swallow it and she paused, her orgasm still rushing through her, her empty pussy clenching then releasing, wanting that firm, thick cock inside her.

Not that she had any clue whether he was thick or not, but this was her fantasy, right?

Not too long, but nice and fat.

Just right.

Did she just rhyme that? Idiot.

She moved her fingers away from her pussy, concerned that he'd heard her groan.

Please be asleep.

Please be asleep.

She knew she'd never be able to face him in the morning if

he'd heard her make sex noises. There was no coming back from sex noises.

But he didn't call out or knock on the door, so she let out a sigh of relief. Okay, he was obviously asleep. Thank goodness.

Still, probably better if she did that sort of thing when she was on her own from now on. Getting out of bed, she hopped carefully into the attached bathroom and used the toilet before washing her hands. She needed to change her panties since they were soaked. Just as well she'd brought plenty of pairs with her.

She had a feeling this could be a constant occurrence.

11

"Are you sure you'll be all right?" Razor asked the following morning.

"I'll be fine." She was finishing up the scrambled eggs he'd made her. Damn, she could get used to this. The man could cook. She thought she'd mastered scrambled eggs, but all she'd done was stir some eggs together and put them in a pan with butter.

Razor had taken them to the next level, mixing in some cream and chives and serving them on thick cuts of sourdough bread.

She was in heaven.

"Lois, my next-door neighbor, will check in on you a few times. I'm also going to come home at lunch as well."

"No, you're not," she countered. "I don't need anyone to check up on me."

"You need toilet breaks."

"I'm not a dog." She glared at him.

"Luna will need toilet breaks too," he pointed out. "Lois is in her seventies. She can let Luna out, but she can't carry you to the toilet."

"Nobody needs to carry me to the toilet."

"Then how are you going to get there?" He reached for her empty plate, putting some more eggs and buttery toast on it.

"I couldn't fit more in," she protested, out of politeness than any genuine belief that she was full.

"Eat. You need to keep your strength up."

"I'm not taking part in a marathon," she told him. She swallowed the forkful of eggs that she was unaware of putting in her mouth. "And I can hop or crawl to the toilet." It wouldn't be nice on her grazed knees and hands, but she'd manage.

"I don't like it. You could fall."

"How am I going to fall if I'm crawling?"

"You shouldn't be crawling. I mean, not unless you like crawling."

What? What was he talking about? He took a sip of coffee. She reached for the smoothie he'd made her. Wow. That tasted so good.

"You have to teach me how to make this."

"I will." His lips twitched. "You finished?"

She glanced down at her empty plate. Well, darn it. When had she eaten all of that? Now she was full. She might need to lie down for a while. She fidgeted in her seat. It was going to be so hard not being able to jog.

"I don't suppose you have any weights or anything?" she asked Razor.

"Weights?"

"I get antsy sitting around. Lots of restless energy. That's why I jog every day."

"When do you find time for that?" he asked as he loaded the dishwasher.

"I go each morning," she told him as she checked her emails on her phone. Full of the usual junk and scams. She knew she needed to call Jared. Better he find out from her that she'd hurt herself. "I usually wake up around five-thirty then head out. I run for around an hour."

There was silence and she looked up from her phone to stare over at Razor, who was glaring at her. What was his problem?

"It's still dark at five-thirty in the morning."

"The street lights provide plenty of light," she countered. "And it's starting to grow light by six."

"Who do you go with?"

"Um, no one."

His eyes looked like they were about to bug out of his head. "No one? No one!"

Wasn't that just what she'd said?

"Yes, I go on my own."

"And you think that's safe?" he asked in a low voice that had her sitting up straight. He was angry. Why was he angry?

"I have my pepper spray and stun gun, as well as my cell phone."

"That makes all the difference then."

"Are you being sarcastic?"

"Yes, I'm being sarcastic! Tabby, that's not safe. Anyone could attack you."

"But I told you, I have my pepper spray and stun gun!" Now she was starting to get mad. She wasn't stupid.

He ran his hand over his face. "And what if you couldn't get to the spray or stun gun in time? What if they were too close for the pepper spray but too far away to stun? What if there was more than one attacker? What if one person distracted you while the other one snuck up behind you? What if they had a damn weapon!"

"Well, I . . ."

"You didn't think of any of that, did you?"

It wasn't that she hadn't thought of it. It's just that she thought it unlikely.

"There are usually other people around. There's one guy that usually jogs at a similar time. And people commuting to work."

"And if someone dragged you into an alley? If that jogger decided to attack you? What then? Baby, fuck!"

She rubbed at her ear in agitation. "I like running in the morning. It's quiet and peaceful. I thought I was pretty careful."

"Not careful enough, if something happened to you . . . you know that people would care, right?" he asked.

No, she didn't really know that. Jared would.

"I would care. I'd care if something happened to you, Tabby."

"You'd go to my funeral?"

Something frantic filled his face and he placed his hands on the counter and leaned over. "There will be no funeral. Understand me!"

She nodded without thinking, wanting to placate him. Also, she didn't want a funeral either. For the first time in what felt like years, she actually did care about more than how many people would mourn her loss.

"I don't want to die," she whispered.

"You will not die. I won't have it."

Oh, the arrogance in that statement was . . . delightful. A shiver of pleasure ran through her.

She wouldn't die. He wouldn't allow it.

Of course, he actually had no say. Sure, he was her boss and she was now staying at his house. But she'd go back to her own place, her own life soon enough.

However, knowing that he cared was everything.

"Okay, maybe I shouldn't go jogging so early in the morning."

"You will not go jogging that early anymore. I forbid it."

"Um, pretty sure you can't do that."

"Pretty sure I just did. No more jogging in the dark. You shouldn't be jogging alone at all. It's not safe."

"Who's going to come with me?"

"I will."

"Um." She didn't know how to say this without sounding mean, but ...

"You don't think I can jog? I can jog. Are you trying to call me old again?"

"No. I wouldn't do that." Nuh-uh, she'd learned that earlier. "You're not old. You're very fit looking. Especially for your age. Oh, crap, that came out wrong. It's just, you don't look like a jogger."

"Are you being joggist?"

Was that a thing? No, it wasn't. She narrowed her gaze at him. "How are you going to come jogging with me? You live thirty minutes away."

"I'll figure it out," he muttered. "You're not running on that foot anytime soon, anyway." He glanced at the clock. "Shit. Got to go. Let's get you set up for the day."

"I need to go brush my teeth," she told him.

He carried her to the bathroom and thankfully left her alone while she brushed her teeth and peed. There was a knock on the door and she opened it. He frowned as he stared down at her, balancing on one foot.

"I don't like you hopping around. You could fall over. How are your hands? Do you think you could use crutches?"

"Maybe."

He suddenly picked her up around the waist and carried her over to the counter, sitting her on it. Then he drew the bandage off one of her palms. Crap, they still looked red and sore.

"That's not happening for another day or so," he told her. "But I'll still pick some up for you."

She thought it was overkill, but she was beginning to learn to pick her battles. He lifted her again and ten minutes later, she was settled on the sofa with a couple of books, some bike magazines that she'd insisted she wanted to read. Maybe she'd learn something. The TV remote was in easy reach, and he'd tucked a blanket around her.

Who knew that a tough biker guy could be such a fusspot?

"Need anything else?" he asked after setting her up with snacks, water and yuck, painkillers.

"Nope, I'm good."

"Lois will pop in randomly throughout the day. I'll be back at lunchtime. Be good."

She rolled her eyes. "I'm always good."

"Uh-huh, somehow I don't believe that." He muttered something to himself. She was pretty sure she heard him saying something about running in the dark, but she ignored him.

"Luna, watch Tabby."

The dog sat up with a short yip. Jeepers, did everyone obey him?

SHE DRANK down the last of her water. "Right, better get some more before I get back into this book."

Damn, Razor had some good romance books.

She swung her legs over the edge of the couch as Luna let out a yip and disappeared. Oh, did she want out?

Then Luna returned. With a bottle of water in her mouth.

Tabby felt her mouth drop open. That was freaking insane. How had she done that? Luna dropped the bottle of water into her lap. After she got over her shock, Tabby gave Luna an enthusiastic pat.

"Good girl, Luna. Well done. Aren't you clever?"

She had no idea how the dog had done that. Amazing.

A knock had her turning towards the door. She knew it was locked, Razor had told her he would lock it when he left. So the sound of the door opening had her freezing. Then Luna let out a bark, her tail wagging.

"Helloo, just me, Lois. The next-door neighbor."

Tabby breathed out a sigh of relief. Right, the neighbor who was checking on her.

"Hello, dear, you must be Tabby."

A fit-looking woman with short, white hair strode in. She was dressed in a pair of jeans and an oversized white shirt. She looked gorgeous and stylish. And she was carrying a container.

"Hi," Tabby said quietly.

"Hello, Luna. How are you? I'm missing you. Yes, I am." The woman put the container down as she greeted the dog. Then she raised her head to study Tabby. "How are you doing? Razor said you've hurt your ankle?"

"Um, yes, thank you for checking on me, you really didn't have to."

"Nonsense. I'm happy to drop in. Gosh, with everything Razor helps me with, it's the least I could do. I baked you some chocolate chip cookies. I'll put the container in the kitchen and put a few on a plate for you. Would you like milk or coffee with them?" she called out as she walked into the kitchen.

"You don't have to."

"I know I don't have to, dear." She ended up coming back with a glass of milk and three big cookies. "I'll take Luna out for a walk, but do you need anything first?"

"Oh no, I'm fine."

The woman eyed her. "You can tell me the truth, dear. Last year, I broke my ankle. Such a nuisance, but Razor was such a dear. Did so much for me around the house. Such a nice man, isn't he?"

"He is."

"Reminds me of my late husband, James. Not in looks, but in personality. Poor James wasn't a hunk like Razor is."

A hunk?

Tabby had to hide a grin.

"If I was a few years younger . . . " Lois said with a sigh and a wink.

Oh, she was trouble.

"James had a similar personality to Razor. Quiet but firm. Lord, it took a while in the beginning of our marriage for things to sort themselves out. That man was not afraid to take me over his lap if he thought I was doing something that put myself at risk." She winked at Tabby, who stared at her in shock.

"He spanked you?"

"My, yes. For the first few months, I didn't sit comfortably. Looking back now, I think I goaded him on purpose. But I would never have admitted that to him. Ah, those were the days. Now, I'll go take Luna on a walk."

Wow. She didn't even know what to say to that.

LATER THAT NIGHT, she finished up a second helping of lasagna, which Lois had dropped off that afternoon when she checked in on her again. Razor had made a salad to go with it, which kind of shocked her. A man who ate salad?

They were sitting in the dine-in area in the kitchen. It had a window seat on one side then two chairs across the small table. It was pretty much the sweetest thing she'd ever seen.

"Want any more?" Razor asked, picking up both plates.

"No," she said with a groan, rubbing her tummy. "This time I mean it."

"Unlike all the other times when you said you were full out of politeness."

She blushed. "Um, yeah. Can I help you tidy up?"

"Nope."

"Razor," she grumbled. "I'm not helpless."

"No, you're injured. There's a difference."

She sighed. "Are you still unhappy with me?"

When he'd come home at lunchtime, she'd been making her way back from the bathroom, hopping along the hallway.

"You already scolded me."

It had gone on a good five minutes. She'd started to think she'd rather have taken a spanking. Okay, it seemed Lois had gotten into her head. Also, she'd recently read a spanking scene in one of Razor's romance books. Sheesh, that was hot.

"If I can't rely on you to behave yourself, I'll need to have someone come and stay with you all day," he told her.

She let her lower lip drop out. "I'll behave. Did you know that Luna got me some water today? I didn't know she could do that."

"Luna's a clever girl, aren't you?" He patted the dog's head as he moved around, tidying up.

He settled Tabby back on the couch. "Want something to drink? Beer? Wine?"

"You have wine?"

"Got some red."

"Yes, please. A small glass."

He returned with a glass of red for her and a beer for himself. They settled in to watch some episodes of the house renovation program they both liked. When one episode finished and he'd gotten a new beer, she turned to him.

"Did you know that Lois' husband spanked her?"

Beer burst out of his mouth and he started coughing. "W-what?"

"Oh, sorry, I should have waited for you to swallow. Maybe I shouldn't have said anything. But she didn't seem like she was telling me a secret."

"Um, yeah, I did know that. I knew James. He was a good man. He wasn't abusing her."

"No, I gathered that. She said she used to provoke him to get a spanking."

"Brat. She could have just asked if she wanted one. I'm sure he'd have been happy to give her that."

"I didn't know people did that. I mean, outside of BDSM. I didn't know that someone could like that. I didn't like it when Luther hurt me."

"What Luther did to you was abuse," he said firmly.

She nodded. She knew that.

"What was between Lois and James was consensual. When they first started dating, he told her about the sort of relationship he wanted. One with a domestic discipline element. She agreed to it, even if it sounds like she found it hard to get used to in the beginning."

"Sounds like she came to like it."

He nodded. "Some people like having rules, having boundaries and consequences if they're broken. Others enjoy pain. Some like to be submissive or dominant in the bedroom and nowhere else. Some might like to go to a club to play in a safe setting. They might enjoy submitting as a way of releasing stress. Maybe they don't want to be in charge for a while, they want to let go. Others enjoy something that goes beyond the bedroom. Everyone is different. But there should be consent. Abuse is something very different."

"I had no say in anything. I didn't even get a say in whether I wanted to marry Luther or not. My uncle just told me what was happening. At the time, Jared was living in Boston. He wasn't even talking to my uncle. I'm sure he would have gotten me away from Luther if he'd known how bad things were. But like I said, he thought he was protecting me by staying away. He's not a bad person, my cousin. Everything he does isn't good. But he has changed things about my uncle's operations."

Razor didn't look like he agreed.

"Luther kept me mostly locked up in his house. The abuse wasn't just physical. He systematically beat down my self-esteem. I started to think all the things he said about me were true. That there was no one to help me. That no one cared. That no one would ever care or love me. That I was worthless."

"Tabby-baby." He came over and crouched in front of her, taking her hand in his. "You know that's not true, right? You are infinitely lovable. You are worthy of love. And there are people who care about you. Including me."

"I know that now. I didn't then. He got so far into my head, I didn't even think about trying to tell Jared."

"My mom was in a relationship with someone who abused her. We were young at the time, but I can remember seeing her with a bruised eye. Can remember the yelling at night. Waking up to find stuff smashed."

"What happened?" she whispered.

"One day, I came home to find him hitting her. I ran into my bedroom and picked up my dad's baseball bat. I rushed out, swinging it at him. Only, I was young and no match for that asshole. He easily took it from me, then he started hitting me as well."

"Oh no!"

"Yeah. I ended up covered in bruises, a broken nose, and black eye. When he left, my momma called my uncle. My dad's brother. He came over, saw me, and then he disappeared. That asshole never came back."

"What happened to him?"

"My uncle ran with a bad crowd. Guessing he and his friends killed him." He eyed her as he said that, but she didn't flinch. "I just wished I'd been big enough to protect her, you know?"

"Oh, Razor. I'm so sorry. Can I . . . will you let me . . ."

"Spit it out, Tabby-baby," he said quietly.

"Will you let me hug you?"

"I'd love that."

Then she found herself enveloped in his arms, held tight. And it was heaven. Her heart wept for that younger Razor.

Eventually, he drew back, but he didn't move far. His face was a few inches from hers. "Don't ever think that you don't have worth, Tabby. Or that someone doesn't care. All you need to do is say it and I'll be there for you. No matter what."

She didn't really think about it. She just acted on instinct. Leaning up, she placed her hand around the back of his neck and kissed him. Her lips brushed against his and a shot of pleasure ran through her. Moaning softly, she parted her lips, and that seemed to be some sort of signal to him. His lips moved against hers. Fireworks shot off through her blood.

She melted. She'd never been kissed like this. With such passion. When Luther had kissed her, she'd felt ill. One time, she'd actually started gagging. He hadn't really tried again after that. And she'd been thankful.

But with Razor . . . holy heck. It was like her entire body just suddenly lit up. She felt so damn alive. It was exhilarating.

Then he drew back. She murmured out a protest, waiting for him to return, but he moved away from her and she opened her eyes, feeling a dark chill fill her as she took in the closed-off expression on his face.

"I'm sorry. That was fucking wrong."

Tabby flinched. Wrong? Here she was thinking about how amazing the kiss was, how she'd never felt better and he thought it was wrong.

Hurt dug its way in deep. She quickly built up a protective layer to hide the pain from him.

Never let anyone see you in pain. They'll use it against you.

Luther had thrived on her pain. He'd used her emotions against her. To manipulate her.

So she wrapped up her hurt in layers and kept herself from

doing what she really wanted to do. Which was to reach for him. To hold him tight. To beg him not to let her go.

"I apologize. That shouldn't have happened. I didn't mean to take advantage of you."

She frowned. Take advantage of her? He didn't take advantage of her. Hell, if anything. it was the other way around.

"I'll be back soon."

Before she could tell him that she should be the one apologizing, he'd left the room.

What the hell?

HOURS LATER, Tabby lay in bed unable to sleep.

She tossed and turned, playing that kiss over and over in her mind. Why had she kissed him? She'd ruined everything.

He'd pulled back from her. The rest of the night had been awkward. They'd been overly polite with each other. And other than when he'd carried her to bed, he had been careful not to touch her.

Did she really want to stay here anymore? Where she wasn't wanted? Where she was a burden.

Sitting up, she wondered if it was better to go now. It would probably be a relief for him to wake up in the morning and find her gone. She didn't know how they were supposed to work together.

Which was just the situation he'd been trying to avoid, and now look what she'd gone and done.

Shit.

Moving to the side of the bed, she pulled back the covers and swung her legs around. But when she attempted to hop towards the bathroom, her foot banged into the bedside table.

Ow. Shit. Mother-fucker! She let out a strangled cry, trying her best to keep quiet as she sat back down on the bed and held onto her foot with both hands.

Ouch. Ouch. Ouch.

She didn't want to cry out and wake him. A knock on the bedroom door told her that she'd failed.

"Tabby? You okay?"

"Fine."

"Sure? I thought I heard you cry out."

Shit! He'd really heard that? Thank God he'd been sleeping last night when she'd made sex noises. How embarrassing would it have been if he'd heard her?

"I'm coming in, all right?"

No, it wasn't all right. But before she could protest, he walked in. The bathroom light was on, but she couldn't see his expression as he moved forward.

Was he annoyed? Probably.

"What happened?" He crouched in front of her, then switched on the bedside light. He took hold of her foot in his hands.

"Nothing. Just banged my big toe."

"Can you wiggle it?"

"It's really fine. I—"

"Can you wiggle it?" he asked more firmly.

Well, sure she could. With a huff, she wiggled the toe back and forth.

"Not broken, that's good." He gently prodded the toe and her foot. "Doesn't look too bad."

"It's just a stubbed toe, I'll live." Although if he kept touching her then she might just throw herself at him and beg him to kiss her again.

Pathetic, Tabby.

"What were you doing? Did you need the bathroom?"

She couldn't tell him she'd been going to sneak out. Now that she thought about it, she wouldn't have done it. It would be a really shit move to just leave like that. She couldn't be that rude when he'd been so nice to her.

"Ah, yeah." She crossed her fingers behind her back.

"You should have called out for me."

"I didn't want to disturb you. I thought you might have been asleep."

"I was. But I'm a light sleeper." He picked her up, carrying her to the bathroom. "Call out when you need me."

Wait. A light sleeper?

She used the toilet, so she wasn't such a liar. Then she washed her hands before hopping to the door.

A light sleeper.

Her crying out just before had woken him? Which meant . . . had he heard her last night? Did he know what she'd been doing?

Oh. Holy. Fuck.

She opened the door and he frowned at her. "You should have called out."

"Sorry." He carried her back, settling her under the covers before tucking her in. A flush of pleasure ran through her at the caring gesture.

"I hope I haven't been making noises in my sleep and keeping you awake," she said, fishing.

He stared down at her for a moment. Were his lips twitching? They were, right?

"There were a few noises last night. But they didn't disturb me." He turned out the light. "Night, Tabby. Sleep well."

Shit.

How was she meant to fall asleep after that?

12

Tabby stared at the black TV screen.

She'd barely spoken to Razor this morning. She'd been too embarrassed after learning he'd likely heard her pleasuring herself the night before last.

And he'd been reticent. Closed-off. Probably regretting opening up his house to her. Hell, at this point, he likely regretted giving her a job.

She wished she'd never kissed him.

With a sigh, she picked up her phone. She'd better call Jared.

"Hello? Tabitha?"

"Yep, it's me. How's it going?" she asked cheerfully.

"It's going fine," he replied. "How are you?"

"Well, don't freak out because I'm fine."

"What happened?"

"I just twisted my ankle," she said hastily. "That's all."

"You need to come home. I'm sending someone to get you."

"No, I'm not coming home." She grimaced. Not that she considered it home. "The doctor said my foot would be fine in a few days."

Jared grunted.

"I just wanted to let you know."

"If you need help, you're to let me know immediately."

"I will."

"Funny, you should call. I was just looking at your credit card statement."

Oh, shit.

"Is that right?" she asked.

"Yeah, you bought a pet?"

"Yes, some fish. Is that okay?"

"Of course it's okay," he replied, his voice softening. "You can buy what you like. I see you also bought some toys?"

Fuck!

"I'm an adult! I can buy toys if I want!" she defended.

"What? I wasn't saying that you couldn't. They're for you? I thought you might have met someone with children."

"You're talking about toys." Actual toys, not her vibrator. Shit.

"Yes, what did you think I was talking about?"

"Nothing, gotta go." She hung up, her heart racing.

Idiot.

She slumped back. She was losing her mind.

Luna suddenly went on alert as the front door opened.

"Heelllooo, I'm here!"

She frowned. That wasn't Lois. The voice sounded too young. But it was familiar.

"Come on, Mr. Fluffy. No, I'm not carrying you. You're too heavy. You can sleep when you're inside."

Luna gave an excited bark as Millie walked into the living room, half-carrying a big dog that bore a marked resemblance to Luna. Obviously the same breed. Although the dog Millie was trying to convince to walk seemed even larger than Luna.

Millie stood and the dog flopped to the floor then rolled onto his side. Millie stretched out her back then rubbed her shoulder.

"Darn it, Mr. Fluffy, Spike is going to be mad if I hurt my shoulder or back trying to move you around. He's going to send you to that behavioral specialist for dogs, you know. The vet said there's no physical reason for you to be so lazy." She waggled a finger at the dog.

Luna raced over, pouncing back and forth as though trying to get Mr. Fluffy to play. But the other dog just lay there, watching Luna. Then he yawned.

Tabby found herself giggling. Mr. Fluffy *was* lazy.

Millie turned, smiling widely at Tabby. "Oh, Tabby! I'm so glad to see you."

The other woman wore a blue and white polka-dot dress with buttons down the front. It was cinched around her waist with a big red belt. Millie had gorgeous curves and a body that was made for the fifties style dress. Her long, dark hair was pulled up into a high ponytail and she wore a red cardigan. On one arm she had a pale blue handbag that was in the shape of a triceratops.

"Hi, Millie," she said shyly. "Love your handbag."

"Thanks, Spike got it for me. Usually, I use the bag my friend, Mrs. Spain, made for me, but this is just too cute not to use."

It was cute.

"I didn't know you were coming to visit today."

Millie paused. "You don't mind, do you? Razor said it would be okay. He seemed to be worried about you being here all day by yourself. But if you'd rather Mr. Fluffy and I left . . ."

"No, please stay," Tabby said, leaning forward. "I've thought about you a lot since that night."

"You have?" Millie asked, looking amazed. She came and sat on the sofa next to Tabby. Then she glanced over at the dogs as Luna whined. "Sorry, Luna. He's not into playing. They're brother and sister, you know."

"Oh, I didn't know."

"I've thought about you a lot too. Wondered if you were all right."

"I'm sorry I never called you. Life was just . . ."

"It's all right. I get it. Life can be shit. But you're here now and you're all right, which is the main thing. Well, other than your poor ankle. How is it? Do you need anything? Razor said you're not supposed to walk on it but that you can't use crutches because of your hands? He sounded very concerned about you."

"I'm fine. He's just being overzealous. It's only a sprain."

"Overzealous." Millie grinned. "I like that word. Most of these guys are overzealous when it comes to their women."

"But I'm not Razor's . . . um, woman."

"Yeah? So what is going on between the two of you?"

"Nothing. I just work for him."

Millie leaned back with a wide grin. Crossing her legs, she flicked one leg back and forth. "That so?"

"Uh, yeah, it is."

"Because a few months ago, one of Razor's guys broke his arm. Strangely enough, he didn't insist that Big G move in with him so he could take care of him. And he didn't organize people to come in and check on him."

"Well, would you want Big G staying with you?" she joked. Big G was one of the quieter guys who worked for Razor and more than a little intimidating. "He'd terrify the neighbors."

"He is scary. But my point is that Razor didn't move you in here because you work for him. He feels something for you."

"He doesn't," Tabby said.

"Totally does. I know these things. Reverend Pat says it's just that I'm nosy, but it's not. I have a sick sense for it."

"Do you mean sixth sense?" she asked.

"That too."

Tabby grinned. "Reverend Pat?"

"Yeah, he's a friend from my old town. I come from this place called Nowhere. It's a great place. I loved living there. But my friends visit when they can. Hey, you want anything? Hot chocolate? I thought I'd order in for lunch. Spike is on this health kick, so do you think we can order pizza?"

Millie gave her a pleading look.

"Sure, pizza sounds good."

"Yay." Millie clapped her hands. "I'll make us hot chocolates. I hope Razor has the right ingredients. A hot chocolate just isn't right without whipped cream and sprinkles. Oh, it might be best to order two pizzas as I'm a vegetarian. Most people like meat on their pie."

"That's okay. I can eat a whole pizza on my own."

"Really?" Millie asked, looking down at her. "That's impressive."

Tabby just shrugged.

"Right, we need a hot chocolate in order to figure out what is going on with you and Razor."

"There's nothing going on with Razor and me."

"Uh-huh. Sure there's not. Denial isn't healthy, you know. It'll give you diarrhea. That's what Mrs. Spain told me and I'm certain it's true. Mr. Spain denied for ages that he was organizing Mrs. Spain a surprise birthday party for her seventieth birthday and he spent most of those two weeks on the toilet. The man lost ten pounds."

Tabby didn't know what to say to that. Then she couldn't say anything due to the noise that Millie was making in the kitchen.

When the other woman returned, she was carrying two large mugs topped with so much whipped cream that Tabby was worried it was going to tip down the side and spill everywhere.

But Millie managed to get the two cups to the coffee table. Tabby saw that copious amounts of sprinkles had been spread over the whipped cream.

"Hot chocolate. Spike only lets me have one of these a week. I mean, what's with the health kick? If you can't eat whipped cream then what's the point in living, am I right? It's all Hack's fault. I went in for this check-up and my iron levels were low. I just needed a bit more spinach in my diet. Like Popeye, right? Only Spike freaked that he wasn't looking after me properly. And now, it's all vitamins this, vitamins that. All I had to do was pop a few of those gummy vitamins. Done."

"I love gummy vitamins." Especially since she couldn't take actual pills.

"Swallowing real pills sucks. Why do it when you can chew gummy vitamins, right? But nooo, now it's all veggies and fruit and legumes. I do like a good veggie burger, though. Maybe we should have burgers for lunch. Nah, actually, pizza is good."

She wondered if Millie spoke this much all the time or if it was the sugar in the hot chocolate she was sipping on. Tabby picked hers up and took an experimental sip.

Ooh. That was nice.

She couldn't remember a lot from the night she'd met Millie, maybe she was always this bubbly. Not that Tabby minded. It was so nice to have someone to talk to. Made her realize, more than ever, how starved for human contact she'd been. For affection. Was that why she'd kissed Razor? Because she wanted some human touch?

Yeah, you can tell yourself that, but it's not true.

She was attracted to him. Plain and simple.

"He decided to go on a health kick because you were low on iron?" It seemed like an overreaction, but then Millie said that these guys were all overzealous when it came to their women.

"There might have been a few other reasons," Millie muttered. "You like the hot chocolate?"

"Yeah, it's delicious."

Millie kicked her shoes off and that's when Tabby noticed they had mini T-Rexes on the buckles.

"Those shoes are so cool."

"I know, right? Found them online. I love dinosaurs, in case you didn't realize." She patted her triceratops handbag. "I made Mr. Fluffy this brontosaurus outfit for Halloween. He looks sooo cute in it."

Tabby eyed Mr. Fluffy skeptically. "He doesn't look like he'd be into Halloween."

"Well, he's not into trick-or-treating, that's for sure. Too much walking. I think I'll throw a Halloween party this year, you'll have to come."

She was already thinking about Halloween? It was months away. And a party? Where she'd have to talk to people? Could she do that?

Of course you can. Look at you, you now have a job. You're sitting here talking to Millie. You own fish.

Totally winning at this life stuff.

Except for the fact that the only person she could kind of claim as a friend wasn't really talking to her.

"So, tell me what's going on," Millie said, turning to her with a serious look. "Because you look like someone stood on your toe then punched you in the boob before they stole your favorite stuffie."

Um, what?

Then she saw Millie looking at Scooby-Doo and Snappy who were keeping her company.

"Oh, um, I . . . these . . ."

"No need to be embarrassed," Millie said with a kind smile. "I left mine at home. But Chompers does most things with me. He sleeps with me too. Spike takes up most of the bed, though, so it can be a tight fit for the three of us. I suggested we get a bigger bed, then maybe Mr. Fluffy can sleep with us. Spike didn't agree."

The dog looked like he could almost take up a double bed just on his own. So she kind of had to agree with that.

"You like Scooby-Doo? I do too."

"Yeah, you don't think that's odd?"

"Girl, you're asking the wrong person about what's odd. I have a dinosaur purse."

Tabby had to grin.

"So enough procrastination. Hit me with it."

Could she tell her? Should she? But who else did she have to talk to? And Millie knew Razor, she might be able to give some insight.

"I kissed him," she blurted out.

Millie's mouth dropped open. Then she grinned. Wide. "You did? You go, girl. That's awesome."

"No, it's not awesome. Really not awesome. He pulled away from me."

"Get out."

"Um."

"He did not."

"He did," she insisted.

"He didn't kiss you back? I refuse to believe it. How could he not kiss you back?"

"Maybe he's not into me."

"Nooo." Millie looked shocked at the thought. Which did a lot to soothe Tabby's injured pride. That hurt that she'd buried deep lessened.

"Well, I mean, he did kiss me back for a start," she admitted.

Millie slapped her thigh, making Tabby jump. "Well, there you go. He kissed you back."

"But then he drew away. And he's been acting strange ever since. Distant."

"What a dumbass."

"What?" she asked. Why was she calling her a dumbass? That seemed kind of rude.

"Not you," Millie told her. "Razor. Obviously, he kissed you back because you're gorgeous and he's attracted to you. But then, for some reason, he drew away. It'll be some stupid reason. Like how he shouldn't want you because you work for him and he's in a position of power. Or because you're younger than him. Or because you're vulnerable from what you went through with Luther and he doesn't want to push."

"Wow. You're good at this."

"I know. See, Reverend Pat was wrong. I'm not nosy. I totally have that sick sense."

"You do." She didn't bother correcting her that it was a sixth sense. If she wanted to call it a sick sense, she could.

"Do you really think that's why he's acting funny? Not because he's not actually attracted to me?"

Millie waved a hand. "Totally. Question is, how do we get him to tell you what's going on?" She tapped her chin. "How do you feel about nudity?"

"Um." What?

"That might be too much anyway. I mean, coming home to find you nude in his bed would give him a shove, but he might go all shy. These guys have got delicate feelings. We have to be careful not to hurt them."

She didn't remember much about Spike, but from what she did, well, she wasn't sure he had that many delicate feelings.

"I don't think I'm comfortable with climbing into his bed naked."

"Too bad. It's a nice direct approach, you know. We need something grand and dramatic."

"Or I could just ask him, I guess."

Millie blinked. "Ask him. I wonder if that would work. I'll have to think about it. Could you do that?"

Could she?

"I'm not sure."

"Well, that's a problem, then. How long are you staying here for?"

"I don't know. I thought about leaving last night. I couldn't sleep. But then I figured that would be rude."

"Yeah, and he'd just go after you and drag you back. You're not going anywhere unless he wants you to. These guys are stubborn. And really protective. I bet you're not allowed to lift a finger."

"I'm not. But I should be able to use crutches tomorrow. Maybe even walk on my ankle. Once I can do that, I'm going to go home."

"Or you could come stay with me. I'll take care of you. It would be great fun. We could have a sleepover. We can even invite my friends. Betsy, Sunny, Emme, and Jewel would love to have a sleep-over with us."

"I, um . . ." Was she ready for that? Maybe not yet.

"Once you're ready," Millie said gently. "Sorry, I can be a lot."

"No." She shook her head. "No, you're perfect. It's me. I'm just not used to having friends. I'd like some, though. I'm kind of lonely," she admitted.

Millie reached over and squeezed her hand. "Then I'd be honored to be your friend. And friends can tell each other anything, okay?"

"Okay," she whispered. "I want to tell you something, but I'm nervous."

"Is it that you're a Little?"

"What?" Tabby asked.

"Oh. That wasn't it? Huh, my sick sense must have been off about that. Drat. It's probably all this healthy food that Daddy has me eating. It's just not good for me. I'm telling you, it's not normal to be that regular."

"What?" Did she just say Daddy?

"Pinky promise that you won't tell other people, I mean other than people who already know, like my friends. And also pinky promise that you won't think it's weird or stuff." Millie held up her little finger.

"You're going to tell me something that you think I'll find weird and you don't want me to tell other people about?" she clarified.

"Right."

Tabby wrapped her finger around Millie's. "There's nothing you can tell me that will make me think you're weird. And I would never betray a confidence."

Millie beamed. "And that's why we're gonna be best friends."

They were? That sounded like fun.

"So, here it goes. I'm a Little."

"Okay." She wasn't sure what that meant. Or what she should say.

"I like playing with toys. I sleep with a stuffed dinosaur. Sometimes my Daddy cuts up my food small and feeds it to me. I like using a pacifier and not just because it can help with my migraines. I'm a Little and Spike is my Daddy Dom. He cares for me, loves me, looks after me. So. Do you think that's weird?"

"No. I mean, I've never heard of it, but that doesn't make it weird." Something niggled in the back of her mind, but she pushed it aside.

"Some people do. But it's . . . it's something I need. Going into Little headspace is a way for me to let go of all my adult worries, you know? I can just play and have fun, and Spike is there to take care of me. It's a softer side of BDSM. Sure, there are still punishments and consequences. But I feel safe with those. Like, I know the boundaries and if I push them, then Spike is there to reinforce them. It's nice to know someone cares if I'm late getting home and don't call. Or if I'm tired and stressed, he'll hug me and make sure I rest."

It sounded amazing.

"I've always been a bit different, I guess. My best friends before I came here were all over the age of sixty-five. I'm impulsive and a bit crazy, and I can be a lot to take. But Spike loves me just as I am. He just makes sure that I stay safe and healthy and happy. And sometimes, playing with my toys is what makes me happy. That's not wrong, is it?"

"No, it's not wrong at all. In fact, that sounds amazing."

Millie beamed at her.

"Thought you might think that."

Tabby blinked at her. "Wait. Do you think that I might be a Little?"

"I wondered if you could be. No pressure for you to be. You don't have to be in order for us to be friends, okay?"

"All right. Why would you think that?"

"Well, there's your stuffies." Millie pointed to Snappy and Scooby.

"Lots of adults have stuffed toys."

"True."

"Only." Tabby chewed at her lower lip. "Is there stuff you can read about Littles and Daddies?"

"Sure, I can recommend some books, if you have an eReader or an app."

"I've got one on my phone." She pulled it out and bought some of the books that Millie suggested.

"I've probably overwhelmed you. Sorry."

"No, you've actually given me something to think about. I, um, I have something I need help with."

If Millie could be brave, so could she.

"Sure, what is it?"

"I need to know what the soundproofing is like between the walls of the bedrooms. Could you maybe go into Razor's bedroom and tell me if you can hear me?"

Millie blinked then grinned. "Oh, girl, what did you do?"

"Something horribly embarrassing."

Millie helped her into her bedroom then she left to go into

Razor's bedroom. She waited a few seconds before letting out a noise that was close to the same level she thought she'd made the other night.

"Was that the noise?" Millie called out.

She groaned loudly. "Yep. You obviously heard."

"Um, yeah. Wait there."

Millie walked into her room a few seconds later. Tabby was lying on the bed with a pillow over her face. She felt the bed move then Millie grabbed hold of her hand.

"You made that noise in bed, didn't you?"

"Yep."

"While you were, you know what, right?"

"Yep."

"Were you using a toy?"

"Nope."

"Well, I have you beat then, I was."

It took a moment for those words to sink in then Tabby sat up and stared down at Millie. "What?"

"Yep. I stayed with Spike for a while because, well, that part doesn't matter. But anyway, I was in the bath and I thought I'd use my dino vibrator. Because being close to Spike had made me horny."

She got that.

"I cried out when I came. He knocked on the bathroom door, worried about me. I told him there was a mouse."

"A mouse?"

"Yep. A mouse." Then I slipped getting out of the bath. He had to rescue me. Long story short, he cleaned up in the bathroom for me and found the dinosaur vibrator."

"Oh, God, Millie!"

"Yep. He figured out there was no mouse."

Tabby couldn't help it. She burst into laughter. She buried her face in the pillows next to Millie, who started laughing as well.

Then she patted Tabby on the back. "So you see, your story isn't that bad. At least he didn't find your vibrator."

Tabby rolled onto her back, wiping at her eyes. "I guess I can be thankful for that."

They were silent for a long moment.

"Razor's a good guy, Tabby. If you really like him, then don't give up on him, okay?"

"I won't."

"But also, don't hurt him. Cause I like you, I wouldn't like to have to rearrange your face."

"Noted."

Millie rolled over to face her. "Come to Reaper's this weekend."

"What?"

"Yeah, we're setting up a karaoke station. The guys don't know yet. It's one of those ask for forgiveness rather than permission deals. Jewel is going to set it up. She's good at being sneaky like that. Sunny isn't. We haven't even told her yet. Emme's good at keeping a secret too, but we're not sure she can make it. It's not exactly safe for her."

It wasn't?

"Her dad is . . . well, she just got reunited with him, and he has enemies. One warned Jewel that if Emme's father kept coming after him that he would retaliate. It's why we all need to be watched."

"But you're here."

"Yeah, but Spike drove me and he'll pick me up. And I'm not allowed to leave. Oh, and there's a guard outside."

"What? There is?"

"Yeah, Emme's dad arranged for us all to have guards when our guys can't be around, ever since Mr. X, that's the name of the bad guy, it's a good name, right? Anyway, since that warning, we've all been under close watch. Normally, Spike would stay but he had some stuff to do. He doesn't really like me leaving the house anymore. But we'll be safe at Reaper's. We'll be surrounded by Iron Shadows guys. They're a bit rough, but mostly harmless."

"I don't know. I'll think about it."

"I wonder if Emme's dad needs to arrange a guard for you, seeing as Razor is interested in you."

"We don't know that he is, though," she pointed out.

"He is. We just have to give him a little push. Don't worry, we'll figure this out. There's nothing I can't do once I put my mind to it. Just ask Reverend Pat, he'll tell you. I get shit done."

That's kind of what she was afraid of.

13

W hat was she doing?

Was she seriously going into a biker bar? She stared out of her car windshield at the sign. This place looked run-down and some of the guys walking inside appeared rough, to put it mildly. But Razor was in there.

And Millie.

She should have told Millie that she'd changed her mind and asked her to pick her up. She'd returned to her apartment yesterday, after she'd shown Razor that she could walk fine.

To her surprise, he hadn't put up much of a protest. Which had made her think that Millie was wrong. He wasn't interested in her. He was just being kind because he felt sorry for her.

So she'd gone home to her quiet, empty apartment and her fish.

And she didn't think she'd ever felt more alone.

Razor had told her that he didn't want to see her back at work until Monday, so she'd spent all of today sitting around feeling sorry for herself. Until she'd made the last-minute decision to come here tonight.

So, here she was.

Dressed in a pair of tight jeans and a sparkly top. Her hair was up in a ponytail and she'd even put on some make-up.

She could do this. How hard could it be to walk into a bar alone?

"Really hard," she muttered to herself. "Should have stayed home with the fish. They aren't scary and they don't judge. Well, much. I'm pretty sure that Shaggy is a bit judgey. It's in the beady eyes."

And now she was talking to herself. She was going to become a crazy fish lady.

Truth was, it might have been only thirty-two hours since she'd last seen Razor and Luna, but she missed them.

If only she hadn't kissed him.

Such an idiot.

Climbing out of her car, she locked it and glanced around. With a sigh, she limped towards the front door where a huge guy stood, watching her. His eyes narrowed as she drew closer. Probably wondering who the hell she was and what she was doing here.

Because she was a complete fish out of water.

"What happened to your foot?" he barked, surprising her.

"Um, I twisted it."

"Someone hurt you?"

"No." Were these normal questions for a bouncer to ask?

"Should you be walking around on it?"

"The doctor said it was fine to start walking on it for short periods of time after a few days."

The big man just grunted. This was very weird. "Got ID?"

She fished around in her sparkly handbag and drew out her ID. He gently grasped hold of her hand, turning it over. "What happened to your hands?"

"I fell over when I twisted my ankle." She'd taken the bandages off, but the grazes were still visible.

"You clumsy?"

"Not usually," she said in a bewildered voice.

Another grunt. Was she supposed to know what that meant? He checked her ID then handed it back to her. "Why're you here?"

"Um, a friend invited me."

"Yeah? Who's that?"

Did she have to tell him to gain entrance?

"Her name is Millie."

His eyebrows rose. "You know Millie?"

"Yes. Do you?"

"Yeah. She made this shirt for me. Find it hard to get shirts the right size."

She could see why.

"It's very nice," she told him, since he seemed to be waiting for her to say something.

"Yep. You go on in. Have a nice night. If anyone bothers you, come get me. I'll knock their heads together."

"Okay, thank you." Was that the appropriate response? He seemed happy with it.

She stepped into the room. Oh, crap. She'd expected just a few people drinking in groups and at the bar. She'd thought she would immediately see Millie. Or Razor. Or someone she knew.

Maybe there was a good reason the bouncer had told her to let him know if anyone bothered her. Because as soon as she moved into the room, people turned to stare at her. A grizzled-looking man wearing baggy jeans and a leather jacket with the arms cut off walked past with a grunt. "You lost, girlie?"

"Um, no," she replied as he stared at her tits with fascination.

"Who you lookin' for, cause I'm sure I can make you a better offer."

Ew.

"I know you definitely can't," she replied.

He narrowed his gaze, reaching for her. She dodged around him and pushed through two big, smelly guys. Yuck. She couldn't believe this was where Millie wanted to hang out.

Both men stopped their conversation to stare down at her. "Excuse me."

A hand slapped down on her ass. "No worries, sweetie."

Let it go. Walk past. Don't say anything.

But, damn it, she was sick of people thinking they got to do what they liked to her. This asshole had just snapped the last of her control.

She whirled, hands on her hips as she glared up at the big, bearded guy. "Did you just slap my ass?"

"Did you like it?"

"No, asshole, I didn't like it."

"You know, you should watch the way you talk to me, little girl. That'll get you into trouble."

"You shouldn't go around touching women without their permission. That will get you into trouble."

"Fuck, girly, you don't want to talk to Curly like that." It was the guy with the baggy jeans. Suddenly, she was surrounded on three sides by rough, mean-looking bikers.

Just awesome. How did this keep happening to her? And where the heck was Millie?

"Listen to me, you cu—"

"You don't want to finish that sentence, Curly," a deep voice growled from behind her.

Instantly, she relaxed. She knew that voice.

Curly took a step back, hands coming up. "No harm meant, Razor. We're just having a chat."

"Tabby, come here."

Turning, she looked up at Razor and winced at the cold, calm look on his face. Oh, he was mad.

"You know her?" Curly asked, attempting to sound casual.

"Didn't realize. We were just talking, right, Tabby?"

"Don't talk to her. And you stay where you are, Rat. I'm not finished with you."

Tabby turned to see the wiry older guy was trying to move away. His name was Rat? Seemed fitting.

"Tabby. What'd I just tell you to do?"

Um. Oh, right, go to him. She wasn't so sure that was a good idea.

"Tabby. Here. Now."

Or maybe she should go to him. Yep, keeping him happy was probably the best thing to do. She walked slowly over and he gently drew her behind him. "Stay there."

So. Bossy.

But she'd wait to tell him her opinion.

"Problem?"

A big, bald-headed man walked up. Spike. Her mind flashed back to that night.

Luther hitting her. Pain. Fear.

Sneaking up on him with that poker. Smack!

Fear and elation filling her as he slid to the floor. She'd wanted to kill him. Had been sad when she hadn't. What sort of person did that make her?

Spike storming into the house. The look of relief on his face as he held Millie.

What would it be like to have someone care for her like that?

"Tabby? Baby, you okay?"

She suddenly realized that everyone was staring at her. She nodded at Razor, who had a fierce frown on his face. "Did they touch you?"

"Um, Curly slapped my ass."

Something scary filled his face. He turned back to the two men.

"Hey, man, I didn't know!" Curly cried.

"Spike, watch her. But don't touch her. Gonna go have a chat with these two assholes."

She opened her mouth to protest. She didn't want to leave Razor. She needed to stay with him. And she didn't want him dealing with these assholes. There were two of them and only one of him. What was he going to do? He wouldn't just talk to them, right?

But then Spike was in front of her, blocking her way.

"Um, I really need to speak to Razor."

Spike just shook his head and crossed his arms over his chest. Damn, the man was like a brick wall. She stepped to one side, wincing as she put too much weight on her sore ankle. Ouch. He followed her movement, still blocking her. She moved to the other side, keeping her weight off her injured foot, but he slid in front of her again.

"For such a big man, you sure are light on your feet," she muttered. Her cheeks were growing red as she realized they'd gained an audience. "Please move."

He shook his head.

"You should have been a ballerina."

"Oh my gosh, he'd be so cute as a ballerina."

Tabby turned to find Millie had walked up behind her. "I can see it right now. I wonder if they make tutus that big, though."

Spike scowled fiercely at the other woman and Tabby put herself squarely in front of Millie, ready to defend her. Thankfully, she'd said those words really quietly. Which was a shock since Millie didn't seem to have a quiet button. But Tabby didn't think anyone else had heard over the rest of the noise in the room.

Spike's eyebrows rose at her move.

"Um, Tabby. What are you doing?" Millie asked.

"Just stay behind me," Tabby told her. "I know how to take a punch."

Was it her imagination, or did the whole bar go quiet? She

knew they hadn't. But it felt that way.

"What? Tabby, Spike isn't going to hit me." Millie moved up beside her. Tabby attempted to get in front of her again, but the other woman wasn't having it. Spike's scowl had turned fierce and she wasn't sure if it was because she was keeping Millie from him or because she thought he might hit the other woman.

"Of course. I know that."

She hadn't, though. She'd acted on instinct. That she was now kind of regretting, given the looks both of them were giving her.

"Millie, take Tabby to the others," Spike commanded.

Millie nodded, reaching out to take Tabby's hand.

"But what about Razor?"

"Razor can take care of himself," Millie reassured her.

"Where did he go with those men?"

"Took them outside for a chat," Spike told her, walking behind them. He was careful not to get too close.

She looked at him over her shoulder. "Both of them? What if they try to hurt him?"

Spike gave her a look of disbelief. "Razor can take them."

Shaking her head, she tugged on Millie's hand. "I need to go help him. He could get hurt."

And it would be her fault. All because she'd decided to come here. This had been a stupid mistake. But she wouldn't let Razor get hurt because of her.

"I have to—"

"He's fine," Spike told her. "But I'll go if you stay."

"You'll go make sure he's okay?"

Spike nodded.

"All right, but hurry."

Spike just eyed her then turned to Millie. "Stay with Jewel and Jason."

"You got it!" Millie said cheerfully, tugging her over to a corner table where she could see some other people sitting. She didn't recognize any of them. Where were the guys from work? Were any of them here? Then she spotted Sav over by the bar talking to a dark-haired man. Sav noticed her at the same time and his eyes widened. He looked over across the room as though searching for someone.

Then he turned his gaze back to her and crooked a finger.

She shook her head. She wasn't going over there. If Sav found out what was going on then he might feel the need to get involved, and he couldn't afford to get into trouble because he was on parole.

Millie tugged at her hand. "Why is Sav trying to get you to come over to him?"

"No idea, let's go sit with your friends."

"Uh-oh, he doesn't look happy."

"Does he ever?" she asked desperately.

"True. He's not the most cheerful person. Still, maybe we should go over there."

"Nope."

"Are you scared of him? He won't hurt you. And Duke's right there. He's Sunny's fiancée. Remember, I told you about her."

"I'm not scared of Sav. I just don't think it's a good idea for him to know what Razor is doing."

"Why not?"

"Because he might decide to get involved and he can't."

"Oh. I wish I understood any of that. But okay."

Tabby turned away and headed back in the direction they were going. This time, she was pulling Millie along.

"Uh-oh."

"Uh-oh? Nope. No uh-ohs," she said desperately. She wished she could move faster, but she was still limping, and being on her ankle for so long wasn't doing it any favors. Especially with the way she'd played dodge'ems with Spike.

"He's headed this way."

Tabby quickly slid into a seat next to a gorgeous, blonde-haired woman who was impeccably dressed. Seriously, Tabby needed some pointers because she looked like a model. Next to her was another blonde-haired woman who wore a T-shirt with a sequined unicorn on the front.

Next to her was a stunning woman with darker hair. She wore a tight, red top and an amazing necklace that Tabby instantly wanted to touch. The woman's gaze narrowed in on Tabby, studying her.

There were two men leaning against the wall behind them, chatting. One of them was covered in tattoos and had his hair longer on top and shorter at the sides. The other guy was bigger and looked younger. He had his long hair pulled back

Nerves flooded her. What was she doing?

"Hi, I'm Tabby."

"Hi, Tabby, I'm Sunny." The girl with the sequined top waved at her. "This is Betsy." The gorgeous woman on her left gave her a quiet hi. "And Jewel." The dark-haired woman nodded, then her gaze moved up to the man that Tabby could feel looming up behind her.

Millie took a seat next to Jewel and Duke moved to stand behind Sunny, putting his hand on her shoulder.

"Tabby, didn't you see me?" Sav asked.

"So, what are you all drinking?" she asked everyone. The two men that had been talking moved closer to the table. The bigger guy stood behind Jewel. While the tattooed man moved to Betsy. Right, now she thought she had a good idea of who was who with what Millie had told her.

"Um, Tabby, Sav is talking to you." Sunny leaned forward with a small smile.

"I know."

"Oh. Aren't you going to talk to him?"

"Nope."

Sunny's eyes widened and her gaze moved from Tabby up to Sav. Tabby wasn't going to turn around and see what he looked like after she declared that.

"Why not?" Millie asked. "Was he mean to you?" She glared up at Sav as she said that.

"Oh no, Sav is very nice."

"He is?" Duke asked, a funny look on his face. "Nice, huh?"

She thought she might have heard a grunt from behind her, but she wasn't checking to look. Where were Spike and Razor?

"Yep," she replied, with a fake-cheerfulness. She thought she'd done a crap job by the way everyone was looking at her.

"Sooo, what were you all talking about?" she asked desperately. "Please, go ahead."

"Wow, you're really crap at small talk, huh?" Millie asked.

"Millie!" Sunny said. "Maybe she's nervous."

"Oh, she's nervous all right," Jewel drawled. "But I think it has more to do with the big guy looming over her."

"Is Sav making you nervous?" Sunny asked. "Sav, maybe you should back up a bit."

"No," Sav bit out. "Tabby, where is Razor?"

"I don't know. Shouldn't you know? I just arrived. How would I know?"

They all stared at her.

"What's going on?" Jewel asked. "Is Razor in trouble?"

"Nope. No trouble."

"I'm going to find him," Sav declared.

"No!" Tabby popped up out of her seat and clasped Sav around the waist. He froze. "You're not going anywhere!"

~

"Do you understand me?" Razor snarled in Curly's face as he pinned him to the wall.

"Yeah, yeah, I won't ever look at your missus again."

Razor didn't correct him. It served his purposes for Curly and Rat to think that Tabby was his. It would give her some protection.

From them. But not from their other enemy. He had to remember why he was supposed to be keeping a distance.

Damn, it was hard, though. The other night when he'd kissed her, he'd wanted to keep going. So he'd quickly drawn away.

And look what happens when you do that. She goes and gets herself into trouble.

Maybe he didn't need to worry about Mr. X hurting her when she seemed intent on putting herself into dangerous situations.

Perhaps Reyes was right. Maybe he could have her and keep her safe. Perhaps staying away from her wasn't the best idea. But was she ready for what he wanted?

She did kiss you.

And that had shocked the fuck out of him. But what did he really know about what she wanted? About whether she wanted a relationship? Especially one with someone like him.

He didn't want to take advantage of her. Didn't want to be like every other man in her life.

He dropped Curly. The other man grabbed Rat and they scurried away. Rat held his arm across his stomach. Razor had reinforced his orders with a bit of violence. But he'd held onto his control.

"Thought they'd leave here bleeding."

Razor turned to find Spike standing there.

Rat and Curly were idiots, they were part of a group who had supported the old leader, Smiley, and had stayed on.

"I made my point," Razor said, clenching and unclenching his fist. In his younger days, he'd have taken it further than a few nasty threats. But he was older and wiser.

Kind of.

"What are you doing out here? You're meant to be watching

Tabby."

Spike raised his hands. "She sent me out here. She's worried about you."

Razor grunted. "I can take care of myself. She's the one that needs watching. What the hell was she doing, coming here alone?"

"Millie invited her."

"What? Why didn't you tell me? She shouldn't be walking in on her own. Hell, the walk from her car to the front door is fucking dangerous at night in this neighborhood."

"I know, man. Said she wasn't coming. Didn't know."

Razor let out a deep breath, reminding himself that this wasn't Spike's fault.

It was his.

He should have been keeping a closer eye on her.

"Damn it. She has no sense of self-preservation. What was she thinking?"

Spike just shrugged and headed back inside. Razor followed him. Part of him thought he'd be better off taking a few minutes to calm down. But a bigger part of him needed to see her. To ensure that she was all right.

"What's she doing?" Spike asked.

And he looked up. His mouth dropping open as he took in Tabby. And Sav.

Tabby had her arms around the other man, holding on tight. Sav was staring down at her in shock.

What. The. Fuck.

Two things stopped Razor from attacking the other man. One, Tabby was in the way. And two, was the way Sav had his hands up. He looked shocked.

It was clear he didn't want to touch her.

Yeah, that saved him. Because Razor had had enough. No one was touching his girl. Getting near his girl.

Done. He was done.

14

"Let her go."

The demand came from behind her. Razor's voice flooded Tabby with relief. He was all right.

"Not touching her," Sav replied. "Don't know what she's doing, but it has nothing to do with me!"

Why did Sav sound worried? Nothing much ever seemed to concern him.

"Tabby, let Sav go."

Huh? Oh shit! She hastily let go of Sav then stumbled backward, her bad ankle giving out beneath her. Razor grabbed her and she suddenly found herself in the air and over his shoulder.

Um, what the hell!

"Razor, put me down!"

"If you say one thing about my age, I'm going to spank your ass right now," he growled.

"Razor!" Millie scolded. But Tabby thought there was something funny about her voice. Was she trying not to laugh?

"Tabby and I are going for a chat," Razor told them. "All of you, stay out of it."

Then he turned and walked away. Strangely enough, he managed to walk through the room without anyone getting in his way. As he moved out of the main bar, she thought she heard laughter. Someone must have told a funny joke.

She sighed. She could use a funny joke right now.

"Razor, put me down," she demanded. He strode along a passage, then stopped and knocked.

"Come in," a voice she recognized called out. "Razor. Well, hello, Tabby."

"Hi, Reyes," she said quietly from where she still hung down Razor's back. She tried to move. "Will you please let me down?" Reyes was likely getting a lovely view of her ass.

"No. Stay still," Razor told her. "Reyes, I need your office for ten minutes."

"Only ten minutes?" Reyes asked with amusement. "You're losing your touch."

"I didn't bring her in here for that," Razor said.

For what?

"Ah, good to know. Take as long as you want. I'm leaving. Emme isn't pleased that I wouldn't bring her tonight. She's got some of Markovich's guards at home with her. She's getting antsy, always being under guard."

"Poor girl," Razor said.

Um, hello! She was still here. She wiggled around. If he was going to just stand there having a chat with his friend, then she was out of here.

Smack!

Her eyes widened as Razor's hand landed on her ass. It wasn't hard. It didn't hurt. But it did shock her. He never usually touched her without warning her and tonight, he'd not only swung her over his shoulder, but he'd smacked her ass?

It was like something had snapped with him.

"Give you two some privacy." Reyes crouched down to look at her. "Be good to him, Tabby."

What? What did that mean?

"I'm just an employee."

Reyes grinned. "Not for much longer."

What did that mean? Oh no, was she going to lose her job? But she was coming to love it. Sure, in the beginning, it had been tough trying to figure it all out. However, she enjoyed getting out of her apartment each day. And most of the guys were good to work with. Well, except for Weasel Dick.

The door clicked shut and Razor eased her gently over his shoulder, putting her down on the desk.

"You should be more careful of your back," she scolded him as he placed his hands on either side of her on the desk.

"No."

"No? No, what?"

"No."

"Razor, are you all right?" There was a tic by his right eye.

"No."

"I'm sorry. Is there anything I can do to help?"

"Yes."

She straightened. She would be glad to help him after everything he'd done for her.

"What is it?"

"Never touch Sav again."

Her mouth dropped open. "What?"

"Don't touch Sav again. Don't touch any man again. Understand me?"

OKAY, fuck.

He needed to rein it in. He'd done such a good goddamn job of keeping his insane possessiveness towards her under control that it was no wonder she was looking at him like he was cuckoo.

He'd look at himself like that too.

Only, now that his possessive side was raging, he was going to have trouble pulling it back in.

Shit. She can't handle this side of you. Not yet.

Control. Calm.

"You don't want me to touch another man?"

"Yep. Look, I know—"

"But I was just trying to stop him from going after you."

"What?"

"You said that Sav is on parole and can't get into any trouble. So I was just trying to stop him from going after you. I figured you weren't just having a chat with those guys, right? How are your knuckles? Do they need ice?"

The way she talked so casually about his 'chat' with Curly and Rat both made him sad and happy. Sad, because it showed how used to violence she was. Happy, because it meant that when she heard his full background, she was more likely to understand it.

"My knuckles are fine. I really did just chat with them. Mostly. You were trying to keep Sav out of trouble?"

"Yes."

The knot in his stomach eased.

"Why do you care if I touch him? I mean, I know he didn't want me to touch him. That was easy to tell from the way he held himself. But I was doing it to help him."

Lord, she was sweet. And she'd come so far in a few short weeks that it shocked him. From the girl who would barely look up from her feet, who would jump at a loud noise and didn't talk to anyone if she didn't have to, to someone who would literally attach themselves to a friend to stop them doing something foolish.

"I did something wrong?"

"Fuck, baby. No, you didn't do anything wrong. I'm just acting crazy, all right?"

"Because of your chat with Curly and Rat? They didn't touch me. Well, other than Curly slapping my ass."

"Bastard's lucky I let him keep that hand," he snarled.

Her eyes widened.

He was scaring her. That was the last thing he needed to do. He cleared his throat. "That was a joke."

She gave him a suspicious look. He tried to appear innocent. It wasn't easy. Especially not when he was thinking about chasing Curly down and giving him more of a lesson in not touching what belonged to him.

If the bastard tried anything again, he was a dead man.

"That was really good of you, Tabby."

She blushed. "It was?"

"Yeah, baby. But next time, just let him go, understand? It's not your job to keep him out of trouble. Sav's a big guy. He can look after himself."

"But you tried to keep him safe the other day from that detective."

"Well, yeah, but I'm his employer and friend."

"Oh." Her shoulders slumped and he wondered what he'd said that saddened her.

"What is it?" Reaching out, he tilted up her chin. He realized then that he'd been touching her a lot without asking her first.

He'd slapped her ass. He was lucky that he hadn't terrified her.

Be more careful.

"I thought that maybe he and I were friends. But that's silly. We're work colleagues."

"Sav likes you." He felt terrible now for making her think differently.

"No, it's okay. You don't have to say that to make me feel better." She tried to give him a tremulous smile.

Oh, hell, she was killing him here.

"Stop it," he told her.

"Stop what?"

"Trying to hide when something hurts you. You shouldn't hide shit from me."

"I shouldn't?" Her eyes widened in surprise.

"No. In fact, you should tell me everything. Every little hurt, pain, fear. Give them to me and I'll make them go away."

"What? Why? How?"

"You forgot when and where," he said with amusement.

"Razor Samuels! Wait! How do I not know your real name? Oh shoot, it's not Razor, is it?"

He burst into laughter. Funny, that's the last thing he'd felt like doing when he'd carried her through the door of his office, but Tabby had a way of turning things on their head.

"What's so funny! Are you laughing at me?" A hint of hurt entered her gaze and he immediately sobered. He couldn't have that. It had taken him a while to realize that she had very tender feelings hidden beneath that hard shell.

"I'm not laughing at you." He cupped the side of her face. "My real name is Jeremiah."

"Jeremiah? That's a lovely name."

His smile grew. "My mother thought so."

Her face softened. He ran his thumb over her jawline.

"Razor?" she whispered.

"Yeah, baby?" Leaning in, he nuzzled his nose against hers.

"What are you doing?"

"Well, I was about to kiss you."

"You were?"

"Uh-huh."

"Why?"

He stared at her for a moment before grinning. "Because I want to."

Then he pressed his mouth to hers.

WHAT THE HECK was going on?

Razor was kissing her. Kissing her! And it was amazing. Even better than their last kiss. This time, he put his hand around the nape of her neck as he tilted her slightly back. He tugged at her lower lip with his teeth gently. She opened her mouth on a gasp and he slid his tongue inside.

And boy, did that man know how to use his tongue. He kissed her until her head spun. Her entire body lit up. And she clung to his T-shirt, her hands wrapped up in the material.

When he drew back, his face was inches from hers as he breathed heavily.

"W-what was that?" she asked.

"A kiss."

Well, duh, she knew that.

"Are you going to pull away and go all weird again?" she asked suspiciously.

His eyes widened. "No."

"You sure?"

"Yes."

"I don't know that I believe you."

He sighed. "I promise I'm not going to go all weird on you again."

"Why should I believe you?" she demanded.

"Because I give you my word. I know I've acted weird these past few days since you kissed me."

"Didn't you like it?" she asked.

"What? No, baby. That's not why I pulled away. I loved it."

"Then why did you draw away? Why did you kiss me? And why don't you want me touching anyone? And why did you pick me up and carry me in here and slap my ass? I don't understand what's going on."

"I like you, Tabby."

"Well, that's nice, I like you too, Jeremiah."

"Razor," he told her firmly.

"What?"

"Nobody calls me Jeremiah but my mother. Most of the guys here don't even know my real name. I'd like to keep it that way."

"There's nothing wrong with the name Jeremiah."

"I know," he said softly. "But it doesn't inspire quite the same response that Razor does."

That made sense. "Oh. Right. Okay."

"When I said I liked you, it wasn't as a friend. I'm attracted to you. When you kissed me the other day, I wanted to keep going, but I knew I shouldn't."

"You did? Wait, why shouldn't you? If it's because you're my boss, that's just silly. You're not taking advantage of me, Razor. You've never tried to use me for something. Or manipulate me. Or put pressure on me to do something you wanted me to do. Well, okay, sometimes you're kind of bossy. But that's always when you're worried about me or want me to be safe. You put me first. And I've never had that. But it's a bit frustrating that you're so hands-off and careful when it comes to anything else."

"Oh, it is, is it?"

"You don't have to be so careful of me. I won't break."

"I don't want you to think I'm like him."

How could he think that? "Never. I'd never think that."

"I don't have a pretty past, Tabby. There are things I did that I'm ashamed of. Decisions I made that hurt other people."

"Have you ever hit a woman?" she asked.

"No. Never. I've never harmed a woman or a child." He cleared his throat. "You know that I'm a Dom. I belong to a BDSM club, although I haven't been in a couple of months."

"And you play with women? Scene with them?"

"What do you know about scenes?" he asked.

"I've read some books," she admitted, feeling her cheeks heat.

"That so?" he murmured. "And how did those books make you feel? Were you interested in anything that happened in them?"

"I couldn't go to a club and do something with a stranger. I wouldn't trust them enough."

"You won't be going to a club and interacting with a stranger. I forbid it." He scowled.

She huffed out a breath. "You realize you don't have the right to forbid me to do anything."

"I will soon," he replied ominously.

Oh, the arrogance of this man.

It was enough to send a shiver of delight through her. She didn't know why. It just did something to her. His confidence. His surety in who he was and what he could give her.

But she couldn't let him get too carried away. Damn man would think he was always in charge.

"I don't think so, buddy." She pointed a finger into his chest. "You won't ever have the power to forbid me to do something."

To her surprise, he just grinned.

"Why does that make you smile?"

"You please me, Tabitha."

"I do? Why?"

"Because you're so fucking brave. Your courage never ceases to amaze me. Look at you. Look at what you've accomplished."

"I haven't accomplished that much," she whispered, shocked at his words.

"No? I know how hard it was for you to look for a job. To start from scratch with no experience. To interact with people you don't know on a daily basis, some of them rough and difficult to deal with. You're constantly thrown into scary situations, but you come out swinging. And look at you now, telling me what's what. I mean, you're wrong. But you also make me proud."

Well, sheesh. Was he trying to make her blush?

Mission. Accomplished.

She placed her hands on her hot cheeks, trying to cool them down.

But he gently tugged her hands away. "Don't hide or be embarrassed. You're amazing, Tabby-baby. Don't ever forget that."

And then he kissed her again. A softer kiss this time. Sweet and far too short. She let out a murmur of protest as he drew away.

"Much as I want to keep going, we've got to get some stuff sorted."

She sighed, giving him a disgruntled look. "I think we should just keep kissing."

"Yeah?"

"Yeah, cause then you can't say stupid stuff like you forbid me to do something."

He gave her a stern look. "But then you'd just keep getting into trouble."

She had a feeling that would happen whether he forbade her to do something or not.

"Tabby, it's important that you understand that nothing happens without your consent. I know I can be bossy. I like to be in charge. But I don't ever want to be a controlling asshole. If I ever cross that line, you need to tell me."

"Is this about you being a Dominant?"

"Partly," he told her. "There are things I'd want in a relationship. Things I also think you need."

"Do you think I'm a sub?"

"I think so."

Her cheeks grew warm. "I also read some books that Millie suggested to me. They were about Daddy Doms and Littles."

Razor gave her a surprised look. "Millie talked to you about that?"

"Yeah. Was that wrong? Should she not have?"

"If Millie wanted to tell you that, then she must trust you," he reassured her.

"I'd never heard of it, but the way she talked about it, about Spike being her Daddy, well, I ... maybe it's silly to want that."

"It's not silly at all. Tabby, I'm a Daddy Dom as well."

Her mouth dropped open. "You are?"

"I am. What did she say that appealed to you? Did you read anything you liked?"

"Just how, well, she said she liked being in Little headspace because it felt like she could let go of everything else for a while. She said it made her feel so loved and safe, like she was wrapped in a giant blanket and surrounded by an army of stuffies keeping her safe."

"Army of stuffies, huh?"

"I think all the stuffies were dinosaurs, so I'm not sure why she felt so safe."

"I think if dinosaurs still roamed the earth that Millie would be their queen," Razor said seriously. Then he winked at her, making her giggle.

"And I guess the fact that Spike cares so much about her. Looks after her. Helps her with things she needs. That could be nice."

"I think you could use some boundaries and rules."

"I grew up with lots of rules. It wasn't fun."

"No, but those rules were all about other people's needs, not about your own. Any rules I gave you would be strictly to keep you safe or happy or healthy. I want to see you smile, to hear your laughter, for you to know that someone has your back. Always."

"And I'd have yours."

He grinned. "Yep, baby. You'd have mine. You'd be my baby girl and my sexy mama." He wriggled his eyebrows.

She blushed. "Not so sure about the sexy part."

"I am."

"My only experience with sex is with Luther and that was . . . awful."

"Then we'll have to replace the bad memories with good ones. But that's not something you have to worry about right now.

"Jared goes to a BDSM club. I never really paid much attention. But I did overhear him talking to his assistant once. And now, I think maybe he was also his sub."

"Your cousin is gay?"

"Maybe. Or perhaps he's bi. I'm not sure. But he called him his good little boy. I also think he spanked him at least once. When Jared was home for dinner, North would normally eat with us. And he'd sometimes be unable to sit still. And they'd share this look." She sighed. "I didn't pay a lot of attention. I kept to myself a lot. I didn't want anyone to really notice me."

"Did you never talk to someone about what happened?"

"Someone? Like a therapist? No. We don't talk to strangers in my family. Heck, I probably shouldn't even be telling you all this."

He cupped her face between his warm hands. Her whole body sighed. It still amazed her how much his touch could ground her, center her. How much she craved it.

"You can tell me anything. And if you don't want me to tell anyone, then this is as far as it goes. All right?"

"All right," she whispered.

"I'm here for you, Tabby-baby. You come first."

Tears entered her eyes and his eyes widened. He moved his hands down to her shoulders. "Don't cry."

"You can't just command someone not to cry."

"Why not?" he asked, looking perfectly serious.

"Because that's just silly. Besides, I'm not crying. I never cry. I'm fine. It's allergies." She crossed her fingers.

Her vision blurred, but she noticed him frowning down at her. "Little one, did you just lie to me?"

"It's not a lie."

He handed her a tissue from the box on the desk. "I don't want you to tell me something just to make me feel better."

"So no white lies?"

"No white lies either."

"What about if the person telling the white lie also crosses their fingers? Doesn't that make it okay?"

"It does not," he said firmly. "No matter how cute that is."

Darn it.

"Tabby, do you think you'd want to explore being my baby girl? That you could trust me to help you? Guide you?"

"Yes, I want to do that. I want to try."

"And you're not just saying that because it's what I want?" he asked suspiciously.

"I'm really not. I've been thinking about it ever since Millie told me she's a Little. And I couldn't try with anyone but you. Out of everyone I know, you're the person I trust the most."

"That means so much, baby."

She licked her lips nervously. "I don't remember everything from that first night we met, but I do remember how wonderful you were. Kind and patient. And sexy." She grinned. "I've gotten to know you over these past few weeks and I think you're amazing."

"I'm not that amazing, Tabby-baby. Like I told you, there are things I've done that I'm not proud of. Things I should tell you. I should give you the option of walking away."

"I can't walk away."

He rubbed his nose against hers. "Thank God, because I wasn't going to let you."

She had to smile at that. He was insane.

Razor drew back, staring down at her. "Can't let you go. Even if I should. Even though it would be safer for you."

She frowned. "Safer?"

"I tried to distance myself. Told myself it was better for you. And it likely is. Only thing is, I can't stay away. I need you."

"I need you too. Razor, the things I feel for you . . . they're like nothing I've felt before. When you drew away from me after I kissed you, I was devastated."

He grimaced. "I was trying to protect you. Being with me could put you in danger."

"In danger? You're not talking about that Mr. X, are you?"

His eyes widened. "Just how much did Millie tell you?"

"Don't be mad at her," she said hastily. "It's my fault."

He raised an eyebrow. "How is it your fault?"

"Um." That wasn't something she had a quick answer for.

He cupped the side of her face. "It's not your fault. You don't need to protect her from me. I'd never hurt her."

"I know you wouldn't. I'm sorry."

"It's all right. I know it's going to take a while for you to feel safe. There's no time limit. So Millie told you about Mr. X's threat?"

"Yes, and how the women are all guarded now in case he comes after them."

"Therefore, me being with you puts you in danger."

"Razor, that's nothing new to me. I've always been in danger. Being in my family doesn't generally come with a long life-span."

He scowled. "It will for you."

She gave him a soft smile. "All I'm saying is, being in danger isn't something that is unusual to me. It doesn't scare me. Being with you is worth the risk."

"I won't have you in danger. I can't." He paced back and forth. "I need to make sure you're safe."

"My apartment is secure. And when I'm not there, I'm usually at work. The only other places I go are for jogs, which I can't do yet with my foot, or to the supermarket, and I can get my groceries delivered."

"No jogging alone."

"Okay." Maybe she'd have to buy a treadmill.

"You still have to go back and forth to work. It's risky."

"I always park in the garage, and remember, my car has bullet-proof glass. I'm as safe as I can be."

"I want to have Ink look at your security system."

She bit her lip. "Can he do it without Jared noticing? I don't think it would be a good idea to tell him about you just yet."

"I'll talk to Ink. In the meantime, I want you to stay with me again." He was now standing, facing her. He looked like he was ready for a battle.

"All right."

He blinked. "Yeah? Just like that?"

"Just like that."

His shoulders dropped and relaxed. "Thank God."

"If it makes you feel better having me close and having Ink check my system, then that's what we'll do."

"I thought you'd argue."

"Over you keeping me safe? No."

"Thank you, baby." He moved forward and placed his hands on the desk on either side of her. Gently, he gave her quick kisses. "Thank you for letting me protect you."

Her insides melted. Surviving Mr. X didn't seem hard. Surviving staying with Razor again without her vibrator? Yeah, much harder.

But then, maybe she didn't need her vibrator anymore. As nervous as she was about sleeping with him, she was also excited.

"I've never had someone put me first. Luther was forced to marry me, and we know how that went. My mother loved me, but when we lived with my father, she was always taking care of him. And after we went to live with my uncle, she kind of zoned out.

She'd sleep most of the time and she took a lot of drugs. That's how she died. She overdosed."

"Fuck."

"You should have always been put before anyone else. You have worth, Tabby-baby."

"I'm coming to realize that."

"It kills me that you didn't already know that. Just like it's nearly torn me apart every time you've put yourself into a dangerous situation. I want that to stop, understand? You get hurt and I'm going to be pissed. I've worked long and hard to get my temper under control."

"You don't have a temper."

"Used to, when I was younger. And it cost me everything. But you get hurt and I just might lose it. So you need to be more careful with your own safety, understand?"

"I understand," she whispered. "I'll try. I guess I have something to live for now, huh?"

"You always did. Now you just have more incentive. Because put yourself in danger, and then you'll be in trouble."

"What sort of trouble?"

"How do you feel about me spanking you?"

15

U m, did he really expect her to answer that?

By the look on his face, he did.

"Like you just did to me before?"

He looked confused. "That was just a slap on the butt to get you to pay attention. It didn't hurt, did it?"

She shook her head. "No."

"I'd never harm you. I'd never hit you in anger. Not ever. Not for any reason. And if I ever did, you leave and you go find Reyes or Spike, you tell them what I did and you let them take care of it. Then you stay far, far away from me. Promise me."

"I promise."

"You can't stand the idea of me spanking you, or it scares you, then it's off the table. We don't need to do that. I can find other ways."

"Other ways?"

"To reinforce boundaries. To make you think twice before you break the rules. Did Millie talk to you much about that?"

"Not really."

"Spike cherishes her. He would do anything for her. But he

wants her to be safe and to feel secure. So they have rules and consequences. That's not all that this sort of relationship is about, though. And it's not a one-size fits all. I've been a Daddy Dom for a long time. Spent a lot of time in clubs, helping with Littles. But I've only ever been in a relationship with one Little. My wife."

"Your wife?" she whispered. He was married? But he couldn't be.

"I was married a long time ago. Sandy died in a fire when she was far too young."

"Oh, Razor, I'm so sorry." Her heart broke for him.

"Thank you, baby. I wish I had been a better husband and Daddy to her."

"What do you mean? I'm sure you were wonderful."

"No, Tabby-baby, I wasn't. I was arrogant. Thought I knew it all. I didn't do the proper research. I didn't speak to other Doms in the lifestyle even though I had offers from people I knew. I didn't listen to what Sandy wanted. I really don't deserve you."

"Says who?"

"Me. You deserve someone better. Younger, with fewer stains on their damn soul."

"You're an idiot."

He gave her a shocked look.

"You're an idiot," she repeated. "Fewer stains on your soul. Razor, you're the best person I know."

"Yeah, well, Tabby-girl. No offense but that doesn't mean a lot."

Damn. He had a point.

"Just tell me. Please."

He sighed and started to pull off his T-shirt. She stared at him in shock, wondering what the heck was going on. Then her mouth went dry as she took him in. The man was solid. His biceps had to be as big as her thighs. His shoulders were broad and his skin looked so smooth.

I want to lick it.

Whoa. Where did that come from?

"I didn't realize we were at the stripper part of the evening," she commented.

He stilled then grinned. "Sorry to disappoint you, but I never did learn how to use a pole."

She pouted. "Too bad. I'd have paid at least a dollar to see that."

A huge bark of laughter filled the room and she tingled inside. She'd done that. She'd made him laugh.

"Damn, baby. A whole dollar, huh?"

"Well, I'm not sure how good you'd be. You don't seem very aerodynamic."

He just shook his head. Then he sighed and turned to his side, lifting his arm. He pointed to a spider web tattoo. "Any idea what sort of tattoo this is?"

She had a suspicion. "Gang tattoo?"

"Yeah. Gang tattoo. I told you my past wasn't pretty."

He then showed her the inside of his arm. There were two dates written along the inside of his forearm. "And this?"

"I . . . the dates you were in the gang?"

"Close. The dates I was in prison."

"You were in prison?" she whispered.

He nodded.

"I'm so sorry. Was it scary? Did anyone hurt you? Actually, I'm not sure I want to know that."

He stared at her. She wanted to check out his other tattoos, but the look on his face kept her where she was. He looked confused. Shocked.

"Did I say something wrong?"

"When I tell people I was in a gang and that I spent time in jail, their usual response is to ask what I did wrong or what gang I was in or if I'm still in it. Not to ask me if I was scared or was hurt."

"Oh. Sorry."

"You got nothing to be sorry about, Tabby." He studied her for a long moment. "It doesn't turn you off? Make you scared of me?"

"I'm supposed to be scared of you?"

"I thought you might be."

She grimaced. "I guess that's a normal reaction, huh? There doesn't seem to be much that's normal about me."

"And I'm damn grateful for that."

"You are?"

"The last thing I want is for you to be afraid of me."

"I've lived with monsters, Razor. With true evil. You help people. You give them a chance when many wouldn't. You're more than just a boss, you're their friend and mentor. Whatever you did in the past, it's turned you into the person you are now. And I happen to think the person you are now is amazing."

Heat filled her cheeks as he said nothing. Then he strode over to her and picked her up. She wrapped her legs around his waist as his lips met hers.

Holy. Hell.

Sitting on the sofa, he continued to kiss her. She wrapped her arms around his neck as she straddled his lap. This was the most intimate position she'd ever been in with a man. Luther would never have held her like this.

When he drew back, his face was filled with hunger, with amazement.

"Fuck, baby girl. What did I ever do that was good enough to deserve you?"

She gave him an exasperated look. "Is your memory going? I think I just told you everything you did."

"Was that a dig at my age?"

"What? No!" she said with fake shock. "I would never."

He grinned. "I like this sassy side of you."

"Oh, yeah? That's good since you might be seeing more of it."

"I hope so." He ran a finger along her lower lip. "And you're more than a prize. You're the fucking pot of gold at the end of the rainbow. Only the rainbow has been more like a rollercoaster in and out of hell. But it was all worth it to find you."

She reached up to touch him, then hesitated.

"You can touch me as often as you want to. Don't hesitate. I won't ever push you away."

"Really?"

"Really."

She ran a finger down his forehead and cheek, then over to the shell of his ear, exploring him. "Sometimes it seemed like you were going to touch me, then you'd pull away."

"That had more to do with wanting to respect your boundaries, with worrying that I might scare you than not wanting to touch you. All I've thought about for the past few weeks is how I want to touch you. I want to strip you naked and kiss every inch of you. I want to wrap my hand around yours and never let go. Sometimes, I've wanted to lay you over my knee and spank your ass."

She sucked in a breath.

"That worry you?"

"I'm a bit nervous. But I know you wouldn't harm me."

"The thing with a relationship like this is that you always have the ultimate control."

"I do?"

"Yeah, you choose a safeword. And any time you say it, I stop what I'm doing. Immediately. I know it requires trust. But I will always honor your safeword."

"Even if it's a punishment?"

"Even then."

"What would it be?" she asked.

"How about just red," he suggested. "Yellow to slow down, red to stop. And you can use it for anything. All right? Promise you'll use it. Because I couldn't stand knowing that you were hurting or frightened and didn't say anything."

"I promise."

"I won't betray your trust. Ever."

"I'm not sure how I was lucky enough to find you. You're like no man I've ever met."

"I hope that's a good thing." He winked at her. "After your first spanking, you might not think so. There are other methods of discipline I can use as well, like corner time or writing lines."

She wrinkled her nose. "Those don't sound fun either."

"Kind of the point. Ever heard of edging?"

"No."

"It's where you're brought to the point of orgasm, but you're not allowed to go over. And it can happen over and over until your Dom is sure you're properly repentant. Of course, it's not always used for punishment. It can also be a way to make the pleasure intense when you're allowed to come."

"I don't think I like the sound of that either. I've just learned how to come again after Luther. I don't want to be denied an orgasm."

"What do you mean, you've just learned to come again?"

HER FACE WENT BRIGHT RED.

"I, um, well . . . I never orgasmed when I was with Luther," she blurted out. Then she placed her hands over her cheeks. "I can't believe I just told you that."

"I'm not surprised you didn't orgasm while with that asswipe. Probably couldn't find a clit even if it had a giant arrow over it and a sign saying, touch me."

She giggled at that. But then her gaze ducked down. Nope. He wasn't having that. Reaching out, he tilted up her chin. "Don't hide from me. Tell me."

"It wasn't just with Luther. Actually, we didn't, um, after the first few times he went elsewhere. He claimed I was like a wet fish in bed. I don't know what he expected, considering I had no choice in any of it. I didn't enjoy anything he did."

"He was your abuser, your jailer. There's a big difference between what he did and being with a partner who wants you to feel pleasure. Who wants to show you that you're a fucking queen. Who will fucking worship you."

Her breathing grew rapid and he wanted to take her home and show her exactly what he meant.

Easy. Take it slow.

"After he died, I still didn't feel any urges. At least, not until . . ."

"Not until when?" he asked.

"You," she blurted out.

Christ. He could feel himself puffing up like a rooster. She now resembled a tomato, so he decided not to tease her.

"No edging then. At least for a start. What other punishments could we use? Hm, ever heard of figging?"

"Um, no."

"It's where I'd insert a piece of peeled, raw ginger into your bottom. Then I'd probably put you in the corner or have you bend over something while the ginger burned."

"That's terrible! I'd rather take the spanking."

He grinned. "I'll remember that punishment for when you've been really naughty."

"Sheesh," she muttered.

Reaching up, he ran his thumb under her eyes. "You sleep okay last night?"

"Not really," she admitted. "It felt weird being home on my own."

"I didn't sleep much either. You fed the fish today?"

"Yes," she replied.

"Good, we'll go back to your place tomorrow and get some stuff so you can stay until Ink checks your security."

"All right." She looked slightly stunned.

He raised an eyebrow. "You okay, Tabby-baby?"

"Yeah," she said. "I don't think I've ever been better."

He drew her close and kissed her again. "Baby, you keep saying sweet things like that and I'm going to end up spending all my time kissing you."

"That's okay with me."

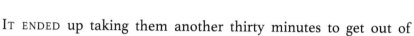

It ended up taking them another thirty minutes to get out of Reaper's.

"I knew we should have snuck out the back," he grumbled, his hand wrapped around hers as he led her through the bar to the front door.

He winced as the guy singing karaoke reached a high note. Somehow, Jewel had managed to sneak in a karaoke machine. He was pretty sure that Jason helped her.

When they'd first returned, Millie had been up there belting out a song. Girl could sing. Afterward, she'd blushed when everyone had clapped. Spike had drawn her onto his lap, whispering something in her ear that had made her grin. Millie had tried to talk them into staying and singing a song.

That wasn't happening.

They stepped outside, and he nodded to Butch, who gave Tabby a curious look.

"You don't like karaoke?" she asked.

"Not particularly," he replied as he led her to his bike.

"You can't sing?"

"I can hold a note. But I don't sing in front of others."

"Would you sing for me?" she asked.

"Maybe, if you were a good girl."

"Oh." She licked her lips, and he groaned.

"Stop trying to tempt me into kissing you, brat."

Her eyes widened. "I wasn't. Although I do like when you kiss me."

The look she gave him was a shy one, and he had to keep reminding himself of her innocence. Sure, she might not be a virgin, but she'd only experienced violence and coercion.

Razor hoped he was doing the right thing. Because walking away from her now was impossible.

She might be in danger from Mr. X. But like Reyes said, he could protect her.

And while his past wasn't pretty, if anyone could handle it, it was Tabby.

He was going to make certain that he never did anything to undermine her trust in him. But he also knew he couldn't let her go now. Something inside him had snapped tonight. She was his.

End of story.

He'd do whatever he had to in order to keep her. He'd kill that fucker, Mr. X, if he had to.

Nothing and nobody threatened his girl.

"You ever ridden a bike before?" he asked her.

She shook her head, bouncing up and down on her feet. "No, I've always wanted to, though. But I brought my car. I should drive that back to your place."

Shit. He hadn't thought of that. He didn't want her leaving her car here.

"I don't like you driving at night," he grumbled.

"Why?"

"You could get tired, fall asleep, and drive off the road. Some drunk could plow into you. You might get blinded by someone's lights and cross the center—"

She reached up and put her hand over his mouth. "I promise, I'll drive really carefully." She dropped her hand.

"Fine, you remember the way home?"

"Yes."

"I'm going to be behind you the entire time. Don't worry about losing me, I'll keep up."

"All right, but . . ."

"Yeah?"

"Will you take me for a ride another day?"

"You bet, baby. It'll be a date."

"I've never been on a date."

"That needs to change. Come on, I'll walk you over."

"It's fine. My car is just there." She pointed at it.

Grasping hold of her hand, he escorted her over to her car. She sighed, but didn't say anything.

He opened her door, then buckled her in. "Wait for me to be ready before you leave. I'll see you at home."

Damn, that sounded good.

16

Home.

That's what he'd called his house and as she stepped through the door after him, that's what it felt like.

Luna came rushing out at them, greeting her excitedly. She bent down and got a full lick in the face.

"Ew. Nice. Thanks, Luna. I missed you too."

"She moped all day today," Razor told her. "I swear she was looking at me like I'd stolen her best friend. You want a drink, baby?"

She yawned, and her tummy rumbled. Embarrassed, she put her hand over it. "Sorry."

"Did you eat dinner?"

"Um, yep."

Razor just grinned. "Come on, I'll make you a snack."

He walked into the kitchen and she followed along.

"I can get it myself. You don't have to wait on me."

"But I like waiting on you. Besides, if I let you make it, then you'll probably give yourself salmonella."

"That only happened once," she muttered.

Of course, she hadn't tried to cook with chicken again.

He grasped her around the waist and lifted her onto the counter. She let out a small gasp, caught by surprise at the sudden movement.

Don't flinch.

"Sorry, should have warned you."

"No." She shook her head. "I'm just still getting used to being touched. But I like it. Don't stop. Please. I don't want to be treated like I'm fragile."

"I know you're not fragile. You're fucking strong."

She wouldn't go that far. But she felt like she was getting stronger every day.

He moved between her legs, parting them wide around his big body. He ran his hands up her thighs. A shiver raced through her as he grew close to her upper thighs. "I won't treat you like you're fragile, but I will treat you like you're special. Because you are. My special baby girl."

Damn. He was killing her. He moved away, and she watched as he fixed them both grilled cheese. He cut hers up into triangles which was super cute. Then he picked a triangle up and blew on it.

That was the craziest, sweetest thing she'd ever seen.

"You okay, Tabby-baby?"

"Ah, yeah."

"There you go, it's cooler now." He held the sandwich out to her and she grabbed hold, taking a bite. Her eyes nearly rolled back in her head at how good it was.

"Will you show me how to make them?"

"Course I will, baby." He turned to the fridge and poured her a glass of chocolate milk. It had become her favorite treat.

"Yummy, thank you," she said in a surprisingly sweet-sounding voice.

"You're welcome. I don't have any straws, I'm afraid."

"Oh, I like straws," she said excitedly. "Especially the ones that go around and around. Swirly-twirly ones."

"I'll see if I can get some."

"You don't have to." For some reason, she felt a bit shy about him buying them for her.

"I know. I want to."

She took three big gulps of the chocolate milk and put the glass down. With a smile, he reached over and wiped his thumb over her top lip. "There, that's better."

"Oh no," she cried.

"What is it?" he asked, turning from the dishwasher where he'd just put the dirty dishes.

"Nothing, it's fine." She crossed her fingers behind her back.

Wait. Oh, drat.

Razor gave her a stern look. "No hiding things from me, remember? That's now a rule."

"It is?"

"Yep. And there will be consequences for breaking it."

A shiver ran up her spine. One of anticipation. "I wasn't lying. Exactly. It's just," she bit her lip, feeling like an idiot, "I don't have Snappy or Scooby."

"Oh, shit. I'm sorry, Tabby-baby. I should have thought of that. Do you need them to sleep?"

"I think I'll be okay. I didn't sleep with Snappy when Luther was around. If Luther had known about him, then he would have destroyed him for fun."

"But you shouldn't have to sleep without him. I'll go get him and Scooby for you."

Her mouth dropped open. "You can't do that!"

"Course I can. It will take me about an hour, though. I don't know about leaving you here alone."

"Razor, you don't need to go into the city to get my toys. I'm fine."

He frowned. "A girl needs her stuffies."

Damn. Damn. He had to stop. "If you keep being so nice, I'm going to start crying."

Leaning in, he nuzzled his nose against hers. Oh, Lord. That was so sweet. She loved when he did that. Her eyes fluttered shut and he kissed each lid. Her nose. Her cheeks. Chin. Then her lips. She sighed happily as he drew back and she opened her eyes.

"I don't want you to cry."

"They're happy tears."

"Happy tears. Never did understand the concept," he grumbled, making her smile.

Poor Razor.

"Didn't your sisters ever cry happy tears?"

He let out a huff of breath. "Oh, they shed all sorts of tears. Sad tears. Happy tears. Angry tears. Ecstatic tears. Then there was all the screaming, the laughing. Our house was never quiet."

It sounded like fun.

"I don't want you to go," she confessed.

He gave her a thoughtful look. "My job is to make sure you have what you need."

He was crazy. He couldn't do that all the time. "I'll be—"

"If you say you'll be fine, I'm going to turn you over my knee," he growled at her.

He was joking. Right?

She wasn't so sure. He definitely looked serious. "That's not very nice."

"I'm not very nice."

She huffed out a breath. "Now who's telling fibs, Daddy?"

Shock filled her as the word came out. Her cheeks heated and she squirmed on the counter. The ridiculous urge to hide came over her. But he grasped her hips.

"No."

No? What did he mean by no?

"Look at me."

Yep, that wasn't happening. She kept her gaze down.

"Damn," he muttered. "You know how good it feels to hear you call me that?"

Her eyes shot to his without her permission. "Yeah?"

"Yeah, Tabby-baby." He looked bewildered. "Why wouldn't it? I want to be your Daddy, Tabby-baby. You know that."

What was she doing? Acting like an idiot.

"I'm sorry. I don't know what happened. As soon as I said that, I had this urge to hide. It's not that I thought you would hurt me. I don't know what happened."

"Guessing you felt vulnerable and unsure. You tend to hide your gaze when you're worried or scared." He grasped hold of her chin. "It can be hard to open up. I get it. But you don't ever need to hide from me. I want all of you."

She shuddered out a breath. "Okay."

"Now, stay there. Promise."

"Promise."

"'Cause if I have to chase you down, there's going to be trouble." He tapped her nose with his finger then left the room.

She wondered what he was doing. He soon returned with something held behind his back. When he drew it out, it was a soft toy replica of the Mystery Machine. She gasped.

"I know it's not Snappy, but maybe it will do for tonight?"

Tabby hugged it against her. It was squishy and soft and delightful.

"I love it, Daddy. It's perfect."

Just like him.

∾

"Where are you going, baby girl?" Razor asked Tabby as she headed towards the spare bedroom.

"Oh, um, I thought we were going to sleep." She looked confused and sleepy. A big yawn overtook her and she gave him an embarrassed look. "Sorry."

He'd break her of that habit of saying sorry for shit she didn't have to apologize for. And for brushing aside her own needs as unimportant.

"You're not sleeping in there," he told her as he tugged her down the passage to his bedroom.

"I'm not? Where am I sleeping?"

"With me." He opened the door and Luna shot in. Then he realized what he'd just done. *Way to bulldoze her, asshole.*

It was his natural inclination to take charge, but he had to remember that she was still feeling her way with him.

He wanted her in his bed every night from now on. Just the thought of her sleeping somewhere else made a growl rumble its way up from his gut.

Hide the crazy, man.

Turning, he found her staring up at him in shock.

"Unless you don't want that," he added. "Nothing happens that you don't want, remember?"

She nodded.

"Just sleeping. Nothing else."

"That's too bad," she muttered.

"What?" He couldn't have heard her say that, right?

Something strange came over her face. "Okay, I want to sleep with you."

"Good." He walked into the bedroom. Luna climbed into her bed, spinning around a few times before she plonked down. Tabby giggled at the dog's antics, making him smile. He led her over to the bathroom and found her a new toothbrush in the cupboard under the sink.

"Brush your teeth, baby girl. I'll get you something to wear."

All of his stuff was going to swim on her, but she couldn't wear her clothes to bed. He grabbed a T-shirt that had shrunk in the wash and walked back into the bathroom to put it on the sink.

"I'll go use the other bathroom, be back soon." He couldn't help but run his hand over her ass. Despite her slim, athletic build, she had an ass that just didn't quit. Christ. He was going to be hard-pressed to keep his hands off it now.

He squeezed one cheek, then gave it a light pat before forcing himself to exit the bathroom. God damn it. Did he have time for a quick, cold shower? He adjusted his straining cock and moved through the room.

"Don't look at me like that," he muttered to Luna as he grabbed some pajama pants and a sleeveless tank top. He usually went to bed naked, but Lois had given him these pajama pants last Christmas, and he thought that Tabby would be more comfortable if he wore them.

When he returned after using the spare bathroom, he found her standing awkwardly by the bed, hugging the stuffie he'd given her. She had her hair tied back in a braid.

She looked over at him shyly. "Wasn't sure what side you slept on."

"Side closest to the door, baby girl." Taking her hand, he led her to the other side of the bed. "Always between you and the door."

She gave him a surprised look, but he bent to draw back the covers. "In you get."

"Thank you."

After she'd climbed in, he tucked her in, then moved around to the other side. He turned off the main light, and she sucked in a breath.

"Need a light on?" he asked.

"Um."

"Honest answer," he said firmly. This had to stop.

"Yes, please. If it won't bother you."

"Doesn't bother me." He remembered from when she'd stayed here that she'd had the bathroom light on. He turned it on and half shut the door before climbing into his side.

As he lay down, he realized how stiff she was. She'd never sleep like this.

"Come here, Tabby-baby."

"What?"

"Come here. Lie next to me."

She moved slowly over. Razor forced himself to be patient. She was so unused to touch, and yet, he thought she was starved for it. Touch that didn't hurt, anyway. She lay on her side with her head resting on his chest. He wrapped his arm around her.

A soft sigh left her.

"Better?" he asked, reaching over to massage her scalp.

"Uh-huh."

"I want you to get used to my touch. Because keeping my hands off you has been fucking hard. And it's only going to get harder. I'm going to lift you up."

He waited for her agreement. Then he lay her on top of him and rubbed his hands over her back.

"Ohhh," she moaned.

"You're all tense, baby girl. You're going to cause yourself an injury."

He moved his hands over her back, feeling for each knot and working on it until it released. Gradually, she relaxed completely. He figured the best idea was to be firm and steady in his approach. Go slow, but also show no hesitation. Because if he was confident in what he was doing, it would make her feel safer.

Decision made, he moved his hands down to her ass. She jolted, but he didn't pull back as he squeezed and rubbed her butt cheeks. Yep, operation 'get Tabby used to his touch' was going well.

"Razor?"

"Hm?"

"Will you tell me about her one day? Your wife?"

He stilled for a moment then sighed.

"Sorry. Forget I asked." She was growing tense again and he slapped her ass.

"Stop that. You can ask me anything." It was his fault she'd grown all worried, though, so he rubbed the cheek that he'd just smacked.

"Even how you ended up in jail?"

"Yeah, baby girl. Even that." He continued to run his hand over her ass as he thought about where to start.

"Remember how I told you about my uncle and his friends getting rid of that asshole who hit Momma?"

"I remember."

"Well, they were in a gang. My momma, she loved her brother, but she didn't like his life choices. She tried to keep us away from anything to do with the gang. But that night, it changed something in me and in their relationship. She started letting him come around more often. He spent time with all of us, but mostly me. Momma didn't know, but he often took me to the gang's headquarters. It felt good. I felt like I was part of a family. I mean, I had a family, but I was the only guy. But as I got older, I became more entrenched in that lifestyle. Momma argued with me about it a lot. But that just made me more determined."

She lightly patted his chest next to her face. "That must have been hard on you both."

"I put her through hell. I was young and rash and stupid. So fucking stupid."

"You were a kid who looked up to his uncle. It's not so stupid to want to feel safe and accepted."

"But I had a family who loved me. I just thought that my

momma was making a big deal out of nothing. I thought I knew it all."

"How old were you?"

"When I first initiated, I was seventeen. I'd left school already, gotten a job working at one of the gang-owned businesses. It was a front for everything else they had going on. Mostly drugs. Figured I was old enough to make my own decisions. It's a wonder Momma put up with me. I moved out of home, and eventually I stopped going around because I knew Momma would just lecture me. I met Sandy, my wife, through one of the guys. We were both twenty. She was his cousin. Took one look at her and I knew she was the one."

"Did she feel the same about you?"

"Hell, no. Pretty sure she hated me as soon as she saw me."

She laughed. "I'm certain that's not true."

"Oh, it is. I came over to where she was hanging with her friends at one of the parties at the club house. Had this swagger going on. Some cheesy line came out of my mouth as I moved up behind her and squeezed her ass. She turned around and slapped me."

Tabby giggled. "Oh no."

"I know. But I was a persistent little ass. I knew I could win her over. Took me a whole year before she agreed to date me. By then, I was fully entrenched in the gang. Sure, I was low in the ranks. But I was loyal and willing to do anything."

He shook his head with a sigh. "I'd always liked control in the bedroom, but Sandy wanted to take it further. She'd heard about this BDSM club opening from a friend and she talked me into going. It was like I'd found something that helped center me, you know? I could be rash and impulsive, but I also liked to be in charge. It wasn't until we'd been going for a while that she met Sheena and Mark. Sheena was a Little. Sandy and Sheena just clicked. Became best friends."

"And that's when she brought it up with you?"

"Yeah. I wasn't sure about it for a start. Sandy wanted me to talk to Mark about it, but I wouldn't. Too arrogant and full of myself. Reckoned I could figure it all out myself. I could tell Sandy was disappointed, but I wouldn't change my stance. We got married. Life had its ups and downs, but on the whole, things were pretty good. And then I got arrested."

"What for?"

"Just remember, I'm not this person anymore."

She leaned up on her arms to stare down at him. "Razor, I know you're not that person anymore. You don't have to tell me if you don't want to."

He just shook his head. "No, I need to tell you. I was the getaway driver for an armed robbery. But I was the only one caught. I refused to roll over on the others though. Fortunately, I wasn't armed and I didn't have the goods. But I still went away for five years. I came out a different man. Sandy found it hard. It was difficult for her when I was away. Things weren't good between us. We fought a lot."

He put his hand over his face and her heart broke for him. "It's all right. You don't have to say anything more."

She didn't want him to hurt.

He let out a deep breath then removed his hand, looking up at her. "No, I need to tell you. We fought one night. Bad. She . . . she'd met someone else. I couldn't believe it. I was enraged. I stormed out after telling her to fuck off."

"Oh, Razor."

"I returned to find she was gone. She'd packed up all her stuff and left. I told myself I didn't care. Drank myself into a stupor. Two days later, the cops turned up to tell me that she'd died. Turns out, she'd gone to stay with her sister in this trailer park. Crappy place. No smoke alarms, no sprinklers. It was a dry summer. They think someone must have flicked a lit cigarette onto the ground. Place went up in flames. Everyone in the trailer died, including Sandy."

"Oh no, Razor."

"That was the wake-up call I needed. She'd still be alive if I hadn't lost it and thrown her out. I don't know why she didn't go to him, this guy. Sometimes, I wonder if she made him up to get at me. I don't know. I got lost in the bottom of several bottles. The guys came around in the beginning, all full of sympathy. But then they started getting annoyed because I couldn't just get over my wife's death. The last straw was when I came home from the bottle store and found a naked woman in my bed. A present from the guys. They thought some sex was all I needed to get over Sandy. The next day, I grabbed my stuff and left."

"I'm so sorry. But she must have loved you. I'm sure she did. It wasn't your fault that she died."

"I might not have lit the fire, but it was my fault she was there."

"What about your family?"

"I haven't seen them since. I didn't say goodbye. Things hadn't been good between us for a while. When I went to jail, my Momma came to visit me. She told me that I needed to sort my life out. I got angry. Said things I didn't mean. Took me over a year or so before I even called them to let them know I was okay. We rarely talk. I've never gone back to see them."

"I'm so sorry." Her heart hurt for him so much. She remembered how bad it had felt, losing her dad then her mom. And her mom had already checked out of life when she'd died. She couldn't imagine how he felt, knowing his family was there but out of reach. "I'm sure they miss you."

"When I left there, I wandered around for a while and eventually found myself here. Like I said before, I've played with Littles in clubs. But I've never been in a relationship again. I'm a much better person, a much better Dom. I promise, I won't make the same mistakes."

"I'm not worried about that. I know you're a good person."

She wished he knew that too. She leaned her face against his chest with a sigh. He ran his hand down over her ass, squeezing it. After a while, he moved his hands lower, rubbing the backs of her thighs.

"Razor," she moaned. "So good."

"Yeah, you like my massages?"

"Uh-huh. You could make good money giving massages," she muttered.

"If the motorbike business ever goes under, I'll keep that in mind."

"But I don't want you touching any other woman," she replied, sounding grouchy. "So only I'll pay you."

He laughed. "I'll be your personal masseuse, huh?"

"Yep. I'd pay you like fifty cents a massage."

"So generous."

"I especially like when you massage my bottom. Much better idea than spanking it."

"Oh, so you think when you're naughty, I should just give you a butt massage?"

"Yeah," she said brightly. "Good suggestion, Daddy. Let's go with that. You're so clever."

"Brat." He gave her ass a sharp tap. "Flattery is not getting you out of punishment."

"Darn it," she muttered, then let out a soft sigh as he rubbed away the sting. "Razor?"

"Yeah?"

"I'm really glad I kept your card all these months."

"Me too, baby girl. Me too."

17

"Thanks man, I appreciate all your help." Razor ended the call with Ink.

Fuck it. Not the news he wanted.

Standing, he moved to the doorway of their offices so he watch Tabby as she worked. Luna was lying at her feet.

Maybe he should just not tell her. Why did she need to go home? She had everything she needed with him. He could watch over her, take care of her. After just three nights at his place, she was starting to get used to him touching her more. He did it every chance he got. Although he tried to be more circumspect at work.

So far, he'd mainly just had glimpses of her Little, but he had something planned for this weekend. Something he hoped she liked.

He hadn't heard anything from Detective Andrews about finding those assholes who'd broken into the garage. But they'd managed to clean everything up and he'd changed the code for the gate.

She turned, saw him standing there, and smiled. Her eyes lit up and his insides settled. Tabby was his. It didn't matter how far apart they were; he wasn't letting her go.

However, he couldn't keep shit from her.

"Hey," she murmured. "Everything okay?"

"Will be once you come over here and kiss me."

A blush lit her cheeks, but she rose eagerly and moved towards him. She stepped around Luna.

When she drew close, he grasped her around the waist and pulled her into him.

Hell.

Every time he touched her, it was getting harder and harder not to go further than he knew she'd be comfortable with. Each night, she slept with him. Usually, he would wrap himself around her back, spooning her. His back to the door, keeping her safe in his embrace.

And every morning, he woke up with his hard cock pressed against her. He was turning fifty at the end of the year, for God's sake. That shit shouldn't happen anymore.

But it was her. Her scent, the way she'd shift against him, the small murmurs she'd make in her sleep. Sometimes, she'd thrash against him and he knew she was having a nightmare. All it took, though, was a few words from him to soothe her back into sleep.

And didn't he feel like a fucking king when he managed to do that?

Moving his hands to her ass, he squeezed it, rubbed it. His dick pressed against her stomach. Christ. He picked her up and she wrapped her legs around him. The kiss deepened and she put her arms around his neck, holding on tight. He turned and stepped to the side so he could press her against the wall.

Hell. Yes.

"Hey, I—oh, fuck. Sorry to interrupt, boss."

Tommy.

Razor drew back as Tabby stiffened in his arms. She might be getting more used to his touch, but she was still shy around others.

When she tried to wriggle down, he shook his head. He didn't want her moving. He didn't want anyone else seeing her right then. That just-kissed look on her face, her slightly swollen lips and messy hair were for his eyes only.

No fucking way did Tommy get to see her right then. It was unfortunate that he had to be the one to walk in on them. Tommy was a smart ass, and Razor had come close to firing him a few times. But he was the cousin of a good friend who'd begged him to take Tommy on. Still, he better not say anything about Tabby, or he'd be out on his ass.

And he definitely wasn't getting a look at his Tabby while she was like this. Plus, Razor needed a minute to chill.

"What do you want?" Razor snapped.

"Just letting you know that the Smithson job is close to finished. You said you wanted to come check it over. Of course, if you're too busy . . ." There was a sly note to Tommy's voice he didn't appreciate.

"Be out in a minute."

"I need to talk to Tabby."

"No, you don't. Go away."

He heard the door slam. Tabby's gaze had dropped. Shit. He probably shouldn't have done this at work. Last thing he wanted was for her to feel like a play thing.

Stepping away from the wall, he walked into his office, slamming the door shut with his hip. Then he moved to his chair and sat with her on his lap, straddling him.

She was stiff and unyielding.

God damn it. If Tommy had undone all his good work, he was going to punch the asshole. Wasn't like he didn't deserve it.

"Look at me."

Her gaze didn't rise.

"Tabby. Look. At. Me."

To his shock, a huff of displeasure left her mouth and she folded her arms over her chest as she stared at him. "You can't always get your way."

He raised an eyebrow. "Why can't I?"

"Because . . . maybe I don't want to look at you."

"Why? You mad at me for kissing you at work?"

"It's not very professional."

"So? I'm the boss. I get to do what I like."

"Yes, but what if the guys think I'm getting special favors or something . . . ?"

"I don't care what the fuck they think." He grasped hold of her chin to keep her face up. "All I care about is what you think. Did I embarrass you? Make you feel like I was using you? Pressuring you?"

"What? No!" She gave him a shocked look and the tension in his stomach eased. "You'd never use me."

"Good. I might be your boss, but you can always say no. Hear me?"

"I know. Shouldn't you go out there?"

He sighed. "Yeah."

Her lips twitched. "You don't sound very enthusiastic."

"Eh, I'd rather stay in here with you." He ran a finger over her cheek. "Maybe I should have you sit right here while I work."

"I have work to do too."

"I'll hire someone else to do it."

She grinned. "So you're going to pay me to be your lap warmer?"

"Hm. Well, you'd be required to kiss me too."

"I think that might be an added-on extra."

"So what you're saying is that it will cost me?" He raised an eyebrow.

"Uh-huh."

"How much?"

"I dunno. Fifty bucks a kiss."

"Fifty bucks! You were only going to pay me a dollar for a pole dance."

"That offer still stands."

"Brat." He grasped the back of her head with his hand, then nuzzled her nose. "Fuck, you're beautiful." With a sigh, he leaned back. "Got something to tell you."

She tensed. "What is it?"

Immediately, all the happiness bled from her face. He hated seeing that.

"Easy," he soothed, running his hand up and down her thighs. "I just got off the phone with Ink. He said your security is some of the best he's ever seen. Reckons you'll be safe there."

"Oh."

Was that a disappointed oh? He liked to think it was.

"So I guess that means I can move back into my apartment."

"Yep." He tried to figure out whether that was what she wanted or not. She had a good poker face.

"All right. What about my stuff? Should I get it tonight, or . . ."

"I guess so."

Tell me you want to stay with me.

She smiled. But it didn't reach her eyes. There was a knock on the door as he opened his mouth to ask her what she wanted to do. He scowled. "This isn't the place for private conversations."

"Or kissing," she scolded.

"I'll be back soon." He lifted her off his lap and turned her towards the door. "Get back to work, brat."

"I thought sitting on your lap was work."

He slapped her ass, making her jump. "Hush, you. Or I'll put you to work doing something else." Leaning in, he whispered in her ear. "Having you suck me off while I sit at my desk is number two on my fantasy list."

He winked as she blushed. Then he strode to the door.

Ask me. Ask me.

"What's number one?"

"Spreading you over my desk and eating you out."

He left after telling her that. God. He was in for a painful few minutes while he got his hard-on under control.

TABBY SAT BACK in his chair, her hand pressed to her chest as she tried to slow her breathing.

Dear. Lord.

The man could kiss. She couldn't believe he'd picked her up like that, pressing her to the wall. His strength still shocked her. And sitting on his lap, well, that might just be her favorite thing of all.

But doing that sort of thing at work probably wasn't a good thing. Especially in front of Tommy.

Although he'd actually sought her out to apologize the other day. And she'd barely seen him since. Maybe he was just one of those guys that didn't know how to talk to women, so he acted like an asshole thinking they'd find it attractive. She wasn't sure. She was just glad that things were better between them now.

Maybe now that she was with Razor, he'd behave.

Her core was still throbbing. That kiss had lit her from the inside out. She was finding herself starting to crave his touch more and more.

How was she meant to go back to her apartment now? Over the past week, she'd only spent one night there alone. She didn't want to go back.

She wanted to stay with him. But could she tell him that? Was she brave enough? Did he want her to stay? That would be like moving in with him and it was too soon for that, right?

Right.

Urgh.

She closed her eyes. She couldn't get any time alone to take care of her problem. She'd attempted to a few times in the shower, but the orgasm had been tiny and unsatisfactory. She needed her vibrator.

Or maybe she needed him. She needed him to . . . to . . .

Spread her across the desk and eat her out. Her cheeks were hot as she stared at the desk in question. Could she do that? Nobody had ever done that to her before. Ew, not that she'd wanted Luther's face near her pussy.

Just thinking about it made her want to gag.

She'd also never sucked a cock before. But if it was Razor's dick, though. Yeah, she thought she might like that. A wash of heat flooded her and she found herself fanning herself. This was crazy. If she didn't get some relief soon, she might self-combust.

Maybe going home wouldn't be a bad thing if she could use her vibrator in privacy.

Then again, if Razor would just do more than touch and tease her . . . that would be even better.

Truth was, she didn't want to go back to her apartment. That wasn't home.

Home was with Razor and Luna. That's where she belonged. Where she wanted to be.

TABBY WAS NEARLY in tears as she followed Razor into his house. He turned off the alarm, then reached back for her hand. She'd noticed that he liked to hold her hand or that he'd place his hand on her ass when they were walking together. Even when it was just through his house.

"I'll go pack up my stuff," she said. He didn't reply, and her shoulders slumped. "There's really no need for you to come back to my apartment with me when I have my car here."

He simply grunted.

Awesome. Feeling completely dejected and more alone than ever, she made her way to his bedroom.

They'd gotten some of her stuff last Sunday. He'd taken her on a long bike ride and they'd ended up eating lunch at this gorgeous restaurant. It had been the best day she could recall in a long time.

Pulling out her backpack, she started packing up her stuff. Luna padded into the bedroom and sat at her feet, whining. She held her ball in her mouth. This was her favorite game with Tabby.

"I'm sorry, Luna," she said sadly. "I don't think I can play today." She had to go home to her cold, sterile apartment. At least her fish would be happy to see her. Could fish express happiness? She did feel kind of bad that she was never around for them.

She just finished putting her clothes into her backpack when Razor came in.

"Almost done," she said as cheerfully as she could.

He picked up her backpack, then reached in and drew out the clothes, putting them back into the drawers he'd emptied out for her.

"Razor? What are you doing?"

He grabbed the empty backpack and stuffed it up onto the highest shelf in the wardrobe, the one she had no hope of reaching without a stool.

Tabby just gaped at him. He didn't say a word as he was doing this. Then he grabbed her hand and drew her out of the room.

"What's going on? What are you doing? Am I not going home tonight?"

He shook his head and led her into the kitchen, then lifted her up on the kitchen counter. The same place she always sat while he was making them food.

"What do you want for dinner?"

Her mouth was open. She probably looked like an idiot as she sat there, staring at him.

"Um."

"Might grill some steak. Want baked potatoes and salad?"

"Um."

"Drink?" He moved to the fridge and opened it, glaring into it. "No chocolate milk left."

"Um."

"You need a snack while I cook?" He aimed a look at her. "Who am I talking to? Of course you do."

"Razor!"

"Yep?" He stilled, crossing his arms over his chest. He looked like he was prepared for battle.

"What's going on?"

"You're not going home."

"I'm not?"

"Nope. You're staying here."

"I am?"

"Yep. And I don't want to hear any arguments."

"You don't?"

"No. I'm putting my foot down."

"Can you do that?" she asked curiously.

"Damn straight I can." He pointed a finger at her. "I forbid you to leave."

With that said, he stomped past her and headed outside towards the grill.

Tabby waited until he was outside to let a smile slip free.

She wasn't going back to her apartment.

Because he forbid it.

Silly man.

But boy, did she adore him.

18

Tabby wrapped her arms around his neck as he kissed her.

So good.

She couldn't believe that she'd never realized how wonderful kissing could be. That she could feel this much for someone.

It was Friday night. They had the whole weekend to spend together. She couldn't wait. They'd been working long hours the last couple of days in order to clear some workload, so Razor could have the weekend off.

Razor liked to grumble about her working too much when she insisted on staying late with him, but she'd rather be with him. And she knew he wouldn't be happy with her going home on her own.

They were still going back to her apartment every second day to check on her fish. She wondered if it was even worth keeping the apartment. But then, it was too soon to think about getting rid of it, right?

Not that she ever wanted to think about going back there. That would be devastating. She couldn't imagine life now without Razor.

Nope. Not happening. But she wouldn't mind postponing that conversation with her cousin for as long as possible. It wasn't something she could just bring up during their weekly catch-ups.

Razor drew his lips away from hers. "Time for bed, Tabby-baby."

"All right." If he wanted to move this to the bedroom, she was all for that.

"You need your sleep. I've got a busy weekend planned."

"You do?" she asked while frowning. Sleep? Who wanted to sleep? Her body was on fire. She needed to come more than she needed to rest. "What is it?"

"That's a surprise." He tapped her nose. "What's that pout about?"

"Nothing." Climbing off his lap, she sighed. She guessed she'd just go get ready for bed.

He grabbed her hand. "You know better than to say that nothing's wrong. Talk. Now."

So far, other than a few threats to pop her ass, he hadn't really gotten stern with her. Definitely hadn't punished her. Then again, she'd been careful to be on her best behavior. The last thing she wanted was to annoy him.

"Tabby," he warned. "I'm going to count to three, then you better spit it out. One."

She bit her lip.

"Two."

"Don't you want to have sex with me?" she blurted out.

His mouth dropped open, his eyes widening as he stared up at her. Great. She'd rendered him speechless.

Good job, Tabby.

"You think I don't want to have sex with you?" He sounded so incredulous that she started to think she'd misread the situation.

But if she had, then why hadn't he moved beyond kissing and touching her?

"Baby girl, why do you think I take an extra-long shower every night before bed?"

"I don't know." She had noticed him taking a while.

"And have you not noticed how hard I am every morning when I wake up?"

"Isn't that a normal male reaction?"

"Maybe when you're nineteen, not fucking forty-nine. I've had so many damn hard-ons in the last week that I'm starting to think I'm going to strain something. Maybe my hand from rubbing one out so much." He stretched out his hand.

It was her turn to gape at him. Did he seriously just say that? Or had she misunderstood?

"Do you mean, are you saying that . . ."

"There's a reason my showers are extra-long? Yep."

"Oh my God! Why!"

"What do you mean, why? Because it was getting damn painful, plus I didn't want to come to bed with a hard-on and scare the shit out of you."

"But I would have . . . I could have . . . I'm right here! Why wouldn't you want me to do that?"

A wave of rejection filled her. She lowered her gaze to her feet.

His hand cupped her chin and he raised her face. "Jesus, baby. Who the hell do you think I'm thinking of while I'm jacking myself off? I close my eyes and I imagine it's your hand around my dick. Your mouth. That you're underneath me, riding me, that I have my mouth on that pussy which I just know is going to be lush and perfect."

She flushed. He couldn't know that. And just the thought of doing any of that with him was making her squirm.

"I want that. All of it. What I don't want is to push you too far too fast."

"You're not," she insisted.

"You were in an abusive relationship. The only sex you've known was forced on you. The last thing I want is to reawaken old nightmares. To hurt you."

Reaching up, she cupped his cheeks. "Remember how you said I wasn't weak and you wouldn't treat me like I was? I know what I want. It's you."

"Then why the fuck didn't you say so earlier? Would have saved me getting repetitive strain."

She gaped at him. She couldn't believe he'd just said that. Then he grinned at her, his perfect white teeth flashing at her.

The ass.

She whacked her hand against his chest then sucked in a breath. Ouch!

"Shit! Did you hurt yourself?"

"Nah, it's fine." Damn, that was embarrassing. Just what was he made of? Concrete?

"Let me see." He grabbed hold of her hand and gently inspected it. "I've got just what you need to make it feel better."

To her shock, he raised her hand to his mouth and kissed it gently. "There, Daddy's magic kisses will make it all better."

She swallowed, trying to wet her dry throat. "Does he have any other magic kisses?"

"He does. Where would you like these magic kisses?"

She didn't know if she could say it out loud, so instead, she grabbed his hand and placed his fingers on her mouth.

"Anywhere else?" he asked as he moved forward, pushing her backward. He placed one hand on her hip.

She lowered his hand to her neck.

"Oh yeah."

Then down to her breast.

"Baby, yes. I've been dying to get my mouth on your breasts."

Lord help her. She bravely reached down over her tummy to her pussy. She pushed his fingers against her mound.

"Christ, that's it. I'm picking you up."

The warning came two seconds before he had her in the air. She wrapped her legs around his waist, holding on tight. Turning, he carried her into the bedroom.

Carefully, he placed her down on the bed then he lay next to her. His lips lowered to hers. "Tell me if there's anything you don't like."

"Just don't make me wait. I can't go another week or two without coming."

"You mean you haven't been playing with yourself?" he asked.

"What?" she squeaked.

"Do you have a vibrator? Or have you just been using your fingers?"

There was something in his gaze. Something cheeky and knowing.

"Oh my God!" she yelled. She tried to get away, but he held her tight. "You heard me that night, didn't you? Oh no. I'm so embarrassed!"

He let out a low chuckle. "Baby girl, I just told you that I've been jacking off each night in the shower, how is admitting that you made yourself come while you were staying in my spare room any more embarrassing?"

"I don't know!" she wailed. "It just is. We weren't together then. And you heard me . . . heard me . . . oh my God! I'm mortified!" Grabbing the neckline of her top, she drew it up over her face, hiding herself from him.

So, hiding under her clothing was a new one. Covering her face was another way of hiding from him. And he couldn't allow it.

"Would it help if you saw me jack off?" he asked casually.

His balls were already aching at the thought of her watching him.

For a moment, he thought she hadn't heard. Or that she had heard but it made no difference. Then she peeked out over the top of her shirt.

Damn, that was cute.

He tapped her nose. "Come out here." He kept his voice soft but firm. "You know that hiding isn't allowed."

She mumbled something under her breath. Something that sounded rather sassy and naughty and likely would have earned her some corner time under other circumstances.

"You're riding close to a punishment, little girl. It's only because I know that you need to talk about this that you aren't standing in a corner right now."

"That's not fair!"

"I don't want you hiding from me," he said firmly. "And I don't like how you just curled in on yourself. There isn't anything you can't tell me, remember?"

"Yes, but . . . we weren't together then."

"So? You want to know what I did when I heard you cry out like that?"

"I suppose so." She didn't look too sure.

"I took myself off for an icy shower."

"You did?"

"Fucking hottest thing I've ever heard. In fact, it kept playing over and over in my mind." He drew her up onto his lap so she straddled him. "I want to hear you make that noise again."

"Really?" The tension and embarrassment in her face eased.

"Yeah, only I want to hear you scream those noises. And I want it to be my name that you yell."

She flushed.

"I'm fucking hard just talking about this."

"Can I see?" she whispered shyly.

"Hell, yeah, baby. You can see. You can touch. You can do whatever you like. Sit up for a second."

As she drew her weight off his legs, he undid his jeans, pulling them and his boxers down to his knees. She took in a sharp breath and he waited for her to say something.

"Have I shocked you into silence with how magnificent my dick is?" he drawled. "I mean, I get it. Can't blame you for being awed."

"W-what?" she said then she burst into laughter. "Magnificent? Awed? Is that what you think, huh?"

He loved when she smiled. She looked so carefree. So sweet. Happy. That was how he always wanted her to look.

All he wanted was her happiness.

Reaching down, he grasped his dick around the base.

"You don't think he's magnificent? You'll hurt his feelings."

"Oh, your dick has feelings, huh?"

With each ridiculous thing he said, the tension left her shoulders and the red retreated from her cheeks. If he had to make an idiot out of himself to make her feel less self-conscious and more at ease, then that was just what he was going to do.

"Sure does. And right now, he's sad."

She raised her eyebrows. "He doesn't look sad. He looks enormous."

"Well, now he feels happier."

"Your dick has emotions?"

"Darn right he does." Reaching out with his other hand, he tilted up her chin. "I'd never hurt you."

"I know. But wow, sometimes I can barely take my vibrator, and you're way bigger."

"You sure know how to flatter a guy's dick."

"Oh, he's happier now, huh?" she asked.

"Look at him. He's on top of the fucking world."

She rolled her eyes.

"Where's your vibrator?" he asked.

She bit her lip. "It's back at my apartment."

"We'll get it when we next go back. You want to touch?"

"Yes," she whispered. Her gaze darted from his dick to his eyes then back to his dick. "You'll tell me if I do anything wrong?"

"You'll do just fine." He moved his hand away, leaning back against the headboard to give her more room. And then she was touching him. Holy shit. Lightly at first. So light it was like the worst of teases. Softer than a butterfly's wings.

"Baby girl?"

"Yeah?"

"He won't break."

"Oh. Right." She wrapped her hand around his cock and squeezed. "Better?"

"Yes. Now, if you'd just move your hand, I'd be damn ecstatic."

She ran her hand up and down his dick. "He's so hard yet soft." She ran her thumb over the head. "So pretty."

"He's not pretty."

"Yeah, he is."

"Dear Lord, you're gonna give him a complex."

She giggled. "I think he'll survive. Can I take him into my mouth?"

Killing him. She was killing him.

"Yep," he said on a low groan as she moved. He drew off his pants and boxers then spread his legs. She got onto her knees between his thighs. Leaning over, she grasped hold of the base of him again, she took him deep into her mouth.

"You have no idea how fucking good that feels. That's it. Take me deeper. Hell."

His breathing started to quicken. He was so hot, he was sweating. Pulling off his T-shirt, he tried to move as little as possible, so he didn't jolt her. Then he lay back against the headboard, enjoying the feel of her mouth wrapped around his cock.

. . .

OKAY, she liked this way more than she thought she would. The feel of him in her mouth somehow settled her. It was weird. She felt almost powerful. As though she could do anything. Maybe she liked being in charge. Was that it?

No, not really. She didn't want to tell Razor what to do. She scoffed at the idea. Yeah, she had no inclination to do that.

But there was something about this that made her feel good, deep inside. She pushed aside the thought as she concentrated on giving him pleasure. Moving her hand to the base of his thick shaft, she ran it up and down his cock while she took the head into her mouth, sucking strongly.

"Baby. Fuck, yes."

She had to smile at the breathless tone in his voice. He definitely enjoyed what she was doing. Maybe that was it? She got a thrill out of pleasing him? He was always doing stuff for her.

Maybe she simply liked pleasing him.

What else could she try? An idea came to her, but she wasn't sure how he'd feel. She pulled her mouth back. "Can I touch your balls?"

She kept her eyes on his chin.

"Meet my eyes and then ask again. This time say please."

The command in his voice shocked her, even as it sent a jolt of pleasure through her.

She forced her gaze up. Met the heat in his. "Please, can I touch your balls?"

"Sir," he added.

"Can I touch your balls, Sir?"

"You can. Now, get back to sucking my cock."

Oh yeah. That commanding tone just did it for her. She decided it didn't matter why. It just was. She lowered her mouth to his dick, moving her hand so she could lightly cup his balls.

Damn, she loved the feel of him. The way his breath hitched. She wanted to make him lose control. She constantly felt out of control around him, so it was only fair, right?

"That's it. Baby, I'm going to wrap my hand around your braid. Just to guide you, not force you. I need you to tell me if that's not okay."

Oh Lord. Her stomach melted. She loved that he always took care of her. No matter what.

"It's fine, Sir."

"Good girl. You'll tell me to stop if you need to." He wrapped his hand around her braid and tugged lightly. He paused, waiting to see how she'd react. But there was nothing but heat. She returned to his dick, bobbing her head. He lightly guided her and she moved with him. Slow then faster. Then slower again.

"That's it. Fuck, yes, baby girl." He groaned, a deep noise that she longed to hear over and over.

It was going to become an addiction. She could feel it.

"All right, baby girl. Pull back. I'm going to come." He tugged lightly on her hair, but she shook her head and felt him let her braid go.

"Sure, baby? I can't hold back."

She took him as deep as she could without gagging then he released in her mouth. The taste wasn't bad. Sweet and salty. Sounded weird. But it worked.

When he was finished, she drew back and stared down at him. He was panting slightly, relaxed. He looked like some kind of God, resting on his throne. Gorgeous. Sexy. Ripped.

And all hers.

Without even thinking about it, she licked a line along his dick, then placing her hands on his shoulders, she sucked on his nipple.

She moved to the other nipple.

"That feels good. But there's no way for him to get hard again this quick." Reaching down, he drew her head up so he could kiss her. He didn't seem to care that he'd just come in her mouth. Then he drew back. "Now it's my turn."

"You don't have to," she whispered.

"Uh-uh," he scolded. "There's no going shy on me now. And why the fuck wouldn't I want to worship every inch of your body? It belongs to me, doesn't it?"

She mustn't have answered him quickly enough because he grasped hold of her chin. His touch was light but sure against her skin. "Doesn't it?"

"Yes, it belongs to you. Like yours belongs to me." Because she would never be someone's possession again. Not unless they belonged to her as well.

"Damn straight it does," he told her. Then he leaned in and kissed her. Her entire body tingled from the tips of her toes all the way to the top of her head.

"Now, I want you to get off the bed and strip," he commanded.

Oh hell.

19

He waited to see what she would do. If she wasn't ready for this, then he wouldn't push her. This had to be at her pace.

But shock and pleasure filled him as she climbed off the bed and stood next to it. Her hands shook as she attempted to strip.

"Would you like some help?" he asked, wanting to ease her stress.

"Yes, please," she whispered.

He got off the bed and drew her top over her head. All she wore underneath was a lacy, black bra. It stood in sharp contrast to her creamy skin. Reaching around her, he undid her bra, pulling it off her arms. He leaned in and placed a kiss on the top of her shoulder then down her collarbone. He moved lower until he got to the top of her breast.

Slowly, giving her plenty of time to protest, he crouched and pulled her pants down until they pooled at her ankles. Her panties were a deep burgundy. Plain but sweet. Grasping her around the hips, he laid a kiss on her mound.

With a gasp, she tried to move back, but he held her. She probably shouldn't be standing on her ankle for too long, though. He tugged her panties down her legs.

"Fuck, baby," he muttered as he bared her. "You're so beautiful. Put your hands on my shoulders so you don't fall while I help you."

She held on as she stepped out of the rest of her clothes. Then she was standing there, naked. He wanted to take his time studying her, but he could tell she was already feeling shy. She was growing tense, her hands clenching and unclenching as though she was fighting the urge to cover herself with her arms. Standing, he wrapped an arm under her ass and lifted her against his chest so he could kiss her. He cupped the back of her head and held her steady until the tension left her and she melted against him.

"That's better," he murmured after he drew back. "I know this is new, but you don't have to be shy around me. You're so sexy."

"You're sexy," she whispered. "I'm just plain. Me."

He set her down on the bed then lay next to her, kissing his way down her neck while his hand cupped her breast.

"So precious."

He pinched lightly at her nipple.

"Tell me if there's anything you don't like. Or want to try."

"I don't . . . I don't know."

"Think about it."

He moved his mouth down to her breast, sucking on her nipple.

"Oooh," she cried out, her back arching.

"You like that, baby girl?"

"Yes, please, more."

"Damn, you're so responsive."

He lightly pinched one nipple as he sucked and tongued the other one. Tabby wriggled around on the bed. Tiny groans escaped her. He loved the way she didn't hold back. He played with her until her cries grew deeper, louder. Until he could hear her panting.

He wanted to get her to the point where she was so aroused that she couldn't think. Couldn't worry.

He ran his hand down her stomach, towards her pussy. "I'm going to make you feel so good."

"Or my money back?"

He grinned. "You want a refund for that whole dollar?"

"Nah, I'd pay you a buck fifty for this experience."

He threw back his head and laughed. She wriggled and gave him a small smile.

"You're a crazy girl," he whispered.

"You like crazy?" she asked as he kissed along her jaw.

"Yep."

"That's insane. You should run from crazy."

"You think I should run from you?" He leaned up again to peer down at her.

"You should definitely run from me."

"Why would I run from you when being with you is the one thing that makes me feel alive? All I want is to protect you, lift you up, help you shine."

"I don't shine."

"You will." He winked at her before moving down her body.

"Wait! Razor!"

He paused, glanced up at her. Her nerves were clear to see. Poor baby. That bastard, Luther, had a lot to answer for. If resurrecting the dead ever became a thing . . .

"What is it, Tabby-baby?" he asked, running his hand up and down her tummy with butterfly light touches.

"What if you don't like it?" she whispered.

"Not possible." Enough procrastinating. If he kept letting her think, then she'd talk herself out of this. Out of everything.

He slid down onto his knees and drew her closer to the edge of the bed. Then he spread her legs and looked up at her. "Get those two pillows and put them behind your head. When I glance up, I want to see your eyes on me. Understand?"

She nodded.

"Words, Tabby-baby."

"Yes."

"Yes, what?"

"Yes, Sir?"

"That's my girl. I'm going to eat you out and I'm not going to stop until I've had my fill. You're going to come as often as you like, understand?"

"I . . . okay," she whispered.

"But if I look up, you'd better be staring down at me. Otherwise, I'm going to turn you onto your tummy and you get five spanks."

"Oh Lord, help me."

"Baby girl, there's no help for you now."

He ran two fingers down the lips of her bare pussy. "Waxed?"

She tensed. Why did that upset her?

"Laser. Uncle Fergus made me."

He hid his face as anger flared hot and hard. That utter bastard.

Razor might be possessive. But he'd never treat her like a possession. Not like her uncle had.

"He made you get laser treatments?" he asked when he had his anger more under control.

When she didn't answer, he moved his head, forcing himself to look up at her. She was staring up at the ceiling, not down at him.

"Tabby-baby, what did I say about looking at me?"

She gasped and glanced down. "Are you going to spank me? I thought that was only while you were . . . oh God. I'm not sure I can do this."

"You can do this," he whispered. "One warning." He definitely wasn't going to spank her when she was stressed. He wasn't really looking to punish her, but to gently teach her to obey him. That she should look to him. And he wanted her to know who was touching her.

He kissed his way up her thigh as she shuddered. "So beautiful. Damn, you smell so good."

"I do?" she asked shyly.

"You do."

"Do you like me bare?"

He paused then placed a kiss on the top of her slit. "I like you whatever way you come."

"Uncle Fergus said men like women bare down there."

"Uncle Fergus was a dick. And the only way he could get a woman was to buy her or intimidate her."

"That's true," she whispered.

"Can we not speak of your uncle when my mouth is an inch from paradise?" he asked right before he ran his tongue up her slit.

"Razor!"

That was better. That cry was filled with shock. With hunger. Using his fingers, he parted her lips, taking her in. Plump, pink, and delicious.

Precious.

She groaned as he lowered his tongue to her clit, flicking it. He ran his tongue around her clit then rubbed it back and forth over the nub. Her hips thrust up.

When she didn't answer, he looked up her body at her. Her eyes were closed, head thrown back.

"Tut-tut," he said after drawing back. "Where are you supposed to be looking?"

Her eyes flew open and she stared down at him, her mouth open. "No! Razor! I need another warning."

With a mock sigh of sadness, he shook his head. "I'm sorry,

Tabby-baby. No more warnings allowed. Now, are you going to take your punishment like a good girl?"

She pouted. "But Daddy . . ."

Oh, that was sweet. She thought that by calling him Daddy, she'd get out of her punishment. Too bad for her, all that did was firm his resolve.

"Eyes on me." He leaned over her, placing his arms on the bed as he stared down at her. He wanted to make sure that she was all right. To his surprise, panic filled her face and she started pushing at him.

Immediately, he rolled to his side, away from her.

She curled up into the fetal position. Shock filled him as he stared down at her. Her eyes were wild, she held her body tight, defensively.

"Tabby-baby? What's wrong?" He wanted to touch her, but he was afraid of frightening her further.

"I . . . I . . . damn." She closed her eyes, her body shuddering.

He hated this. That she was scared. That he'd done this.

He hated that she'd curled up, as though protecting herself from him.

That wasn't the way this was going to work. Nope. Nuh-uh. She came to him for protection.

"Sorry. Sorry. It was you being over me. I know you wouldn't hurt me, but that just . . . it . . ."

"Triggered you? Made you flashback?" he asked gently.

"Yes," she whispered.

"I'm going to touch you now," he warned before he moved up onto the bed and lay next to her, facing her. Then he gently cupped the side of her face. She flinched slightly but he didn't let that deter him. There were going to be obstacles. There were going to be moments like this.

All he could do was be here for her. Be patient.

"I'm so sorry," she whispered.

"It's not your fault. It's mine for not checking if you had triggers."

"Not your fault. You're perfect."

He let out a scoffing noise. "Baby, I'm the very definition of not-perfect."

To his surprise, she reached out and placed her hand over the Superman shield on his upper hand. He'd been young when he'd gotten that.

He'd thought himself invincible.

How wrong he'd been.

"Superhero."

"No, baby. Nobody's hero. Just a guy who's done plenty of stupid things in his life and made too many mistakes. And wants to rectify that. Wants to grasp hold of anything good, little as he may deserve it, and never fucking let go."

She was silent. Just breathing, her cool hand over his shoulder. She was cold. He needed to warm her up.

"This is meant to be fun, pleasurable for us both." He ran his hand up and down her arm gently until she started to relax. She let go of her legs, lowering them.

Razor lay on his back and opened his arms. "Come here."

Gradually she moved over, snuggling up next to him. He kissed the top of her head, grateful that she showed him enough trust to do this. To let him hold her, touch her. After all that she'd been through, this trust she had in him was a freaking miracle.

"Baby girl, at any time you can stop me. No matter what. We should have talked before we dove into this." He rolled to his side so they faced each other.

She wrinkled her nose. "I don't know, orgasms sound so much better than talking."

"Agreed. But talking is important. I need to learn your triggers. Your limits. There needs to be rules in place."

"I think with time, I can work through it," she told him. "But at the moment, it might be a limit. As well as not punching or kicking me, but I wouldn't be with you if you were going to do that."

He let out a low growl before he could help himself. "Don't fucking joke about that."

For a moment, he thought he'd made a mistake. Her eyes widened and he worried she was going to flinch away in fear. But her face softened and she patted his chest gently. "I won't. I'm sorry."

"What he did to you . . . baby, I would never . . ." He sucked in a breath, unable to go on.

She leaned in and kissed him gently. "I know, I'm sorry for joking. I know you wouldn't. I wouldn't be here if I did. Truth is, there might be things I don't think will trigger me until they do . . . like you being over me. I didn't think that would be a problem."

"If there are any issues, anything I do that scares you, then say your safeword. Promise me."

"Promise," she whispered. Her gaze moved over him. "I wish I hadn't just freaked."

"In the morning, we're going to talk more about limits and rules. And I want you to think about talking to someone."

"Jared would never allow it."

"Jared can kiss my ass," he growled. "You'll be doing whatever the fuck you want."

"Oh yeah? I'd pay to see that." She gave him a trembling smile.

"That so? How much would you give me for that?"

"Oh, at least five dollars."

"Five whole dollars. Wow. You really want to see that."

"It is a fine ass."

He rolled onto his stomach so she could pat his ass. She let out an exaggerated sigh of admiration. "Damn, that's fine." She gave it a squeeze. "So firm. So hard."

"That could apply to another part of my anatomy, too," he muttered as her small hands kneaded his buttocks.

"Yeah?" She moved her hands up his back, massaging and rubbing.

Shit. That felt good.

"Shocking, huh?"

"Definitely," she agreed.

"Hey," he protested. "Brat!"

She giggled. Damn, he loved that sound. She didn't laugh enough. But he was going to remedy that.

"Sorry, Daddy. It's just at your age . . ."

"Do you need a spanking," he mock-growled. "I'll be happy to oblige."

"Nope, not me, Daddy. Now, hush. I'm massaging you."

Maybe he had the wrong idea before. He should give her a chance to get to touch him. Explore.

She moved her hands over his shoulders.

"Baby, that feels so good."

"Yeah?"

"Yep. I get all tight at work. Was thinking of putting in a hot tub."

"Ooh, that could be fun."

"Yeah? Help me pick one out?"

"Really?"

"Uh-huh," he murmured. Christ, she was massaging him into a coma. Then she slid her hands to his thighs.

"You're so hard."

"You've got that right."

"I meant your back and thighs. I think your thighs are bigger than my waist."

He knew they were. She was tiny. He didn't know where she put all that food she ate.

A groan escaped as she kneaded down one leg then the other.

When she ran her knuckles over the sole of his foot, he thought he'd fucking died and gone to heaven.

"Roll over," she told him.

Moving onto his back, he kept his eyes closed as she started at his shoulders. Next were his pecs, then she skipped down to his legs. Then he felt the warmth of her mouth surrounding the head of his dick.

"Holy shit!"

"Sorry."

Yeah, right. She didn't sound sorry. There was definitely a brat lingering under that shell of hers. She might keep herself apart and reserved, but then the real Tabby would unexpectedly shine through.

Like when she wrapped herself around Sav to stop him from doing something that might get him in trouble. Touch didn't come easy to her. But she'd gotten past that to protect a friend.

The more time he spent with her, the more he saw through the cracks. And the more she smiled and relaxed. A cool finger ran down his dick and then her hand cupped his balls.

"Ah, Tabby-baby?"

"Hm?"

"I don't think my balls need a massage."

She paused then stared at him, her lips twitching. "No?"

"No."

"You sound nervous."

"Little girl," he warned. "You don't want to find yourself in trouble, do you?"

"I'd say you're the one in trouble, Daddy. I've got you by the balls." She giggled after saying that and his heart soared at the carefree sound.

"You won't always have me by the balls. And your butt might feel the sting of my palm."

"Ah, Daddy. I'm starting to think you're bluffing." She lightly squeezed his balls. The damn things were aching, the need to come riding him hard.

She was a freaking aphrodisiac.

"I'm not bluffing, Tabby-baby. I still owe you five, remember?"

"Uh-huh." Leaning down, she drew his dick into her mouth again.

Fucking hell. Was he going to let her get away with this? But he was loving the confidence she exuded as she took him deep. And he didn't want to smother her or have her hesitate with him.

This required a delicate balance. Not exactly easy for a man who'd been known as Bulldozer in his earlier years.

"Enough, baby girl." He tugged her back.

"You didn't like it?"

"You kidding? Why wouldn't I like that? Look at my dick. He hasn't been this happy in years. Him being so happy all the time makes it damn hard to concentrate on paperwork, though."

She let out a strangled noise. "You mean, at work, you've been sitting in your office and . . ."

"Yep. And without any privacy to take care of matters. Do you feel sorry for me?"

"Not really, since I've been in the same boat."

"Is that so?" he murmured.

She cleared her throat. "Would you . . . would you try touching me again?"

He studied her for a long moment. "You're sure?"

"Yes, I trust you."

"Promise you'll tell me if I do something that scares you."

"I promise. I want to try again. Please."

"All right, baby girl." He cupped her breast as she stared down at him, licking her lips. "So have you been thinking naughty thoughts while sitting at your desk? Have you thought about me?"

"Y-yes," she whispered.

"Were they about me spreading you over my desk and eating you out?"

"M-maybe?"

"You don't sound so sure. I think you've had other fantasies, what were they?"

She cleared her throat. "I, um . . . I thought about you touching me."

"Yeah? Touching you where? Kissing you?"

"Yes."

"All over?" he asked.

"Yes."

"And those thoughts made you wet?"

"Yes," she groaned. "Damn."

"Are you wet now, Tabby-baby?"

"Oh Lord."

"Well?"

Her breathing grew faster. "You like to talk a lot during sex, huh?"

"That wasn't an answer to my question," he warned. "When I ask a question, I want an answer. Unless you tell me your safeword."

"Yes, I guess so."

"You guess so? That sounds like I'll have to check. Remember my fantasy? The one where I knock everything off the desk then lay you out naked? Then I spread your legs and eat you out?"

"Yes, I remember your other fantasy too."

"Do you? What was that?"

"You mean you've forgotten already? Perhaps we should get your memory tested." She shook her head at him.

"Brat, if you think I'm not keeping track of your sassy-pants answers, then you'd be mistaken. Sit back against the headboard," he ordered.

She moved into position, sitting back against the bed. He

grabbed the pillows and put them behind her back so she was more comfortable.

"Spread your legs."

For a moment, he wasn't certain she would obey. But then her legs drifted apart.

"Good girl." He knelt between her legs and cupped her face before kissing her. He drank from her, his lips light against hers. He kissed her until she wrapped her hands around the back of his neck, holding onto him tight.

"What was my other fantasy?" he asked her.

"Where I got down on my knees while you sat at your desk and sucked you off."

"Yeah, baby. Although now I'm thinking I'd pick you up in my arms and press you against the wall and fuck you. Or maybe I'd bend you over my desk and fuck you from behind. Because that ass of yours is amazing."

"Razor," she murmured.

"Put your hands behind your head," he commanded. "And remember, you can say your safeword if it's something that scares you or makes you uncomfortable."

He figured she likely would. It wouldn't hurt her to learn that saying her safeword was fine. That she could say it and he'd listen. She hadn't said it earlier, when he'd triggered her.

So it shocked the hell out of him when she moved her hands behind her head. Satisfaction flooded him at her sign of trust. At her submission to him. Bending down, he sucked on her nipple in reward.

"Good girl," he murmured, moving to her other nipple. He lightly brushed his beard over her nipple. "Such a good girl for Daddy, aren't you?"

"Please," she begged.

"Please, what?"

"Touch me. Don't stop."

"Trust me, I don't ever want to stop." He moved down until he was lying on his stomach on the bed, his face inches from her pussy.

"Bend your knees and put your feet flat on the mattress," he commanded.

Without a grumble, she moved her legs up. This spread her and he could already see the dew glistening on her lips. His mouth watered.

He knew she was going to taste delicious. He parted her lips with his fingers and then ran one up her slit.

"Oh yeah, my baby girl is wet. Did you have any other fantasies about what I might do to you? About what you would want?"

"Well, I, um . . ."

"You can tell me. I told you mine."

"I was thinking, maybe I like the idea of you having me suck you off while you work." She blushed bright red. "That's probably not a good thing to fantasize about, right?"

"Who said it's not?" he demanded. "You can fantasize about whatever you want. That's the whole idea. It's what you want. Even if you never do it. Although that one we can definitely make come true."

"I like the idea of hiding under your desk and doing that to you. It feels naughty, but also like . . ."

"Like what?"

"I dunno. It sounds silly."

"It's not silly. What?"

"Like I'd feel safe. I guess I like knowing that I can bring you pleasure. It makes me feel . . . important? Are you sure that's not silly?"

"Nope, not silly at all."

"I like doing that to you."

"Damn, baby girl. I like it too. But right now, I want to taste you. So, hush."

"Hey, you're the one who keeps talking."

"You want another five for arguing?" he grumbled at her.

"Another five?"

"You earned five for looking away from me. And now you've earned five for keeping me from my treat."

Her mouth dropped open, staring down at him in shock. He took that opportunity to take a long lick of her.

"Hell, yes. Delicious."

She groaned as he flicked at her clit. Back and forth. Fast then slow. He didn't want her to come too quickly. And at the same time, he wanted to see her lose it. To see her in the throes of pleasure. Her eyes were starting to shut.

He drew back.

"No!"

"Keep your gaze on me," he warned.

"I can't. It's too much."

"You can. You will."

"Why?"

"Because I want you to know who is giving you pleasure. I want to see your eyes. I don't want you hiding from me."

He slid a finger deep into her passage and she clenched down.

"Oh God. Oh God."

"How many times can you come with your vibrator in one session?" he demanded

"Three. But that was only once, the first time I used it."

"First time?" he asked as he added another finger, sliding them in and out of her slick passage.

"I bought it a few weeks ago," she told him.

He sucked on her clit and she screamed as she came.

"You're so passionate, baby girl. So beautiful. I love hearing you come, having your taste in my mouth. I need more. I'm moving you." He tugged at her hips gently, drawing her back down the bed so she was in a similar position to before. Once he was on his knees on the floor, he dragged her legs back with his hands and started devouring her again.

Just as he'd thought, her taste was addictive. The sounds she was making were killing him. They spurred him on, he drove his fingers in and out of her. Damn, he couldn't wait to get his hands on her vibrator. Maybe he'd get her one of those eggs to wear at work.

Might be pushing the employer-employee boundaries. He didn't much care. The idea of turning it on while she was sitting at her desk. Of walking into her office and finding her all flushed and pink . . . fuck, he wouldn't want anyone else seeing that though.

Okay, maybe after hours he could do that. But not while the guys were around.

"Razor! Razor!" she screamed.

He moved her legs over his shoulders so he could drive his fingers in and out of her pussy until he felt her clenching down as she came again.

As she breathed heavily, her legs slumped over his shoulders, he removed his fingers from her pussy and ran his tongue over her entrance as he used his finger on her clit.

"It's too much! I can't!"

Like hell she couldn't. If she could come three times with her vibrator, she could come that many times with him. He thrust his tongue into her pussy while he reached up with one hand to pluck at her nipple.

"I can't," she groaned.

He drew his tongue from her pussy. "You can." He stared at her, his gaze infusing her with the knowledge that this was what he wanted.

And she would do it.

"No! No!"

Pulling back, he gently drew her legs off his shoulders, then he half-rolled her and popped her ass several times. Not hard. Just light smacks to let her know he meant business.

"You can. Trust me?"

"Yes," she breathed out, shuddering as he rolled her back. "Holy fuck, how was that hot?" She sounded so bewildered that he had to grin.

"Liked getting your bottom heated, did you?"

She squirmed and he knew she was wondering if she shouldn't have.

"Don't worry about why you feel the way you do or if it's right or not and just feel."

"Easier said than done."

"We'll see about that. Get over onto your hands and knees."

He stood and waited with a raised eyebrow as she rolled and presented her ass to him. There was a slight pink tinge from his handprint. He hadn't hit her hard. This wasn't about punishment. It was about testing what she liked.

Another two smacks had her groaning. He reached between her legs to play with her clit. With his other hand, he smacked her again.

"Oh. Ohh, Razor, I can't!"

"You can. One day soon, I'm going to get you a clit tickler that stays in place with straps. I'll insert a vibrator in your hungry pussy. Then I'll spank this naughty ass."

Two more smacks. Then he drove two fingers into her.

"Razor!" she screamed as she came again. This time, she collapsed forwards and he figured she was done. Holding her hips up with his hands, he kissed each warm cheek. Fuck it, one more taste. He knelt again and drew her hips back to lap at her. She let out small murmurs as he cleaned her up. Then he let her slide down onto her side. He curled around her, wrapping his arm around her waist.

He kissed her shoulder. "Thank you, baby girl."

"Shouldn't I be the one saying that?" she teased.

He chuckled. "Maybe. I did just about orgasm you into a coma."

Reaching back, she attempted to slap him, then she groaned. "Remind me to give you a smack later."

"Come on, Tabby-baby, time for a shower."

"No, just leave me here. Unless you want," she looked over her shoulder at him, pressing into his cock, "to take care of that?"

"I can wait. You're exhausted."

"I usually have a lot of energy." She yawned. "You've exhausted me tonight."

"Ah, so that's what I have to do," he teased. "Give you orgasms to help you sleep."

"Insomniacs the world over will be lining up for that treatment. Why, you might be able to charge them a whole ten bucks."

"Brat!"

She squealed as he popped her ass. He felt himself grinning. They might have a ways to go. There were still hurdles to be crossed. But he knew it would all be worth it. All those years alone and trying to atone, and he'd been given his salvation.

This beautiful, broken girl was all his.

And he'd kill to protect her.

Tabby woke with a gasp, startled.

Unsure where she was, she glanced around. Then she realized her nightlight was casting shadows of stars across the ceiling. Razor had spotted the nightlight when they'd grabbed her stuff, and he'd insisted on setting it up in their bedroom. She'd worried that it might keep him awake. He'd just kissed her and told her not to stress.

Speaking of Razor, his arm was around her waist and he had

her tucked up into his body.

He was murmuring to her quietly and she realized she must have had a nightmare. She'd woken up the other night from a nightmare to find him talking to her, telling her that she was safe, that nothing would harm her with him here.

And he thought he wasn't a superhero?

Huh.

Maybe not for anyone else, but for her he was.

She lay there, letting her breathing grow more even, hoping he'd be able to go back to sleep, even though she knew she wouldn't. She couldn't get up and go for a jog, but maybe she could do some sit-ups or something.

Anything to burn up the energy now buzzing through her.

"I can hear you thinking," Razor murmured.

"Sorry," she replied quietly. "I'll get up so I don't keep you awake."

He tightened his arm around her waist. "No, you don't."

"I won't go anywhere, I'll just make the coffee and watch some TV or something."

"You should go back to sleep."

"I won't. I'm too wired."

"I have an idea how to help." He cupped her breast through the T-shirt she wore. It was one of his. She liked being surrounded by him. She'd put it and some panties on after their shower. "Take your panties off and slip your leg back over mine."

"Razor," she muttered.

"Do as you were told," he replied firmly.

She sucked in a breath. He'd used that tone a few times with her last night, even though he'd been less demanding than she'd thought he would be.

"Unless you want to see if a spanking has the same effect. Personally, I'd want the orgasm."

"No, no," she squeaked as she slipped off her panties and then pushed her leg back over his.

"Good girl. Now, close your eyes." He pushed his hand up under her T-shirt. "From now on, no panties in bed."

"What?"

"Unless you're on your period. Then I'll allow it."

Allow it?

Mr. Bossy was back.

"Allow?"

"Allow," he said firmly. "Now, are your eyes closed, or do we have to test whether a spanking will help you sleep?"

"They're closed." She crossed her fingers then she realized what she'd done.

Shit.

"They weren't closed, but they are now," she hastily said.

His hand paused in its movement under her T-shirt.

"Good girl."

"For closing my eyes?"

"For telling me the full truth."

Warmth filled her that turned into a raging volcano as he teased her breasts. He wouldn't let her move, wouldn't let her touch him. His fingers plucked at her nipples before lightly teasing them. By the time he moved away, she was breathing heavily, her body so ready to come it felt like it was a wire pulled taut.

At breaking point.

He moved his fingers down to her pussy. "Someone is very wet."

"Please. Please."

"Do you need to come?"

"Yes."

"Ask nicely."

"Please, Daddy, let me come."

"That's my good girl. Now come for me. Come nice and hard."

She was happy to say that she obliged.

20

"I've got a surprise for you," Razor told her the next morning as they sat drinking coffee in the living room.

"You do? What is it?" She gave him a worried look.

"Come here." He crooked a finger at her, not liking that look on her face. He knew it was an impossible dream to hope she'd never had to worry again. But he'd do his best to mitigate most of her concerns and fears.

If anyone deserved to live a carefree life, it was Tabby. She was the most loyal and self-sacrificing person he'd ever met. He knew she'd give the shirt off her back to help someone else. It was up to him to ensure she didn't go too far.

"Oh, that sort of surprise." She smirked at him as he lifted her onto his lap.

"No, not that sort of surprise, brat," he told her. "I don't constantly have sex on the brain, you know."

"You don't? That's disappointing."

He gave her a light slap on her thigh. "Give a girl a few orgasms and it gets her sassiness going."

"Hm, must be all the blood moving around my body."

"Must be," he murmured, kissing her cheek. Then he nuzzled his nose against hers. "You're gorgeous when you smile."

"I haven't had a lot to smile about. Until you."

"I'm glad I make you happy, baby girl. But I do have another surprise. I just need another hour or so to make it happen. Can you wait out here like a good girl?"

She narrowed her gaze. "You have to leave?"

"Nope, I'll be in the spare bedroom."

"The one I slept in?"

"No, the other one down the end of the hall. It's smaller."

They'd gotten up earlier than he'd intended. He didn't like how little sleep she got. He needed to think of a way to help her relax.

They'd ended up spending an hour or so in his home gym in the basement, with him keeping a close watch on her so she didn't use her foot any more than she should be. When he'd checked it this morning, it hadn't been swollen which pleased him. He'd hate to think they'd hurt it further last night.

After showering, he'd made them both breakfast. It was only ten, so he had plenty of time to do what he wanted with her.

"Promise you won't peek. I want you to get the full surprise."

"I promise."

"Good girl. You're going to like it."

SHE WATCHED as he walked away after setting her down on the sofa. He had the juiciest butt she'd ever encountered. And those shoulders. Don't get her started.

Then there were his hands.

His mouth.

His tongue.

The man was just multitalented. That was for sure.

She wondered what the surprise was. She was feeling surprisingly relaxed after their gym session. It wasn't a jog, but maybe the workout combined with all those orgasms was helping keep the buzz of energy at bay.

After about forty minutes, she looked up to see him walk into the room.

"Right, give me five minutes then come knock on the door, okay?"

"All right," she said slowly. "This isn't one of those things where I knock, then open the door and you're naked, right? I mean, not that it's a problem. Just checking."

"Give a girl a few orgasms and she turns into a freaking smart ass," he muttered as he turned and walked away.

She grinned. She definitely felt freer than she had in forever. The longer she spent with Razor, the more the heavy veil over her lifted.

And the real Tabby could shine through.

After five minutes, she moved down the hallway. Luna padded along behind her and she placed her hand on the dog's head as she knocked on the door.

"Close your eyes," Razor commanded.

Nerves filled her. Then she told herself not to be silly. This was Razor. He wasn't going to do anything to frighten her. And he'd seemed kind of excited about whatever the surprise was.

"My eyes are closed," she told him.

She felt a shift in the air as the door opened then he took hold of her hands. "Follow me."

He led her into the room and she had to fight hard not to tremble.

This is Razor. Trust him.

"All right, open them. Luna, that's not yours," Razor scolded.

She opened her eyes and the first thing she saw was Luna sitting in front of her with a stuffed fish in her mouth.

Tabby burst into laughter as Luna looked sadly up at Razor.

"Don't laugh. She knows that's not for her." Razor sighed as both she and Luna turned to stare at him. "I swear, the two of you think you can wrap me around your little finger and tail ..."

"You mean, we can't?"

He grunted. "Fine, Luna. Go." He turned to her as Luna trotted off with her loot. "You do realize you gave her one of your toys. And now you're probably going to have to guard the rest of your stuffies from her."

"I'll share my stuffies with Luna," she said slowly, turning around. "As long as it's not Snappy, Scooby, or my squishy Mystery Machine. What is this?" She'd done a full circle and she still couldn't take it in.

There was a corner seat with storage underneath that ran under the window and down the next wall. On the walls, decals had been plastered everywhere with all the characters from Scooby-Doo. In one of the corners, there were a few stuffies, some fish, an octopus, and a shark. Across the ceiling, fairy lights had been strung. But the very best thing was against the other wall.

"A Mystery Machine bed?" she asked, turning to look at him. It was a raised bed. She climbed in and gasped as she took in the fairy lights that lit up the space. He'd put some cushions in here along with book shelves.

It was magical.

"I thought if you wanted, you could read in there. Or play. You know, when you needed downtime."

She crawled back out and then she realized she could climb into the driver's side of the Mystery Machine.

"The steering wheel works!"

"Yep, and toot the horn."

When she pressed on the horn, the Scooby-Doo theme music played.

"Daddy! This is amazing!"

"You like?"

"Like! I love it!" She climbed out and threw herself at him. He hugged her tight.

"Good, I wanted you to have your space. Somewhere where you could chill and your Little would be happy. I thought she might be more relaxed in here."

"I think it's perfect." Looking around, her eyes blurred with tears. "I can't believe you did this for me."

"Come here." He tugged her close, hugging her tight. "Why wouldn't I do this for you? I'd do anything for you."

"But what about the bed? Will I sleep in here sometimes?"

"Never," he growled. "I won't have it."

She rolled her eyes at him. He bopped her lightly on the nose then pointed a finger at her. "Did you just roll your eyes at me, baby girl?"

Reaching up, she nipped his finger. Then her eyes widened in shock.

"Did you bite me?"

"Sorry, Daddy," she squealed.

"See that corner." He pointed at the one corner of the room that didn't have anything in it.

"Yes."

"That's the naughty Tabby-baby corner. I think I'll get a wall decal made up saying that."

"No, Daddy!"

"Yep. That's a good idea. Rolling your eyes means getting sent to the corner. Understand?"

"Yes, Daddy."

"And you won't ever spend a night apart from me. You'll spend every night in our bed, in my arms."

Happiness filled her at his over-the-top caveman demand. Because that was when she felt safest. In his arms. And she didn't want to think about sleeping without him.

"Then what's the bed for, Daddy?"

"That's for naps."

She burst into laughter. "Oh, Daddy. You're so funny."

"That wasn't a joke." He folded his arms over his broad chest, giving her a look that said he meant business.

"I'm a big girl. I don't need a nap."

"You're a Little girl. My baby. And yeah, you do. You don't get enough sleep as it is."

She frowned. Well, she couldn't deny that. And honestly, when she thought about it, there were days when a nap didn't sound so bad. But she didn't think she could sleep.

"I'll never sleep, Daddy."

"We'll see. I have ideas to help with that."

"Like orgasms."

"Greedy baby." He grinned as he lightly smacked her bottom.

Yeah, she was getting orgasms to help her sleep. Honestly, she was a bit worried she was getting addicted.

"There's more. Go have a look in the drawers under the corner seat."

She opened up the drawers and found them filled with puzzles and board games. And then she pulled out a box that made her squeal. "It's a detective kit!"

"Sure is." He gave her an indulgent smile as she opened it all up. Inside was a magnifying glass, spy glasses, two small cameras, a fingerprinting kit, crime scene tape, and an invisible ink pen. "Now, if there are any mysteries, you'll be able to solve them."

"Daddy, this is awesome! I need a mystery to solve."

"We'll see what comes along." He winked at her. "And there's more in the closet."

Moving to the closet, she opened it, staring in at the clothes hanging on the rail and folded in the cubby holes.

"Didn't buy you too much. Wasn't sure what you'd like. But there're some shorts, skirts, and tops since we'll be coming into summer soon. Oh, and I bought you another onesie."

She drew it out with a squeal. "It's a turtle. I love it."

"Yeah?"

"Yes, Daddy, you're amazing. I don't know how you managed this."

He shrugged. "I had some help. And you know how Sav came into the office yesterday and sat with you?"

"Yes. He was grouchy the entire time. He wouldn't even talk to me. I don't think he's forgiven me for touching him. I don't know if he likes me."

"Well, we set this all up then. The hardest thing was the bed, but Spike picked that up with his truck for me. And we've talked about Sav. He likes you just fine. He just doesn't know what to do with you. He's not used to someone sticking up for him. And now he's surrounded by all these people with more loyalty in their little toe than most other people have . . ." Razor shrugged "He'll get used to it. I did."

"Okay, I'll be patient with him."

"There's some chalk under the window seat too, as well as some painting and crafting materials. Thought you could try different activities. See what you liked. Since you didn't get to do much in your childhood." He shrugged as though it was no big deal.

But it was. It was a huge deal.

"Daddy, this is the nicest, most amazing thing anyone has ever done for me."

"Yeah?"

"Yeah." She turned and hugged him again, climbing him so she could wrap her legs around him.

"Careful of your ankle," he warned.

"If I hurt it, you'll carry me everywhere."

"Course I will. That doesn't mean you get to be careless, though."

"Okay, Daddy."

"There's something else we need to do." He set her down then went into one of her drawers and pulled out some chalk. She was puzzled when he stopped by a black patch painted on the wall near the naughty corner.

Gah, naughty corner. As if she'd need that? She was going to be perfectly behaved.

Up at the top, he wrote something in pink.

Tabby's rules.

Oh.

She shuffled from foot to foot. "We don't have to write them up there, Daddy."

"Oh, but we do. Have you thought of any more limits?"

She cleared her throat. "No humiliation. And I don't think I could deal with being tied down. Not yet, anyway. Also, nothing over my eyes. I don't like the dark. Or being left alone. I couldn't stand it if you suddenly stopped talking to me or something."

"I'd never do that as punishment, baby girl."

She let out a relieved breath. Even though it hadn't been exactly like that with her mom, it kind of felt that way. If Razor did that to her . . . well, it would be hard for her to cope with.

"Right. If there's anything else, you tell me."

He wrote out some rules as he spoke. Number one was not hiding if something upset or hurt her. Number two was realizing her worth.

"Realizing your worth means that you don't throw yourself into dangerous situations and that you keep yourself healthy. Because you know that I would be devastated without you."

"Okay, Daddy," she whispered.

Rule three was she had to respect herself. "That means no putting yourself down."

"All right, Daddy."

"Good girl. Rule four is no going anywhere alone."

"Because of Mr. X?"

"Exactly."

"Rule five is that you must call Daddy a hottie at least once a day. And hug and kiss him at least five times a day."

"Hold up there, buster."

"Yeah? What's wrong with that?"

"You've gone a step too far. A hottie once a day?"

"Shall I make it twice?"

"Your ego is going to be impossible, isn't it?"

He just grinned at her. "I think that will do for now. We'll add to them if we need to.

"Can I put on one of my outfits now if we're done with the stinky rules?" She started rifling through them.

"You mean the rules that Tabby needs to be safe?" he countered. "Yes, we're done and you can put on whatever you like. It's all yours."

"Yay! But you've got to wait out in the living room."

"I thought I'd help you get dressed."

"Nuh-uh, I'm going to do a parade."

"All right then, baby girl. You do your parade. But first, gimme some sugar." He tapped his cheek and leaned down for her to kiss it. Then he turned his head to the other side so she could kiss that cheek. Then his lips.

"You can have sugar anytime you want, Daddy."

"How do I look?" she asked shyly as she walked into the living room, where he sat on the sofa.

She was wearing the Scooby socks he'd bought her. They went up to her knees and had these dog ears that flopped out. She wasn't wearing any shoes. A dark blue skirt nearly reached her knees and was paired with a blue and white striped top with long sleeves.

"You look so good, baby girl," he murmured, taking her in. She'd put her hair into two braids and tied them with blue bows. "Good enough to eat. Do a twirl for me."

She went to spin.

"Slowly," he barked. "Your ankle is still recovering."

She rolled her eyes. "Daddy, you need to stop worrying. My ankle is nearly as good as new. See?" Balancing on one foot, she held the other out and turned it. "I think I could go running tomorrow."

"I think not," he told her firmly. "When you can move around without wincing, then we'll talk," he told her firmly. "Now turn. Slowly."

"Well?" she asked after moving around until she faced him once more.

"I think you're so damn gorgeous that I can't believe you're here with an old man like me."

"You're not old." She walked closer and he drew her onto his lap so she straddled him. Her skirt went up her thighs. Oh yeah, he liked this outfit.

"Number on my driver's license says different. Same as the gray hairs in my beard."

"I think they're sexy. You'd make a great Santa Claus." She lightly tugged at his beard.

He raised his eyebrows. "Because of my belly full of jelly?"

"Don't worry, Daddy. It only jiggles when you laugh."

"Why, you little," he spluttered.

She giggled, then buried her face in his chest as she laughed.

"That deserves a spanking," he growled at her. "My belly does not jiggle."

He rolled her onto the sofa then knelt on the floor and started to tickle her. She tried to fight him, pushing at his hands as she laughed. He managed to get her onto her tummy, and gave her a few sharp smacks on her ass.

"Daddy, no! That's no fair! No spanking Tabby."

"Tabby needs to be a good girl then, doesn't she?"

"Tabby is always a good girl, Daddy. It's Daddy who has to be good."

"Oh, I do, do I? And what would I have to do to be good?"

"Hm." She sat up and tapped a finger against her chin. "Buy Tabby ice cream."

"Really?"

"Yes." She nodded. "And let her go running."

"Yeah, that's not happening. And if Tabby tries to go running before I let her, then she's going to have a very hot bottom."

"See, that right there isn't being good, Daddy."

"You don't think a good Daddy would spank your behind when you do something to put your health at risk?"

"Exactly. No spanking. It's settled then. Wanna cookie?"

"No, I don't want a cookie, you brat. So I'm guessing in your mind, Daddy would be a pushover, huh?"

"Well, only when it comes to his Little girl."

"His Little girl?"

"Yes, Daddy," she huffed. "And by the way, that's me."

"Ahh, that's who you are."

"Daddy!" She stood and stomped her good foot but standing on her weak ankle made her wobble. Razor quickly grabbed her, drawing her onto his lap.

"Easy, baby girl. You're going to hurt yourself." He hugged her tight. "Of course, you're my Little girl. And I want to do the best job I can to take care of you. Which means making sure you follow the rules."

She sighed. "Rules schmules. Shall I go put on the next outfit, Daddy?"

"Yep, can't wait to see it. Then after your parade, how about you get your chalk? I've got some jobs to do outside and you can draw me a picture on the pavement while I work."

That sounded perfect.

SHE LOOKED DOWN at the hopscotch she'd drawn on the pavement. She'd already completed her fashion parade of every outfit in her wardrobe. Daddy had loved every one, of course. He'd insisted she wear something warm to come outside, though. So she'd put on some tights and a long-sleeved jumper that ended mid-thigh. It was soft and cozy.

Hm, she needed a stone. Daddy was doing something with the gutters. Which was really boring and after he'd told her that she wasn't allowed up on the roof, she'd stopped paying attention.

She'd have to use her left foot to jump on since her right foot was still healing, so she wouldn't be able to do the four and five and the seven and eight properly since both feet were meant to go down. Still, she thought she could figure it out.

But yeah, she needed the perfect stone. Moving towards the garden, she took a look around. It was really pretty out here. Just what she'd expect from grandma's house.

Then she came across it.

A massacre.

Opening her mouth, she let out a screech of horror.

It was terrible. Shocking.

Sobbing, she moved back towards the house.

"What? What is it? Tabby, where are you?" Razor demanded, climbing down the ladder. Turning, he caught her just as she threw herself at him.

"Daddy, it's horrible."

"What is? What happened? Baby girl, are you all right?" He ran his hands over her as though searching for injury.

"Daddy, there's been . . . there's been a murder!"

He froze, then to her shock, he picked her up, putting her on his hip. "What? Where? Who? Fuck, let me call the cops."

Oh.

Whoops.

"Daddy, not an actual murder," she said as he started carrying her inside.

"What the hell? Who is it? Shit."

"Daddy, it's not a person who's been murdered," she told him urgently.

He stilled. Then he set her down on her feet and grasped hold of her shoulders. "What?"

"It's not a person."

"Then what is it?"

"One of my stuffies!"

"What?"

"It's one of my stuffies! It's been murdered."

"Not Snappy or Scooby," he said, looking worried.

Okay, that was sweet that he was so concerned about her favorite stuffies.

"No, or the Mystery Machine, thank goodness. It's Octy."

"Octy?"

"The octopus." Obviously. "He's been slaughtered. Torn to pieces."

Razor frowned. "Is that so? Well, I can guess who—"

"I've got to solve the mystery," she interjected quickly.

"The mystery?"

"Uh-huh, I'll get my detective kit."

Understanding filled his face. "Right, yes, it's best you do that. You won't get upset dealing with a murder victim, though, will you?"

She sniffled. "It is very distressing. But it's my job as a detective to get to the bottom of this mystery. I'll be back in a moment. I have questions for you."

"Questions? For me? Surely, you don't think that I had anything to do with this." He gave her a shocked look.

"Daddy, everyone's guilty until proven innocent."

"Um, baby girl, I think that's the other way around."

She glared at him. "Who is the detective here, Daddy?"

"Well, you, baby girl."

"Then let me do my job."

As she turned away, he gently grasped hold of her wrist. "One moment. I need to talk to you about something."

"Daddy, it's a murder. This is very time-sensitive. The murderer could be getting away."

"I understand. And I'll let you go in just a moment. But first, I need to ask that next time there is a murder, perhaps you could lead with the fact that it was a stuffie that was murdered, not a person."

"A stuffie is important too, Daddy."

Razor raised his hands in the air. "Oh, I know. I agree."

"They have feelings. Their life has meaning."

"Definitely. But just, to save Daddy from having a heart attack? Please?"

"Okay, Daddy. I'll take that under advisement. But, for now, please go sit outside and wait for me to conduct my investigation."

Fifteen minutes later, she'd set up the crime scene and dusted for prints. Scooby was acting as her assistant. She'd taken Daddy's fingerprints for analysis. She had one more witness to interview.

"Well, Luna, where were you between the hours of eleven-thirty and twelve-thirty?"

The dog let out a bark and she gasped. "Daddy!"

"What? What is it?" He walked quickly out of the house. He was carrying a plate of sandwiches.

"I've found the culprit. And she's got the evidence of her crime, in her teeth!" She pointed to Luna.

"Uh-oh." Razor came over and stood beside her. "Luna, did you sneak into Tabby's bedroom and steal Octy?"

Luna woofed.

"And did you murder poor Octy, Luna?" she asked.

Another woof.

Tabby shook her head. "What do you think we should do with the guilty party, Daddy?"

Razor sighed. "Well, I think we'll have to ban her from your bedroom."

Luna whined.

"Daddy, I don't think we need to be so harsh. Poor Luna." She dropped down and put her arm around the dog. "She didn't mean to."

"She's just going to get more of the stuffies, baby girl. Do you want to risk their safety?"

"No, I guess not. I'm sorry, Luna. No more stuffies for you."

Luna licked her cheek.

"I guess she's not too cut up about it."

"Come on, time for lunch."

Standing, she put her hand in Razor's and let him lead her to the outdoor table.

"You did a good job finding the guilty party, baby girl."

"I know, Daddy. I'm an excellent detective. Do you think I could join the Scooby-Doo gang?"

"I'm sure they'd love to have you," he said as he pushed in her chair then handed her a sandwich. "Unfortunately, Daddy just couldn't spare you. I need you here with me."

"You would be lost without me, Daddy."

"That I would."

"Daddy, where are the Scooby snacks?" she asked, looking around. "Scooby's been working hard, and he needs his snacks."

"I'm sorry, Scooby. Let me go see what I've got." He returned with a bowl of Luna's food. She wrinkled her nose. "Doesn't look very appetizing."

"It's dog food and Scooby is a dog."

She gasped, putting her hands over Scooby's ears. "Daddy! You'll hurt his feelings." Removing her hands, she gave Scooby a pat. "I'm sorry, Scooby. Daddy isn't a very good waiter."

"Excuse me?"

"I agree, Scooby. We should dock his pay."

"Oh, how much money are you taking?"

"What do you say, Scooby? Shall we take two dollars an hour off him?"

"Jeez, that's harsh."

"What's even harsher was that you were only on a buck an hour," she told him. "So now you owe us money."

She giggled as Razor shook his head.

"You and Scooby are a bad combination."

21

Tabby tried to stifle the yawn as she climbed into the truck on Wednesday morning. Razor, who held the door open for her, turned her face towards him, staring down at her with concern.

"You're exhausted. You need more sleep."

"It's hump day."

He snorted. "Right. And that's meant to explain everything?"

"Everyone's tired on hump day. They're waiting to get to the weekend. Everyone knows this, Daddy."

"Right. Or, it could be that you don't get enough sleep and then you get up and exercise, so you're exhausted before you even start the day."

"I'm sorry if I keep waking you up."

"Hey, that's not what I'm worried about. If you keep running on fumes, then you're going to get sick. Maybe I should leave you at home today."

No. She didn't want to stay home. She loved Razor's house, but she didn't want to be here alone.

"I'll be fine, promise."

"I don't know. I don't want you wearing yourself out. But then, I don't want to leave you on your own, either. I wonder if someone could come sit with you."

"I don't need a babysitter, Daddy," she told him, affronted at the thought. How embarrassing would that be?

"That's exactly what you need. If I leave you alone, you'll get up to all sorts of mischief."

"That's just not true."

"Maybe you could take a nap at work."

Yeah. That wasn't going to happen. "If I can't nap at home, I'm not going to be able to nap at work."

His face lightened and he smiled happily at her.

"What?" she asked.

"You called this place home."

"It is, isn't it?"

"It absolutely is." Leaning in, he kissed her and she melted into the seat. When he drew away, she had to fight the need to drag him back to her. He was doing his best to help her sleep with endless orgasms. But he hadn't made a move to fuck her. Maybe that was the problem.

"Not being fucked is the problem?" he asked, amusement in his voice.

"Oh God! I said that out loud?"

He threw his head back and laughed. Even when he stopped laughing, his eyes were twinkling. "I'll take that into consideration."

Her breath caught. "Really?"

"Really."

Oh hell yeah.

"You know what else might help me sleep?"

"Besides sex?"

"Um, yep." Her cheeks grew hot. Sheesh, she sounded like such a hussy. "Being able to go for a run."

He immediately frowned, shaking her head. "Your ankle isn't fully healed."

"Daddy, it's fine. You're being a fusspot."

"A fusspot? If you go running too soon, you'll reinjure yourself, and then you won't be able to run for weeks."

Drat. He had a point.

"Maybe we can leave a bit earlier today," he told her. "You can have a nap. Besides, I'm hoping that something will arrive today to help you relax."

"What is it?"

"It's a surprise."

"Okay, Daddy."

"No questions?"

"I like your surprises."

"I'm glad, baby girl. Because I love surprising you. Now, let's get to work." Leaning in, he kissed her, then did up her seatbelt.

JUST BEFORE LUNCHTIME, she knew something was wrong. Her tummy started to cramp.

Shit. Shit.

Tabby hastily grabbed out her handbag and jumped up, rushing into the bathroom.

Well, crap.

Just awesome. She searched through her handbag for a tampon, letting out a sigh of relief when she found one. Her period had never been regular, so it generally caught her unawares.

Only problem was, one tampon wasn't going to last her until the end of the day. Even if Razor still planned on leaving early. After cleaning up, she moved back into the office and closed down her computer. She'd go out and grab what she needed.

Ouch. Ouch.

Damn, the other issue of having irregular periods is that they were often painful as hell. She slowly made her way out to the workshop. She left Luna in the office. The poor dog whined at her, but if she had to walk down to the store, she didn't want to take her.

Razor was standing, talking to Sav and Dart. Trying to look like her insides weren't being twisted by a giant hand, she made her way over to them.

Razor had his back to her, but Sav was facing her. He frowned, his gaze roaming over her.

"What's wrong with you?" Sav barked, making her pause.

"Wrong? Nothing's wrong." She smiled widely.

Now all three of them were staring at her.

"Baby girl? You're awfully pale. Aren't you feeling well?" Razor asked with concern in his voice.

"I feel fine."

They all gave her looks of disbelief.

"I need to go out. I'll be back soon. You want me to get anything?"

"You need to go out?" Razor asked incredulously.

"Yep. I'm going out."

Razor crossed his arms over his chest. "You're not going out."

As he spoke, she noticed that Sav nodded in agreement. What was with that?

"Razor, I need to go out."

"Why?"

"I don't have to explain why. I'm not a prisoner," she snapped.

She wished the words back as soon as she said them. Crap. Shoot.

Razor's eyes narrowed. "Of course you're not. But I don't want you going out on your own. And you know why."

Damn it. What were the chances this Mr. X guy would come

after her? And while she was out getting sanitary products? That wasn't likely, right?

Did Sav and Dart know about Mr. X? Likely not if he wasn't mentioning his name. She didn't think that Dart had anything to do with the Iron Shadows.

Another cramp hit her then and she groaned.

Dart's eyes narrowed.

"I just need to go out for a few minutes," she said. "I'll be back soon. I don't even have to drive, I can go to the convenience store down the block."

She was starting to wish she'd just gone instead of telling him. But she'd known he would flip out if she did that.

"What do you need to get?" Razor asked. "I'll send one of the guys instead."

"No way!" she squealed.

Several people turned to look over at her. Oh, Lord. She was acting like a crazy person. It was just tampons.

But that was something that Tommy was most certainly not going out and buying her. Ew.

She could feel her cheeks flare red. Dart leaned into Razor and said something quietly to him. Probably telling Razor that she was insane and he should run. She wouldn't blame him. Then Razor stared at her again. He nodded.

"I'll be back soon," he said to Dart and Sav. Dart just nodded back while Sav appeared confused.

Razor wrapped an arm around her, leading her over to his truck. "You have everything you need?"

"Ah, yes," she said confused. He led her to the passenger side of the truck.

After opening the door, he lifted her in and buckled her seatbelt. She wasn't sure why but he liked to be the one to fasten her seatbelt. And it was such a sweet thing to do that she didn't protest.

It was like he was confirming that she was safe. In fact, he usually tugged at the belt afterward as though ensuring that she was properly buckled in.

He climbed around into the driver's seat. "Where do you want to go?"

"Just the convenience store is fine."

"Sure?"

"Yes, I'm sure. Razor, you've got more important things to do. You really don't need to drive me. I can go on my own."

"You're not going on your own. You know it's not safe."

"What are the odds that Mr. X would come after me? I mean, I'm no one. I don't mean as much to you as Millie does to Spike, say. Or Emme to Reyes."

He moved his truck to the side of the road, about half a block from the convenience store. Kind of odd to park here when he'd insisted on driving her. She really could have just walked.

"What did you just say?" he whispered.

Oh shoot.

She realized too late that he was furious. Turning, she saw he had his hands clenched around the steering wheel.

Taking in a deep breath, she reminded herself that Razor wouldn't hurt her. Obviously, he was upset with what she'd just said.

Although she wasn't entirely sure why. It was just the truth, right? How could she be as important to him as the others were to their men?

"Repeat what you just said, Tabitha."

Uh-oh.

Girl, you are in so much trouble right now. She could practically feel her bottom cheeks warming as she sat there.

"I don't think that would be a good idea," she whispered.

"Why is that?"

"Because you already look like you're gonna explode."

"And why would I explode? Hm? Why would I find it so upsetting for you to tell me that I don't love you as much as Spike loves Millie? That losing you wouldn't completely devastate me? Wouldn't turn my world on its axis? Make everything darker? Huh? Why wouldn't that upset me?"

She swallowed.

"And please stop looking at me like I would hurt you. I would never . . . I could never. . ." his voice was a soft whisper. "Please tell me you know that." She could hear the plea in his voice.

"I don't think you're going to hurt me. I promise. Sometimes I just forget. Momentarily. I think it's an instinct thing. It's not like I'd be with you if I truly thought that you would harm me."

"Good." He stared out the window for a long moment.

"You really love me?" she whispered. Her? He really loved her?

"It kills me that you say that with such disbelief. As if I couldn't possibly love you." The more agitated he became, the thicker his drawl. "Why wouldn't I love you, baby girl?"

She licked her lips. "That feels like a trick question."

He laughed, but there was no humor in the sound. Just sadness. She'd let him down. She hated that she'd done that. And now she had to fix it.

"I guess I'm not used to being loved."

He nodded.

"I didn't realize that you felt that way."

He tensed.

Shit. She was messing this up. Leaning back, she put her hands over her eyes. "I'm such a fuck-up. I don't know what to say to make this better. Am I supposed to apologize? I don't want you to be upset with me. I'm terrified of losing you. I love you so much that it would be impossible to carry on without you. I do—"

She was cut off as he slammed his hand over her mouth. Then he reached down with his other hand and undid the buckle on her belt. Suddenly, she was picked up and pulled onto his lap.

"Razor! What on—"

"You love me?"

She blinked. "Of course I love you. How could I not?" She threw his words back at him.

"Maybe because I'm a bossy old man, who's over-protective and likes to spank?"

"Oh."

"Oh? Oh what?" he demanded.

"Well, I figured those were your best qualities."

He stared down at her for a moment before grinning. "They are. Brat."

"I love you, Jeremiah," she told him quietly. "You're the best thing to ever happen to me."

"God, baby girl. Don't ever tell me that you're not as important to me as the others are to their men. I might just lose it, understand?"

"Lose what? Your marbles?"

"That too," he told her dryly. "You're precious to me. And I'm sorry if that means I get stifling, that you're not allowed to go to the convenience store on your own or to sleep a night away from me. But that's just the way it has to be. Because nothing is going to happen to you. Understand?"

"I'm sorry if I was being difficult," she murmured as he rubbed his hand up and down her back. "I just needed to go to the store. Alone."

"You don't need to do anything alone. What do you need?"

"I've got my period. I need some stuff."

"All right, let's go then. Are you in a lot of pain? Cramps? Do you need a heating pad?"

"What? No. I just need some pain relief and other stuff. I'll be fine. Actually, I can just walk from here. I'll be back soon."

He held her, not letting her climb off his lap. Shoot. She knew it wouldn't be that easy.

"Look at me, baby girl."

She tilted her head back, staring up at him. He studied her. "You get that I was married?"

"Yes." What did that have anything to do with her period?

"And I have four sisters? I grew up in a household with five women?"

"Right."

"You think I haven't bought tampons before? Or fetched heating pads? Or been sent out for chocolate and painkillers? Baby, I've done all of that. You think I wouldn't want to give you whatever you needed? Help you how I could?"

"Oh. Sorry. I guess, I'm not used to anyone helping me."

"What happened when you got your first period?"

"Razor!"

"Sorry, do you need to go get the stuff right away?"

"No, I found a tampon in my bag. It's just . . . I'm not used to talking about this."

"Who explained everything to you? Your mother was still around then?"

"Ah, no, my mom died before I got it."

"Oh, baby. So who helped you?" he asked softly.

"Jared," she whispered.

"He did?"

"Yeah. He found me crying in the bathroom and figured out what was wrong. I mean, technically, I knew what was going on. I went to a private school and we learned about it in health. But I had no idea what to do. Jared told me to hop in the bath. Then he went out and bought me stuff. When he came back, he helped me go through it and figure it all out. I don't know what I would have done if it wasn't for him."

Razor grunted. "Don't want a reason to be thankful for the bastard." He kissed the top of her head. "Hop back in your seat and I'll drive closer."

She moved over.

"Seatbelt," he commanded.

"But we're only driving a minute down the road."

"And you're going to put on your seatbelt."

There he was, being all overprotective.

"Or I could get you some sort of harnessed baby car seat. That could work too."

"I'm fastening it, I'm fastening it," she said hastily, clicking the belt into place.

"Thought you might see it my way."

When they got to the store, she didn't expect Razor to follow her down the aisles, although she should have. He seemed really paranoid about this Mr. X.

There was no reason to think he'd come after her. But she guessed Razor was extra worried about losing her because of Sandy. Sympathy filled her at the thought and she promised herself that she'd be more careful from now on. She didn't want to stress him out.

"Shoot," she muttered as she stood in front of the shelves with pain relief.

"What's wrong?"

"The kind I like isn't here."

"What kind do you usually have?" he asked as he grabbed a packet.

The kind that wasn't pills.

"I'll be fine without."

"No, you won't. Get this stuff. Unless you have an allergy?"

She thought about lying, but instead, she shook her head.

Tell him the truth.

"I don't like taking pills," she blurted out.

"What?" He turned to look at her.

"I don't like swallowing them."

"But when you had your sore ankle . . ." he trailed off as she gave him a guilty look.

"I didn't take them," she confessed.

"So you can't take any of these?"

"No."

"Right, we need to talk. Come on." He left the pills behind and they moved to the cash register.

She reached into her handbag. But before she could even get her wallet out, Razor had paid with his credit card.

"You didn't have to pay for me." She scowled at him.

"I already had my card out." He grabbed the bag with one hand and her hand with the other, then led her out. "I have a heating pad at home, but if you want to go get one now, we can."

She shook her head. "My periods are pretty irregular, so sometimes they can be quite painful and heavy, but I think I'll be all right until we get home."

He opened the door and lifted her in, placing the bag at her feet before he did up her seatbelt. "So that's why this period is only three weeks after your last one?"

Holy hell.

Why hadn't she thought of that? And how had he possibly remembered?

Who was she kidding? This is Razor. Nothing got past him.

She waited until he was in the driver's seat to turn to him. "I lied."

"About taking those painkillers? Yeah, I got that."

"Not that. I lied about my period. I didn't really mean to. It was just a little white lie and I crossed my fingers. See, I told you I had my period three weeks ago, but I didn't. I'm a lying liar-pants liar," she wailed.

"Okay, calm down. Why did you tell me you had your period?"

"I don't know, it just popped out. I wasn't getting groceries. Instead, I bought my fish and Scooby. Just like I lied when I said I was listening when you asked me to order a part that first week I started working. And I hate swallowing pills. I only like liquid pain relief."

"Why didn't you tell me?"

"What? That I'm a big baby who can't swallow pills because my asshole ex-husband drugged me?"

"Tabby, you should have said something." He looked at her, aghast.

"I've always had issues with taking pills. Something about the taste and texture. But after Luther drugged me, I can't even look at them without feeling nauseous."

He leaned over to hug her awkwardly.

"I'm so sorry, baby girl."

"It's not your fault," she whispered.

"I wish you'd told me. I only want to take care of you."

"I know." She felt terrible.

"We'll go to the pharmacy and get some liquid pain relief."

"We don't have to . . ." she trailed off at the look on his face.

Right.

Hush, Tabby.

He gently grasped hold of her chin and turned her face towards his. "No lies, not even small, white ones, understand?"

"Yes, Daddy. I understand."

"And you're getting fifteen."

"What! But, Daddy, you can't spank me! The lies happened before we were together."

"That's why you're only getting fifteen. I wouldn't normally punish you for things that happened before we were in a relationship, but this is important. However, I'll wait until the cramps have stopped."

Wow. That was so generous of him.

22

B y the time they pulled up to his house later that afternoon, she was feeling miserable. Not because of her period. Well, partially because of that. But mostly because she felt like she'd really messed up.

Razor parked in the garage and hopped down, letting Luna out of the backseat. Then he came around and helped her down.

"You're quiet, Tabby-baby," he said, taking hold of her hand. "Not feeling great?"

"I'm all right." Urgh, what was she doing? She shook her head. "Actually, no, I'm not feeling great."

"You need some more pain relief?"

"It's not that." She spotted two boxes sitting on the doorstep and it distracted her. "What's that?"

"Something I ordered for you."

"Great! Now I feel even worse," she cried as he opened the door. She stormed in and put in the code for the alarm. "I'm a terrible person."

"You're not a terrible person," he said as he carried the boxes in and set them down on the dining table.

She sat on a chair at the table and lay her head on her arms.

Razor placed his hand on the small of her back. "Come here."

He lifted her and then took her seat, settling her on his lap.

"I don't deserve you being nice to me," she muttered, even as she buried her face in his neck.

"Oh, you don't? You want me to be mean to you?"

"It's what I deserve."

"You don't think you're being a bit hard on yourself?"

"No." She sniffled.

"Okay. Then is there something that might make you feel better?"

She shook her head.

"You know the point of a spanking?"

"To hurt someone's bottom."

"Well, I guess, but not really. It's a deterrent for future behavior."

"Right."

"And it's a way for the person who is being spanked to be punished. To let go of any guilt they hold. To wipe the slate clean. Once a punishment is given, then all is forgiven."

"Really? But what if the person doing the spanking brings it up again?"

"I guess that happens," he conceded. "But with you and me, I want it as a way to move forward. Living with guilt isn't fun. For anyone. It can make you sick. It can make it hard to sleep. It can eat away at you."

"Yeah, I guess that's right." She sat up straight. "So what you're saying is I'll feel better if I'm punished."

"That's the hope."

"What if you do something wrong? Who spanks you?"

"Nobody spanks me. But you're right, there should be a consequence if I do something wrong."

"Like what?"

"Have you got any ideas?"

"Maybe you should have to piggyback me everywhere I want to go for a day."

He gave a solemn nod. "I can see where that would be a just punishment."

"Are you going to spank me then?" she whispered.

He rubbed her lower tummy. "I don't want to while you're already feeling yucky and down. Probably doesn't help that you're sleep-deprived."

"I think you should just do it. I don't wanna think about it anymore."

"All right, if you're sure."

"I'm sure." Nerves filled her as he put her on her feet.

"Go use the bathroom. When you come back, I want you to go stand in that corner and wait for me."

She looked to where he was pointing, but she was slightly confused. "Not the naughty corner in my playroom, Daddy?"

"Nope. I have something to set up in your bedroom." He got up and picked up both boxes that had been on the doorstep.

"But, Daddy . . ."

"Yes?"

"I don't deserve any more nice things."

"Just because you make a mistake or break a rule doesn't mean that you don't deserve nice things," Razor told her gently. "That's just nonsense. Besides, Daddy enjoys doing nice things for you. You wouldn't take that away from me, would you?"

"No, Daddy."

"Right, go use the bathroom. Then come back out. I expect to find you in that corner. Actually, wait. We'll get you changed first."

"Changed?"

"Yeah, after your spanking, you can take a nap."

"Daddy, that didn't go so well last time."

"I have an idea for this time. Although it might not be so fun with a hot bottom. We'll see. Go to the bathroom and meet me in your room so we can get you changed."

After using the bathroom, she walked into her room. He had a drill set and a stepladder in there. What was he doing?

"Come here."

He gestured at her and she saw he had an outfit on her bed. It was an all-in-one pajama set that had a drop seat.

"Take off everything except your panties and then we can get you dressed."

She slowly started to strip. He helped her, tugging off her top then getting her to hold onto his shoulders while he tugged off her pants. Soon she was just wearing her panties. She couldn't help but feel slightly self-conscious as she hugged herself.

"No need for that, baby girl," he murmured, helping her step into the outfit. It was blue with fish all over it. Really cute. He drew it up and helped her get her arms through the sleeves before doing up the short zip at the back.

"Perfect. Now, take yourself off to the corner in the dining room while I take care of this."

With a sigh, she turned. He landed a heavy slap on her ass making her squeal.

"Get moving, brat."

Fine, she was going, she was going.

Sheesh.

Corner time was weird.

She'd thought it would be boring, and it was. In fact, she fidgeted something fierce for the entire time. First, her foot itched, then her nose. Then she started to worry she might have some sort of rash. Then her back ached and she had to stretch.

"You really can't be still, can you?"

She gasped and turned suddenly, wincing as she landed heavily on her sore ankle.

"Shit! How did I forget about your foot? I should be shot. Are you all right?" Picking her up, he carried her over to the kitchen counter and set her down on it. He then gently grasped hold of her foot, checking it. "It doesn't appear swollen."

"Cause it's not. It's not sore either. I wasn't fidgeting because my ankle was sore. I just have excess energy."

"I still should have had you sit in the corner. You're sure your foot is fine?"

"Hunky-dory."

His lips twitched. "Hunky-dory? Really?"

"What's wrong with saying hunky-dory?"

"Nothing, if you're eighty."

"Well, I might be now that I'm living in grandma's cottage."

"You brat." He tickled her as she giggled and tried to push him away.

"Enough! Enough!"

"You're right. It is enough." Drawing back, he gave her a stern look. "Time for your punishment."

Uh-oh.

He lifted her down, putting her carefully on her feet. Taking hold of her hand, he led her to the table. Drawing out a chair, he sat and patted his lap.

"Maybe I need more corner time practice."

"You do," he confirmed. "You're not supposed to fidget around while standing in the corner. You're supposed to be thinking about what you did that resulted in you getting put in the corner."

"It's so hard, Daddy. I have ants in my pants."

"I know you do. Come here, now."

With a sigh, knowing she wasn't going to get out of it, she took his hand and he helped her over his lap. As soon as she lay on his thighs, she expected him to start whaling on her ass. But instead, he rubbed her lower back.

"How is your period pain? Got cramps?"

"It's all right, Daddy," she whispered. Would he ever cease to amaze her with his caring? Would she ever come to take this for granted? She sure as hell hoped not.

Because he was special.

And hers.

"That's good. I'm going to do this quickly, so we can get you settled and down for your nap with the heat pad." As he spoke, he undid the drop seat on her pajamas.

"I still don't think I'm gonna be able to nap, Daddy," she told him, tensing as he pulled down her panties until they were just under her cheeks.

"We'll see. The count is fifteen. Ready?"

"Yes, Daddy."

Before she even finished speaking, he started. His hand landed several smacks on her ass. It wasn't until about the third one that her brain seemed to catch up with what was happening. She let out a loud cry that had Luna howling.

Two more smacks landed, then Razor stopped, rubbing her lower back. "Luna, she's all right."

Tabby sucked in a breath. All right? She wasn't sure that she was all right. Her ass was already on fire. And there was more to come.

But she turned her head, trying to smile at the dog. "I'm okay, Luna."

"I might have to put her out," Razor said. He stood her up. "Sit for a moment, I'll be right back."

Was he for real? Sit? She wasn't sure she'd sit again. However, she did take the opportunity to rub at her bottom. Ouchy.

Razor was quick to return and he raised an eyebrow as he saw her. "No rubbing."

Her mouth dropped open. "That's not a rule."

"Oh, it definitely is." He took his seat again. "Rubbing is not allowed. Now, where were we?"

"You'd given me twelve already."

"Are you crossing your fingers?" he asked suspiciously.

She groaned. "It's like a sickness. Seriously. I don't even know I'm doing it."

"It's a habit we need to break, Tabby-baby. Now, we have to start over."

"What? Nooo," she groaned. But he began smacking her ass again. This time it was worse. This time, it felt like her bottom was a giant ball of fire. It was tender as hell. She didn't know how many spanks he got in before she was kicking her legs and trying to wriggle away from him.

"Daddy! Daddy!" she cried out.

He paused and she sucked in a sobbing breath.

"Okay, baby girl?" he asked, rubbing her back.

"N-no!"

"What's wrong? What hurts? Your foot? Your tummy?"

"My bottom!" She really thought that should be obvious. "Oh."

Oh? That's all he had to say? Oh?

"What do you mean, oh?"

"Well, your bottom is meant to hurt," he told her.

"Yes, but . . . it's worse than I thought."

"I'm sorry about that. But there wouldn't be much point if it didn't hurt. Right, you've got seven more to go."

Seven more?

This was terrible.

Then he began again. Tears dripped down her cheeks about three smacks in. She gave up on fighting. She knew this was going to happen no matter what. And once she relaxed and gave in, the spanking actually became easier to take.

Sure, her bottom might be hot. But she did deserve this. Strangely, the guilt started to melt away. Maybe it was a mind trick or something, but did it matter if it worked?

Razor gently turned her over on his lap until she was straddling his legs, facing him. She curled up against his chest and cried. It felt like she hadn't cried in years. In fact, she couldn't remember when she'd just let go like this.

Sure, when Luther hurt her, she'd often cry. And there had been times after he'd died that she'd wake up with tears dripping down her cheeks. She'd shed a few tears here and there. But nothing like this.

This felt cathartic.

"That's it, let it all out."

Funny, she'd expected him to tell her to stop. Or to hush. But Razor just held her, rocking her slightly back and forth. She loved being in his arms. He was so big, so strong, it was like nothing could touch her when he held her.

"Let's get you some tissues."

Great, she probably looked like a mess. He picked her up and carried her against his front with his arm under her ass.

"There, there, baby girl. You're all right now. Daddy has you. You're okay," he told her.

They were the same words that he often told her during the night, she realized. When she had a nightmare and he'd hug her tight and tell her that he had her.

They ended up in the bathroom and he handed her some tissues while he wet a washcloth. After she'd blown her nose and cleaned herself up, he wiped her face down with the cloth and then her hands. As she became more aware, she realized that her ass was still uncovered.

"Daddy, my drop seat is open." She attempted to pull up her panties, but he grabbed her hands, keeping them in front of her.

"Don't pull them up yet. I want to check your bottom."

Surely, he wasn't serious.

"My bottom is fine," she hastily told him. "It's right where you left it. You know, when you were pummeling it. Is your hand made out of concrete, by the way? Because I'm pretty sure I'm not going to be able to sit for at least a week."

He gave her an amused look. "I think you'll be okay. I didn't spank you that hard."

Didn't spank her that hard? Was he insane? She was serious about the not-sitting thing.

"Now turn around and bend over the counter."

"Why?" she asked suspiciously. "You already gave me the spanking. And I'm thinking you gave me extra. How are your counting skills?"

"I've been counting to fifteen since I was four," he told her.

"Four! Sheesh, I couldn't do that at four. Numbers are tricky."

"Yes, I know you have problems with them. I've seen your spreadsheets."

She gasped in shock. "Daddy! That's just mean."

"But true."

Well, she couldn't dispute that. Unfortunately. Numbers. Gah.

"And you got extras because we had to start again. Now, turn." He twirled a finger in the air.

Lord help her. She couldn't believe he was making her do this. "Daddy, this is just mean."

"No, this is what happens after every spanking to make sure you're all right."

"I think you just want to look at my butt."

"That too." He winked at her. "It's a mighty fine butt."

Well, she couldn't argue that either. So she turned and bent over the counter, pressing her hot cheek against the cool counter. Razor ran a finger over her warm bottom, making her jump and squeal.

"Looks good to me, Tabby-baby." He pulled up her panties and did up her drop seat before she stood and turned. "There's one thing we haven't spoken about."

"What's that?" she whispered.

"Anal play. I know I mentioned figging to you a while back."

"Yeah, I don't think that sounds like much fun, Daddy. I was always told don't mess food up with umm, butt stuff."

"Really? Who gave you that advice?"

"Oh, well, um, I think it was a cartoon."

"That's an interesting cartoon you were watching. Are anal punishments and play a hard limit?"

She opened her mouth to say yes. Then she thought about it. Was it a hard limit?

"I don't know. I've never done anything like that, so I don't know if I'll like it or not."

"But it's not a trigger?"

"I don't think it will be. Luther never did anything to me there."

He gently tilted her face up. She hadn't even realized that she'd ducked her gaze down.

"We'll see how it goes then? There's no rush. And if there is anything that makes you uncomfortable or scares you, then what do you do?"

"Say my safeword."

"Good girl. Now, let's go have a look at your surprise.

"Are you sure it can take my weight?" she asked as she watched him position the swing, which really just looked like a long piece of material that was looped over at the bottom and attached to the D-ring at the ceiling.

"Do you really think I'd allow you on something I hadn't tested myself?" he asked her.

"You mean it took your weight? Whoa, it must be strong."

"Are you calling me fat, brat!" he demanded.

"Never, Daddy. You're just big," she took in the look on his face and hastily added, "big Daddy. Big, handsome Daddy. Big, sexy, handsome Daddy with a cherry on top."

"Uh-huh, you keep trying to get yourself out of trouble."

"It's not working, Daddy?" She sniffled. "You don't think I'm cute?"

He shook his head. "You're too cute for my peace of mind. Thinking we need to make a few changes for when you leave the house."

"Like what?" she asked, puzzled.

"Long sleeves and pants. And a hat. Maybe a scarf that covers the bottom of your face. Yeah, that should work."

"So you want me to dress like a snowman?"

"I don't think snowmen wear pants. They don't exactly have legs."

"I wouldn't know," she sighed pathetically. "I've never made one."

"Never?"

"Before I moved to Chicago, we lived in Florida."

"How didn't I know that? But when you moved to Chicago, surely you could have made one."

"I guess. I was probably too old by the time I moved to Chicago, anyway."

"Never too old for a snowman. We'll make one when it first snows."

"Which won't be for a while."

"Hm. Come on, test this out." He held open the sides of the swing. "This is meant to make you feel safe, like you're being hugged. And it's fun."

She wasn't so sure, but she trusted him. She climbed in, sitting in it like a swing. It was surprisingly gentle on her poor bottom. It was fun when she swung, but she wasn't sure she got it.

"Lie back in it."

Turning, she put her legs up and lay back. He gently pushed her.

Oh.

Ohhh.

She closed her eyes and lay there, going back and forth gently through the air. It was like a giant hug. It was amazing. Then he drew the curtains and turned off the lights, so just the fairy lights twinkled.

Soothing music filled the room. Her limbs grew heavier as she started to relax. Maybe she could even sleep in here?

The swing was stopped and she frowned up at Razor. But it was as though he had read her mind because he had a heating pad, Snappy, and a fluffy, bright yellow blanket. He gave her the heating pad and she placed it on her lower tummy. He quickly tucked the blanket around her and then kissed her forehead, setting her off again.

This was amazing.

And she owed it all to him. How was it that he always knew what she needed without her even asking?

RAZOR PEEKED into the swing as he heard a quiet sigh come from her. Her eyes were closed, her face peaceful. A smile curled his lips up.

She was adorable.

So much for her not being able to nap, hm? She was fast asleep, and to his shock, she was sucking on her thumb. He was tempted to snap a photo to show her but figured that might embarrass her. Still, it was cute.

After waiting a while to ensure that she was in a deep sleep, he moved into the closet to grab the item he'd set up on the top shelf. It was a baby monitor. He wasn't sure exactly how she'd feel about it. But he wanted to be able to keep an eye on her while she slept. It was one of those camera ones so he could see her. He'd intended to mount it to the wall above her bed but now, it would be trickier.

Instead, he sat it on the corner of the bed, aiming down. He wouldn't see her face, but it would give him an idea of when she was starting to wake up.

Tiptoeing out of the room, he found Luna waiting on the other side. The dog was sulking from not being allowed in the bedroom. But Razor thought it was better to keep the space dog-free.

Especially since Luna was a stuffie-destroyer.

"Oh no, Daddy, they're making a mess of this renovation," she called out from where she lay on her tummy on the sofa.

"They are?" he called out from the kitchen.

Normally, she'd sit on the kitchen counter while he cooked, but Razor had insisted that she lie down while he cooked tonight. Probably a good idea, given the state of her bottom. To her shock, she'd slept for nearly two hours this afternoon in her swing.

That swing was incredible. Not just because she'd managed to nap in it. But because of how it made her feel. Weightless. Without any worries or stresses. She could just let go.

After Razor had helped her out of it, he'd shown her the baby monitor he'd used to watch her. Tabby wasn't entirely sure she liked the idea of it. But in the end, she guessed she could live with it.

She just hoped she didn't do anything embarrassing in her sleep.

"Hell, what are they doing?" Razor walked into the room,

wiping his hands on a towel. He winced as he saw the mess the two people were making of their house reno. "They're gonna regret that."

"Uh-huh."

He moved over to her and picked up her glass of chocolate milk. It had a swirly-twirly straw that he'd surprised her with. "Want some more, Tabby-baby?"

"No thanks, Daddy."

She had a heating pad under her tummy and had taken some more pain relief earlier so she was feeling pretty good.

"I'll get you some ice water. Let's just check your bottom first."

"Daddy, you don't need to be checking my bottom. It's fine."

He raised his eyebrows and she huffed out a breath. "Okay, Daddy. You can check it. But it's the same as it was an hour ago."

"It's about to be redder than it was an hour ago if Tabby doesn't watch her sassy tone."

"Sorry, Daddy. Don't you have to cook dinner?"

"It's in the oven. It will be another half an hour."

"Hm." He undid the drop seat. "Whoever invented these was a genius."

Uh-huh.

He drew down her panties. "All right, looking good." He ran a finger over her cheeks then down between them. She stiffened as her clit throbbed in reaction. Did she want him to touch her there?

"Some other things arrived today."

Had they been in the smaller box?

"What was it, Daddy? More toys? I don't need any more."

"Actually, it is more toys. But not for your Little."

Oh, holy hell.

He pressed his finger against her asshole and she groaned, clenching down.

"Would you like to experience some anal play?"

"I . . . I . . . I've got my period."

"I know some women don't like to play while they're on their period. And others who do. I thought we could try the smallest plug in your bottom. I've also got an egg with a remote. Instead of putting it inside you, I could put it against your clit. What do you say?"

His finger was still pressing against her bottom hole, and she had to admit that it felt really good.

But did she want to do any playing?

"All right, I'm not sure I'll like the plug, though."

"You might surprise yourself," he told her. "I'll be back."

That didn't sound ominous or anything. When he came back, he held some things in his hands. She watched as he put a tube of lube on the floor, then a small remote. He held up the egg for her to see. "Don't worry, I washed my hands before touching anything."

Well, she hadn't even thought of that.

"Let's put a cushion under your tummy."

She rose up as he positioned the cushion and her heating pad. Then she lay down.

"Spread your legs," he commanded.

She moved them slightly apart, and he slid the egg between her legs and up against her clit. The way she was lying kept it in place. He removed his hand, then touched the remote. It started buzzing, and she groaned.

"Feel good, baby girl?"

"Yes," she moaned. It felt so good. She thought it wouldn't take long for her to come. But then the egg stopped and she let out a protesting groan.

"Daddy, turn it back on."

He gave her a stern look. "Who makes the decisions around here?"

"You do."

"That's right. I'll decide when it goes back on." He picked up the plug and started coating it.

"That's a small one?" she asked.

He grinned. "Yep."

Lord help her.

"Now, I'm going to use my finger first. I want you to try to relax."

She gave him a skeptical look.

"I know, I know," he said. "That seems impossible, but it will help." He moved next to her and parted her bottom cheeks.

Okay, could she do this? Did she want to do this? Then she felt some cool lube being applied to her back hole before a finger prodded at the entrance.

"That's it. Fuck, this is hot. Good girl, nice deep breath, then let it out." As she let out her breath, he inserted his finger.

Oh, hell.

That felt good. He moved his finger in and out of her ass a few times before withdrawing it. She had to bite back a protest. But before she could feel too empty, she felt the tip of the anal plug against her asshole.

"Good girl. Let's make this a bit more fun." He must have hit the remote because the egg started buzzing again.

Her breath came in sharp pants. She was so close; it was embarrassing how quickly she'd gotten there.

"Deep breath in," he commanded.

She took a breath in.

"Now out. Good girl. There you are. You took that perfectly. Baby girl, you look amazing lying there with a plug in your bottom."

She didn't care about the way she looked. This was all about how she felt.

She felt amazing.

The orgasm took her by surprise, rocking through her body and making her gasp and whimper.

"That's my girl." He kissed her lightly as she lay slumped there. "Normally, you wouldn't be allowed to come after a punishment, but you took your plug so beautifully, that deserves a reward. I've got to wash up and check on dinner. Stay right there."

She noticed that he took the remote with him. Did that mean he was going to push it while he wasn't even in the room? Holy shit.

Lord, she hoped no one came to the door while she was lying here like this. All she needed was Lois to walk in while her plugged butt was on display. Mind you, from what Lois had told her about her past, maybe she wouldn't be all that shocked.

Tabby attempted to concentrate on her show, but that damn egg went on and off infrequently. She'd be so close to coming, then it would shut down.

"Daddy!" she said demandingly as he walked in carrying a plate of food and a glass of water.

"What is it?"

"The egg keeps turning off when I'm close to coming."

"Does it? Well, that is unfortunate, isn't it?" he said as he sat on the floor next to her head. He held the straw in the glass of water to her mouth and she gulped down eagerly. It was her second glass of water since he'd plugged her. Being sexually frustrated was thirsty work, apparently.

"Well?" she asked as he put the glass down and picked up the plate and fork.

"Well, what?"

"Aren't you going to do something about it?"

"Like what?" he asked before he blew on the forkful of food.

"Like let me come."

"Oh no, I'm not going to do that."

"Why not?" she wailed.

"Because you were punished earlier. You were allowed one orgasm as a reward for taking your plug, but you're not allowed anymore."

"Daddy! That's so mean."

"Maybe you'll think about this next time you go to break a rule." He held the forkful of food to her mouth. "Open up wide."

"I don't think I'm hungry."

"You're always hungry," he pointed out.

Well, yeah. But this was a protest.

"No sulking," he warned. "Or I'll think you need some corner time."

Sheesh. He really didn't play fair. She leaned up on her forearms to take the bite of the cheesy chicken casserole. That was delicious.

"Daddy, will you teach me to cook this?" she asked.

"You know that I'll teach you anything you want to know."

"Even how to ride a motorbike?"

He turned to give her a wide-eyed stare. "You want to learn how to ride?"

"Yeah, I was thinking I might get one of my own. Will you teach me?"

"No."

"No? Why not?"

"Because I've seen you drive."

"So?"

"You get easily distracted."

"I do not."

"Baby girl, you do. There's no way you're riding a bike."

She huffed out a breath, her lower lip dropping out. "Please."

"No, and don't even start that pouting with me. No motorbikes."

"Don't you trust me?"

"Not with this. Nope."

"I'd just like to point out that you're being a hypocrite."

"Noted. It's not changing my mind. The only time you're on a bike is when you're behind me."

Well, at least he wasn't saying she could ride at all.

Still, maybe one day she'd get her own bike. After all, if she bought one, then he'd have to teach her, right?

23

"Tabby-baby?" Razor called out as he walked into her office.

She turned in her seat. "Yep?"

He had his hand over the receiver end of the cordless phone.

"Could you run and grab Dart for me? Nobody's answering the phone in the shop."

"Yep. I'm on it." It was close to closing and the guys were starting to pack up.

She left the office, Luna trotting along behind her.

When she got to the shop, though, Dart wasn't around. Where was he? Maybe he was out back in the bathroom. She guessed she could just check. She knocked but didn't hear anything. So she pushed open the bathroom door.

"Dart?" she called out without looking.

Nothing.

Okay. Where else could he be? Out back smoking? Did Dart smoke? She wasn't sure.

"Best check just in case," she said to Luna as she opened the back door and headed into the alleyway. Then she sighed. Crap. Tommy.

Just her freaking luck.

"Tabby, you looking for me?"

She reminded herself that Tommy had been nothing but polite to her since his apology a while back. So she should stop holding a grudge against him. Give him the benefit of the doubt.

"Nope. I'm looking for Dart. Have you seen him?"

"He just popped around the corner. Should be back any moment."

"Can you tell him to come to the office when you see him? Razor wants him."

She turned, but she wasn't quick enough. He grabbed hold of her arm. Hard.

Luna growled.

"Shut up, dog."

She sucked in a breath. "Let me go!"

"What's your hurry? We can have ourselves a little chat. Or do you need to go and suck the boss man's dick?"

Did he really just say that? Shit! So much for turning over a new leaf, huh?

Turning, she glared at him.

"What? Don't tell me that you didn't do that to keep your job after messing up so much? Sending me to the wrong place for that part? Messing up that big order?"

She gasped as it all became clear. "You did that?"

"Dumb cunt. Of course I did. Teach you not to be an uptight bitch with me."

"Fuck you."

He squeezed her arm and she cried out.

Luna snarled.

"Shut up, mutt. Stupid dog has always fucking hated me."

Oh, she wondered why.

"Maybe because she's got good taste."

Whoops. She didn't actually mean to say that out loud.

"What the fuck? What the hell does that mean!" He shook her, growing agitated.

She rolled her eyes. Really? Could he be this stupid?

"It means that you're a petty little asshole and Luna can sense that. Now, let me go before I scream for help."

His hold tightened to the point that tears entered her eyes. She tugged on her arm, but he pulled her around, slamming her up against the building.

Ouch.

"Not so fast, bitch. I'm not done with you yet. You know how hard it's been trying to be nice to you, bitch? But I'm done. Dart thinks he can give me another warning? Tell me that one more mistake and I'm out? Not. Happening."

Luna started barking and he kicked out at the dog, who thankfully dodged his foot. But that was enough for Tabby to see red.

"Don't kick my dog," she yelled at him. She swung at his throat with her free hand. Somehow, she got in a good hit and he staggered back, struggling for breath, his hands clawing at his throat. Not wanting to waste any time, she ran around the building, her breath sawing in and out of her lungs. She ignored the twinge in her ankle, it would hold up.

"Luna, come!" she yelled. As she raced past the workshop, she saw Razor standing there, staring around in concern. Sav was next to him.

Relief filled his face as he saw her. Sprinting over, she threw herself into his arms.

Immediately, his arms wrapped around her.

"What is it? What's wrong? What happened?"

Luna was whining, nuzzling at her.

A feeling of safety infused her. Nothing would happen to her now.

"What's going on?" Sav snapped.

"I don't know. I sent her to find Dart, but when she didn't come back, I came out here to find her. She came running around from out back. And now she's trembling. Baby girl, tell me."

"I . . . I . . . Tommy," she whispered.

Razor stilled. "What do you mean, Tommy?"

"Out back?" Sav growled. "Tommy was just out there."

Razor stared down at her for a long moment. "Did he touch you? Hurt you?"

She knew better than to pretend otherwise. Slowly, she nodded. What she wasn't expecting was for Razor to pass her to Sav. "Watch her."

And then he was gone.

Wow. He moved pretty fast for a big guy. Then she realized what was happening. She blamed it on shock that she was so slow. She took off after him.

Well, she attempted to.

In reality, she found herself hanging in the air with a solid arm around her waist.

"Let me go!" She pulled at Sav's arm, but he wasn't budging. The man was solid.

"No."

"Damn it, Sav! Let me down. I've got to stop him."

Sav shook her gently. "Stop it. You'll hurt yourself."

She wriggled around madly. "Do you think I care?"

"You might not. He will."

"Put me down!"

By now, she was aware that everyone had stopped what they were doing and were gaping at her. She didn't care.

"Go home," Sav barked. They all hastily finished and moved to their vehicles.

"Put me down!"

"No. I put you down, it's my ass on the line. Not happening."

"God damn mother-fucking bastard!"

"Girl, you need your mouth washed out," he growled.

"Shit!"

"What's wrong?" Dart asked. He didn't look concerned, but he didn't waste any time in moving over to them.

"Take her. Razor's gone to deal with Tommy. He touched her."

"Dart, make Sav let me go!" she demanded.

"Quiet," Sav told her. "You're going nowhere."

"I'll go. Both of you stay here," Dart commanded and rushed off.

Suddenly, Sav picked her up, throwing her over his shoulder.

"Hey! Let me down!" She slammed her fists against his back. Then she immediately felt bad. "Sorry." She rubbed the spot she'd just hit. "Did I hurt you?"

Sav muttered something she couldn't hear then carried her into the office. "Luna, come."

Luna whined, obviously wanting to go to Razor. Tabby totally understood.

"Sav, I need to stop him."

"Dart has it."

He set her gently down on her feet. Immediately, she attempted to move around him, but he blocked her then leaned against the door. A big, unmovable wall in front of her.

"Grr." She slammed her foot on the ground. Unfortunately, it was her still healing one and she couldn't hide a wince.

Sav narrowed his gaze. "What did you do?"

"Nothing. Let me by."

"No."

"Fine, then you go check on him. Stop him from doing anything crazy."

Sav just gave her a look. One that said he wasn't buying her bullshit for a moment.

"Damn it, Sav!"

The door suddenly opened and Sav would have gone flying backward if he didn't have great balance.

Then she didn't care about Sav or his balance as Razor walked in the door. She couldn't read anything from his face.

"Razor! What happened? Where's Tommy? Dart? Are you all right?" She moved towards Razor and he held up a hand.

"Stay away from me."

She froze. She felt ill. Oh my God. Did he blame her for what happened?

"Razor," Sav warned. Suddenly, he moved in front of her. Was he blocking her from Razor? Or protecting her?

What was going on?

"What?" Razor snarled. "What are you doing?"

"You told me that you'd never push me away. That I could always touch you," she whispered.

There was silence. Then a long breath of air left Razor. "Fuck."

She waited. Not sure what was going on. What if he did blame her, though?

"Sav, move."

"Not sure that's a good idea," Sav replied.

"Move," Razor demanded.

Sav slid to the side and Razor's gaze pierced her, held her in place. "Baby girl, I'm not rejecting you. I promise. I just," he put his hands on his head, letting out a breath, "I need to get myself back under control."

She noticed a patch of something wet on his black T-shirt. Blood? Hard to know. His knuckles on his right hand looked scraped and swollen, though.

Moving from foot to foot, she tried to give him that time. But damn, it was hard.

"I'll just go outside for a moment, wait here."

He disappeared before she could say anything. Sav turned to look at her. "You gonna let him do that?"

"What?"

"Shut you out."

Oh.

"No."

"Then go to him now."

She nodded numbly. Then she moved out of the office, looking around. There was Razor, leaning against the wall of the workshop. His legs were bent, his hands on his knees.

"Razor."

"Tabby-baby. Just a bit longer. Then I'll take care of you."

She shook her head. She wasn't the one who needed taking care of right then. Moving closer, she placed a shaky hand on his shoulder.

Please don't reject me. Please don't.

He was her safe place, and she couldn't stand it if he pushed her away.

But all he did was shudder then lift his head. "Baby girl . . ."

"No, don't tell me you need a bit longer. You don't need to be on your own. You need me." She used a firm tone, as though she believed in what she said. In truth, she wasn't entirely sure. Maybe she was the last thing he needed.

All he did was look at her, though. Then he drew up his hands and she was shocked to see they shook.

"I don't want to touch you with these hands. I need to wash them. To be clean before I touch you. I need . . . to find my control again. I won't risk harming you."

"Bull-pucky."

"What?"

"I call bull-pucky. You'd never harm me."

"I lost control. I haven't done that in years."

"Because of me," she whispered.

His gaze met hers. "Because of him. That bastard. I should

never have hired him. It was only as a favor. He's been nothing but a pain in my ass from day one."

"Where is he?"

"Dart's taking care of him."

"Does he need help?" she asked.

Razor raised an eyebrow.

"You know, to dig the hole," she half-joked. "I could call Jared, he probably knows of a hundred ways to dispose of a body."

"He's not dead. And we definitely won't be calling your cousin."

"Okay, that's good. So you didn't lose control that badly."

"I would've killed him if Dart hadn't stopped me. He touched you." Suddenly, he stood. "Are you all right? Did he hurt you? Fuck, I should be taking you to the hospital."

"No, no, I'm fine. Really." He ran his hands down her arms and sides, as though checking to ensure she was telling the truth. "Daddy, I'm fine."

He held out his arms for a hug. Then seemed to think better of it. "Wait."

She paused. Please don't tell her he was going to give her more bullshit about not being in control. But he whipped off his T-shirt instead. "It had his blood on it."

She eyed the T-shirt he'd chucked on the ground. "We should get rid of that."

"My little detective in the making."

Actually, she thought that had more to do with being the cousin of a crime boss than her love of a good mystery. But she pushed that worry to one side as he took her into his arms and held her tight.

"What if he decides to press charges?" she asked.

His hand cupped the back of her head, drawing her close. The heat of his skin warmed her. She hadn't realized how chilled she'd become.

"He won't. Don't concern yourself."

How could he say that? Of course she would concern herself.

"We should clean you up, just in case. Get that shirt in the wash. Are there any cameras? What about Dart, can he be trusted?"

He drew back, putting a finger over her lips. "Will you just let me worry about all that?"

"But I don't want to lose you."

"You will never lose me. Come on, I need to talk to Sav, then we're going home." He grasped hold of the T-shirt and she made a mental note to get it into the washing machine as quickly as possible.

Razor went to grasp hold of her hand then paused. She barely refrained from rolling her eyes, grabbing his hand with hers.

"You're really not upset by the idea that I hit Tommy?"

"You did it for me. How could I be?"

With a nod of his head, he entered the office. Sav was tapping on his phone as he leaned against her desk. Luna was sitting at his feet. The dog jumped up and practically pounced on them both. Razor bent down and gave her some pats and Tabby crouched, hugging the dog who licked her face.

"Poor Luna nearly got kicked by that asshole," she told him.

"What?" Razor asked.

"She was barking at Tommy when he had me pinned to the wall. He tried to kick her. She dodged in time, but then I got mad and punched him in the throat."

Both men were gaping at her.

"What?" she asked. "You would have done the same. He nearly hit her."

"Damn, baby girl. That's how you got away?"

"Yeah, I went out back looking for Dart. Tommy was there. He said Dart had gone around the building. But I didn't want to walk past him, so I told him to tell Dart to come see you. But when I tried to leave, he grabbed my arm and said a few nasty things."

"Like what?" Razor demanded.

"Just about how I was a bitch and how Dart had given him a last warning. I think he didn't care anymore because of that. Oh, and he also said he deliberately messed up some of my work stuff. Then he slammed me back against the wall and was looming over me. Luna barked, and you know the rest."

"Show me your arm," Razor demanded.

"There's nothing wrong," she said hastily.

"Show me."

She had a button-up blouse on and she couldn't easily pull up the sleeve, so she started to undo the top buttons.

"Whoa, what are you doing?" Razor demanded, grabbing hold of her blouse and glaring over at Sav.

"It will be easier to pull it down rather than push my sleeve up," she explained.

"Sav, turn around."

Razor waited until Sav had turned, before letting go of her blouse. She gave him an exasperated look but tugged the top of the blouse down to show him her upper arm. It was definitely red from where that asshole had grabbed it.

"Fucking bastard. Did he touch you anywhere else?"

"No. But he pushed me against the wall. There might be a small bruise on my back."

"Show me."

She quickly showed him. He lightly ran his fingers over the sore spot. "It might bruise."

"I'll be all right."

She did up her blouse as he turned away to pace. His hands clenched and unclenched. Then he stopped and leaned his hands against the wall with his back to her. He bent over, taking in deep breaths.

"Razor," she said.

"One moment."

Sav turned back, studying her.

"He put his hands on you," Razor groaned. "It was my job to see to your safety and I let that bastard touch you."

"Razor, that wasn't your fault."

"Has he touched you before?" Sav asked.

Razor spun, staring at her. "No, he hasn't touched her. Because if he'd touched her like that, she would have told me. Isn't that right, Tabby-baby?"

"That's right. He hasn't touched me."

Razor gave an arrogant nod.

"And he apologized for the things he said when I first started here, so I thought everything was fine."

"Fuck," Sav muttered.

"What things?" Razor asked.

"Oh, um, just calling me sexy thing."

Sav grimaced and glanced over at Razor. "Don't kill me, but he called her that the day she came to see you about the job."

"Why didn't you tell me?"

"Because I fucking warned him. Thought that was enough."

"Was there more?" Razor asked her.

"Ahh, yeah. He asked me out. Told me I'd have a good time with him and then got angry when I said no. But that's the way guys talk. I mean, I've heard some of Jared's guys speak about women like that. They'd never say that to me, of course. Or in front of me. But I'm working with all guys, I thought . . ."

"You thought what? That it was something you had to put up with? You should have told me."

"I . . . you're right, I should have. But I wasn't certain that it was something to be concerned about. And then he apologized and he hasn't said anything since. I'm really sorry." She felt terrible. If she'd told him, then she could have prevented this.

Razor sighed and her stomach dropped. She was going to be sick.

Then he held out his arms. "Come here."

She flew into his embrace and he tightened his hold on her. "Never again, understand me? From now on, you tell me every damn thing."

"I will. He seemed so contrite. It just didn't seem important."

"You don't decide that, I do. It's just better if you tell me everything. I'll filter through it. Got it?"

"Got it."

24

R azor held her hand tightly as they walked into the house. Instead of moving into the kitchen as he usually did, he led her to their bathroom. Grabbing her around the waist, he lifted her onto the counter.

He started washing his hands. He'd brought in the T-shirt that he'd been wearing and had tossed it in the hamper. She'd wash that soon.

"Razor?" she asked softly. She knew he was still fighting himself. He'd been quiet on the ride home. Was he angry with her? For not telling him about Weasel Dick? She couldn't blame him.

Drawing her knees up to her chest, she pulled the top of her blouse up over her head.

"Baby girl, no hiding."

"I'm so s-sorry, Daddy! I don't d-deserve you!"

"Hey, now, what's all this?" He tugged at her blouse. "Come on, let me see that beautiful face."

She shook her head.

"Tabitha," he said in a low voice. "Let Daddy see you."

Popping her head out at the command in his voice, she sniffled and wiped at the tears in her eyes. "Today was all my fault!"

"No, it was Tommy's fault. He touched you. Did you want him to do that?"

"No!" She shuddered at the idea. "But I should have told you what he said to me."

"You should have. But I know you didn't trust me fully back then. And you didn't feel comfortable telling me things like that."

"But once we were together . . ."

"Did he say anything like that after we got together?"

"No, he apologized like I said."

"And you thought he was genuine."

"Yes," she whispered. "I thought I should give him a second chance, you know? You've given all of your guys a second chance. I thought it was only fair I did the same. I was wrong."

"Making mistakes is okay, Tabby."

"But look what it did to you! You thought you couldn't touch me. You were forced to hit him."

He huffed out a breath. "I wasn't forced to hit him. No one forces me to do anything. I wanted to."

"But . . . but . . ."

"It's all right. I knew what I was doing. Afterward, yeah, I had problems pulling myself back together. Regaining control. But that's my issue, not yours."

"I didn't mean to keep it from you. If he'd said anything more, I would have told you."

"Good. I wish I'd never hired that bastard. Should have listened to my gut. This is my fault too."

She shook her head. He'd only been trying to do the right thing. Like he did for all his guys.

He cupped her face between his hands. "I love you, Tabby-baby."

"I love you too."

Turning away, he filled the bath.

That was it? Wasn't he going to punish her?

"Daddy? What are you doing?"

"I need to take care of you. Will you let me? It helps center me. I need to feel in control right now."

"Okay, Daddy. I'll do anything you need."

"What about what you need? Did Tommy grabbing you trigger bad memories? Of course, it did, what am I saying? What do you need?"

"I don't . . . I don't know." She gulped as disappointment flashed in his face. What did she need? "I need you. To hold me and tell me everything is all right."

"Yeah?"

"Yeah. And Snappy and Scooby. Some Little time. I think that would reassure me."

"That's what I thought too."

She hoped that would be enough to get rid of this gnawing feeling in her stomach.

Somehow, she worried it wouldn't be.

RAZOR BATHED HIS LITTLE GIRL, praying it would soothe the beast still raging inside him. He got out the bath toys that he'd bought for her when he'd created the playroom.

While she tried to play, it was clear her mind wasn't in the right place. She was tense, worried.

Was she scared of him now? Was she concerned he'd lose control around her?

Helping her out, he dried her off then dressed her into the panties and all-in-one pajamas he'd fetched as she'd played.

"You need to use the potty, baby girl?" he asked.

She gave him a surprised look, probably because he'd called it a potty. She didn't tend to go that young in Little headspace, but he felt she might need to tonight. Or maybe that was what he needed.

He waited out in the bedroom for her, pacing back and forth. Maybe he should go work out in the gym. Perhaps that would help him control the residual fear and anger still raging through him.

He'd failed to protect her.

"Daddy?" she asked quietly, making him turn.

He stared at her for a long moment. She started trembling.

"You're scared of me," he said in a raw, pained voice.

Her eyes widened. "What? No!"

"You're trembling. Are you worried I'll lose control around you? I promise I won't. I was upset because he touched you, but I'd never lose it like that with you."

"Razor. Daddy. No," she said firmly. "No, I'm not scared of you. I could never be afraid of you. Not when everything you do is for me. I know you only got so mad because he touched me. How could I possibly be afraid of you?"

"Don't be. I'd never harm you. I promise."

"Jeremiah," she said softly. "I know, honey. I know." She slowly moved closer, as though she didn't want to startle him. And then she slid her arms around his waist.

And all was right in his world.

He hugged her back, picking her up so she could wrap her legs around his waist. She held on tight.

"Tabby-baby, I couldn't stand it if anything happened to you."

"It won't. Not with you around."

He shook his head, he'd nearly failed her.

"Daddy, it wasn't your fault. It was his."

"Baby."

"No, it was. And I know what else I need to feel better."

"What's that?" he asked, figuring she'd want some more Little time, maybe some hugs and comfort food.

"I need you to punish me."

Razor drew his head back, staring down at her in shock. "I don't think that's a good idea."

She tilted her head up, looking straight up at him. She wasn't hiding. Wasn't trying to keep her thoughts away from him.

"It is. I have this aching feeling in my stomach that won't go away. I know what it is. It's guilt. And if you punish me, then hopefully that feeling will disappear."

"You were just attacked. You shouldn't be spanked right now."

"I'm not going to settle until this feeling goes away. I did something wrong. I broke the rules. Please."

He took in a deep breath and let it out. "Fuck. All right. I get it." And he did. If anyone knew what it was like to have guilt eat away at you, it was him.

"This is what we'll do. You're going to go and stand in the naughty corner of your bedroom. I'll order us some dinner because I'm not in the mood to cook. Then I'm going to come in and punish you. Understand?"

She shuddered against him and he almost changed his mind, but then he heard her sigh. She sounded relieved.

"Yes, Daddy. I understand."

TABBY HATED CORNER TIME.

Thinking wasn't fun. Everything kept coming back to her. Tommy grabbing her. Pushing her against the wall. She was still shocked that she hadn't panicked. That she hadn't tried to retreat into her head. That's what she used to do with Luther. Go somewhere in her head where he couldn't reach. Couldn't harm her.

Except for when she hit him over the head with a poker. Yeah, she hadn't retreated that night.

And the same with today. She'd fought back. She'd stuck up for herself and for Luna. And she was proud of herself for that.

The door opened and she stilled, knowing Razor was in the room now.

"Come here, baby girl."

Turning, she saw that he'd carried in one of the dining room chairs. She swallowed heavily.

But she walked over, reminding herself that she'd asked for this. And she knew she'd feel better afterward. Instead of pulling her over his lap as she'd expected, he sat her on his knees. His arms encircled her, holding her tight.

"Are you sure about this?" he asked.

"I'm sure, Daddy," she whispered.

"What were you thinking about while in the corner?"

"About how I fought back. I never fought back with Luther. Well, except for that last night, when he hurt your friend and threatened Millie. I always just let him do what he wanted in the hopes it would end quicker. But with Tommy, I fought back. And I'm proud of myself for doing that."

"I'm so proud of you too, baby girl. You're a fucking fighter. You're amazing. But I want you to do me a favor, to save me from having a heart attack."

"What's that?"

"Don't get into another situation like that again."

She smiled up at him. "I'll try not to, Daddy."

He groaned. "You're going to turn Daddy gray."

"I think you'll look sexy gray." Reaching up, she kissed him lightly. "You'll be my sexy silver fox, Daddy."

"I'll have earned every gray hair chasing after you, brat," he growled. Then his face softened. "You ready for your punishment?"

"Yes, Daddy."

"No cramps? Stomach pains? Soreness anywhere else?"

"No, Daddy, I only get cramps the first day of my period," she reminded him.

He nodded then lifted her off. He helped her onto his lap and then she saw something she'd missed before, sitting on the floor next to him. It was in a plastic bag. What was it?

As he undid the drop seat and pulled down her panties, it finally registered.

Ginger.

Oh, hell.

"Daddy, wait!"

"What is it, baby girl?"

"Is that ginger?"

"Sure is."

"But . . . but Daddy . . . I don't need ginger in my butt!" she wailed.

"Daddy thinks you do," he told her.

Smack! Smack!

"He doesn't like that you're feeling so guilty."

Smack! Smack!

Ouch. Crap. He really wasn't holding back. Several more spanks landed before he spoke again.

"And since you have trouble remembering not to hide things from Daddy, that you have worth, he wants to make this memorable."

Smack! Smack!

"It's already memorable, Daddy! I'm not going to forget it!" she cried as he continued to spank her.

Her ass was throbbing and hot. She started sobbing as he continued to give her smack after smack.

"We're going to make sure that this doesn't happen again. Daddy has to take care of his girl."

"But I only need the spanking!"

"The ginger is going to impress on you how serious Daddy is. How much he loves his girl and never wants anything to happen to her. She has worth. More worth than all the gold and jewels and treasure in the world."

Damn. How could he say such nice things while turning her butt into something you could fry bacon on?

Finally, he stopped and she lay on his lap, sobbing her heart out.

"Good girl, let it all out. That's it. Good girl."

He leaned over and picked up the bag, and her cries increased. She was crying so loudly that she must have missed hearing the bag open. Then her bottom cheeks were parted. She tensed automatically.

"Easy. Just relax."

Right. That was going to happen. But she felt him prodding at her bottom hole so she took a breath in, letting it out on a sob as the ginger sunk in.

Okay, that wasn't so bad. There was no burning. Not like the outside of her bottom, that was for sure.

"You're going back into the corner. Is your foot all right, or would you rather sit?"

"My foot is fine, Daddy." He helped her up and then turned her towards the corner as the doorbell rang.

"That will be dinner." Standing, he landed a heavy smack on her ass that had her yelping and clenching down on the ginger.

Okay, now there was some warmth building.

"Off you go. Corner."

She shuffled to the corner as he left. She kept her buttocks tightly clenched as she moved, worried the ginger might pop out. As she made it to the corner, though, she realized that would have been a blessing. Apparently, clenching down was bad. Bad. Bad. Bad.

She whimpered. Now it was really starting to burn. How long was she expected to stand here? Shifting from foot to foot, she glanced over at the door. Where was Razor? When was he coming back? This was horrid.

The door opened and he raised his eyebrows as he took her in. "I see the timer has to start over. Face back in the corner. Ass pushed out."

"But Daddy, it burns," she cried.

"This is a punishment."

Well, it sucked. She was never going to do anything that might result in her getting ginger up her butt again. Taking deep, shuddering breaths, she stood with her nose in the corner and her poor bottom on display.

Hours later, okay, it was likely only minutes, he came over to where she was in the corner. He ran his hand up and down her back.

"I want you to bend right over and I'll take the ginger out. Stay in the corner while I get rid of it and clean up."

Her cheeks grew hot, but really her need to get the ginger out overrode her embarrassment. Bending over, she touched her toes. He parted her bottom cheeks and withdrew the ginger

"There you are. Stand back up."

With a sigh of relief, she rested her face back in the corner. She felt exhausted, spent. And also, blessedly light. The gnawing feeling in her tummy was gone.

"Come here, Tabby-baby." Razor turned her, engulfing her in a tight hug before he picked her up. She clasped hold of him. "Are you feeling all right? You've been punished now. All the guilt should be gone."

"It is," she reassured him. "I feel so much better. Thank you, Daddy."

"You're welcome, my precious girl."

∾

TWENTY MINUTES LATER, she sat on his lap while he fed her bites of sesame chicken. Her bottom hung off the end of his thigh, it was still hot and way too tender for her weight to rest on it.

"Want any more, Tabby-baby?" he asked her.

"No, Daddy. I'm full all the way to the top." She held her hand up to her head. "I gots no room left."

"Really? Not even for some chocolate?"

Hm. She thought about that. "Well, there is a special tummy for chocolate. So, I think I could fit it in."

"I thought that might be the case. Why don't you go lie on the sofa while I clean up?"

"Okie-dokie, Daddy." Getting up, she moved into the living room and surfed through the channels. "Daddy, our favorite program isn't on tonight."

"Why don't you choose a movie, then?"

"Can we watch the Scooby-Doo movie?"

"For the fifteenth time? Sure, why not?" he replied with amusement as he walked into the living room. "You should go get Snappy and Scooby so they can watch too."

"Good thinking, Daddy. You're not just a pretty face."

He gave her thigh a light smack as she walked past him. "Brat."

Giggling to herself, she grabbed Snappy and Scooby from their bedroom. Happiness filled her. Who'd have thought she would go from being lonely and having no one, to this? And the change had all started when she'd met Cat.

Oh, fuck. Cat.

RAZOR RAISED his eyebrows in surprise as his girl came trudging into the living room. When she'd left to get her toys, she'd been bright and happy. Now she looked sad.

She stood in front of him, twisting her foot around as she kept her gaze on the floor. She heaved out a big sigh.

"Baby girl, what's wrong?"

"I have something else to tell you, Daddy."

He stiffened. Jesus. Was he going to have to sit her down at the end of each day to check in with her? Actually, that wasn't a bad idea at all. That way, he wouldn't miss anything.

"What is it?"

"Before I tell you, I'd just like to point out that this happened before I met you. The second time, I mean. It was a few days before I came to the shop to ask about the job."

"Okay," he said carefully.

"And I haven't even really thought about it since. It's not like I kept it from you on purpose or anything."

"All right, just tell me. I'm not going to get upset."

"Will your spanky hand start getting itchy?" she asked.

"Are you at risk from what you have to tell me? Is it something that threatens your health or safety?"

"Oh no, Daddy. Not anymore. I mean, I'm not even allowed to go jogging at the moment. And when I can, I know I can't go on my own. Especially in the morning."

Right. He really wasn't going to like what she said. But so far, his spanky hand didn't itch, as she'd put it.

"Come here." He crooked a finger at her.

"Nuh-uh, Daddy. I think I'll just stay here."

"Little girl, I'm not going to spank you. Come here."

With a sigh that he thought was touching on being a bit too sassy, she slowly moved towards him. So slowly, that he rolled his eyes.

"Unless you *want* me to spank you?"

Suddenly, she managed to move much quicker.

"That's what I thought," he murmured as he lifted her onto his lap so she was straddling his legs.

"Tell me." He grasped hold of her chin as she attempted to hide her face with her dark brown hair, which was currently a wild mess around her face. He'd need to try to tame it later.

"You know how I used to go running early in the morning 'cause I'd wake up and wouldn't go back to sleep."

"Yes, something that won't happen anymore."

"You can't spank me for that, Daddy!" Her hands, which still held Snappy and Scooby, went behind her back to protect her bottom.

He sighed. "I'm not going to spank you. Now, put Scooby and Snappy down and just tell me."

"Okay, Daddy, I'm trying to, but you keep interrupting and saying you're going to spank me."

He hadn't once done that. But he decided that arguing at this point would be counterproductive.

"Keep going."

"Well, the Thursday before I came to the workshop, I went out running, and I heard this person calling out for help."

He groaned.

"Daddy, stop interrupting."

"I'm really not going to like this, am I?"

She chewed her lower lip. "Maybe you better sit on your spanky hand, just to make sure it doesn't get itchy."

"Little girl, Daddy doesn't spank because his hand gets itchy. Now, spill."

"Okay, well, I was going to keep running but then I thought about how often I wished someone would have help me."

"So, you ran towards the person yelling for help," he said.

"Yep."

It was what he'd expected her to say.

"Then what happened?"

"I saw this man trying to force someone into a car. So, I ran over there, yelling, and he let go. I sprayed pepper spray in his face then took off to hide. The person he'd been trying to kidnap turned out to be a woman. She asked me if there was somewhere safe we could go."

"Please don't tell me you took her home to your apartment."

"Of course not, Daddy. I'm not silly. I took her to the local diner."

"All right." Not as bad as he'd expected. At least it was in a public place. "Then what?"

"We ate a delicious breakfast. I should take you there. The eggs were cooked perfect and the hash browns were—mmphm." He put his hand over her mouth, cutting her off.

"Focus, baby girl."

She didn't generally have focusing problems and he knew it was a mix of Little headspace and not wanting to tell this story.

"Sorry, Daddy," she told him as he dropped his hand away. "She used my phone to call someone. She spoke in Spanish, I think. And then someone came to pick her up."

"Who?"

"Her dad. But I didn't see him. She wiped everything off my phone except for her phone number. She said to call if I needed anything. Then she told me to leave before he got here because he might want to take me with him."

"What?" he barked.

She shrugged. "I don't know why, but I left. That's when I decided that things needed to change. Because if I'd died helping her, do you know how many people would have gone to my funeral?"

"You will not die," he whispered harshly.

She patted his cheek lightly. "Of course not. But the answer is three! Maybe four. Jared, his guards, and perhaps his assistant, North. That's it. Isn't that so sad?"

"You will not die."

"Daddy, you're not understanding my point. I decided that I

wanted to do more with my life than stay secluded in my bubble of one. I helped Cat. Me, the person who couldn't even help myself. I saved her. I felt powerful and useful. If it wasn't for that encounter, I might never have turned up at the garage that day. So, we should really be thankful it happened."

Really? That's how she wanted to play it?

"First of all, you shouldn't have been jogging in the early hours of the morning alone."

"Yes, you've told me. Many, many times."

"Does someone need more time with a ginger plug?" he warned.

She straightened up. "No. Promise!"

"Then watch the tone." He tapped her nose warningly.

"Sorry, Daddy. But I won't do that again. You'll be coming with me next time, right?"

"Right." He wasn't looking forward to that. His body wasn't made for jogging.

"If you hear someone calling for help, then the appropriate response is to call 911 and me. Then wait."

She chewed her lip. "I don't know if I can do that. I mean, what if you need help?"

"Call 911 and then call Reyes or Sav or Dart."

"But what if you need help straight away? I couldn't stand by and let you get hurt."

He cupped her face in his hands. "I couldn't stand it if you got hurt trying to help me, understand? It would wreck me."

"What if it's Millie or one of the girls?"

He closed his eyes, looking pained. "I just don't want you to get harmed. What if that guy had a gun?"

"I had my pepper spray. I would try to be as safe as possible, but if someone was hurting someone I cared about, then I couldn't stand by."

"Fine, if it's someone you care about and you can safely help them and you've already called for help, then you can do it. But if you get hurt, I'm going to be really, really mad."

"All right, Daddy. Hopefully, it doesn't come up."

"With the life we seem to lead . . . I swear you Littles will be the death of us," he muttered.

She patted his cheek. "You'll survive. Because if something happens to you, I'll be soooo mad."

"Brat. Just try to keep yourself safe, huh?"

"Okay. So, ummm . . ."

"What is it?" He didn't know how much more he could take.

"How's the spanky hand feel?"

"You're safe from it, brat. At least for the rest of the day."

"Whew. Because otherwise, I was gonna suggest we go get a cream for it."

"A cream?"

"For the itchiness."

"There's no cream that will fix this itchiness," he told her.

"Now, Daddy, don't give up so easily. I'm sure we can find a cure."

"The cure is you following the rules."

"I'm sure we can find something easier."

He just shook his head. "I want to see your phone."

"Why?" she asked suspiciously.

"I want to see her number."

"You won't erase it, will you, Daddy?" Alarm filled her face.

"Of course not," he told her. "Please go get it for me."

After searching through her phone, he couldn't find any trace of calls or text messages.

"What's wrong, Daddy?" she asked.

"Just wondering if it's worth having Ink's tech expert take a look at your phone."

She frowned. "But why? Cat's no threat. She was grateful to me for helping her and I'll probably never see her again."

"Yeah, I guess you're right. Come on, it's been a big day and I have a surprise for you tomorrow."

"Another one?"

"Yep."

"You're the best Daddy in the world, you know that?"

"Thank you, baby girl."

"Someone might even put that on a mug for you."

"Well, I'd have to be very lucky for that to happen."

"Uh-huh, you sure would."

25

I t's just a barbeque.

No need to be nervous.

Razor lifted her from his truck and Luna jumped out behind her.

"Luna, heel," Razor commanded. The dog whined. He turned to Tabby. "Emme is coming today and she's scared of dogs. She's getting better and Reyes has been helping her, but it would be better if Luna didn't rush around the back and frighten her."

Poor Emme.

Tabby understood what it was like to be afraid. Right now, she was worried about what she was going to talk about with everyone. She didn't know how to do small talk.

She took a look around at Sunny and Duke's neighborhood. It was cute and normal. Similar to where Razor lived. As Razor led her past the open garage, she came to a stop. "Is that a motorbike? A pink motorbike?"

"Oh yeah. Don't get any ideas. Sunny isn't allowed to ride it."

"Why not? Why buy it if she can't ride it?"

"A friend sent it to her," Razor said. "Duke wasn't happy."

What kind of friend sent you a motorbike? That seemed a strange and expensive gift. But she shrugged it off as they walked around and came out into the backyard. It was a warm day today and Duke was already grilling on the porch. Chairs had been set up and the girls were all together down at one end, the men around the grill.

Oh no. She couldn't stay with Razor? This was worse than she'd anticipated.

She clutched his hand.

"It will be all right, baby girl. Promise."

Yesterday, his surprise for her had been to take her to the aquarium. She'd loved it and he'd even bought her a new stuffie. An octopus to replace Octy.

A dog gave an excited bark and she glanced over to see Luna playing with two other dogs while Mr. Fluffy lay sunbathing. She had to grin. Mr. Fluffy didn't care about what anyone else was doing. He did his own thing.

She respected that.

"Tabby!"

A loud yell made her jump, then she turned just as Millie threw herself at her, greeting her like a long-lost friend. Razor's quick reflexes stopped her from being thrown backward as the other woman squeezed her tight.

"I've missed you so much!"

"You saw me a week ago," Tabby pointed out Millie took hold of her hand.

"Yeah, a whole week! It's been forever. We have to set up regular dates. Come on, come meet Emme."

Millie tugged her towards the girls. She quickly glanced back at Razor, who winked at her. She was introduced to Emme, who was a gorgeous-looking woman with wild, curly hair. Tabby didn't notice her showing any concern about the dogs, although when

Luna came over to sit on Tabby's feet, she did stiffen a bit before relaxing.

"Spike said that Razor did you up a playroom," Millie said loudly.

Spike walked over and put his hand on Millie's shoulder. "She might not want everyone to know that, baby doll."

"Oh, shoot. I'm sorry, Tabby."

"It's all right. Really." She looked at Spike. "Thanks for picking up the bed."

He just nodded then squeezed Millie's shoulder. He left, returning a few minutes later with a pitcher of pink water and glasses.

"Fairy juice!" Millie said cheerfully. "Have you had this before?"

"No," Tabby said. "Does it have alcohol in it?"

"It can if you want," Jewel told her with a wink. "Be kind of gross though."

Millie just giggled. "No, it's special water that helps you see fairies. I have a fairy garden at my house. You need to come over and see it. All of you should."

Everyone nodded in agreement and she felt herself relaxing. Even if she wanted to fade into the background, Millie wouldn't let her. No one was ignoring her or making her feel awkward because she was the new girl.

Soon the food was ready and Razor held her plate while she put some food on it. She copied how much Sunny took, not wanting to be greedy.

"That's not enough, baby girl," he told her quietly. "Put as much on it as you'd normally have."

With a blush, she piled the food up. Razor carried it to her chair for her, before filling up her glass with more fairy juice. Millie plonked down beside her and Spike handed her a plate.

"Wow."

Tabby waited for a comment about how much food was on her plate.

"This food looks so good, Sunny," Millie said. "Thanks for my vegetarian sausages."

"I think I like them better than actual sausages," Sunny replied. "Especially when you dip them in ketchup. Yum, yum."

They all started chatting. Millie leaned over into her. "Things are really good with you and Razor?"

Tabby smiled. "They're the best."

"Told you. Sick sense."

"Oh, I'm a total believer."

They grinned at each other.

WHEN THEY LEFT, it was getting close to dark. Tabby sighed happily as they drove down the street.

"Have a good time, Tabby-baby?" Razor asked. Luna was already asleep in the backseat, completely worn out.

"Uh-huh. I really did."

"Told you there was nothing to worry about."

"You were right, Daddy."

"Daddy normally is."

She snorted at that.

"Need to stop at your apartment on the way home and feed the fish. Thought we should have a talk about something."

"What is it?"

"How do you feel about moving in with me? Permanently?"

She turned to look at him. "Really, Daddy?"

"Really."

"I'd love that."

"Yeah?"

"Yeah." She nodded excitedly. "I don't ever want to leave. Your house feels like home."

"Good. Because I wasn't actually planning on letting you leave."

"Daddy." She rolled her eyes.

"Why don't we pack up some of your stuff tonight, then stop for dinner on the way home?"

"Sounds good, Daddy. Oh, have you got a spot for the gang?" she asked, meaning her fish.

"We'll find one," he promised her.

"There's just one problem," she said as he drove into the garage under her building.

"What's that?"

"Jared. I haven't actually told him about you."

"I'll tell him."

"No, no, I think that would make it worse. I'll do it."

"I want to be there when you call him. I won't let him speak badly to you or try to intimidate you."

"Okay, Daddy. That sounds really good." She wouldn't mind the backup.

They managed to pack up her remaining stuff. She didn't have a lot. Razor piled it into the back of his truck. They'd have to move the fish another day. She didn't think she'd be hungry again after all the lunch she'd eaten. But she managed to fit in some Pad Thai.

They were nearly home when Razor's phone rang. Frowning, he looked at the number then pulled his truck over rather than using the Bluetooth.

"Hello, Jeremiah Samuels. Yes. What? Fuck. Yes, we'll be right there."

He ended the call then swung the truck around.

"Razor? What is it?"

"The shop is on fire."

26

S he felt so helpless.

Tabby sat in the truck with Luna and stared out at the garage. By the time they'd gotten there, the fire brigade already had the fire under control. Razor had jumped out, telling her to lock the doors and stay put, before he'd raced towards the fire. But a couple of firefighters had stopped him. Now he was standing there, his hands behind his head as he stared at the destruction.

She couldn't take it any longer.

"Stay, Luna."

Climbing out of the truck, she headed towards him.

"Razor." She moved up beside him.

"How did this happen? Look at it! Everything that I've worked towards. Gone."

She shook her head and hugged him around his middle while facing the building. The office was completely destroyed since it had been made of plywood. At least the shop had been concrete. So the building itself was all right. But what was inside it might not be.

"What the fire didn't destroy, the water likely has." Razor let out a deep sigh. "At least most of the finished bikes went out on Friday."

But there were still all the bikes they'd been working on.

"I'm so sorry, Razor," she said quietly.

"Thanks, baby girl." He hugged her as one of the firemen walked towards them. "I better talk to them." A bike approached. She glanced over to see Dart climbing off. Razor nodded to him, then gestured to her.

Dart let out a low whistle. "Fuck."

"Yep. Stay with Tabby for a while?"

"Sure."

She didn't want to let him go, but she forced herself to stay back with Dart while he talked to the firemen.

How had this happened?

Several hours later, with no answers, they pulled into the driveway at Razor's house. Both of them were exhausted. They stunk of smoke, and could barely even manage to stumble into the house. After a quick shower, they collapsed into bed.

T ABBY OPENED HER EYES.

Her heart was racing. She looked over at the clock. It was just after five. That was practically a sleep-in for her. Had a nightmare woken her?

Then she heard the knocking at the door. Luna barked.

"Razor?" she said.

"I heard it." He got up with a groan and grabbed a pair of pajama pants, pulling them on and a T-shirt. He'd started sleeping in just boxers lately. "Luna, stay."

Luna whined as he walked past.

In her gut, she just knew that something was wrong. Climbing out of bed, she hastily pulled on some clothes.

"What the hell?" Razor snapped. "What the fuck are you talking about?"

"Turn around and put your hands behind your back, or we'll have to use force."

Oh fuck. She recognized that voice. Not wanting to leave Razor alone with Detective Andrews, she ran down the passage to find Razor and the detective glaring at each other. Two police officers stood with the detective.

"What's going on? What's the matter?" she asked.

"Turn around and put your hands behind your back," the detective ordered.

"What? Why are you arresting Razor?"

"Nothing to do with you, ma'am," the detective said slimily.

"They think I set fire to my own garage," Razor snarled.

"That's ridiculous. Razor would never do that. And he was with me the whole time."

"I don't think you're a very reliable witness, Ms. Smarts. How is your cousin, by the way?" Detective Anders gave her a smirk.

Oh shit. He knew who she was? That Jared was her cousin? No wonder he didn't consider her reliable.

"Besides, I have a witness," the detective added as Luna kept barking. "Cuff him, and shut that mutt up."

"Luna, quiet," Razor ordered.

"No, don't! Please!" she cried.

"If you don't stand back, Ms. Smarts, we'll have to arrest you as well," Andrews told her.

"Wait, I'll fucking cooperate. You assholes. Just leave her the fuck alone."

Razor turned so they could cuff him. Detective Andrews read him his rights as they led him out, and she ran after him, panic filling her. "You can't arrest him. Why would he set fire to his own shop?"

"Insurance money, of course," Andrews replied as they placed Razor into a cop car.

"Tabby, call Reyes. Tell him what's happened. Stay here. Wait for him to come get you."

"What about a lawyer?"

"Reyes will organize it. Just stay inside where it's safe. Got me? Go to your apartment or stay with Reyes. Stay safe."

She stood on the pavement and watched as they drove away with him. Panic threatened to overwhelm her.

Get it together, Tabby!

She couldn't help him standing here like an idiot. Ignoring the way the stones bit into her bare feet and how she shivered in the morning cold, she raced inside with Luna at her heels.

Rushing into the bedroom, she grabbed her phone. Fuck! She didn't have Reyes' number. Her fingers shook. She had Millie's, though. And she'd know what to do. All she knew was that she needed to help Razor. Immediately.

LATER ON THAT AFTERNOON, Tabby sat outside the courthouse. The sun was shining, but she felt chilled.

Reyes was on the phone next to her, speaking quietly into it. After calling Millie, she'd fed Luna, then dropped her off with Lois, promising to keep the older woman updated.

Spike sat on her other side while Sav paced up and down the pavement.

"Can't we go inside?" she asked.

"Best we wait out here," Duke told her as he approached with a bottle of water and a muffin. "You need to drink and eat."

"I can't eat anything, thank you."

She thought she'd be sick if she tried.

"This will be over quickly," Duke tried to reassure her. "And Razor will be unhappy if he comes out and finds you looking like this. He'd want us to take care of you."

"I just can't. Sorry."

"Leave her be," Sav said gruffly. "You wouldn't be hungry in her position."

Duke sighed, but backed off. She sent Sav a small smile.

"Fuc—flipping bad timing that Duncan is away on holiday," Duke muttered. "Anyone know if this lawyer is any good?"

"Don't know," Reyes replied. "I didn't get a good feeling talking to him. Might be best to look for someone else or fly Duncan home."

"He'll be pissed about that," Duke replied.

"Don't care," was all Reyes replied.

"Reyes," Spike said. Turning, she saw an older man in a suit walking towards them. He was frowning. That knot in her gut tightened. This wasn't good.

"What happened? Did he get bail?" Reyes asked, putting his phone away.

The man, who she guessed was the lawyer, shook his head. "With his previous conviction, the judge decided he was a flight risk and refused to grant bail."

No. No, this couldn't be happening. The world around her spun, and for a moment, she was worried she was going to pass out.

"What the fuck," Sav snapped. "That was fucking years ago, and he didn't take off then."

"I don't know what to tell you," the lawyer said. "The judge wouldn't budge. Does anyone have it out for him? Judge Fallows is never usually that harsh."

"The detective," she said. Everyone turned to look at her.

"Detective Andrews, he arrested Razor. He hates him. Did you tell the judge that I was with him all day?"

The lawyer gave her a condescending look. "That will have to wait for trial."

"So he's just stuck in jail until he goes to court?" she asked. "There must be something more we can do. I don't understand who this witness is. They have to be lying."

"I've got to go. Call me if anything changes."

The lawyer hastily left. That was it?

"Fuck," Reyes said. Then he took hold of her shoulders with his hands. "Don't worry, Tabby. I have other resources I can tap. We'll fly Duncan back. We'll get him out. I promise."

She nodded numbly. But they wouldn't get him out today. He'd have to stay at least one night in jail. It wasn't fair. She just knew that Detective Andrews had done something to ensure he didn't get bail.

She'd love to teach that asshole a lesson.

"Let's go get some of your stuff," Reyes said. "You can stay with Emme and me until Razor is out."

Stay with him? No, she didn't want to stay with him.

"She'll stay with us," Spike said. "Millie wants her."

"Sunny already told me to bring her to our place," Duke added.

She stared around at them all in amazement. Not that long ago, she'd been all on her own. And now, here they were, practically arguing over who got to take her home. It might all be for Razor, but it still filled her bucket up just a bit more.

"I want to go home," she whispered.

"It would be better if you were with someone," Reyes told her. "It's not safe on your own."

"I . . . I . . . please."

"I'll stay with her."

She looked over at Sav gratefully.

"That okay with you, Tabby?" Reyes asked.

"Yes," she said in a hoarse voice. "I want Sav to stay with me."

"All right. Try not to worry too much, okay?" Reyes said to her. "We will figure this out. We'll get him out."

She nodded numbly.

Spike had picked her up in his truck, and he dropped her back off with Sav following on his bike. Sav and Spike spoke quietly as she went across to grab Luna from Lois. The other woman hugged her tight, telling her to call if she needed anything.

But there was only one thing she needed.

Razor.

LATER THAT NIGHT, she lay in bed staring up at the ceiling. There was no way she could sleep. She was too worried about Razor.

What was she going to do?

Sav was asleep in the spare bedroom. She didn't want to get up and wake him. Besides, it wasn't like she could go for a jog at eleven-thirty at night.

Razor would kill her.

She missed him so much. Rolling over, she grabbed her phone and went through the texts she'd received from the girls today. There were so many, she hadn't been able to answer them all. Finally, they'd added her to their group chat.

She never thought she'd have this. She just wished they had a way of helping her.

Then it suddenly occurred to her. Cat! She'd said to call if she needed help.

But what could she do? There was nothing, right?

Except, what if she could do something and Tabby didn't call her?

Oh hell. What was the worst that could happen? She

wouldn't answer? She'd tell her that there was nothing she could do? At least Tabby would have tried something. And right now, she felt so helpless that she'd do anything to alleviate this feeling.

Climbing out of bed, she moved into the bathroom so that she wouldn't wake Sav. This ache in her stomach hurt. It hurt worse than anything Luther had ever done to her, that was for sure.

The phone rang.

"Tabby? What's wrong?" Cat's voice came through the phone as clear as though she was sitting across from her.

Tabby's throat seized up. She couldn't answer.

"Tabby? Are you all right? Wait, is someone threatening you? Grunt once for yes, twice for no."

Someone else spoke in the background, their voice deep. A man. Cat replied in Spanish.

"Tabby?"

"I'm all right," Tabby managed to get out.

"You sure? Say the word or grunt the grunt and my Papi will come rescue you."

"No, no, it's not me that's in trouble."

"But someone is, or you wouldn't be calling me. I'm almost hurt."

Tabby thought she was teasing. She hoped she was. But at the moment, it was difficult to tell. She was just too exhausted and heart sore to work out the finer nuances of what Cat was saying.

"My boyfriend, he's in jail."

"What'd he do?"

"He didn't do anything. This detective has it in for him. He arrested him for setting his business on fire. The detective said he has a witness, but he can't because Razor was with me the entire time."

"Wow, that detective sounds like a real dick."

That deep voice said something again.

"Papi, it's not swearing if it's the truth," Cat complained. "Sorry, keep going, Tabby."

"I don't know what to do. I don't know why I called you. The judge won't give him bail because he was in jail years ago. Our lawyer doesn't seem like he even cares. I just . . . I can't be without him, Cat."

"I get it, Tabby. Let me see what I can do. Hold on."

Tabby paced, needing to get rid of some excess energy.

"Tabby?"

"Yes?"

"You know Bert and Ernie, the guys who kidnapped me?"

"Yeah?" she asked, wondering why she was bringing this up.

"They ended up dead. And it wasn't my Papi."

She thought her father would kill them. Tabby's eyes widened. Then that deep voice spoke again.

"My Papi is going to send someone to help, okay?"

"He is? Who?"

"A lawyer, he's the best. You can trust him. He'll call you when he arrives, okay?"

"All right."

"He can be a complete asshole, but he's also the best there is."

"I don't care if he's an asshole as long as he helps. What's his name?"

"Reuben Jones."

27

T abby sat at the dining table the next morning, poking at the scrambled eggs Sav had cooked.

"You should try to eat something," Sav told her.

"I know, I'm sorry. I wish I could."

Sav just grunted.

Her phone started ringing and she jumped for it. "Hello?"

"Is this Tabitha Smarts?" a sharp-sounding voice asked. He sounded impatient, hurried.

"Yes. Who is this?"

"Reuben Jones, I was told you were expecting my call."

"I was. I didn't expect you to get here so quickly."

"Well, you have friends in high places with big pockets. And their own private plane."

She did? Who? Jared? No, that made no sense. He meant Cat. Shoot. She probably did need to eat something, she was slow on the uptake today.

"Miss Smarts, I'm tired and hungry. I want to get this done. I have other things to do."

"Okay. Sorry."

Cat warned you he could be an asshole.

He sighed. "No, I'm sorry. I don't mean to be rude. Truthfully, it just comes naturally."

"Um, okay. It's all right."

She was aware of Sav giving her a curious glance, so she forced herself to smile at him.

"I think it would be easier if we met in person. I'm going to have to twist some arms to get things done today and I want to start as soon as possible. Can you meet me by the police station? Is there a good café near?"

"Um, there's a diner on the corner across from it."

"Good. Forty-five minutes?"

"I'll be there."

FORTY MINUTES LATER, Sav pulled up outside the diner.

"Don't know about this."

Sav hadn't wanted her to come meet this guy, hadn't liked any of what she'd told him about Cat and her Papi. But in the end, he'd brought her. However, he'd also called Reyes to let him know what was going on. One of Ink's people was researching Reuben Jones.

She didn't care who he was or what he'd done, as long as he got Razor out of jail.

"It will be fine."

She climbed out of the passenger side of Razor's truck. Sav stomped around, frowning at her. "You should wait for me before you get out."

"Sorry. Come on. I don't want him to leave." She walked into the diner, coming to a stop as she realized that she had no clue who this guy was. Then she spotted a dark-haired, handsome man over in the corner. He was working on his phone and he looked tired.

Somehow, she just knew it was him.

She moved swiftly over to the corner, aware of Sav behind her. The man looked up, frowning. That frown turned into a scowl as he spotted Sav.

"Who is he?"

"A friend. Mr. Jones?"

He grunted. "Call me Reuben. Sit. I don't have long. I'm going over the detective's head. What an asshole. If we can get to the district attorney, I could get these charges dropped."

"You can do that?" Sav asked.

"I can do anything. Who are you?"

"This is Sav," she said hastily, slipping into the seat across from him. Sav remained standing beside her. This didn't seem to intimidate Reuben at all, who just smiled up at him. With a lot of teeth.

Yikes.

"Do you really think you can get this overturned? You believe that Razor didn't do this?"

"It doesn't matter to me if he did or didn't do it. But I don't like some of the things I've learned about this Detective Andrews. After I've resolved this, I think I'll go after him."

She glanced up at Sav.

"How can you know anything about him? Didn't you only learn about him a few hours ago?" Sav asked.

"About ten hours ago. I can do a lot in ten hours. I don't sleep. I don't like shady cops. At all. So, tell me what happened."

She started with the call about the fire to Razor getting arrested.

"He said he has a witness?" Reuben asked.

"Yes, but I don't see how. Razor was with me the whole time."

"Any way you can prove that?"

"I don't know how," she said, bewildered. "Why isn't my word enough?"

"Does the detective know who you are?"

Sav let out a low warning noise that Reuben ignored.

"Yes, he mentioned it. You know?"

"I do. You don't think you can be friends with Cat without Alejandro doing a complete background on you, do you?"

She didn't point out that she wasn't actually friends with Cat. Who was Alejandro? Her father?

"He'll try to discredit you. We need indisputable evidence. A timeline. I need to find out the approximate time the fire was lit. Also, who this witness is since they're lying. Razor have any enemies?"

"Other than the detective? I don't know . . . I don't think . . ."

"What about Tommy?" Sav asked quietly.

"Who is Tommy?" Reuben asked.

"He's a guy who worked for Razor until recently," she explained.

"He was fired? He might hold a grudge?"

"Um, yes, Razor also hit him because he touched me."

Reuben stared up at her from where he was taking notes on his phone. "Right. That's interesting."

That was all he had to say? She shared a look with Sav.

"Give me the timeline of where you went yesterday from lunchtime until that call."

She rattled off the places.

"Wonder if the restaurant had cameras."

"Cameras? Oh my God! Why didn't I think of that? My apartment. It has cameras."

"Yeah? Good. That might be too early for when the fire was lit, but it doesn't hurt to get the footage. Can you grab it?"

Shoot. Did that mean she'd have to ask Jared? Maybe. But it would be worth it.

"Yes, I can."

"Good. I'm going to go check on a few things. I'll be in touch." He packed up and left.

She stood and looked up at Sav. "Do you think he'll be able to help?"

"I don't know, but he's confident and he seems ruthless. Surely, he can't do any worse than that other lawyer."

She guessed at this stage, she'd take that.

"What do you want to do now?"

"Can we go to my apartment? I'll set up the automatic feeder for my fish and then I'll call Jared. I might need to be there to do something with the cameras."

Sav just nodded.

She grasped hold of his forearm as he turned away. "Sav? Thanks for helping. And for being here with me."

"Razor would want me to take care of you. Besides, we're friends, right?"

"Right."

~

As soon as she walked in, she knew something was wrong. But before she could figure out what was going on, she was staring at Sav's back.

"Tabby, run."

"What? What is it?"

"I suggest you move away from my cousin, Mr. Miller," a smooth voice warned.

She shivered, hearing the deadly intent. She knew that he wouldn't hesitate to hurt Sav if he thought that he was a threat to her.

"Sav, it's okay. This is my cousin. He won't hurt me." She stepped to the side so she could see Jared.

He was sprawled on her sofa, looking deceptively casual. But she knew that he was on alert for any threat or danger. And his two bodyguards, Bill and Bentley, were as well.

"I know who he is," Sav said, grasping hold of her arm.

Jared's gaze immediately went to where he was holding her arm.

"Sav, let go of me."

"No. You're not going near him."

There was something in Sav's voice that told her he wasn't entirely here. As though he was looking at Jared and seeing someone else.

"I won't," she reassured him. "Why don't you go wait downstairs?"

"No. I have to protect you."

"I'm not in danger from Jared. Trust me."

Sav looked down at her, then he let out a shuddering breath. He gazed around at Jared and his men. "Fuck. Fine. But I'm not leaving."

"All right."

Jared's eyes narrowed, but she sent him a quelling look. "Jared, what are you doing here?"

"I've come to collect you," Jared told her smoothly. "Go and get your stuff. You're coming home with me."

She gaped at her cousin. Had he lost his mind? Why would he think she'd go with him?

"We had an agreement."

"Yes, and that agreement said that if you got into danger that you would move back home."

"I'm not in danger."

"You don't think that rescuing Cat De Leon from a kidnapper is getting into trouble? You could have been hurt. What if he'd had a gun?" Jared had stood at this stage; his voice hadn't risen, but it was clear to see he was upset. Sav must have thought so as well because he took a half-step forward.

Okay, she couldn't have that.

"Sav, my cousin isn't going to hurt me," she snapped at him. "Stand down."

Sav stared at her. "Tabby, you don't know—"

"I do," she insisted quietly. "I've lived in that life for years. I know who my cousin is. And he's not like my uncle. He won't hurt me."

Jared sighed. "This is getting tiresome. You're coming home, Tabby. I can't have you in danger. What were you thinking, jogging in the early hours like that?"

"You sound like Razor."

"And we have to talk about this boyfriend of yours. That's going to end."

"It's not."

"It is. He's no good for you. Look at what he's got you messed up with."

"He didn't set fire to his garage, and even if he had, you wouldn't care. So what's your objection?"

"He's too old for you."

"Try again."

"I don't like who he hangs out with. He has a record."

"Oh, come on, Jared. That's just laughable."

"Fine. I want you to come home. I can't protect you out here. I did my best with this apartment and your car. I did think of getting someone to follow you."

She gasped. "You promised you wouldn't. You never break a promise."

"And I didn't break this one." He gave her a furious look. "That promise was bogus, though. I should never have promised that. Obviously not since they would have dragged you back home after you threw yourself at Cat De Leon's kidnapper."

"I didn't throw myself at them," she muttered. "How do you know Cat? How do you know about the kidnapping if you weren't following me?"

"De Leon," Sav muttered. "She's not . . ."

"Alejandro De Leon's girlfriend?" Jared asked dryly. "Yes, she is. Tabby rescued the wife of the leader of the most powerful crime syndicate in the United States."

"I what?" she said in a strangled voice.

"Alejandro De Leon is powerful and ruthless," Jared told her. "He's also indebted to you."

"You spoke to him?"

"Yes, he called me in the early hours of the morning to tell me everything that happened. Something you should have done. Apparently, Cat didn't tell him about you until you called her for help. Why did you call her and not me?"

"Because I didn't think you would help me."

Jared snorted. "We're going home."

She was still reeling that Cat was the wife of some powerful criminal. She wondered why she'd never mentioned him? The only person she'd talked about was her Papi.

Oh.

Surely not?

Was Alejandro her Papi?

Mind. Blown.

"Why did De Leon call you?"

"We have business dealings. That sort of thing requires some honesty when family is involved."

Right.

"I'm not going home with you, Jared. Cat organized a lawyer for Razor. But I've got to see if I can get the camera footage from here so Reuben can build a timeline."

"Reuben?" Jared asked. "Not Reuben Jones?"

"Yes, why? Do you know him?"

"I know of him. He'll get your boyfriend out. Unfortunately, you'll need to break things off with him. You're coming home with me."

"No, I'm not."

"I'm afraid I have to insist," Jared replied. "For your own safety."

"She said she doesn't want to," Sav told him.

Jared's guys reached for their guns. Fuck. Fuck. Fuck.

This was going to end really badly.

"Oh, goody, I didn't miss the show."

She gasped at the voice that came from behind her. Turning, her jaw dropped open.

"What the hell are you doing here?"

28

B oth of Jared's guards had their guns out and trained on the new guy, who didn't seem to care. He strolled inside with a whistle and tapped at the glass of the fish tank.

"You're not supposed to tap the glass," she told him.

Sav shot her a look.

What? You weren't.

"Who the fuck are you?" Jared snapped. "How did you get in here?"

That's what she'd like to know.

"Oh, you aren't?" the man asked her instead. "That's too bad. You know, I'd quite like to get a pet but I'm never home. How often do they need to be fed?"

"Every day," she told him. "Although you can get an automatic feeder."

What was going on? Why was he here? This felt surreal.

As usual, he wore a cap low on his face. His beard had gotten longer since the last time she saw him.

"Perhaps I should get a human instead."

Get a human? What the hell?

"Reynard? What are you doing here?" she asked.

He rocked back on his heels. "Oh, I'm here to talk to your cousin."

"I don't know you. Definitely don't want to talk to you. Oh, and you're not leaving here alive," Jared snarled. "How did you get in here? You need mine or Tabby's fingerprint to get through the system. You broke into the wrong house."

"It's amazing what you can get off a metal surface."

What did that mean? Oh, wait.

"Off the water bottle you handed me? You took my fingerprint and somehow used it to get through my security?"

"You're clever," Reynard told her with a wink. "I see why Razor likes you."

"You know Razor?"

"Hm."

What kind of answer was that?.

"You've been following me? That's why I often saw you out jogging?"

"You were the weak link, you see. I was going to use you to get to your cousin."

"Get to me?" Jared asked.

"You have something I want," Reynard said. "I have something you want."

"You don't have anything I want."

Reynard turned back to her. "I was going to take you as leverage. But then you got interesting."

"Interesting?"

"Not every person I know would run off to help someone in trouble. And then that person turns out to be Cat De Leon. That was very interesting."

"How did you know who she was?" Cat had been careful to keep her face hidden.

"Oh, I had a chat with her kidnappers."

A chat? Did he mean he forced the information from him? Had he been the one to kill them?

Reynard looked over at her cousin and his guards. "Boys, you're not going to shoot me so put the guns away."

"Why shouldn't they shoot you?" Jared snapped while she stared at Reynard in shock.

"Because like I said, I have something you want. Or someone."

"There's no one I care about you could have."

"No? Not a certain blonde bombshell?"

Jared stiffened.

Who was Reynard talking about?

"Where is she? What have you done with her?" Jared stormed towards Reynard, who didn't look worried.

Was he insane?

Seemed that way.

Sav stood half in front of her and she peered around him, not wanting to take her gaze off either man.

"Oh, she's safe. For now. But if you'd like to know where she is, there's something you have to do for me."

Jared clenched and unclenched his hands.

"And before you think to kill me, I should warn you that would be a bad idea. For her."

Her mind spun.

Reynard had been going to use her as a pawn in a game that she didn't understand. But then she'd become interesting to him because she'd helped Cat escape from Bert. Who was now dead. Killed by Reynard. Who'd lifted her fingerprint from a metal bottle.

"Why did you keep following me?" she asked in a strangled voice. "After I helped Cat, I mean."

"Ah, that was for a different reason. I had to make sure that your cousin hadn't sent you to spy on Razor."

Her mouth opened and shut.

"Why would I care about that old biker and his garage?" Jared asked.

"Hey!" she protested. "That old biker is the man I love. Be nice."

Reynard grinned. "Yeah, be nice. Anyway, this is how it's going to go, Bartolli. You're going to get me an invitation to the auction run by the Russian. And I'm going to look after your blonde friend until after I've been to the auction. Then I'll send her home to you." Reynard pulled a phone from his pocket and handed it to Jared. "Don't lose this. It's how I'll get hold of you."

With that, he turned and wandered out.

"Bill, follow him. Grab him," Jared commanded. "Don't kill him, though. I need him alive."

Bill raced out. But she had a feeling the bodyguard wouldn't find him. There was something about Reynard that told her he wasn't as casual as he pretended to be.

"Who the fuck was that guy?" Jared snarled. "How do you know him?"

"I don't know him. I just saw him jogging a few times. He stopped once when I wasn't feeling well and tried to give me some water. He told me his name is Reynard."

There was the noise of someone climbing the stairs. It sounded like two sets. Satisfaction filled Jared's face, until the door opened and Reuben walked in.

But it was the man behind him that filled her vision. He looked exhausted. Grouchy. But he was here.

"Razor!" She raced towards him, throwing herself into his arms.

He caught her, holding her tight.

"I was so worried. I thought I wasn't going to see you again. I'm so happy you're here. Don't ever leave me." She sobbed as she spoke. She had no idea if he could understand a word she said.

But it didn't matter. He was here. He wasn't going anywhere.

Razor lifted her up and she wrapped herself around him. She wasn't ever letting him go. Wherever he went, so did she.

"Does someone want to explain what the fuck is going on here?" Razor demanded.

RAZOR GLARED at the men in his girl's apartment.

What the fuck?

Had Reuben known that Tabby's cousin would be here? Razor wasn't sure how Reuben came to be his lawyer. He guessed Reyes had hired him. Reuben hadn't told him anything except that they should go talk to Tabby.

Which was fine with him.

But now he had her and she was fine, someone was going to answer his questions.

Like what the fuck her cousin was doing here.

"Someone talk. Now. And why does that fucker have a gun out in front of my girl?" He glared at the goon he guessed belonged to Jared.

Razor remembered Jared from the night he and Reyes had dropped Luther and Tabby off to him. He didn't like the fucker then, and he fucking hated him now.

"You're Jared Bartolli," Reuben said.

"Yes," Jared said. "Reuben Jones?"

"Yep. What are you doing here?" Reuben asked.

"How did the two of you get up here?" Jared demanded.

Yeah, he definitely hated the fucker. Couldn't he just answer some damn questions without asking questions of his own?

"Some guy was coming out and we grabbed the door as he walked past," Reuben told him.

"Did he have a ball cap on?" Jared asked urgently.

"No," Razor replied. "He looked like a goon-for-hire."

Jared scowled at him. Razor just glared back.

"What's going on?" Razor snapped. "Sav?"

"What's going on is that my cousin is coming home with me. You don't need any of this stuff, Tabby. I'll buy you new stuff. Let's go."

"Like fuck she is," Razor roared. "She's going nowhere with you."

Suddenly, Jared's guard turned his gun on him. Only, Tabby was directly in the line of fire.

"Put your fucking gun down," Razor yelled, seeing red. Fucker was dead. So dead.

Jared turned to his goon with a frown. "What the fuck are you doing? Put your gun down!"

"I could take him out."

"Well, you're not going to risk hitting my fucking cousin. Put it down, now!" Jared demanded.

The man lowered his gun and Razor's heart rate started to slow. He still wanted to murder the bastard, though. How dare he have a gun aimed at his girl?

He needed to get her out of here.

Footsteps sounded on the stairs and he turned.

"Baby girl, get behind me." He managed to get her down, pushing her gently behind him so her back was to the wall and he was in front of her. Protecting her.

The same guy that had let them in downstairs came into the room. He was panting, sweating.

"Well?" Jared demanded.

"He disappeared, boss. I don't know where he went."

"Mother-fucking bastard."

Who disappeared? He looked to Sav who just shook his head. Right, he'd get the full story later.

Jared turned his gaze to Razor. His eyes narrowed as Tabby peeked around him. "Get out of the way. She's coming home with me. It's not safe for her here."

"She won't be staying here," Razor countered. "She's moving in with me."

"With you? And how will you keep her safe? You can't even keep yourself out of jail."

"Actually, all charges have been dropped," his lawyer said, flicking some imaginary lint from his sleeve. "They were completely bogus, which helped. Perpetuated by a disgruntled ex-employee and a corrupt detective."

"What?" Sav asked. "Completely dropped?"

"Neighbors had cameras," Razor told him. "Because of all the graffiti recently."

"And on the video feed, you could clearly see who lit the fire. A Thomas Mancetti," Reuben added.

Tabby moved up beside him. "Tommy?"

Razor kept an eye on Jared and his guys. Tabby leaned into him as though she was too exhausted to stand on her own. He put his arm around her.

"Yep, not only did he light the fire, but he was also Detective Andrews' key witness," Reuben informed her.

"It was a weak case that never should have gone that far. That detective obviously thought you couldn't or wouldn't fight back. Don't worry, I'll see he pays for that." Reuben smiled. "Starting with taking his badge. That's already in the works."

"You're scary," Tabby breathed out.

Reuben nodded his head at her. Then turned to Razor. "You're just lucky that your girlfriend has friends in high places."

"What do you mean?" Razor asked. "I thought Reyes hired you."

"I don't know a Reyes. I was hired by your girl's friend, Cat."

"Cat?" Razor asked her.

"I'll tell you later," she whispered. "But Cat has connections."

"Now that my job is done, I'm going to leave. Unless you need me here." Reuben looked to Bartolli. "I'm certain that De Leon won't want Tabitha upset. And it sounds like leaving with you would greatly upset her."

Had the lawyer just threatened Jared? And with De Leon? The only De Leon he knew of was Alejandro De Leon. But that couldn't be right. Could it?

But Jared gave a stiff nod.

"Good. Now that's settled, I'll be leaving."

"Thank you," Tabby said. "Really."

"This was actually fun. While I'm in Montana and have a private jet at my disposal, I think I'm going to go visit my sister and her men." He whistled as he left.

HER MEN?

Tabby shook that off. Not important. She turned to Jared, who appeared about ready to blow. She took in a deep breath, then tried to step away from Razor, thinking that might help her cousin feel better.

But Razor held her tighter, shaking his head when she glanced up at him.

"No."

"But—"

"No."

"I wasn't going to—"

"No."

"Stop telling my cousin what to do," Jared ordered. "You have no right to control her."

She huffed out a breath. What right did Jared have to say that?

"He's not trying to control me," she told him. "He's keeping me safe. Who was that blonde that Reynard was talking about?"

Jared's face closed down. "No one."

Uh-huh.

"Reynard?" Razor asked.

"Explain later," Sav told him.

Razor didn't look happy, but he nodded.

"Right. You have your secrets, and you have a lot going on. I have my life. And my life is with Razor. Not you," she gentled her voice for that last bit. "I love you, Jared. I always will. You've always been like a big brother to me. But I can't live with you forever. And I can't do what you want this time. I want to be with Razor."

Jared just stared at her for a long moment and she thought she hadn't gotten through. Then he suddenly nodded. "Fine."

"Fine?" she repeated, shocked.

"You can go with him—"

Razor let out a scoffing noise and she squeezed him, asking him silently to be quiet.

"But he needs to guarantee your safety."

"He can't guarantee that," Tabby protested.

"Done," Razor said.

"And I want a promise that you'll come to me if she ever needs protection or is in danger," Jared added.

Her mouth dropped open. What the hell? Were they just going to leave her out of these crazy negotiations?"

"All right," Razor said. "But you won't interfere in our lives. No watching us. No cameras. I don't want her involved with your shit."

"Fair enough," Jared said stiffly. "I still want her to check in regularly. She hasn't been doing such a good job of that lately." He shot her a look, but she couldn't deny it.

"Fine," Razor agreed.

"Hey!" she protested. "I'm right here. Is anyone going to ask what I want?"

"Do you object to any of that?" Razor asked.

"Well, no, but I'd still like to be asked."

Jared smiled suddenly. "She's going to be a handful."

"Fine with me. I like her the way she is."

Tabby huffed out an irritated breath. But both men ignored her.

"Now that you're going to be family. We need to talk about how you're going to support my cousin."

"Family?" Razor asked.

"You are going to marry my cousin." There was no question in Jared's voice. Just a firm demand.

She opened her mouth to tell Jared he'd gone too far.

"I am," Razor agreed, shocking her. "But not because that's what you want."

Jared smirked. "As long as you're marrying her. But how are you going to support her?"

"I can support myself," she muttered, knowing she was losing the battle for control of this conversation.

"What are you going to do now that your business has been destroyed?" Jared asked.

Poor Razor. That business was his life.

"I have insurance."

"That won't be quick enough. You need an investor with plenty of cash flow."

"I'm not taking your money," Razor told him.

"It could be a good business relationship."

"No."

Jared huffed out a breath. "Fine, I guess I could release Tabby's trust fund."

"That would be good," she started to say, "wait, what trust fund? I don't have a trust fund."

"You do. The old man kept it from you."

"What? How did I not know? Why didn't you tell me?"

"You were hell-bent on leaving the safety of my protection and I didn't want you to go."

"You gave me a credit card, Jared," she said dryly. "With no limit."

"Well, I didn't want you to do without."

She shook her head. "That makes no sense."

Jared growled. "Fine. I don't know if there was a trust fund or not. But if there was, the old man would have taken it, right?"

"Yes. But you don't know if there was or how much it was. You're not going to just give me money."

Jared growled. "So stubborn."

"It seems to run in the family." She smiled sweetly at him.

"Fine. No money. But you better sort out a way of taking care of her, Samuels. My cousin will not be supporting you. And I will not have her living in poverty."

"Jesus, she won't live in poverty, I have money," Razor spluttered.

Jared just eyed him skeptically. Then he started to move towards the door. Bentley, one of his guards, moved ahead of him. Razor drew her behind him before slamming out his arm to stop the guard.

"One thing."

"What?" the guy asked, turning with a sneer. "Get the fuck out of the way."

Razor drew his arm back then punched the other man in the face. She winced at the crunch of fist against nose. That had to hurt. Bentley bent over with a groan.

"What the fuck!" Bill, the other guard, yelled.

Jared held up his hand to Bill, though. "He deserved that."

"He fucking did," Razor said in a low voice. "You ever point a gun in my girl's direction again, hell, you even look at her again, and you're a dead man."

To her shock, instead of getting mad at the threat, Jared just nodded. He gave Razor a look of respect while Bentley stood, his hand over his bleeding nose.

Should she offer him a towel or something? He was bleeding on her floor. But she had a feeling Razor wouldn't appreciate that.

"We might just get along." Jared met her gaze with his and gave her a small nod. She got it, he wouldn't hug her in front of his men. It was a whole crime boss etiquette thing or something like that. But she nodded back. They might not have had the relationship they once did and likely never would. But she still loved him.

And he loved her as much as he could.

They disappeared down the stairs.

Razor turned and picked her up again, holding her tight. "Let's go home, then someone can tell me what the fuck is going on."

THEY ENDED UP AT REYES' office instead of going home after Razor called and told him the good news. Now, they were all crammed in here. She was sitting on Razor's lap in a chair. Reyes was sitting across from them, while the rest of the guys were spread throughout the room.

Reyes stared at her as they all remained silent, taking in everything she'd just told them.

"You rescued Cat De Leon from a kidnapper," Duke said slowly.

"Well, yes. But I didn't know that she was married to some crime boss," she said. "I thought she was a regular person."

Sort of.

"A regular person who got kidnapped," Ink said dryly.

"Regular people get kidnapped, right? Although she was very calm about it all. And she said that it wasn't her first time. Okay, there were a few signs. Still, I had no idea who she was when I called her for help."

"So why call her?" Reyes asked curiously.

"I don't know. I just had a feeling, I guess. Maybe I was just desperate to help Razor and wanted to try everything." She leaned her head against his chest.

"You did good." Razor kissed the top of her head.

"She's on De Leon's radar now, though," Reyes warned. He was frowning. "I'll have to talk to Markovich, see what he knows about him."

"Don't think he's a risk to us," Sav said.

Everyone turned to look at him, including her. She felt like they had a bond now, her and Sav.

"He's grateful to Tabby. He used his resources to help her. I don't think he'll hurt her."

Reyes nodded. She let out a relieved sigh. She didn't want to think she'd put them all in hot water with her choice to call Cat.

"Can't believe how quickly that lawyer got you out," Duke said. "He on the up and up?"

"No," Ink said in a sharp voice. "Brody looked into him. He's ruthless. Savage. Defends some seriously crooked people. But he's good. Also, I got news that Detective Andrews is on unpaid leave while they look into his conduct."

Good. It was the least that asshole deserved.

"I want to know who the hell this Reynard is," Razor said. "It sounds like he knows me. And he was following Tabby. He could be a threat."

"I don't think he is, either," Sav said.

"Why? Did Tabby help save him too?" Ink asked dryly.

"No. I barely know him," she said.

"I did a quick search on the word, Reynard. Any ideas what came up?"

They all stared at him.

"Fox. From some book or something. I didn't read much past that."

She didn't understand why they all grew tense.

"Mother fucker," Duke muttered.

Reyes ran his hand over his face. "Fuck. Should have pieced that together. I need some sleep."

He did look tired.

"Does that mean something to you all?" she asked.

"Yeah," Razor told her. "I'll explain it later."

"You didn't say anything to Bartolli?" Reyes asked Sav.

"Nah, seemed if he wanted Bartolli to know he'd tell him himself."

"Is my cousin in danger?" she asked.

Reyes shook his head. "I don't think so. If the Fox wanted to harm him, he could have. He needs him to get into this auction."

"Why the hell didn't Markovich tell you any of this?" Razor snapped.

Markovich? Wasn't that Emme's dad?

"You know he gave the Fox free rein to do what he thinks is best," Reyes replied.

"Emme's dad has something to do with this guy?" This was getting more and more bizarre.

Everyone just stared at her. Okay, no one was going to tell her?

"Because he's dangerous. He killed Bert and Ernie," she pointed out.

"He killed some puppets?" Ink asked.

"No, Bert and Ernie, the guys who kidnapped Cat. He murdered them."

"Fuck," Reyes said. "I'll talk to Markovich, see if he can contact him and find out what the fuck he's doing. He's going too far."

Razor stood with her in his arms. "I'm taking Tabby home. She's exhausted and I want a decent meal and a fucking shower. I feel disgusting."

She clutched at him.

"All right," Reyes said. "I'll keep you all informed. Glad to see you, bro."

Razor nodded at them as they all said something similar. Sav followed them out to where Razor's truck was parked.

"I'll give you a ride back to our place so you can get your bike,"

Razor told him. That's what they'd been doing when they diverted to Reaper's.

"Nah, don't worry. Someone else will give me a ride. You two need some time together." Sav looked down at her and gave her a tiny smile. "You did good, Tabby."

"Thanks, Sav. For everything."

Razor kissed her lightly. "Come on, baby girl. Let's get you home. I need a cuddle."

"You get all the cuddles you want. Free of charge."

He grinned at her. "You're so generous. Those things are priceless."

"I know. But so are you."

29

Tabby's mind was spinning by the time they pulled up outside Razor's house.

"So, this guy, the Fox, is an assassin who Emme's dad hired. And he's trying to track down this Mr. X who you all believe kidnapped Emme as a child. And the Fox thinks getting into one of the auctions where this Mr. X sells women is the way to get to him?"

"That about sums it up. With a few other things in there."

"Mind. Blown. So, the Fox is going to take down this human trafficking ring and Mr. X?"

"Hopefully. But he's uncontrollable and unpredictable."

"Emme's dad must have been desperate to find her."

"He was."

"And the reason the Fox thinks that Jared can get him in is because Uncle Fergus used to attend these auctions?"

"That's what I'm guessing."

"Jared doesn't go to them," she said hastily. "He's not like that."

"I'm sure he's not, baby girl."

"I can't believe you never told me any of this."

Razor reached over and undid her seatbelt, lifting her over onto his lap. "I'm sorry. I was trying to protect you. Any knowledge about the Fox is dangerous. You've had enough crappy things happen in your life. But I shouldn't have kept it from you. I'm a hypocrite."

"I forgive you. But only because you had to spend last night in jail and you look exhausted."

"So, I get a 'get out of jail free' card?" he teased.

"Just this once," she warned. "And I still might make you piggyback me around tomorrow."

"Gladly, baby girl. Gladly."

Opening the door, he lifted her down then climbed down himself. "Let's go get Luna, order a pizza, shower, then sleep."

"Sounds good to me, Daddy. Why don't I go get Luna? Otherwise Lois might keep you there for a while. You order us some pizza."

"Thanks."

After reassuring Lois that Razor was fine, she headed over to the house. Luna had already raced off ahead of her.

She pushed open the door and froze.

"We're gonna wait for that bitch girlfriend of yours, then we're going to have some fun."

Holy. Fuck.

Was that the detective? What did he think he was doing? What should she do?

If I'm in danger, call 911 and then call Reyes or Sav or Dart.

Okay, she could do that. She inched out of the doorway and dialed 911. She told the operator what was happening, but refused to stay on the line. Where had Luna gone? She couldn't hear her barking. Was she all right? Was Razor?

Oh God, what if something happened to him?

She called Reyes, but he didn't answer. She couldn't take it anymore. She left him a message. Then she did the same to Sav.

But she wasn't going to let Detective Andrews hurt her man.

She snuck into the house, moving quietly down towards the living room, where she heard them talking.

"What the fuck are you doing, Andrews?" Razor asked. "Do you want to end up in prison?"

"I won't go to prison. That's where you belong," the detective spat.

"Why the fuck do you have this grudge against me? Because one of my guys hit your brother? Does that really equate to you attempting to kill me?"

"I didn't want to kill you. I wanted to lock you up and make you fucking miserable. After all, if I couldn't have the woman I loved, why should you have the woman you loved?"

"What are you talking about? What woman you loved?" Razor asked, sounding as bewildered as she felt.

"Sandy."

Oh. Fuck.

Now this made sense. But that happened years ago. Why was he coming after Razor now? Did he go searching for him?

"You're the guy that Sandy left me for?" Razor asked.

"Took me months to convince her to leave you. And then when she finally did, instead of coming to me, she went to her sister. Because she didn't want to upset you by moving straight in with me. And before I could convince her to move out of that deathtrap, she died. That was your fault!"

"Do you think I don't feel guilty? That I don't remember her and think about what I could have done differently?" Razor asked.

"Far as I'm concerned, you killed her."

That wasn't fair. The detective had an affair with Sandy. Convinced her to leave Razor. It wasn't Razor's fault she'd decided to stay with her sister and had died in a trailer fire.

But then, the detective wasn't exactly acting all that reasonable or sane, was he?

What could she do to help Razor? She needed a weapon. Her stun gun? Pepper spray?

Shit.

"I didn't kill Sandy, and you know it. Did you track me down? Why did it take you so long to find me?"

"I didn't go searching for you," the detective said. "I mean, I did at first, but you'd taken off and I couldn't find you. I gave up for a long time, then I got a transfer to the police force here. My captain wanted to get rid of me. We weren't getting along, let's say. I came from here originally anyway. I didn't know you were here, not until your boy hit my brother. Then I started to look into you, and discovered who you were. Jeremiah Samuels. Also known as Bull-dozer to his old gang. It was like fate handed you to me. And I was going to make you pay."

"Took you some time."

"I had to wait for the perfect opportunity. That idiot, Mancetti, provided it. Only he fucked it all up."

"You got Tommy to set fire to my shop? And to pretend that he saw me do it?"

"Yep, but the idiot was meant to cover his face. I had everything set up. I've got juicy information on two judges; one of them did your bail hearing. You were going to jail for a long time. Your girl would have moved on, she's too young and pretty for you. And you would have suffered like I did. Now, I have no choice but to murder you like I did Mancetti."

Holy hell. He'd completely lost his mind! She dug around in her handbag. She grabbed her pepper spray in one hand and her stun gun in the other. She switched the stun gun's power on. At that moment Luna started barking.

Where was she?

"Shut that dog up!" the detective yelled.

She peered into the room and saw the detective standing at the far end. Luna was on the other side of the double doors, barking her head off.

"She's gonna alert the neighbors!" the detective screamed. "Shut her up!"

Well, if Luna didn't, then he would with his yelling.

"I have to let her in," Razor said. He started moving towards the double doors. As the detective grew more agitated, he started to pay less attention to his surroundings. He turned as Razor moved. This was it. This was her chance. Ignoring her nerves, she raced forward. The detective spun back at the last moment and she somehow managed to get the stun gun close enough to his stomach to zap him. He tilted from side to side, looking dazed and confused.

That's when Razor tackled him. The gun went flying out of his hand. Tabby quickly raced over and grabbed it, then pointed it at the detective.

"Stay down, asshole!" she yelled, her hands trembling.

"You okay, baby girl?" Razor asked.

"Yeah, Daddy. I'm fine. You?"

"Never better." He took in a deep breath then let it out. "Fuck, I didn't reset the alarm because I knew you'd be coming in soon and the bastard just walked right into the house and drew a gun on me. Mother-fucker."

"Well, seems I'm not needed."

She glanced over to see Sav standing in the doorway. Spike appeared from the kitchen.

"Didn't let us have any fun," Spike said as sirens could be heard in the distance. Luna had stopped barking and was now sitting at the door.

Tabby let out a sigh of relief as she lowered the gun.

Sav took over holding the detective down. Andrews was sobbing and not putting up a fight. Razor came over and took the gun, handing it to Spike before taking Tabby into his arms.

Spike let Luna in.

"Going to be fully gray by the time the week is done," he muttered as he picked her up.

She held on as tight as she could to him. "I told you, Daddy. You'll still be my sexy silver fox. Actually, maybe not. Foxes have taken on a whole different meaning. My sexy silver badger. Nope. That's no good. Sexy silver snake. Hm, no."

"We'll figure it out, baby girl," he said, holding her tight.

"Yep. Together we can do anything."

30

Razor woke up when his cock was surrounded by something warm and wet.

He opened his eyes and looked around, his heart racing.

Home. He was home.

Fuck.

He'd been fucking terrified that he wasn't going to get out of that jail cell.

And if Andrews had had his way, he wouldn't have. Fuck, he couldn't believe that Detective Shane Andrews was the guy that Sandy left him for. And that he'd planned this revenge on Razor and used Tommy to set it up.

He'd confessed to killing Tommy as the cops were arresting him. In fact, everything had come out. Including where he'd dumped Tommy's body. Now, Razor was wondering if Tommy had something to do with those assholes who had broken into his shop. He could have given them the code to the gate.

Fuck. He might never know. And it didn't matter. The detective had been arrested, and Tommy was out of the picture. Tabby was safe. So was he.

Everything was so much brighter this morning. Especially with his girl's mouth around his cock. After the cops took Detective Dick Face away, Sav and Spike had left them to eat cold pizza. They'd praised Luna, then after a quick shower, they'd collapsed into bed.

He'd been asleep before his head even hit the pillow.

"Fuck, that feels good."

She murmured a reply which sent electricity through his blood. God damn it. It wouldn't take much for him to come. He threw off the covers then leaned up on his elbows, so he could stare down at his girl swallowing his dick.

Fuck. Yes.

He'd gone to sleep naked last night, not even having the energy to find a clean pair of boxers to sleep in, and now he was damn thankful.

"Damn, that's the fucking sexiest sight I've ever seen. That's it. Take my dick. Good girl." His breathing grew harsher. He needed to come. Desperately. But he didn't want to come in her mouth. This time, finally, he wanted to take her. To fuck her.

"Please tell me your period has finished," he groaned.

She let him slide out of her mouth and grinned up at him. "Yep."

"Thank fuck." Sitting, he grabbed her under the arms and tossed her onto her back on the bed beside him. Then he froze, worried he might have scared her. But she'd started giggling next to him. His heart began beating again. Thank fuck.

"Get naked and spread'em," he mock-growled at her. "And no more giggling. This is serious work."

"Sorry," she said between giggles as she drew off her T-shirt. It was one of his, he noted. He loved it when she slept in his stuff.

His breath caught when he saw that she wasn't wearing

anything else. Then she slowly spread her legs. He wasted no time diving between her thighs. Fuck, she was already wet and creamy.

And he was in fucking heaven. He parted her lips and licked her juices. She tasted so delicious. He was addicted. He drove his tongue deep inside her as he used his finger to flick at her clit. While he wanted to take his time, savor the taste of her, what he really wanted was to be inside her.

"Tabby-baby, I can't last much longer. I have to have you. Are you ready?"

"I am so ready," she told him. He crawled over to his side of the bed and fetched a condom, quickly rolling it onto his dick. His hands were actually shaking.

Shit. What was wrong with him?

Her. It was all Tabby. She was making him crazy.

"Get on top of me. Ride me."

Her eyes widened, but then a smile lit up her face. "Yes, Sir. Whatever you say, Sir."

He snorted but held out his hand as she straddled him.

"Take me inside you when you're ready, but I want you to keep your gaze on me, understand? Remember who you're with."

She sucked in a breath, staring down at him as she grabbed his dick. She ran her hand up and down the shaft.

"Like I could ever forget. I'm with the man I love more than life."

She knocked the breath right out of his lungs.

"Good," he told her. "Because I love you more than anything, Tabby-baby."

"Oh hell," she groaned. "You're so big."

"You sure know how to stroke a man's ego."

"Is your ego in your dick?" she asked with a cheeky grin, right before she slid herself down over his cock, taking him deep.

He swore that his eyes rolled back in his head. "Fuck, yes, baby. Yes. Move, please."

"You feel so good," she told him. "I didn't know it could be like this. Razor, please. Please."

Reaching down, he thumbed her clit with soft strokes.

"Please, please, please." Her breasts bounced as she slid up and down and with his other hand, he pinched her nipple.

Then he flicked his thumb faster. Harder.

Her movements increased in pace. The need to come burned inside him.

"Get ready. I want you to come. Keep looking at me. That's it. I love you. So fucking much."

He tapped her clit and she came, clenching down around him, her face filling with her pleasure. Fuck, so beautiful. He grabbed hold of her hips and thrust up inside her. Once. Twice. Again and again until he reached that peak and screamed his own release.

Fuck. Yes.

She collapsed on top of his chest and he held her tight, running his fingers through her dark hair.

"That was amazing. I just . . . I didn't know . . . I . . ."

Tears dripped onto his chest but he didn't try to hush her. She had a right to her tears.

She'd earned them.

After a few moments, she shifted and sat up, looking down at him. She ran a finger around his nipple.

"I was so scared, Razor. Terrified that I'd lost you for good."

He sat and drew her into his lap, holding her tight. "Hey now. Nothing is going to happen to me. I'm not ever leaving you. Understand me? The charges were bogus, and even without Reuben's help, they would have gotten thrown out eventually. Detective Dick Face was deluding himself into thinking they wouldn't. But Reuben certainly helped speed things up."

"I'm glad I called Cat. I nearly didn't."

"Yeah, she came through for us."

There was a funny note in his voice that made her draw back to look up at him. "You wish I hadn't called her?"

"No. It's not that. Just wondering what it all means. Whether De Leon will see the debt as paid."

She frowned. "There wasn't a debt, though. I would have helped Cat no matter who she was."

"I know you would have. You might never hear from her again. But if you do, I want you to tell me straight away, okay?"

Was he worried about Cat's husband? That he'd want something? Her stomach rolled over.

"Hey, you didn't do anything wrong. I'm just being cautious, all right?" He tilted up her face, nuzzling his nose against hers. "Don't. Worry."

She huffed out a breath.

He drew back. "But just to be safe, don't mention the Fox to her, okay? Actually, not to anyone."

"I wasn't going to. I can't believe he was following me and I didn't even know. Kind of creepy and scary."

"Yeah, I get it." He rubbed her back, soothing her. "But he won't hurt you. I promise. He's dangerous, but he has an attachment to Sunny. He won't do anything that would upset her."

"So don't piss off Sunny and I'll be fine?" she asked.

"Something like that." He winked. "If it makes you feel better, Sunny doesn't take offense easily." He ran a thumb under her eye. "You look tuckered out."

"I'm all right."

He eyed her.

"I don't sleep well without you."

"Same." He yawned. "I'm still tired despite sleeping eight hours last night. My head feels like it's full of cotton. What say we have a lazy day? Movies. Popcorn. Take-out."

"Can I choose the movie?" she asked, clapping her hands.

"All right. Let me guess Scooby-Doo?"

"Daddy, how did you know?"

"Lucky guess," he said dryly. "Now gimme some sugar to power me up." He pointed to his lips.

Well, if he needed sugar then she had to oblige. Wrapping her arms around his neck, she kissed him.

SHE SLUMPED down at the kitchen table with her third cup of coffee. She felt wrung out. Exhausted. "I don't think I've ever been this tired. Usually, I always have this buzz of energy under my skin."

"Poor baby girl." Razor came over and put his hand on her forehead. "You're not running a fever. Probably just tired out from these past few days. Let me go check the mail then we'll cuddle on the couch."

She nodded. But as soon as he got out of sight, a funny feeling came over her. She couldn't breathe. The room spun around her.

Razor.

She needed Razor.

Stumbling to her feet, she managed to get across the room to find him at the front door, slipping on some shoes.

"Baby girl . . . what . . . ?" He grabbed hold of her. "What is it?"

"Don't . . . can't . . . breathe . . ."

He sat her on the floor then crouched next to her. "It's all right. You're okay. Breathe with me. One, two, three. That's it. Nice and slow. Let's count again."

As he spoke, she started to calm, her throat opened up and she could get air in and out of her lungs.

"Good girl. You're all right." He sat down and drew her into his lap. She buried her face in his chest, clinging to him.

"Sorry. Sorry."

"Hush now," he murmured, his accent thickening. "What happened?"

"I don't know. You left the room and I just panicked. So silly."

"It's not silly," he told her firmly. He cupped the side of her face and she stared up into his dark gaze. "Your emotions and feelings aren't silly. If you weren't having issues, I'd worry about you. Okay?"

She nodded. "What about you, Daddy? Are you having some problems too?"

"Truth is, I don't want you out of my sight either. So how about for today at least, we stick to each other like glue?"

"Okay, Daddy. I think that sounds like a plan."

"Come on, I'm hoping something I ordered has arrived."

Ten minutes later, she squealed as she drew out the Scooby-Doo pajama set as well as a pair of slippers with Scooby faces on the front of them.

"Daddy! I love them! Can I put them on right now?" She pulled off the yoga pants and T-shirt she wore as he laughed.

"I guess that's a yes."

"I wanna wear them while we be lazy all day."

He gave her an indulgent smile. "Okay, Tabby-baby."

THEY'D JUST FINISHED the first movie when Razor's phone rang.

"Hey, man, what's going on? Yeah. He can't get hold of him? Right. Thanks. Yeah, we're okay, taking it easy. I will. Thanks." He ended the call.

"Who was that?" she asked.

"Reyes. He talked to Markovich about the Fox. He didn't know that he was going to use you, but the Fox doesn't tell him all the details of what he does and Markovich, for right or wrong, prefers it that way."

It didn't feel right, hiring someone like that and then giving them free rein. But then, the Fox didn't seem like the type to take orders. At least that's the impression she'd gotten.

"Think he was checking up on us too." Razor sighed as his phone went again.

"Samuels. Right. Yep. Thanks. Okay."

She gave him a curious look. "Detective in charge of the case. They found Tommy's body."

"Oh." She wasn't sure if she was supposed to feel bad or not. Was she desensitized to this sort of thing? Maybe. Was it wrong? Perhaps. But she also wasn't sure that she could deal with much more. And Tommy's death wasn't going to be the thing that sent her over the edge.

"Is it wrong I don't feel bad?"

"No, baby girl. Not wrong at all."

Whew.

"How about we get some popcorn for the next movie?" he asked her.

"Okay, Daddy."

"And maybe some chocolate. That makes everything better, right?"

She managed a small smile. "Right. That and Scooby-Dooby-Doo!"

He groaned, but he was grinning. "You really want to watch it for the hundredth time?"

"Daddy, don't exaggerate." She wiggled a finger at him. "It's only ninety-nine."

He laughed. "What will you give me for watching it again?"

"Hm. Let's see. What could I bribe Daddy with? Well, there's cuddles."

"Always good for bribery."

"And there's sugar."

"Yep. More good currency."

"And there's also making him feel really good while he's watching it." She wriggled her eyebrows up and down.

"Why, Miss Tabby," he said in a high-pitched voice. "Are you propositioning me?"

"Daddy, I meant I'd make you a hot chocolate. What were you thinking about?" She gave him a shocked look.

"Brat!" He leaped for her, his fingers at the ready to tickle. With a squeal, she rolled away from him, laughing. Her phone rang, interrupting them. She grabbed it, answering without looking who it was.

"Hello?"

"Tabby-Cat, it's me! The cat part of the equation."

"Cat!"

Razor froze, staring down at her.

"Thank you so much for your help," Tabby told her. "Reuben was amazing."

"He's an ass, though, right? I mean, he has a good side. And he's completely ruthless."

"He got the charges dropped and Razor out. I'm so grateful. So thank you."

"No problem, Tabby. I'm glad I could help. I don't have many friends, you know? Actually, I have none except for Alejandro's men. I know we can't see each other, but do you think . . . well . . . that you wouldn't mind talking once in a while?"

"I'd love that. We can call and video chat."

"Really? You'd want to do that with me?" The vulnerability in the other woman's voice floored her.

"Of course, I would."

"Yay! You know, Tabby. I think we're going to be the best of friends."

"Hey, it's in the name, right? Tabby-Cat forever."

"Yep." A deep voice called out. "Oh, I better go. Papi is calling me. Bye!"

"Bye, Cat. Thanks again!" After hanging up, she glanced up at Razor. He was gaping down at her.

"Did you just agree to call and video chat with Cat De Leon?"

"She's my friend, Daddy. And she's lonely. Surely, I can be friends with her."

Razor ran his hand over his face. "Okay. Sure. My fiancée is friends with Cat De Leon."

"Wait. Your what?" She glared up at him.

"My fiancée. You heard me say to Jared that we were getting married."

"If you think that's a proposal, you better think again, buster. Because you will be proposing properly. Understand?"

His mouth opened, then shut. "Yes, ma'am. I completely understand."

She grunted. "Too right you do." She caught him grinning. "You think this is funny?"

"I think you are. What happened to that nervous girl who couldn't even look me in the eye? Look at you now, making demands and putting your foot down." He drew her close to him, lifting her up so she could wrap her legs around his waist. "So fucking proud of you."

"That's good, because I have one more demand, and you might not like it."

"What's that?"

"I think we should go see your family."

He sucked in a breath.

"Just listen," she said hastily. "If you propose and if I say yes—"

"If! If?" he interrupted, looking enraged.

"Yes, if. Nothing is guaranteed. Got to ensure you make that proposal good. I don't want anything half-assed."

"What makes you think I'd do half-assed?"

"Um, you just thought that telling my cousin you would marry me was you proposing."

"Oh. Right. Keep going. "

"Don't you want to invite your family to the wedding?"

He was quiet.

"Daddy? What do you think?"

"I think you're right. I think it's time to go see them."

"We could do a road trip. Maybe at Christmas."

He raised his eyebrows. "You'd want to do that?"

"Yeah, Daddy. Please? I want to meet them. But even more than that, I want them in your life. And I think you want that too." The way he looked whenever he talked about them, with sadness and longing, it broke her heart. He'd done so much for her. This was something she could do for him. "Besides, you can't go without me."

"I'd never go anywhere without you, baby girl."

EPILOGUE

I will not plot mischief with Cat.
I will not plot mischief with Cat.
I will not plot mischief with Cat.

SHE SIGHED and shook out her hand. A hundred lines. Ouch. That sucked. Especially since she was having to write them while sitting on a hot bottom. Standing, she yawned.

Swing time.

She'd been sitting for the last few hours writing those lines, she deserved it.

Okay, maybe that was an exaggeration. But still, it felt like she'd been sitting for hours. Moving to her swing, she climbed in and started swinging back and forth on her tummy. A sense of calm came over her as she moved.

She loved the swing. It was still the only place she could nap. Sometimes, when she needed downtime, she'd climb into the area under the Mystery Machine bed and read a book.

But she couldn't sleep in there. There was something about

being weightless that just eased her worries and helped her mind chill out. Which, over these past few months, she'd really needed.

There had definitely been ups and downs. Nightmares, a few panic attacks. Luna had barely left her side throughout. She somehow seemed to sense that Tabby needed extra care at the moment.

They had the shop back up and running now. Things were busier than ever. Razor was even looking to hire some new guys.

"Baby girl? What are you doing in your swing?"

"Oh, hi, Daddy," she said brightly, looking up at him. "Watcha doin'?"

"Well, I was coming in to see if my naughty girl had finished her lines." He leaned against the doorway. He was drinking out of one of the mugs she had made for him.

One said, Best Daddy Ever. Of course. A classic. Another was for when he was at work. That one said, the Biggest Baddest Bossiest Boss. She was pretty proud of that one.

Another mug said, Sexy Silver Saint Bernard. That one always made her smile. But today he was using her favorite.

Daddy, Bringer of the Big O.

He only used that one when they were alone. She didn't know why. He should be proud of the orgasms he gave her. She was certainly proud every time she managed to get him to come. Her favorite was when she'd suck him until he lost control and came in her mouth.

"Are they all written?"

"I don't like writing lines, Daddy," she pouted.

"You're not meant to like writing lines, Tabby-girl," he told her. "You know that you're not supposed to get up until Daddy comes for you?"

"Well, obviously I did not know, since I would have stayed sitting, Daddy. I'm a good girl. I always follow the rules."

"That so? Why are you lying on your tummy, baby girl?"

"Because someone's spanky hand got itchy," she grumbled.

"And why did my spanking hand get itchy?" he asked dryly.

"Um, 'cause you wouldn't use some cream like I suggested?"

"I don't need a cream for it, brat." He walked into the room and set his mug down on her desk.

She sighed. "Because I was talking to Cat."

"Try again."

"Because I was plotting mischief with Cat."

"That's right. That was very naughty trying to help her find a way around one of Alejandro's rules for her."

"I know, Daddy. I'm sorry."

"Can you understand why Daddy spanked you?" he asked.

"Yes, Daddy."

"And put you in the corner with some ginger in your bottom?"

"That was just mean, Daddy. To me and the ginger."

"You'll both survive," he said dryly.

"I don't know about me, but the ginger is traumatized."

He grinned.

"And did I have to do lines on top of all of that?"

"Yes."

"But my bottom hurts."

"Kind of the point. Come here."

He held out his arms and she threw herself at him. Picking her up, he nuzzled her nose with his.

"I love you, Tabby-baby."

"I love you too, Daddy."

He moved out of the bedroom, carrying her down the passage and through the lounge. They walked past her fish tank which he'd made space for and she waved at the gang.

"Where we going, Daddy?" She'd been planning on hanging out in her playroom for a while. Things had been so busy lately, she hadn't had much time for play.

"I have something to show you." He carried her outside. It was getting later in the afternoon. Fall had hit and the temperatures were definitely cooler. She loved this time of the year. Halloween was looming and Millie had big plans for a Halloween party. Tabby had been working on outfits for the three of them.

It was going to be awesome.

He carried her over to the pergola area with their new hot tub.

"What is it, Daddy?" she asked.

He set her down then moved behind a pole of the pergola. Suddenly, fairy lights went on, twinkling above them. Even though it wasn't dark yet, she could see how amazing it would look once the sun set.

"Daddy, that looks awesome."

Music blasted on. She jumped up and down, clapping her hands. "Can we use the hot tub tonight?"

"We sure can. I'm going to go make dinner now. You go play for a while. Then after dinner, we'll hop in."

Awesome.

A FEW HOURS LATER, she was dressed in a bright yellow bikini with a halter-style top. She loved this bikini. It was so bright and cheerful. Razor had bought it for her when they'd gone shopping a few weeks ago.

"I've got Ducky and Snappy's girlfriend, Snappina." She held up the two plastic bath toys. Ducky was a huge, blue duck and Snappina was obviously a turtle.

"Good job, baby girl," Razor murmured, turning the music on low. He ran his gaze over her as he set two towels down on the bench he'd built into the pergola.

"Where are your shoes?" he asked.

"Who needs shoes? I'm only going from the house to the hot tub."

"You need shoes. You can't see where you're walking. There could be glass on the ground. You could step on a prickle."

"Daddy, there's no glass or prickles."

But, ouch, there was a stone.

"You just stood on a stone, didn't you?"

"That can be neither confirmed nor denied."

"For someone that had her butt walloped earlier, you're awfully sassy."

"It's a natural talent, Daddy."

He let out a bark of laughter as he pulled the cover off the hot tub then helped her in.

"Ooh, it's so warm!" she said as she sunk in. Then she shot up. "Ouchy."

"Not good on a sore bottom?" he asked with a smirk.

"It's not nice to laugh at my sore bottom, Daddy," she scolded.

"Sorry."

She managed to get in the second try. It was just a bit of a shock the first time. With a sigh, she settled in and let the jets work their magic. Finally, she opened her eyes and stared over at her man.

Fuck, he was gorgeous.

He grinned. "You think I'm gorgeous, huh?"

"I said that out loud?"

"Did you not want me to know?"

"I don't want you getting a big ego, Daddy."

"I'm sure you'll keep me grounded."

"Well, it would be hard for you to get off the ground with your bulk."

"Little girl," he growled.

She was grinning as she moved over to him. He grabbed her around the waist and lifted her onto his lap so she was straddling his legs.

"Yes, Daddy?"

"You best be nice to me."

"Why, Daddy, is your hand getting itchy?"

"Yep. It sure is."

"Let me see what I can do to make you feel better." Leaning in, she kissed his forehead, then down his nose to his lips. They moved against hers as he deepened the kiss.

"Undo your bikini top," he commanded.

"Out here?"

"Is that your safeword?"

"No, Sir." She reached back and undid the halter neck of her top, revealing her breasts. She reminded herself that the backyard was private and secluded. If anyone arrived, Luna would let them know.

Maybe.

Unless it was someone she knew, like Lois.

"Stop thinking. Do you think I'd let you be exposed or embarrassed?"

Of course he wouldn't. This was Razor. The man who put her first, always. Who protected her. Who loved her.

He cupped her breast, running his thumb over her nipple. She shivered. Her nipples felt extra sensitive and she felt that shock run through her body.

"You have the sweetest nipples. Bring them here." He raised her up so he could lean in and lick her nipples. He suckled on one then the other. Back and forth until she was going insane.

"Sir, please!" she cried.

"Please what, Tabby-baby?" he murmured between laying kisses up her neck. His beard tickled at her skin, sending more pleasure rushing through her.

"Please make me come. Please touch my pussy."

"Poor baby, you are needy, aren't you?"

"I am. Please, Sir," she begged as he reached her jaw, then moved to her lips to kiss her again. With one hand, he reached down to cup her mound. But it wasn't enough. Not nearly enough.

"Fuck, baby girl. I need to have you."

"Yes. Yes."

Standing, he turned and set her down on the side of the tub so that only her lower legs were in the water. She didn't even care about how cold it was as he spread her legs then pushed aside the material over her pussy. Then his tongue speared her, moving back and forth as he rubbed her clit with his thumb.

"Sir! Oh God! Please!" she cried out, trying to be quiet. At least the music should mask most of the noises she was making.

She hoped.

He pushed her up and over into an orgasm that had her shaking, her breath coming in sharp pants.

"That was good," he muttered. "But we can do better." Standing, he lifted her into his arms, then somehow climbed out of the tub without dropping her. He carried her quickly inside then set her down by the black leather couch.

"Shouldn't we dry off?"

"No time. Bend over the couch, put your hands down on the seat." She turned and did what he'd ordered. Her feet were a few inches above the ground. Razor pulled down her bikini bottoms, then he moved in behind her and slid his thick cock inside her. She was now on the Pill, so they didn't have to waste time searching for a condom.

"Fuck, yes," he muttered as he grabbed her hips and drove himself in and out.

She could do nothing except lie there and attempt to remember to breathe. He felt so good, stretching her, pushing her higher and higher.

"I'm gonna come, Tabby-baby. Fuck. Fuck."

Moving one hand from her hip, he played with her clit until

arousal tightened in her stomach. The need to come was over-whelming.

Then she reached that peak, falling over with a scream as he continued to fill her. The room spun, her orgasm went on and on as she clenched down on his thick cock. Then Razor let out a roar as he followed her over.

TABBY'S MOUTH dropped open as she stared out the truck wind-shield. "What is this?"

It was Saturday and she'd thought they would laze around all day, but apparently, Razor had different plans. He'd gotten her up and dressed and bundled into the truck, telling her that he had a surprise for her.

"It's a brand new, indoor ski arena."

"Some crazy person built an indoor ski arena in Montana?" she asked incredulously as Razor lifted her down out of his truck. Why would they do that?

He grinned. "They did. And we're going to go in and build a snowman."

"No way."

"Yes way."

"But will they want us to build a snowman if it's a place for skiing? I don't know how to ski."

"Don't worry about that. The only people who are going to be inside are other people who want to build snowmen too."

Huh? Was there some kind of snowman builders club that she didn't know about?

Ooh. How awesome would that be?

She skipped alongside him, holding his hand, as they moved towards the building. "But what about things to go on the snowman, Daddy? I've got no carrots or sticks, it can't be a proper snowman without those, can it?"

"Don't worry." He held up his bag. "I have you covered."

She squealed. "Daddy, you're the best."

Inside, he helped her get dressed in some warm clothes, including the cutest all-in-one snowsuit with pictures of turtles all over it.

"Snappy and Scooby would have loved this."

"We'll bring them next time," he promised, taking hold of her gloved hand in his.

But she couldn't bring her toys. People wouldn't understand. Right?

Then she walked into the huge area which had a big slope covered in snow as well as a T-rope ski-lift, and she understood. Because standing there, with wide smiles on their faces, were her friends.

"Tabby!" they all squealed and raced towards her. They surrounded her, hugging her tight. And the happiness swelled inside her until she was so full she didn't know where it could go.

That was when she realized she was wearing a huge smile. "You're all here? And we're the only ones here?"

"Our daddies rented the whole place for us!" Sunny told her, clapping her hands. She was wearing a bright pink snowsuit with a unicorn on the front and rhinestones down the arms and legs. "We can be Little, have fun, and build snowmen."

"And have a snowball fight," Millie added in a hushed whisper. "I need you all to cover me. Tabby, distraction."

She had no idea what to do as a distraction. Then her foot started to slip and she wobbled.

"Tabby!" Betsy tried to grab her and ended up wobbling as well.

Then Millie let out a hoot of laughter. "Got you, Daddy!"

Tabby had already regained her balance and grabbed hold of

Betsy when she looked over to see Spike brushing snow off his face. She let out a laugh.

"Yes! Snowball fight!" Emme cried. "To your battle stations, Littles. Let's kick some Daddy ass!"

Thirty minutes later, Tabby had spent so much time laughing that her tummy ached.

"Come on, Tabby-baby. Let's build a snowman," Razor said to her. He helped brush her off first. She wasn't sure who won the snow fight, but she thought it might have been the Littles. Emme had the mind of a military genius.

Razor helped her roll the balls and layer them up, then she used the supplies he'd brought with him to create her masterpiece.

Standing back, she stared at the snowman with satisfaction. Razor came up behind her, wrapping his arms around her. "Well, what do you think?"

"I think he's the best snowman ever," she said proudly.

"I think you're right."

"And that this has been awesome." She turned and reached up to kiss him lightly. "Thank you, Daddy."

"Thank you. For loving me."

"You're welcome, Daddy. And you don't even have to pay me."

"Brat!" he cried, reaching down to scoop up some snow. She took off with a squeal.

After another epic snow fight, he settled her down with her friends. "Make some snow angels, all right?"

He shared a look with Millie that she didn't understand, but shrugged off. She lay down with the girls, giggling as they all made snow angels. Then Razor appeared beside her, holding out his hand. She grabbed it, and he helped her up. Then he cupped her face between his gloved hands.

"I love you."

"I love you too."

"Good." He turned her, so she was staring up at the slope. He was behind her, his arm around her chest as she stared at the message he'd written on the snow with piles of snowballs.

Will you marry me?

With a sob, she turned to him. He was down on one knee with an open ring box in his hand. Inside was the most gorgeous antique-looking ring. There was a yellow stone in the middle surrounded by diamonds. It was stunning.

"Yes, yes, I'll marry you."

Around her, everyone hooted and yelled as Razor kissed her. His grin was huge as he drew back and stared down at her.

"Good enough proposal then?"

"The best sort of proposal."

"Plan b was to put it on a coffee mug and hand it to you with the ring inside."

Her eyes widened with a gasp. "Ooh, I like that as well. Can we do that too?"

"You want a second proposal?"

"Uh-huh. Is that greedy?"

"No, baby girl. You can have as many as you want. As long as you always say yes."

Aww, that was just the sweetest thing.

HER DADDY'S SUNSHINE

Setting the soup down, he put the back of his hand on her forehead. Shit. She was burning up.

"Aw, did you make me soup? I love soup."

"Just heated it up."

"That's so nice. You're so nice. I take back every bad thing I thought about you. Your nickname shouldn't be Sir Grouch-a-lot, it should be Sir Nice-a-lot."

Jesus help him.

"I'm going to get a thermometer. Don't touch that soup."

When he returned a few minutes later, she was fanning her tongue with her hand, and tears were running down her cheeks. "Soup. Hot."

"I told you not to touch the soup." He grabbed her water and held it up so she could drink.

"Sorry." She sniffled. "Wanted to try it. I'm sorry."

"It's okay. Did you burn your mouth?"

"Little bit." She looked so miserable and sympathy filled him. He picked up the thermometer and put the tip in her ear.

It beeped. 103. Shit.

"Am I dying?" she wailed.

"Course not," he reassured her. "Just a bit of a cold. You'll be fine."

"I hate being sick. Being sick is sucky."

"Eat some more soup."

"Hot."

"I'll cool it down." He ended up sitting on the bed and feeding her spoonfuls of soup that he checked first to ensure it wasn't too hot.

When her eyes started to droop, he stopped trying to feed her. She probably needed sleep more than anything.

"Is this your bed?" she mumbled.

"No, baby."

"Cause I can sleep on the sofa," she added.

He frowned. "You're not sleeping on the sofa."

"Don't mind. Where I always sleep."

"When you're sick?" he asked as he tucked her in.

"Nope. All the time."

Made in the USA
Middletown, DE
19 December 2023

46332483R00243